Térata

Michael A. O'Leary Jr.

DEDICATION

This book is dedicated to Kevin Conway, without whom it would not have been written.

Special thanks are also in order to my wife, Cynthia O'Leary, as well Erin Eun Suh Bolton, Theron Muller, Eli Berg-Maas, and Michael Conway for their help with the development of the manuscript.

I would also like to thank the MinnSpec writers group for their support and enthusiasm for speculative fiction.

CONTENTS

Chapter 1
An Autumn of Monsters

Octavio Luis Sanchez's life should have left him in a weedy ditch in Afghanistan, along with most of his blood, his left arm, and his lower half. Killed in action by an improvised explosive device in March of 2010.

But that had not happened. He had been bundled up, stabilized at a NATO trauma center, and evacuated to Germany. In addition to severe blood loss and a triple amputation, his eardrums were destroyed. Burns covered eighty percent of his body, including his face to such a degree that the remainders of his eyelids were sewn shut. Pinpoints of light danced where the sutures couldn't stretch the skin over his eyes. He bit his tongue off.

On the flight to Landstuhl Regional Medical Center, in a drug induced catatonic state, he decided to die. As his conscious mind faded, something intervened. A foreign barrier erected itself, stopping his slide into the unknown. He was somewhere else. His first impulse was to believe that he was having another lucid dream caused by trauma and morphine. Perhaps he was not as close to death as he imagined.

He found himself standing in the back yard of his mother's house in Tulsa, Oklahoma on the day he was to be deployed. Laundry hung on the pentagram clothes line, drying slowly in the humidity of midsummer. Toys used by his sisters' kids littered the yard. His mother was not happy with his decision to join the Marines and she had been cold that day. She was not, however, present. Instead, an elderly man wearing a blue suit stood beside him, considering the laundry. He was an albino with the facial features of a black man. In his hand was a frayed copy of a book. He turned to Octavio and said, "My name is Clarence Elpis."

Octavio stared at him but didn't speak.

Clarence smiled. "I'm here to offer you a choice, Octavio. You can die. And you'll join your father, perhaps, and your stillborn brother in Heaven, provided you receive your last rites. But you have something inside you." Clarence said as he put his hand on Octavio's chest. "And it would be a pity to join them before you unlock what is in here."

Warmth radiated from Clarence's hand. Despite the drugs, Octavio was very aware of the damage to his body. A heavy, lead blanket dotted with tiny spikes laid over him, including the parts that were no longer there. Even standing in this dream he could feel it. That weight lifted. The spikes withdrew. For a moment, Octavio felt like himself. When Clarence removed his hand, the blanket descended.

Still, Octavio didn't respond. He wasn't sure what to say.

"I need you to hold on until you get back to Walter Reed Hospital," Clarence said. "If you can do that, all this pain can be removed. You can start over. You can have your life back, whole and even better than before. I just need you to promise me one thing."

"What do I have to promise?" Octavio asked.

"Help me defeat the cancer that is killing me."

Octavio shook his head and said, "How can I do that?"

Clarence tapped Octavio's chest. "With what you have in here."

Octavio found the scenario confusing, but the offer was simple and, in the face of this choice, he did not want to die.

"OK," Octavio said. "I promise to help you defeat cancer."

Clarence handed Octavio the frayed book. Its cover bore a red hand holding up two fingers with the silhouette of a soldier inside. As soon as Octavio touched the book, the dream froze and disintegrated. His will returned and he resolved to live long enough to reach Walter Reed.

Through countless surgeries, transfusions, and a deluge of drugs, Octavio clung to life. His certainty concerning the authenticity of the dream never faltered, keeping him sane throughout the three week process. After he arrived at Walter Reed Medical Center in Pennsylvania, he was transferred to a private facility in Des Moines, Iowa. There someone removed the sutures from his eyes and applied a lubricant to prevent them from drying. Blurrily, he saw that he was in a medical room that reminded him of the dentist's office. Clarence stood before him holding a cardboard sign that read, "*Despierta*."

Awake. Octavio did. Both he and Clarence kept their promises.

Dusk deepened in the Boundary Waters of Northern Minnesota. The sky was a burnt orange on the horizon and an inky blue elsewhere. Shadows cast from multicolored birch leaves and green pines snaked across the forest floor.

"Look alive now, ladies," Octavio called to the group of five young men huddled around a small campfire.

They burst into a flurry of motion. As part of The Elpis Foundation's Self-Empowerment for Urban Youth Program, they were trained to set up and tear down campsites. Over the last two weeks, they also learned basic survival skills such as Dakota fire holes, edible plants, the use of map and compass, and the vagaries of local wildlife. The native animals terrified the boys. Octavio regularly threatened them with bear and wolf attacks to increase motivation. He taught them what those animals' scat looked like and made sure they found it. They had the camp torn down and the site cleared in less than three minutes. No trace of the fire remained.

"Camp clear," said Ronaldo, a lanky kid from North Minneapolis.

Ronaldo had been a problem at the outset of this trip. Like all the boys, he signed up to do this thinking it would be similar to other charitable programs offered to inner city youth: self-affirming but toothless. Upon learning that he would be sleeping outside for three weeks in the chilly, autumnal Boundary Waters without his smartphone, he'd called Octavio several racial slurs. Octavio explained that such language was unacceptable as he lifted two hundred pounds of gear from the back of the cargo van and dropped it at Ronaldo's feet. He elaborated on the need for mutual respect as he snapped heavy gauge rope with his fingers. For the following two weeks all five of the boys showed him courtesy. Ronaldo himself was exemplary.

"Take the third formation we worked on," Octavio instructed. The boys formed a wedge at either side of the campsite. They piled their tack in front of them, faces apprehensive. They knew that a mock attacker was going to ambush the camp. They knew that the boy who scored the most hits would be the winner of this game. They knew nothing else about the scenario.

"Arm yourselves," Octavio said.

Each boy pulled a paintball marker from his backpack and loaded the hopper with cornstarch pellets. These were the same paintball guns used in law enforcement training. The Elpis Foundation did not spare expenses.

Minutes ticked by and the appointed ambush time came and went. Dusk faded to near darkness.

Where is Aaron? Octavio thought. Usually, the ambush went off at 17:45 sharp. At 18:05 Octavio heard a faint rustling at his 10 o'clock. Despite the fact that this was not a live battle, he found himself lowering his center and filling with adrenaline.

Ronaldo was the first to turn his eyes to the ambush point of entry. Octavio allowed himself a small smile. That boy had potential.

What happened next made no sense. Number 10, not Aaron Black, burst from the twilight woods in a fury of motion, moving too fast for any of the boys to react. He slammed into Ronaldo first, killing him with impact alone. He spun through the other four before they had a chance to scream. Blood and body parts flew across the forest floor. In less than five seconds, the campsite was an abattoir.

What the hell is going on! Octavio thought. *Why is Number 10 here? Why did he do that?*

In his true form, Number 10 was one of the most frightening of the Térata. His eyes oozed red gas and his quilled hair stood up. His skin was rough like the surface of a rock. Short, black horns protruded from his joints and skull. Stubby fingers extended into thick claws. He smiled with jet black lips, revealing rows of needle-like teeth.

"What the fu—" Octavio began.

Number 10 crouched and launched forward.

Octavio hissed and dove, but not fast enough. His right arm tore open beneath one of Number 10's clawed fingers. He hit the log next to Ronaldo and flipped over it, clutching his bleeding, useless arm. Number 10 smiled again and sprung toward him. Octavio moved deliberately this time, making his right arm vulnerable. Number 10 grabbed the arm and twisted. Octavio relaxed his shoulder and allowed the arm to tear free. Now off balance, Number 10 stumbled and lurched sideways. Octavio spun and grabbed the monster from behind with his remaining arm. He leapt onto Number 10's back and wrapped his legs around the monster's waist. Horns jutting from Number 10's spine dug into Octavio's chest.

"This will only hurt for a few moments," he whispered into a thorny, rock encrusted ear.

Number 10 thrashed in an attempt to dislodge him. Tentacles the size of electrical wires emerged from Octavio's missing arm socket. They latched onto Number 10's rocky skin and bored into it like drill bits. Number 10 cried out and rolled to the ground, slamming Octavio against rocks and fallen trees. Octavio absorbed each impact with a mere grunt. His body could take much more damage than Number 10 was able to inflict from this position. The tentacles dug deeper and began to pump out flesh and blood. Number 10 reached over his shoulders with both hands and impaled Octavio's neck with his horned fingers. Blood squirted into the air, but Octavio's grip did not falter.

Careful now, Octavio thought as Number 10's movements slowed. When the monster collapsed, Octavio pulled away, drenched in his own blood. The tentacles retreated back into his shoulder. Number 10 gasped in short breaths. Most of his lungs had been sucked out. Using the fireman's lift, Octavio carried Number 10 out of the clearing and into the woods. A larger tentacle snaked from his arm socket and curled around Number 10's leg to stabilize the load. When Octavio came to the edge of a nearby lake, he dropped the body into the water so only the head remained above the surface. Number 10's breaths shortened and became less frequent. Following his final exhale, an intense heat emanated from his body, culminating in a white hot glow. The water around it boiled. Octavio retreated into the woods. Number 10 exploded, sending a plume of steaming water a hundred feet into the air.

Octavio removed his vest and shirt to inspect his missing arm. Small tentacles squirmed inside the wound. They regurgitated consumed flesh from Number 10, using it to build a new arm. Octavio sighed and returned to the campsite.

There wasn't much left of any of the boys except Ronaldo. Octavio crouched beside him. His brown eyes were open, staring into nothing. Octavio gently closed them. For a moment he entertained the death/suicide fantasies that had plagued him for the last few months. The car crash. The gun to the temple. Falling on a kitchen knife. He stopped the train of thought there. As violent as those ideas were, they became worse if he let them. He assumed those thoughts were a result of residual guilt at having survived what happened to him in Afghanistan, a function of post-traumatic stress disorder. Now he wasn't sure.

Shaking his head, Octavio stood and surveyed the campsite. Such carnage wasn't unfamiliar, but it still caused his muscles to feel flaccid and useless. He was confounded by why it had happened. This was his tenth trip up North as part of The Elpis Foundation's Self-Empowerment for Urban Youth Program. In previous trips, Aaron Black, one of the Elpis Foundation's youth directors and another former

Marine, showed up at the end, scared the kids, and tagged them with paint filled balloons. Octavio would do the same for Aaron's group of boys tomorrow night. Every now and then, one of the boys would land a shot, earning the highest honor in the program. Octavio and Aaron had designed this program themselves. It was a popular, successful character building exercise for kids from economically challenging situations. Clarence had a soft spot for such kids and his charitable foundation had won awards for this program. Why had Number 10 shown and up and why had he done this? It made no sense.

Octavio sat down next to Ronaldo, holding the boy's hand. It was cooling off. Tears rolled down Octavio's face and snot covered his upper lip.

"Espero que halle paz y tranquilidad en el Cielo," he said.

He placed Ronaldo's hand onto the boy's chest.

Octavio wiped his face off with the remnants of his shirt and pulled out a satellite phone. For a moment he just stared at it. He pulled up Number 7's number and hit "send".

"Hello, Octavio," Number 7 answered, her voice firm and distant.

"We've got a situation," he said. The line was silent as she waited for him to elaborate. "Number 10 showed up instead of Aaron."

"What?" she exclaimed. She continued calmly a moment later. "What happened?"

"He killed my kids," he answered. "All of them. I killed him. I need an extraction ASAP. Also, bring a cleanup crew. It's messy."

"Where is Aaron?" she asked.

"I don't know," he said and hung up the phone.

Darkness descended. Octavio walked back to the edge of the lake. The stars were painfully clear and the Milky Way exploded over the lake in an impossible number of white dots. The air was brisk and the woods were almost silent. Octavio noted how quiet lakes in Minnesota were compared to their counterparts in Oklahoma. He took three deep breaths and tried to bring that same quiet to his mind.

As he considered the stars, he felt something shift inside of him. It was a slow shift at first, but after a few minutes facts began to clarify. The picture of his life had been blurry for the last two years. The forms of it were recognizable, but he did not appreciate its exquisite details until this moment. The exact depth of his depression emerged and for the first time he glimpsed its specific source. Until this moment he thought he had done the right thing when he chose to "Wake Up". The events of tonight jarred his thoughts toward his employer. Perhaps, in taking Clarence Elpis's offer, he had made a deal that held darker depths than its altruistic surface appeared. Even if Clarence wasn't responsible for the death of those five kids, someone in his organization was.

Octavio followed the arc of the Milky Way from the far edge of the lake to the tree line behind him. Shooting stars were so common here that he barely noticed them, though seeing any in Tulsa would have sent his boyish spirit heavenward. In the paranoid mountains of Afghanistan he only saw them as totemic warnings and associated them with weapon fire. Here, in the vast and ruthless landscape of northern Minnesota, they were just another part of a sky that had no limits and expected nothing but pinpricks of light among darkness. When the helicopter arrived, he was standing on the edge of the lake, staring at the stars with his mouth open and tears running down his face.

Brenda Jones ran her fingers across the metal grating of the park bench. It was coated with a rubbery plastic, which felt nice against her fingertips. Her daughter, Amber, played on a nearby jungle gym assembly, running and screaming through tunnels and down slides. A few other children swung on the swing set, their mindful parents chatting about the unseasonably warm weather. The first round of autumn leaves had fallen, creating a patchy carpet on the mulched floor of the playground.

She's so lucky, Brenda thought again, *she'll miss him for a while, but forget she ever knew him.*

Thoughts like these still emerged unbidden. Two months was a short time for mourning. Brenda tried to push her mind back to the present, but failed. Again.

He used to stand there—right there—at the bottom of that slide. She could see him, wearing a blue hoodie and dirty jeans and steel toed work boots, his square face framed with a black beard that never quite looked trimmed and too bushy eyebrows and those huge arms…He could just step out from behind that big slide …

No, not that. He's gone. Gone for good and I'm alone with our daughter.

The strength it took to think those words was staggering. Her mind slid into a state of shock and denial, back to the moment she was told Kevin had died in a freak car explosion. Thursday. August 16th. 2012. 7:38 p.m. A kind police officer. His uncomfortable female partner. Both stood at the foot of the stairs leading to the condo Brenda and Kevin bought three years before. *'There's been an automobile accident. Is your husband Kevin Jones? When was the last time you spoke with your husband? Could anyone else have been driving the car? Was anyone with him?'* Brenda had spoken to him near that time via cell phone. He was driving the car at the time and was to be home soon. He had just wrapped up a ten hour shift at the auto repair shop where he worked in Cottage Grove. *'We're sorry to inform you...'* Then she was on the concrete of the landing, clinging to the wrought iron railing.

That moment was bottled up and stored on a shelf in her head. Any time her head shifted, the bottle fell, its top popped off, and she relived the terror of discovering herself without him. She knew that the vibrancy of her pain would fade. She knew that the guilt she felt was unreasonable. Many loving people had affirmed that time would mitigate these feelings. She believed them. She had to.

Without Brenda, Amber had no one. Kevin claimed he had no family and she'd heard from no one following his death. Her own mother was a basket case and her father had been dead for years. She had no siblings. There were some aunts and uncles from her side, but she hadn't seen any of them since leaving Kansas City a decade ago. Brenda had to keep moving through all the anguish. A two-year-old did not have the capacity to understand death. As far as Amber was concerned, her dad would just show back up. He'd often taken trips alone to their cabin. Even two months hadn't dulled the child's sense that her father was temporarily away. Amber asked fewer questions as time passed, but every time she asked when Daddy would be home, all of Brenda's tender scabs peeled away. Brenda refused to let her pain overshadow her daughter's life. Amber would forget her father within a year and must be allowed to do so.

Brenda looked down and realized that she had pushed three fingers through the grate of the park bench and was pulling up. She relaxed her hand, removed her fingers, and took a deep breath.

Amber ran back and forth around a series of elevated platforms meant for bigger kids. Brenda called, "Amber! Time to go!"

The girl froze. Head tilted to the left, she yelled, "No, Mommy! Stay at pa'k!"

Brenda smiled and gathered her daughter, who wriggled in protest. She ran her fingers through the child's thin black hair. "We've got to go, sweetie pie. Mommy's got work tonight."

Amber grabbed Brenda's ear and shook it. "No, Mommy! No wo'k! We can stay at pa'k!"

Had Kevin been there, he'd have held her upside down by an ankle, saying something silly and playful. Amber would have squealed in delight before he smashed her in a hug and she forgot all about being a snotty two-year-old. It was a miracle what he could do with her when she became obstinate. A miracle that had ended.

Brenda pushed that thought back and walked to the car, ignoring her daughter's emphatic protests.

Number 9 sat on the bleachers of a nearby soccer field in the body of a man. He watched Brenda pack her daughter into the car, kiss her, and drive away. His index finger tapped rhythmically against his chin. *The woman and the child...* he thought. *The woman and the child...*

The woman was grieving and distracted. She had retied her dirty blonde ponytail three times in the last half hour. Her scent was riddled with frustration and anger beneath the fryer grease and deodorant. He could have slipped in, grabbed the kid, and been gone before she noticed. But he did not. Not today, not yesterday, and not any of the other times he'd found perfect opportunities to do so. His gut said not to move in situations that seemed ripe otherwise. He worried, though, that his gut had become confounded by the woman. She had a peculiar effect on him. She had obviously had a peculiar effect on his brother, Number 1, as well. Number 1 had married her.

Considering what had happened to Number 1, perhaps Number 9's instincts were warning against a trap. His brother had not died in a car accident. Their kind, Térata, self-combusted when their hearts stopped. Number 1's car had been on fire for half a mile before it flipped into a ditch and no one could explain how the fire started or how it got so hot. The chances of a natural death were nil. Someone had murdered his brother. The timing of this was also disturbing. After more than four years missing, his brother had been killed only a day after he'd been located.

Possibilities concerning the murder abounded. Exposure to humanity at large lead to random death for their family. There were rules that must be followed. If his brother had broken too many of them, the world had swallowed him. The Elpis Foundation, which they called home, had become politically unstable. Perhaps someone within it had something to hide and used the murder to bury secrets. Number 10's death in the Boundary Waters two months ago was chalked up to a massive system failure and resulting psychosis. But Number 9 doubted his younger brother had randomly decided to lash out at Octavio. Were Number 1 and Number 10's deaths related? Two dead Térata at the same time was not a likely coincidence.

Forces outside the Elpis organizations could have been at work. No intelligence concerning supernatural activity had been reported in the Twin Cities, but perhaps Number 1 ran afoul of something unknown and powerful. In the end, what really mattered was that whoever murdered him was dangerous.

Number 9 sniffed the air. Rotting leaves. Lichen on stone. Humans and the chemicals they spread on their bodies. Automotive fumes. A decaying song bird beneath the bleachers, killed yesterday by a stray cat. No indication of a trap. No logical reason to hold off doing what he'd come to do. And yet he did. Logic didn't fare well against his instincts. He'd continue watching with discretion until he felt the timing was perfect.

His patience was paying off. Driving across a bridge earlier in the week, he noticed a man in a trench coat staring off into the distance. A familiar scent wafted from the man's coat to the monster's nose. The scent of a woman he'd known decades before who always had answers. A woman connected to himself and his dead older brother. Victoria Starks. She could unlock the puzzle of the woman and child the same way she'd unlocked the puzzle he'd encountered decades ago. He need only find her. She was the kind of person who was only found when she wanted to be found. Her scent was unmistakable, though, so she had either become careless or she was ready for a second visit from him. The second scenario seemed farfetched. She'd barely survived their first encounter. She wouldn't survive the next. His appetite had flared since coming to the Twin Cities. She would make an incredible meal.

Number 9 trotted down the bleachers and jogged across the park. He followed the main trail for a few minutes before veering off the path into heavier woods. This neglected area of the park was overrun with invasive buckthorn. Its thin, twisted trunks choked off all the lower vegetation and created a mess of unruly undergrowth. His nose told him no one was near, so he stripped off his sneakers, sweat pants, and shirt. Once nude, he shifted into his true form.

His skin peeled away and was absorbed by his body, replaced with a black, leathery hide. Tufts of black fur sprung up from his crotch, his armpits, and in lines running down from his chest and up from his buttocks. His face elongated into a toothy snout and his ears spread out like bat ears. An array of three inch quills pushed themselves out from his forearms, elbows, knees, and ankles. His digits curled into claws. A series of fuchsia horns broke through the hide, starting at his shoulders and running down his back in two bright arches. He was still erect for the most part, but hunched down in the fashion of a gorilla.

This was a freeing moment for him. Taking on other forms was painful to do and uncomfortable to hold. He had no idea how his brother managed to do it for four years. For the next few hours, he would run through the park, flex his muscles, and blow off steam from the stress of inaction. Then he'd pay a visit to the man in the trench coat, Kimm Peters.

Ticket times were running too long. Brenda grimaced at the wheel as a server clipped on another yellow order card and swung it back into position. She usually didn't work the cook line, but tonight she was short staffed and the front-of-house was in good hands. Her assistant manager, Andre, was young but he was a customer service natural. She grabbed a skillet, flipped two eggs, and plated a pile of hash browns with four strips of bacon. She slid the over easy eggs onto the plate, pulled a ticket off the wheel, and set the plate on top of it in the warming window.

"Table 5 up!" she shouted, turning her attention to the fryers. A batch of onion rings hissed in the grease. Not quite done. Jose already had the burgers in the window. She should have dropped them sooner.

"Table 8 up!" she called a moment later.

She'd only taken a week off of work after Kevin's death. Being home had almost killed her. Amber kept asking, "Where Daddy go?" Everything in their condo reminded Brenda of him. The quiet hours when Amber slept lead to sobbing fits. She fled back to the Pit Stop Diner. The first week back she spent too much time in the bathroom crying. But the staff had covered for her and by the second week her work had become a sanctuary. Here her mind was her own, at least for the most part. Tonight, though, wasn't going very well.

"Table 13 up!"

She started to get caught up.

Andre poked his head through the window. "How's it going back there, Boss?"

"Good," Brenda said. "I need a tray of sliced tomatoes if you've got a minute."

"Sure thing," he said.

The restaurant was busy for a Wednesday. A storm had blown in minutes after she'd dropped Amber off with her night sitter. Rain always brought guests in droves. The patterns of the restaurant were ingrained into Brenda. She had started at the Pit Stop as an assistant manager after graduating from the Carlson School of Management at the U of M five years ago. Her promotion to GM came less than six months later. Her mother hadn't been pleased with her career choice. She often wondered aloud how many people got a business degree from a good school only to end up working at a diner. Despite her mother's misgivings, Brenda loved it. She loved the pace and the crew she'd put together. Jerry and Mac, the Pit Stop's owners, planned to open a second diner. She was being allowed to partner into the venture. This was her family. Let her mother rot, zonked out on Vicodin or OxyContin or whatever prescription she could swindle out of her doctors and Medicare. She hadn't even bothered to show up when Kevin died. Just sent a card. A fucking card.

"Your tomatoes, madam," Andre said with a grin as he slid the tray through the window. "And you should be more kind to onions. They have rights, too, you know."

Brenda looked down at the onion she was slicing. It looked like it had been put through a food processor. Jose eyed her sideways from the grill. She scraped it into the trash and pulled another one from the cooler at her feet. "Yeah, you're right..." she began.

Andre's face became serious. "You OK?" he asked.

Brenda nodded, wiped her eyes on each shoulder to prevent using her hands, and tried her best to smile. "If you'd made sure Angel had prepped onions before he left, I wouldn't be crying all over the cook line."

Andre smiled again. "Touché. I'll commit seppuku right after this shift."

"You do that, but make sure it's in the parking lot. Health code violation."

He bowed and disappeared from the window. Brenda grabbed the tomatoes, tossed one on each burger, and slid the tray into the cooler.

"Table 21 up!"

"Oren," Kimm Peters said into his phone, "I really need to talk to you."

"Sure," Oren said. "I'm free Friday night. Want to do Mayslack's again?"

"That would be great," Kimm said. "Is seven OK?"

"Yeah."

"Good! I'll see you then. I love you, son."

"Uh, OK," Oren said. "See you then."

Kimm entered the date and time to meet Oren into his smartphone's calendar app.

He stood on the bridge connecting 46th Street in Minneapolis with Ford Parkway in St Paul. The rain had ebbed, leaving a slick sheen on the streets, sidewalks, and piles of multi-colored leaves. The Mississippi River churned beneath him, reflecting light pollution from downtown. His tie whipped in the wind, which carried a chill but was otherwise tame for October in Minnesota. The wind also made it difficult for Kimm to light a cigarette. After the tenth attempt it sparked to life. He took a deep drag and leaned onto the rail, his eyes on the roiling water below. For the last week, he had come to this spot each night after closing up his used car dealership in Northeast Minneapolis. The first time he'd come, he'd meant to throw himself into the miasma of the river below.

In that moment, the weight of his life felt like a thousand metal coils roped to a thousand boulders. His business was failing and at the age of forty-six he had no other prospects for employment. Seven years ago, his mother died and left him a windfall. He was selling cars for Denny Hecker at the time and decided that was his chance to leap. Over the ensuing years, he found the difference between selling cars and running a business to be an unbridgeable gulf. At the end of this year, he'd be bankrupt. Funny, he thought, that the fruits of his mother's death had driven him to suicidal lengths.

His good looks, the key to so much of what he'd done in his past as a salesman, were fading. The abdominal six pack he held all through his thirties was now a pudgy bulk. His blonde hair was thinning. The smile lines around his eyes looked more like crow's feet. As he shaved every morning, he found the man in the mirror becoming unrecognizable. Who was this old person? He had no idea.

His three kids with his first wife were either in college or about to be. He had no idea how he would make Oren's next tuition payment. He hadn't spoken to his daughters in months. He'd missed almost every important event of their lives.

His second wife died in a car accident just one month before his mother died. That marriage had been on the rocks, anyway. Standing at her funeral with her sister openly staring him down had caused his eye to tick. The unpleasant details his wife had disclosed to his sister-in-law about their relationship were written large upon her face. Since opening Kimm's Auto World, he had spared little time for familial relationships.

On his first visit to the bridge seven days ago, the only thing that kept him from jumping into the Mississippi River was a business card. It was a simple yet elegant card that read "Victoria Starks—Mystic Guide" with a Minneapolis phone number. A tire kicker named Frank had given it to earlier that day. As often happened with Kimm's customers, they ended up talking for an hour.

At the end of the conversation, Frank had said, "Hey, I took one of her cards last time I was in. Here. You should give her a call. It sounds like you need some guidance right now. She's good. For real."

Kimm had laughed in a friendly way and said, "Well, like I said, I don't really believe in that stuff, but you're right about needing some guidance."

As he had stood on the Ford Parkway Bridge that night, he stared at the card and the river. The card was embossed with rich, brown ink on expensive rag paper. Its sense of authenticity convinced him that in the face of oblivion or psychics, perhaps his stoic skepticism could take a back seat. He called the number on the card.

As an accomplished bull-shitter and ruthless manipulator of other people's emotional weaknesses, he expected Victoria to pull all the standard tricks of the trade. At first, she seemed just like he expected. When he finally managed to book an appointment, she made it for a month out. But she called him back an hour later and said she could squeeze him in later that day "due to the seriousness of his situation." Her prices were astronomical. This all sounded like a scam from someone claiming to have supernatural knowledge. He told her nothing about himself, but she probably used the same "seriousness of the situation" line on all new marks. Still, he had said, "Thanks. See you at seven," as if the words were being slipped out of him without his own will being involved. Oblivion or psychics? His own will was long gone.

His first interaction with Victoria Starks had been shocking. From the moment she smiled and shook his hand on the porch of her house in Minneapolis's Longfellow neighborhood, he knew that she was the real deal. Her authenticity was palpable. She never asked him a thing about his life, but she mapped it out with stunning detail on the first reading. He cried for an hour on her floor while she drank tea and waited for him to get it together. She scheduled another reading for later in the week and a third the following week. These two readings, she cautioned, were vitally important since they were the last she would do for him. When he asked her why, she replied, "That's all the cards have for you." He spent the next few days thinking more deeply about his life than he had since his mother died. Such considerations were painful but refreshing. He had returned to the bridge every night since the reading. His chosen suicide site was the best place he could find to think.

His final reading was in an hour and he needed to settle on a question. The previous two sessions had concentrated on all the mistakes he'd been making. This session was about the future, which he found much more confounding than the past. He knew his business would fail. He owed over $100,000 in inventory, the payments on his facilities were three months behind, and the state was threatening to go through his accounts. His house had entered the redemption period of foreclosure. Bankruptcy was the only way out of this mess. But where to go after that? He pitched his cigarette off the bridge into the Mississippi and walked back to the Minneapolis side. His car was parked in Minnehaha Park.

As he stepped from the bridge onto the sidewalk, he bumped into a large man.

"Oh, uh, excuse me..." he began, steadying himself on a handrail. "Hey, Roy, right? You were at my car dealership the other day looking at an Astro van. Funny running into you here, eh?"

Roy was an unkempt, ugly guy whose teeth didn't seem to fit in his gums. Kimm never forgot a name and face, but this one was easy. The guy even wore the same oversized trench coat, sweat pants, and t-shirt he'd been wearing a few days ago when he test drove a van but didn't buy it. The salesman in Kimm sprang to life.

"So you wanna take a closer look at that van tomorrow? I might be able to get a better stereo put in her on the house."

Roy frowned and said, "Well, odd to run into you here now, huh? My car died back at the park." He motioned back to the same parking lot where Kimm's Lexus sat. "I guess I shoulda bought that van from ya the other day. I just live over the bridge, so the walk's not too bad. If they don't tow me, I can get the car tomorrow."

Kimm, feeling good for no reason, said, "Well, let me take a quick look at it. I can give you a ride home if needed. I'm parked in the same lot."

Roy's wiry eyebrows lifted. He said, "Well, that'd be great. Thanks."

They crossed the street and walked into the parking lot. The 1980s Datsun that Roy had been driving the other day sat several spaces away from Kimm's car. For its age and vintage it was a miracle that it ran and wasn't rusted bumper to bumper. What weird luck, Kimm thought. He'd nail this sale down for sure. At least he could pay Victoria.

"So what's wrong with her, Roy?"

Roy shrugged and said, "I was turning the corner at Godfrey and 46th and it just died. I managed to coast into the parking lot, but I had to push it into the space. It may be small, but it's heavy as hell."

Roy popped the hood and Kimm looked inside. For all his years selling cars, he had managed to learn almost nothing about how they worked. He liked to say, "I don't sell cars. I sell the *idea* of cars." This was one of the oldest tricks in his playbook.

"Well, I don't see anything obviously wrong..." He shook the battery cable connections, pulled out the dipstick, and replaced it. "Probably something deeper in the engine. There's some oil coming off the heads, but that's not too uncommon in a car this old." He smiled and said, "Why don't I give you a ride home and you can get this thing towed tomorrow when they won't charge you the night service fee."

Roy just stared at him, which Kimm took to mean that

he'd breached some kind of personal social code.

"I mean, I figured you were walking so you didn't want to call a tow truck now..."

Roy's face was moving as if he were about to sneeze.

"Well, I could call a tow if you want. A good friend of mine, Eddie, doesn't charge too—"

For the few minutes encompassing the rest of Kimm's life, he could not get over how fast Roy moved. One second Roy was standing there with a contorted face. The next he was a blur of motion that caught Kimm up and pulled him deeper into the woods of Minnehaha Park, faster than Kimm could have run in ten minutes. Kimm's glasses flew off his face. When the blur stopped, Roy was larger and uglier, his teeth protruding from his mouth. Kimm would have screamed, but the thumb of Roy's right hand was jammed into his mouth and down his throat. Kimm's back was planted against a tree and his feet dangled six inches off the ground. He couldn't quite focus on anything around him besides Roy's face. It was as if his eyes were still trying to process all of the information that had flown past him in the last few seconds.

"You have a psychic you visit, right?" Roy asked. The extra few inches of teeth didn't affect his speech at all. The words seemed to form in his throat. His lips didn't even move.

Kimm just stared at him. He had never moved so fast in his life. Not even an airplane moved that fast.

Roy growled, "The fucking psychic! Where is she?"

Kimm tried to speak, but the clawed thumb in his mouth prevented it. Roy pulled his thumb out of Kimm's mouth and said, "Where does she live?"

Kimm opened his bruised mouth and said, "Uh..." In a panic he realized that he couldn't remember where she lived.

"Uh. Somewhere in Longfellow."

Roy grimaced, the bones beneath his face roiling like the water of the Mississippi. "Address?"

"I—I—I can't remember," Kimm sputtered. He'd been ready to drive there when he ran into Roy but now he couldn't get there if a gun was pointed at his head. And this was far worse than a gun. This was insane. Even more insanely, it seemed that Roy believed him.

"How did you find her in the first place?"

"Uh, I had a card with her number on it. It's in my jacket. Then I met her at the Blue Owl before we went back to her place," Kimm said.

Deciding that the whole situation was so far out that it couldn't be real, Kimm asked, "How did you move like that? Who—what are you?"

Roy didn't seem to hear him. He was staring off into the woods, lost in thought. Kimm hung there, shocked past fear. His mind didn't know how to process any of this. Eventually, Roy fished Victoria's card out of Kimm's pocket. He looked at it for a moment and grinned. That grin broke the dam of disbelief holding Kimm together.

"Oh, oh, oh..." he blubbered.

Roy tucked the card into his trench coat, looked into Kimm's eyes, and cocked his head.

"Oh, please, Roy! Oh, Jesus."

Roy grew even larger and more horrifying. The twisted grin on his face followed him through the transformation. Kimm began crying as he struggled against the claw that pinned him to the tree.

Roy plunged his clawed hand into Kimm's mid-section and pulled out most of his intestines. He stuffed them into his mouth, which opened so wide it seemed his head was split in two. Kimm coughed and thrashed, blood flying through his teeth in a tangle of spit. His vision blackened. The monster kept thrusting his hand into Kimm, pulling out pieces, and stuffing them into his mouth.

Victoria Starks sat in her living room, legs crossed over an embroidered replica of a fourth century Persian pillow. Yellow scrollwork billowed through a field of magenta silk, interlaced with lions posing for attack. Miniscule, golden poppy flowers dotted the background. A matching blanket covered the floor before her. Tarot cards were arranged on the blanket, following the line of the scrolls in a complicated series of overlapping arcs, breaking each time they encountered a lion. This was a potent reading, meant for a man who wasn't here. He was dead or would be soon. Violently so.

Victoria tapped a lacquered fingernail against the last card she had turned. The Hollow Skull. By itself, even as the last card turned, this was not a sign of his demise. But taken with the Tower three spaces to the left and the Scales over two rows and reversed, there was no other reading. The other cards told much of the story. A reversed Raven. The Twins followed by The Herald followed by The Hand. He'd been murdered by a stranger to himself. His body would never be recovered. The cards showed an unresolved fork, implying that Kimm's life was entwined with his murderer going forward. She did not know what that seeming paradox meant.

Normally in this case, Victoria would have done her own reading. Murdered clients were cause for personal alarm. But the cards before her made that unnecessary. The Fool, which only turned up as a representation of herself, sat reversed before The Twins. Whoever killed Kimm Peters did so to find her. Details beyond that would only make the picture more confusing. Possibilities within possibilities. Also, while often ambiguous, the cards could be cuttingly accurate. Once they predicted death, there was no escaping that prediction. Knowing it only made for more anxiety.

She gathered the cards and placed them in a porcelain box which was also patterned with scrolls and lions. She put the box into an oak chest, which she locked with a small skeleton key. She extinguished the incense that had been burning beside the fireplace and retired to the kitchen for a cup of tea. After twenty seven years, perhaps it was time for her to think about moving.

"Yeah, so this guy complains about the French onion soup tonight, right? He says, 'They don't have anything like this in France. I know. I was there. And if they did, I wouldn't have paid for it there, either.' I just apologized and comped it. But man, all I could think was—all I wanted to do was ask him, 'Bro, did you get that toupee in France? Cuz you shoulda asked for your money back on that shit, too.'"

The table burst with laughter. Andre smiled wide, his white teeth contrasting with his dark brown skin in the low light of the bar. "Oh," he continued, "and he stiffed Janelle."

"That dude was such a prick about everything," Janelle said, leaning into the table. "Why do dudes like that come into diners, anyway? Like, you know, at a place called the Pit Stop where you pay seven bucks for an omelet we're gonna have imported cheese and fillet mignon."

"I don't think they tip in France," Gina piped in. She curled her fingers through her frazzled black hair and took a drink of her seven and seven through a straw.

"That's England, baby," said Andre. "It's impolite. And this ain't France, anyway."

Brenda sat at the corner of the table, nursing a Leinenkugel's. Three servers, Andre, and Jose had gathered for a beer at L'Oeil de Cochon Tavern, their regular haunt following grueling shifts. Brenda's quietness in the situation was not unusual. She never drank more than one beer and rarely took the lead in the conversation. Andre always saw to that, anyway. He could talk for hours about nothing, whipping his hands around and drawing pictures with them. He would make an amazing stand-up comic or actor, but instead worked a dead end job as her assistant manager. He seemed to like playing video games more than going to classes. Perhaps in a few years he'd grow out of that and do something more with his life. Until then, he was a huge asset to her crew.

Gina, who was slurping down booze with alarming zeal for someone scheduled to open tomorrow at 5:30 a.m., giggled and said, "Yeah, wrong place, honey. We got ranch dressing and sirloins."

The conversation went on like that for another half hour. Only Jose and Brenda remained silent. Despite ten years in the US, both Jose's command of the English language and his status as a legal citizen remained questionable. He drank a single Bud Light, but smiled and nodded at the right times.

At 12:30 a.m., Brenda stood up and said, "Well, good job tonight, people. See you on Friday. And, Gina, I better not get a call in the morning about you, huh?" She smiled at Gina, who had entered stages of inebriation that would have laid up a three hundred pound truck driver.

Gina laughed and said, "You know me, Boss. Bright and early for the creepy-old-man coffee routine."

Brenda did know but could not figure out how. That girl

was bubbly even with a hangover.

As she walked to the door, Brenda nodded at Todd, the bartender and owner, who smiled too sympathetically.

"Have a good night, Todd," she said.

He nodded and said, "Thanks. You, too. And be safe, Sugar."

Number 9 decided he would be Daniel Clark as he scrubbed the blood out of his fur. He had used the identity once before on a very smooth, easy job. The sun was just rising on a clear, brilliant morning. He crouched in a deep part of a stream, methodically grooming his teeth and claws through his fur. A clump of torn flesh broke free and drifted downstream. He had been messy last night, but he was full. His craving for human flesh was becoming a bother. He waded out of the stream and trotted back into the woods to find his clothes.

Daniel Clark was a tall, broad man with jet black hair, olive skin, and green eyes. The tall, broad part wasn't optional. No matter how densely Number 9 stuffed himself, he couldn't manage a frame under six feet five inches. Everything else was a matter of concentration. Once he found his discarded clothing, he began the process of becoming Daniel. This would not be the smooth transition to his true form. He lay down.

The joints of his hips and shoulders separated and all the others, including his fingers and toes, loosened. His breathing came in rapid pants. Quills, horns, and fur receded into his skin, which lightened and smoothed. His snout shortened with each inhaled breath and his claws retracted, flattening into human finger nails. For a moment he looked like a naked, broken doll thrashing in the fallen leaves. In jerky movements, his joints reset themselves. His breathing slowed and all the details of his monstrosity faded into humanity. He stood up, stretched his new form, and dressed.

This would be a busy day. Victoria was exposed. With patience and luck, Number 9 could flush her out. She wouldn't recognize Daniel, which was a necessary precaution. Her last encounter with Number 9 would have left a negative impression. He could get what he wanted from her if he handled her correctly. First, he'd need to return to his hotel in St Paul and gather the accruements of his identity.

Andre Bowen sat on his couch in his boxer shorts and a t-shirt, a PlayStation controller in one hand and a joint in the other. Andre had been up since six playing the video game and he had to be at work at ten, a scant hour away.

His roommate, Craig, was splayed across a reclining chair, still in the clothes he had worn to the bar the night before. A half empty Mickey's bottle leaned precariously between his legs. His snores were thunderous, but the sound didn't bother Andre. The pair had closed down First Avenue in downtown Minneapolis last night. Craig insisted they go when Andre got home from L'Oeil de Cochon, despite the late hour. DJ Communist Grizzly always brought out the early twenties crowd on a Wednesday night, and while Andre hated the clever mash-up of European techno and 1980s pop, he couldn't deny that it appealed to the ladies. One of those girls was still in Andre's bed, which was why he was playing video games on the couch. He couldn't sleep with another body in his bed. He was pretty sure her name was Debra, she was a marketing major at the U, and she liked to have more than three fingers crammed into her as deep as they would go. He had no intention of seeing her again once she left his apartment.

Craig struck out with Debra's friend, an art major with nose rings and a haircut only slightly shorter than her torn plaid skirt. Craig always went for that type, which had turned out well for Andre this time, since she had a friend who wasn't like her at all. Usually Andre would wingman that scenario, bailing out before one of those politically charged girls attached herself to him. That ploy often worked out for Craig. His association with Andre was some kind of elixir. Andre thought they all looked like hookers who'd been hit with a lawn mower then spray painted. He had a policy against sleeping with any woman who didn't wear a full set of undergarments. This was one of the biggest laughs he got at the open mic night at The Top Hat in St Paul. He always started the routine with, "And people, let me tell you why I'm careful about the white girls I sleep with..."

This tag team strategy worked well last night until they got the girls back to their apartment. The hipster girl went cold after a hit from the bong. She kept saying, "Debra, let's *go*. You've got class in the morning." At about 3:30 a.m., she left in a huff, slamming the door on her way out and admonishing Debra that she could find her own way home. Andre suspected that she left Craig hanging for reasons beyond weed and interpersonal chemistry.

"That's it," he said to the TV as he switched it off. "No more white girls for the rest of the year."

"Yeah," Craig slurred from his chair. He looked up, blinked through his matted blonde hair, and passed out again. Andre mimed a high five and relieved Craig's crotch of the Mickey's bottle.

Despite the fact that he was running late, Andre spent a half hour showering and grooming. With a wide toothed comb and a bottle of oil he formed his small afro into a perfect sphere. He chose the gold crucifix from the three hanging from the light beside the mirror. The tricky part of getting ready for work would be sneaking into his room, collecting his work clothes, and sneaking back out without waking up a hung over co-ed. He managed it with only a few interrupted snores from the girl he assumed was named Debra. He dressed in the bathroom.

The apartment was in an uncommon state of disarray. A bottle of Stoli's lay on the floor in the hallway, about ten beer cans dotted horizontal surfaces throughout the living room, and half-eaten boxes of Chinese takeout littered the counters in the kitchen. Every ash tray was full. The hipster chick had chain smoked the entire time she was there and Craig could smoke an entire pack in an hour when drunk.

Andre gathered up the beer bottles and Chinese food. He also flipped on the air purifier to cut down the smell of smoke. Two years of food service management had made him a neat freak and he hated leaving for work with a dirty apartment. He would vacuum and wipe the counters when he got home. With an hour of sleep, he was heading into a double shift.

Octavio slid right, avoiding Aaron Black's jab by millimeters. Aaron was a foot taller than Octavio and his reach was amazing. Octavio threw two punches at Aaron's gut to buy himself time to set up for a hook. Aaron stepped back and adjusted his stance to the left, the opposite direction Octavio was trying to move him. With a quick uppercut, Aaron penetrated Octavio's fists and clocked him in the jaw. One of Octavio's back teeth shattered and blood whipped from his lips onto the canvas floor of the boxing ring.

"Oh, sorry about that, man," Aaron said, lowering his gloves. His black, curly hair was slicked with sweat.

Octavio rotated his jaw and pressed his tongue against the broken tooth. Tiny tentacles were already at work repairing it. "No problem," he said. "Nice move. I'd have nailed you if you'd gone right."

"I know," Aaron said, smiling. "That's why I didn't."

The two stripped their gloves. Neither wore headgear. For guys like them, even the gloves were more protection than necessary. They wore them for show and to remind each other that the fight was only a friendly sparring match.

"You want to get a beer with me and Tabitha after work today?" Aaron asked.

"No thanks," Octavio said. "I've got a pile of paperwork that's overdue. Since they moved me out of the Youth Program, I've been buried in Térata BS. It's more of a babysitting gig than the kids were."

Aaron smiled and stuffed his gloves into his gym bag. "Yeah, those creatures are a bit of a problem aren't they?"

"Clarence doesn't think so," Octavio said, shrugging. "They're definitely effective at what they do."

"When they don't go crazy," Aaron amended.

Octavio frowned.

"You know that wasn't your fault," Aaron said. "Those kids. If anybody's to blame, it's Clarence. He knows where his numbered pets are all the time. He tracks them in the Elipsis System. He should have warned you and me that one of those things was on the loose in the woods up there. If one of my kids hadn't broken his leg right before Number 10 showed up, things would have been different. You did everything you could."

Octavio nodded. "I know," he said. "It still bothers me, though. How could it not?"

"Look. It's been weeks since that shit went down. Come out with me and Tabitha. Relax for once. You need it, man."

Octavio shook his head. "I appreciate the offer. Just not tonight."

He gathered his gear and stepped out of the boxing ring.

"Remember," Aaron said. "We're Awake. Everyone you ever knew before thinks you're dead. We're your family now. You don't have to be alone."

Octavio pulled a towel out of his gym bag and cleaned the blood from the mat. Aaron patted Octavio's back and walked to the showers, whistling a jazz tune.

Chapter 2
Incense

The Blue Owl was a coffee shop/wine bar tucked into the Longfellow neighborhood of south Minneapolis. Floral canvases painted by a local artist hung on slate gray walls. The floors were a muted grey checker board and the tables were wrought iron with glass tops. A large chalk board hung behind the bar, spelling out the menu in swirling, multi-colored calligraphy. The air smelled of incense. Number 9, dressed in the skin of Daniel Clark, hated incense. His sensitive nose could filter most of the city's olfactory assault, but incense cut right into his sinuses. He sneezed twice when he walked in.

He knew Victoria was there. Even through the incense, her smell was unmistakable. She sat beneath a large painting of a chrysanthemum, reading a paperback novel. She wore a loose yellow skirt peppered with Asian designs. Dozens of small braids hung to her shoulders and her skin was a rich bronze color, contrasting with her striking blue eyes. Her age was indeterminate, at once youthful yet deep into womanhood. She did not notice him as he entered. Neither did the handful of other customers, each engrossed in their computer screens, newspapers, or books. Even the barista didn't look up from the glasses she was dry wiping.

Daniel crossed the room with deliberate steps, releasing a series of potent pheromones as walked. This was a heavy handed way to get what he wanted, but it would work. Based on the pheromones she exuded, he manufactured a string of his own which would ensure she was attracted to him to the point of sexual arousal. He was halfway to her table when she put the book down and looked at him. Though she remained in a reserved position, the pupils of her eyes widened and she smiled. Several other women, and one man, glanced up at him as well. While their attraction wouldn't be as strong, throwing around body lures always drew attention. Sloppy. He didn't bother to introduce himself as he sat down, but he proffered the business card he'd taken from Kimm last night.

"I have need of your services, Victoria. I was hoping for a private reading this afternoon."

She inclined her head and with a smooth, calm voice said, "Readings are done at their own time. One cannot force them."

"Well, let's bend the rules just this once, shall we?"

He smiled what he knew was a gorgeous smile and exuded a second set of pheromones designed to make her trust him.

She leaned forward and matched his smile. "Well, sir, I suppose exceptions can be made even with the spirits."

Their faces were almost touching and he found himself swimming in her eyes. They were blue like the ocean around an exotic tropical island, exactly as he remembered them from years before.

"Who, may I ask, gave you my card?"

"An associate of mine. Kimm Peters. He also told me I

might find you here in the late morning, if I couldn't reach you on the phone. I'm only in town for today, so I was hoping you could accommodate my schedule."

"Certainly," she replied. "Would you like to follow my car? I'm parked in the red Ford truck outside."

"I was hoping you could give me a lift," he said.

They left The Blue Owl together, Victoria hanging from his arm.

Before anything else, Victoria Starks considered herself a guide. Though the terms medium, seer, or psychic applied to her trade, she was not one of those people. Her senses were sharper and her physical body stronger. Her abilities were rooted in a spiritual plane, not psychological parlor tricks. After more than ninety years of life, she found the term "guide" best described her profession. During card readings, she never told clients what she gleaned. Rather, she created circumspect paths for them to follow, helping them to distinguish the varying shades of difficult choices. When that man walked into the Blue Owl, Victoria knew that she must earn her self-chosen descriptor. If she failed to guide him, he'd kill her. Even without his connection to Kimm Peters, that fact was clear. She had never felt such a physically dangerous presence, even before he hit her with an onslaught of pheromones, a move she considered tacky. Why did he want her to want to sleep with him, anyway? She allowed the chemical assault to overtake her senses. Fighting such powerful biochemistry was impossible, so she relaxed and surrendered. She hoped to wall off a piece of her reason and ride out the emotional wave. If she convinced him that she was smitten, perhaps he wouldn't continue to assault her libido.

"What is your name?" she asked as they walked to her pickup. She slid her hand under his sweatshirt and teased her fingers across the skin of his back. The amount of information the touch gave her almost caused her to trip and fall. This was not a man at all. Something else lurked beneath that skin. She managed to keep her heart rate steady, her muscles loose, and her tone casual. If he suspected she was aware of so much, he'd kill her as soon as he had what he wanted, whatever that was. He would likely do so, anyway.

"Daniel Clark," he said.

Not his name at all. Did creatures like this even have names? She doubted it. As they reached her truck, she disengaged her fingers from his back. That hadn't seemed to arouse him. She looked up into his eyes and widened hers.

"Daniel," she said. "God's judge. It suits you."

That did it. He was trapped in her eyes for several seconds. She could feel his desire for her spark to life. She could guide him with her eyes.

She unlocked his door and opened it. He sneezed twice when she did so. *Odd*, she thought. He'd done that as he walked into the coffee shop as well. Perhaps his nose was sensitive. Her truck smelled of herbs and incense. A bundle of dried *Artemisia annua* she had bought at a local herb shop was stashed behind the passenger seat.

As he climbed in, he said, "Not often a woman like you drives a truck like this, Victoria."

"My daddy was a farmer," she replied when she got to her side. "Some of his habits stuck with me."

Victoria lived on West River Parkway. In the winter, she could see the Mississippi from her living room window. She opened the garage door with a remote clipped to her sun visor and pulled in. As the door retracted, she felt a moment of panic. The jaws of a trap were closing around her. She let the moment pass. Daniel, or whatever he was, did not notice. He was sneezing again.

He has some kind of allergy, she thought. Her garage was a drying room for all sorts of aromatic flowers, herbs, and plants. When they got into her house, he excused himself to the bathroom.

While Daniel was in the bathroom, Victoria formed her entire plan. His absence allowed her to think clearly. She set up her tarot cards, pulled herbal tea from a cabinet, and put a pot of water on the stove. From the depths of her highest cabinet she pulled out a small vial filled with a pinkish powder. Tiny, handwritten script along its side read, *Papaver somniferum.* Based on the strain of the flowers she had grown to get this powder, the vial was enough to blast an entire dinner party to the moon. Her life depended on getting this creature called Daniel to ingest most of it. He'd given her enough time to make a plan. She hoped she would live long enough to execute it. She pulled a lemon from her refrigerator and split it into four pieces, then lit an incense stick on the mantle of the fireplace.

So much incense! Daniel thought, scrubbing his nose at the sink. Her house was the most concentrated pit of the stuff he'd ever encountered. She hadn't had any in her Washington, DC mansion the last time they met. He blew out a satisfying wad of yellow mucus and looked at his face in the mirror. She had fallen for that face. He didn't need his nose to tell him that. Her eyes hinted at what was going on in her mind, and he had decided to find out what some of those things might be before he eliminated her. Those blue eyes were electric, framed by her bronze skin and hair. He'd remember them forever. When he dispatched her, he'd make sure they were closed. He wiped his face with a yellow towel hanging by the sink and let it fall to the floor.

The tea pot whistled as Daniel emerged. His nose clogged at once and he sneezed five times.

"Dammit," he growled. "Put out that fucking incense!"

Victoria was pouring hot water into a chrome plated carafe. She looked up at him, eyes wide, and said, "I'm sorry." She went to the fireplace and stifled the incense. "I've made some tea to help with your allergies. I didn't realize it was the incense."

He stood at the doorway of the kitchen and watched as she steeped the tea. She added honey and squeezed in two lemons. The smell did cut through the incense.

"What kind of tea is that?" he asked, steering his voice back to pleasant territory. He couldn't afford to smash her with pheromones again. It would interfere with the reading. From the way she looked at him, he didn't need to bother.

"*Euphrasia officinalis,*" she replied. "It has anti-inflammatory properties and blocks histamines. Tastes bitter, though, so I've added honey and lemon to take the edge off."

He waved his hand. "Good. Fine."

She put together a tea service tray and nodded toward the living room. "I have prepared your reading, Daniel."

He followed her into the living room, which was, he supposed, very feng shui. Candles burned on sconces on either side of the fireplace. Plants were scattered among tasteful furnishings which looked antique and Oriental. Three abstract paintings hung on the wall, the canvases stained with a myriad of colors.

"Those are Sam Gilliams," Victoria said as she noticed him looking. "Washington Color School in the 1960s..."

He cleared his throat. "Is the tea ready?"

She glanced back at him and their eyes met. For a few silent moments they stared at one another. She smiled and said, "Please have a seat on that cushion."

She set the tea service on the hardwood floor and poured two cups. He sat across from her, admiring her ritualistic and graceful movements. A sublime magic was at work in her hands. He'd felt the same power when she had read for him before. That reading was still crystal clear in his mind, though his other memories of that time were hazy at best. Almost thirty years had passed. He had been weaker then, almost a different being.

She handed him the tea, which he put to his nose before drinking. The clogged sensation lightened as he inhaled. He took a sip and his sinuses relaxed. His sense of smell didn't return, but at least his face didn't feel like a swollen, pinched balloon. For a brief moment, he wondered what else might be in the tea besides *Euphrasia*. But she was drinking with him, and her eyes still regarded him with nothing but guileless desire. When he finished the cup, his sinuses clogged again, although not so badly as before. He set the cup on the tray and wiped at his nose with the back of his hand.

Victoria refilled his cup without comment and pulled her cards from a porcelain box sitting beside her. With nimble fingers she began to shuffle. Daniel was captivated by the fluidity of her movements as she turned the cards back and forth, pulling them apart so that they seemed to float in the air. He picked up his cup and drained it.

His face felt much better. Light as feather, in fact. He shot Victoria a loose smile, which made her shiver as she finished shuffling the cards.

She set the deck before him and intoned, "Please cut the

cards. As you do so, hold firmly in your mind the questions you pose to the spirit world. Do not allow your mind to stray."

Her voice held a rock solid command wrapped in a soft bolt of cloth. He thought of his brother and his brother's supposed child, Amber.

She refilled his cup as he cut the cards. He drained it again. The second cup had cleared his sinuses. Perhaps a third would restore his sense of smell. What was the name of that herb? *Eu*-something. He needed to remember that. It worked miracles. And made him feel wonderful.

"You have three questions," she intoned. "Ask the first."

He said, "Who killed my brother?"

One by one, Victoria flipped four cards from the deck and arranged them on the blanket, which he noticed had a marvelous lion design on it. Those beasts almost appeared to be jumping off of the silk, claws extended, teeth bared. The cards were handmade works of art as well, popping from the red blanket in exquisite detail. The Tower. The Hand. The Carnival King. The Upside Down Sword.

Her voice rang in the room. "All is not as it seems. Death is reversed. You are watched. Home is no longer a safe haven. Ask the next question."

He grimaced at the answers. They were riddles. This was the same as the last time she had read for him, though, and those riddles had told him everything he needed to know. Perhaps he could coax more information from her when the reading was over.

"Who watches me?" he asked, veering from his original questions in the face of this new information.

She flipped one card and placed it in the center of the blanket. The Scales.

"The dead," she said.

That was not helpful at all, but he should have known better than to stray from his original set of questions. Asking questions about answers was never fruitful. Why had he done that? With some effort he refocused his mind.

"Does the child have what my father wants?"

He looked in her eyes as she dealt the cards. They were distant and immeasurably deep, the most amazing things he'd ever seen.

She pulled five cards from the deck and dropped them over the other cards. Two fell face down. One fell off the blanket. The other two dropped face up, one atop the other. The Hollow Skull.

"Yes," she said.

He felt himself smile as if from a vast distance. He looked down at the last card. The top of the skull was cut away. As he watched, it turned up to face him and began laughing. He looked at Victoria. She was panting. With the same grace she used to deal the cards, she slid her blouse off, exposing the tender flesh of her breasts. He didn't notice them. Her lightning blue eyes dominated his entire field of vision.

He lunged across the blanket of cards, scattering them. She caught him, enveloped him, and guided him. His senses smeared as he moved. The world dissolved and lurched. Her eyes were the only solid point. He couldn't look away. Her fingers worked nimbly on his clothing, stripping his jeans in a fluid motion. He was inside her without effort, her eyes everything. His body floated, the muscles in his legs and back caught in spasms. She moaned, her hands locked around him. He growled and his body began to transform. The links in his mind that held the shape of Daniel broke one by one. He had no will, no real sense beyond the intensity of her eyes and a pleasure that hummed with mania. As he reached climax he shouted, "Close your eyes!"

She did not. They remained open, locked to his.

"Close your eyes!"

He could not kill those eyes. He could not! Her own orgasm shook her, but still she kept her eyes on his. So he closed his own eyes and raised a half-clawed hand. His sightless world spun into murky darkness and his senses dissolved. As if from miles away, he could feel her beneath him, writhing in pleasure, digging her fingernails into his back. He brought his claw down on her chest, ripping into her, tearing toward her heart. The smell of her blood burst through the barriers in his nostrils. So sweet, so wonderful. He tore at her, feeling her flesh give, feeling blood run through his fingers. His head crowded with images of her death but her blue eyes floated in the void, perfect and untouched. He came again, the reverberations collapsing his conscious mind. Spent, thrilled, and riding a wave of intense feelings he'd never known, he collapsed onto her.

Bleeding, high from the opium, and shuttering from the throes of sexual intercourse, Victoria pulled herself from beneath the half-man, half-monster. Dark pink spikes protruded from various parts of his body and his skin was partially blackened. His nose and mouth were contorted into a snout. He snored, face down on the floor, his jeans around his ankles. She grabbed what was left of the Persian blanket and pressed it against the three gashes in her left shoulder to staunch the flow of blood. The matching pillow was tatters. The monster who called himself Daniel had destroyed it, thinking he was destroying her. She stumbled to the bathroom, grabbed some athletic tape from the cabinet under the sink, and wrapped the blanket to her wounds. *Thank God for the opium,* she thought.

Her ploy worked, though she was not sure how well, nor why. Once things had started, she'd been forced to move on instinct. Her eyes had been the key. The fact that he couldn't smell her fear probably saved her as well. Whatever was going on in his mind when the opium rage hit might have helped, too. She didn't know. But she needed to leave. He drank enough of the tea to overdose three people, but it didn't look like that would happen. Hopefully he would sleep for a very long time. Killing him as he slept was a tempting idea. However, she had made vows that could not be broken. Never lie during a reading. Never kill. Some technical difficulties may arise with the second vow if he did die from an overdose, but she didn't think getting him high qualified as attempted murder.

The tarot cards had parted as he attacked her. None were bent and not a drop of blood tainted a single one. She gathered them into their case. In her bedroom, she grabbed a packed suitcase from her closet floor. She struggled into a black t-shirt and sport pants, trying to keep as much blood off of them as possible. These injuries might require a trip to the emergency room, but she would figure that out when she was somewhere safe.

On her way back through the living room, she stopped long enough to pull the wallet from the monster's back jeans pocket. She threw it in her purse, stumbled to her truck, and drove north.

At the age of fourteen, Craig C. Miller Jr. escaped his mother and abandoned his two younger half-brothers in Hershey, Pennsylvania. He hopped on a Greyhound with a ticket he bought online with his mom's current boyfriend's credit card. He used the return address on child support payment envelopes to locate his father, whom he had not contacted in five years. Two days later he was on his father's doorstep in Cottage Grove, Minnesota, still sporting a black eye and a swollen ear that remained malformed even after it healed. His mom's boyfriend had been, like those before him, drunk and violent.

Moved by his physical condition, Craig Sr. welcomed Craig into his home. Despite a court order in Pennsylvania, Craig Jr. stayed in Minnesota. With the aid of expensive lawyers, full custody rights were eventually given to his father. This was a watershed for Craig.

Everything about living with his father was better. As a partner at a downtown Minneapolis accounting firm, Craig C. Miller Sr. made stratospheric amounts of money and lived in an idyllic suburban setting. As opposed to the trailer parks and HUD apartments Craig was used to, the new environment felt tranquil and free. The houses meandered through tidy, manicured cul-de-sacs. The people were polite, reserved, and friendly. He felt as if he'd awoken from a nightmare into a flawless world.

There were flaws, however. Over time, the details of his new home tarnished. His father had remarried and fathered two more children, both daughters. Lilly, his wife, was mistrustful of Craig and while she never fought against his arrival, she never welcomed him either. She relegated him to the basement bedroom, two floors below the sleeping quarters of the rest of the house. While she showered her daughters with gifts and praise, she kept a cool distance from Craig. He paid for anything he wanted out of a tight allowance, which depended on his completion of a list of household chores. Still, as far as wicked step mothers went, Craig didn't think she was all that bad. Unlike his mother, she was emotionally solid. She didn't drink, smoke, nor cuss him out at the slightest provocation. While her lipstick and mascara lifestyle rang hollow at times, she never made him feel like a worthless piece of trash.

More disturbing to Craig was his father's emotional distance. Clearly, Craig was his father's burden, a mistake of his misspent youth. For a year after Craig's arrival, his father was forced to send child support payments to his mother. Each month, that check in the amount of $1,598 was left on the kitchen table. The checks unleashed Craig's ire towards his mother. What had she done with all that money? In his mind it was an unfathomable sum. While he wore the cheapest clothes she could find at the thrift shop, ate free lunches at school, and subsisted in the lowest echelons of the junior high social order, his mother had a horde of cash she kept secret. Over time, though, Craig began to suspect that his father was trying to tell him something. His medical bills would also sit on the table for a day, as would receipts for school supplies. He once found a spreadsheet listing the entirety of his expense to the family for the month of October. It totaled $3,459.28.

For his sixteenth birthday, his father bought him a ten year old Mazda coupe ($3,999 + tags, title, and tax). Now mobile, he got a job at Rick's Tire and Battery in a nearby strip mall. With an income, he began to do more than lurk in the basement. He joined an Aikido dojo in St Paul, began dating a girl from school, and forged his first lasting friendship with a classmate, Andre Bowen. This was a second period of intense happiness. However, his grades suffered and his father was not pleased. The evening his report card came out, he found himself in his father's office, where familial discipline was carried out.

"Son," Craig Sr. said from across his vast, oak desk, "life is not a flippant fairy tale. It is a series of decisions, one following the other, each with their own consequences. You're choosing a poor path right now. You'll need higher grades than B's to get into the U of M with a scholarship. My office has generously put together such a scholarship, but we can't grant it to you with a GPA under 3.5. That creates a problem. College isn't cheap—and I know you don't appreciate this—but we really can't just throw money around here. I'm taking the car away until your grades improve. And I want you to quit that nonsense job at that auto place. Focus on your future."

Craig sat stunned in an antique leather chair, picking at the loose rivet under his right hand. His father spoke further about money and trees and decisions, but Craig didn't hear it. His bright spot had been snuffed, leaving a dead blackness. He said, "Yes, Father," and retreated to the basement.

He took the bus to school the next day, enduring jabs from those he thought he had left behind. He focused on his classes, even spending his lunch hour in the library catching up on trigonometry. That night he was scheduled to work 5:00 to 9:00 p.m. He sat on the bus with his mobile phone in his hand and the number to Rick's called up on its screen. Finally, after stumbling from the bus with an unnoticed spit wad stuck in his hair, he hit the "call" button.

"Hello, Rick's Tire and Battery, this is Kevin Jones, how can we be of service this afternoon?"

"Hey, Kev," Craig said. "I'm not gonna make it in tonight."

"What's up, Craig? You sick or something?" Kevin replied.

"No. No, it's worse than that. My dad's making me quit. I can't work there anymore."

"I see," said Kevin. A few seconds of silence stretched out

on the line.

"I'm sorry," Craig said. "I don't want to quit, but my dad's got this scholarship thing, and I can't let my grades fall…and he took my car away so I can't get there anyway."

Kevin cleared his throat and said, "Look. How about this. I'll send Claire over to get you tonight. You can put in your two-weeks-notice like you're supposed to and we can go from there. I'm short-handed right now and I need you here."

"Uh, OK," Craig said. "Yeah. I'll tell my dad that."

"Good. She'll be over in a few minutes."

When Craig got home from work that night, his father's voice rang from the office, "I thought I told you to quit that job, Son."

Craig explained that he needed to give two-weeks-notice and had done so in writing tonight.

Craig Sr. harrumphed and said, "Places like that don't need notice. They aren't some kind of professional setting or anything…still, it's fine as long as your grades don't slip any further."

There was an egress window in Craig's room that led to the back yard. After his two weeks were up, Craig slipped out of that window, snuck down the street, and met his ride to work. The experience was thrilling, but coupled with a sense of guilt. This was the first time since leaving Pennsylvania that he disobeyed his father. Craig invented a series of extracurricular activities and study groups to cover for his absence from the house, though he rarely had to use such lies. His job, and in particular his relationship with his manager, Kevin, had become more important to Craig than his father's wishes.

When his grades came back the next time, they were straight A's. Craig's father gave back the car and Craig was free to go to work without sneaking out the window. The episode produced some casualties. He lost his first girlfriend with the car. Also, a sense of resentment towards his father sprouted in his heart. That resentment festered over the course of the next two years and exploded when it was time for him to go to college.

"You'll be joining the same fraternity I was in," his father said, matter-of-factly. "It's a good house. The chapter here has a sterling reputation. You'll pledge—"

"No, actually," Craig replied from the same chair in which he'd sat through uncountable lectures. "I've already signed a lease with Andre for an apartment in Dinkytown. We're moving in on June first."

His father went on as if nothing had been said. "You'll pledge at the beginning of August and move in to the house around the twelfth, I think. I have all the paperwork prepared. While it's expensive, I think you really need—"

"No," Craig said again. "Thank you, though. I'm sure the fraternity would be great, but I already have other obligations." He stood up to leave the office.

"Young man," his father intoned, "you don't know what obligations are. You have a greater obligation to your future than you do to that black kid or some nonsense lease with a slum lord. The lease can be cancelled. Andre will find another roommate. Now, back to Phi—"

Craig walked out of the office. He got in his car and drove around the Twin Cities for two hours. Over the course of the weeks leading up to the first of June, he and his father locked themselves in a cold stalemate. His car was taken away again. Craig found all the forms to enroll in the fraternity filled out and sitting on the kitchen table. He threw them away. The following day his car vanished from the driveway. A bill for his first semester at the U sat on the table for a week. With a shaking hand, Craig wrote "Paid In Full" on it without being certain what he even meant.

On June first, Andre showed up with his parent's SUV and they packed all of Craig's material possessions in one load. He left his bed, since it had been there when he moved in four years before. He also left his computer, exercise gear, and anything else he'd seen a receipt for on the kitchen table. He bought new furniture with money he'd saved over the course of two years. The same day, he stopped by Kimm's Auto World and bought a fifteen year old Honda with cash.

For the next few years Craig lived off campus with Andre. He became notable for his ability to clear four foot bongs, shoot Jim Beam, and still stand. He continued working at Rick's. He attended college three quarter time, which allowed him to do all this and still maintain a perfect GPA. His lifestyle led to a series of small scale battles between father and son across the table at holidays and family functions. A frosty silence between the pair would go on for a month or two afterwards. Lilly had become more pleasant since Craig left and did an impressive job of playing peacekeeper. While she never took sides, she had a knack for deflating Craig Sr. just before his temper would spoil the afternoon or mar her perfectly orchestrated dinner party. Craig was grateful for her poise and acute sense of what others thought of the inner workings of her family.

The Sunday following his half-sister's twelfth birthday party, Craig and his father had a row. Craig's part time status as a student was the focal point of his father's pontification. Craig found himself in the same office, sitting in the same chair he had so often occupied as a teenager. Like most of their arguments, Craig Sr. did most of the talking while Craig Jr. stared at the screen saver on his dad's computer, an artificial aquarium. Craig fiddled with the loose rivet on the arm of the chair, as he always did.

"You're spending too much time partying with Andre," his dad said for what Craig estimated was the four thousandth time. "And you still work at that stupid tire shop. You need to quit drinking, take a bigger course load, and get a job in one of the labs on campus. You're majoring in biology. How do you expect to get a job after college if you don't have any experience in the lab? My friend, Dr. Julia Winter, takes on students every semester on the St Paul campus and she's said to me more than once at church that she'd be happy to have you. I keep telling her..."

Craig spaced off into the fish screensaver for a few minutes before something his dad said brought him back.

"...and you're turning out just like your mother. Probably doing drugs and sleeping with anything that moves and—"

"Never say that again," Craig spat across the desk.

His father frowned at him and shot back, "Young man, if you think you can speak to me with that tone of voice in my own house, you've got another—"

"I haven't spoken to my mother or seen my brothers in seven years! I am nothing like her and I can't believe you just said that to me!" Craig's voice and hands started to shake. "You don't know a damn thing about me! You don't know a damn thing about me!"

He stood and sputtered, "Fuck you!" before storming from the room. Clutched in his right hand was the loose rivet from the arm of the leather chair.

For the following four days, Craig went into full party mode. He managed to make it to work but blew off every class that week, a first for him. Late Thursday morning, he rolled off the chair he'd been passing out in and took a shot of Wild Turkey whiskey. He wondered how in the hell the whiskey and a handy shot glass got onto the coffee table beside him. He neither worked at Rick's nor had class on Thursdays, so this could be the final, crowning day of a spectacular bender.

Flunking out of college and losing his job were not his goals here. He knew that next week he'd be doing double time trying to repair the damage he had done with this tantrum over paternal disapproval.

Fuck, he thought, *I am Psych 101.* He took another shot. *My Dad's a huge prick and Kevin's dead. Yeah. Still.*

In the two months since Kevin's freak car accident, Craig began to understand just how critical that man had been as a role model. Guilt riddled him. He felt as if he had taken something from Kevin and never bothered to pay for it or say thanks. *Yeah, maybe Psych 202,* he thought.

By 5:00 p.m., Craig was shit-faced. In a moment of what felt like complete lucidity, he decided to steal his dad's minivan. He hated the thing. It was a Dodge, it was new, and it cost forty thousand dollars. How in the hell a minivan could cost that much money was beyond Craig, but that wasn't why he hated it. He hated it because Lilly drove an Escalade that cost half and again as much, yet his father insisted that the Caravan was the superior vehicle. He had walked around it right after picking it up from the dealership and snapped, "I can get more people and more stuff in this thing than any SUV. And it gets twice the mileage. This, Craig, is a good buy for a vehicle." His father's arrogance concerning that van was more than Craig could take.

He knew that his father and Lilly would be at some stupid dinner party at one of their rich friends' houses on Thursday at 6:00 p.m. The van would be parked in the driveway, since Craig Sr.'s spot in the garage was occupied by whatever small, European car from the 1960s he was currently failing to restore. The spare key to the van sat on the shelf by the service entrance to the garage. All he had to do was take a bus to the stop four blocks away and the van was his.

Brown-bagged 40 ounce Mickey's in hand, this is exactly what Craig did. He got the van back to Dinkytown by 7:00 p.m. and began sending text messages. Andre would be home by 9:00 p.m. This would be a great fucking night.

Chapter 3
Victoria's Circle

Victoria Starks sat naked in the lotus position on the floor of her cabin outside of Pine City, Minnesota. Tarot cards were sprayed all around her. Her clothes, along with an apple scented log, burned in the fire place.

Her chest heaved, each breath pulled all the way in and expelled completely. Jagged cuts ran along her shoulder and left breast. The wounds changed colors from deep red to gaudy purple, but they would heal without medical attention. The scar would be impressive, though. Despite her age this would be her first permanent, physical scar.

Psychologically, she was still a mess. The opiate and pheromone deluge dulled her senses. Coherent thought was a challenge. As she breathed, she tried to make sense of the day's events.

This was not the first time Victoria had been raped. Despite her own desires and despite her complicity with the act, she had that same feeling of violation, powerlessness, and self-loathing so intrinsic to the first time it had happened. She grappled with the fact now, rather than rest and sort it out tomorrow. Her mind and body were hot and alive and very dangerous. She couldn't have slept if she wanted to. So she meditated. She breathed. And she remembered.

She sank backward through more than eighty years, each decade falling away until she arrived where, for her, things had really begun.

Life is circles, overlapping, she thought. *The longer I last on earth, the more those circles will crisscross into one another.* This was a circle Victoria had hoped she would never complete. *Sooner or later,* she thought, *we complete them all.*

Tabby Starks abandoned Pikeville, Tennessee, her nine-year-old daughter, and her husband, Basil, for a white man in a carnival show in the summer of 1927. She had been quite light skinned herself and it was the opinion of the rest of the colored people of Pikeville that she fancied herself white. When she absconded with a white man, the community feigned blasé disaffection. "Bound ter 'appen soon er late," sang the woman who cut Victoria's hair. "Such's she's always thinkin' ther on ther way up. Well, mebbe she is." Even Basil acted nonplussed. The object of Tabby's affair had been the man who lit the explosive lights the last night of the carnival. According to Basil, "She always liked shiny things and that fella had on clothes so bright I couldn't even look at him directly." The face of a laughing cat was painted on the side of all the carnival's trucks and wagons. Basil told Victoria later that such was the way of the ignorant and ashamed. She didn't understand what he meant until decades later when she saw that same cat in Chicago.

Tabby's mother, known as Mam-maw to the entire town of Pikeville, took the child under her wing for those things related to the female gender. But even before her mother ran off, Victoria was her father's daughter. Basil Starks was a self-taught exception to the phrenological notions of his time. While his taste in women was suspect, he was able to read, write, and perform advanced math. As a sharecropper, such knowledge allowed him to grow the acreage he planted each year and come out ahead at the end of each season. His ability to isolate his landlord's book keeping "mistakes" and be paid what he was owed contributed to his success. Though blocked from owning land by the local authorities, Basil prospered in a profession designed to be unprofitable. Others in the sharecropping community, even the white ones, often asked him to look over their ledgers, but he always declined. Tweaking the lion's nose was fine. Pulling his tail quite another.

When Julius Rosenwald built the Lincoln School for Colored Students in 1925, Basil ensured that Victoria, who could already read, was enrolled. She quickly stripped the school of all it had to offer and began her own educational journey. There was no library yet in Pikeville, but her father managed to scrape up books for her on his frequent trips to Knoxville.

1929 brought the end of Basil's career as a sharecropper. As crop prices plummeted, he realized that the net loss on that year's yield would outstrip his ability to recoup it. So he packed up Victoria, sold most of his belongings, and joined many others in the Great Migration. The family's first stop was Knoxville, where Basil had family and professional contacts. Eventually, he hoped to move all the way to Chicago. Through his cousin, Basil found employment doing ledgers for a mortuary. His reputation for literacy and precision spread through the Bowery neighborhood in Knoxville. Various other black businesses began enlisting his services. One white man, a tailor, used him as well, but discretely. Basil posed as a cleaner when he went to his store once a week. Once he and Victoria were secured in Knoxville, he liked to boast that he was the only black man in the south who beat sharecropping.

During the years before he and Victoria left Pikeville, Basil found a broker in Knoxville willing to invest the small profits he made each year from sharecropping. He continued to invest once in Knoxville. His portfolio grew over the years, amounting to just over $12,000. This locked Basil into a financial position that allowed him and Victoria to live comfortably despite the Depression.

Victoria loved Knoxville. It featured dozens of shops and a library branch that allowed black people to check out books. She attended a private school for colored girls. With its focus on etiquette and social polish, she found its core banal. However, in comparison to Pikeville, it was urban and sophisticated. She blossomed socially and became active in a variety of school functions.

Throughout this period, she and her father shared a close relationship. He allowed her to drive his pickup truck to and from school on days he didn't need it. He spoiled her with fancy dresses. They lived in a camelback house in the Mechanicsville neighborhood near Knoxville College, where it was assumed that Victoria would matriculate once she finished her secondary education. And the music! It was everywhere on the streets, especially Market Square. Victoria loved the sound of the jazz and hillbilly music floating through the neighborhoods. She and her father took long walks together, enjoying the music and one another's company. While far from idyllic, this period of her life was infused with happiness.

Sitting before the fire in Pine City, Victoria imagined each childhood memory was a sphere of blue light in the air before her. She inhaled them all in a long, measured breath. These blue orbs spread through her, bringing a positive influence to her physical manifestation. She relaxed every muscle in her body and slumped forward so that her forehead touched the floor. Folded, she remained in that position for several minutes.

As if being pulled by an invisible string, her body straightened. Her eyes snapped open. Her muscles tensed. Her arms flew out like the wings of a bird. The fire danced in her eyes. Her mouth twitched. She decided to dive all the way down tonight. Face it all. She fell backwards, arms outstretched. As she fell, her mind tumbled back as well, to the end of that period and the beginning of who she was now; or, rather, who she had been until tonight.

The Bowery neighborhood in Knoxville became increasingly violent and crime ridden as the Depression dragged on. Prohibition laid the foundation by making the neighborhood a center for organized crime, but the general poverty of the Depression pushed the neighborhood further into decline. Several of the businesses that Basil worked for folded. The mortuary was his only steady client by 1937. Still, Basil and his daughter didn't suffer as much as the rest of the community. His investments provided a cushion, preventing them from experiencing austerity pains.

Women, however, continued to be Basil's primary weakness. Particularly, he had a problem with prostitutes. His heart never fully recovered from what Tabby had done to it. When his desires exceeded that which his hand could stifle, he rented a girl in the Bowery for a night. This was not a compulsive habit, nor did it otherwise affect his life until he met Nelly Brown. She was physically to his liking, so he paid her repeat visits.

One night, Nelly overheard Basil talking in his sleep about money he had stashed in the fireplace. She began to suspect that he was financially beyond her usual clientele. She brought the matter up to her pimp, Billy Dillon, suggesting that Basil might make a better mark than client. Billy agreed.

Nelly began to endear herself to Basil. His infrequent visits became common, as she no longer charged for her services. She filled his head with sweetness and feigned love for him. Basil had no desire to reform a prostitute, but Nelly put herself to work on the matter and eventually talked him into at least inviting her to dinner. Though he felt uneasy with the decision, he did not suspect she wanted more than to be with him in a new capacity. What could that hurt?

On a Friday evening in the fall of 1938, Basil sent a car to pick Nelly up and bring her over for dinner with his daughter. Victoria was two months into her final year of primary school and cleared an otherwise busy evening. She had no notion of what Nelly was, only that her father had finally shown interest in a woman. Nelly wore a smashing dress she bought that day, dropped all hint of the Bowery accent from her speech, and did her best to impress. It worked. Victoria was charmed by the woman's worldly wit. Basil was incredulous that a prostitute, even one that claimed to have given up the trade for him, could make such a transformation. Dinner was splendid. Nelly talked the pair into staying up late for a couple of drinks afterward. A few drinks turned into more, and while Basil forbade Victoria from drinking more than one, she was intoxicated by her father's happiness. Not since her mother left had Victoria seen her father smile the way he did that night. The edges of his mustache seemed to reach towards his eyes. This was exactly how she always remembered his face from her earlier childhood.

Late into the evening, Nelly announced that she should be going. She had, in fact, hired a driver that evening to fetch her at this hour. He'd be by any minute. She'd be in the water closet for a few moments, in case he showed up. Later, Victoria would understand the significance of the odd hand gesture Nelly made as she stood up in full view of the front window. At the time it just seemed like an affectation. It was not. It was a signal. As soon as she closed the door to the water closet, a sharp knock came from the front door.

Victoria was seated on the sofa across from her father. The game of Monopoly that had been going on for most of the evening was spread out between them. She shared a moment of tenderness with her father that lasted as long as a glance and would never be forgotten. Basil rose from his chair, placed the dice he'd been rolling between his fingers on the game board, and turned to answer the knocking door. The radio played a big band number—Benny Goodman doing an arrangement by Fletcher Hendersen on the Let's Dance late night radio show.

Back in Pine City, Victoria took a sharp breath. The happenings of that night from this point forward were difficult not only to remember, but also to go through the act of remembering. She pushed the negative energy outside of herself, seeing it as a black fog rolling out of her mouth on the exhale and filling up the room.

Basil opened the door to Billy Dillon. He was six foot five and lean. A scar arched across his forehead, in view just beneath his green fedora.

"Billy..." Basil said, "Guess I didn't expect you to be the—"
Billy grabbed Basil and threw him through the doorway.

"Shut up, nigga."

Basil flew into the family photo album's stand, scattering pictures across the floor. Victoria stood up and started to scream, but Nelly appeared behind her with a knife from the kitchen. She put the blade against Victoria's throat and said, "Lissen here, sweetie, don't you make a noise. I'd like nuthin' more than ta open you up jus' like a pig."

Billy closed the door and kicked Basil toward the living room. He saw Nelly with the knife at Victoria's throat. A steady stream of blood ran off the blade where it broke the skin. "Don't ya kill that bitch, Nelly Brown, or I'll turn ya inside out. I gots use fer a bitch like that."

"If I aimed ta kill her, she'd be dead," Nelly spat.

Billy turned his attention to Basil, who was bleeding from his left ear. "Now, Mista High Class, ya tell me where ya keep ya fuckin' money and we kin make this perty quick."

Basil shook his head and looked into Billy's eyes. "My money's in the bank."

Billy roared and kicked Basil in the ribs so hard he lifted off the ground. "Ain't no nigga in this fuckin' state keeps 'is money in no bank, no matter how high class that nigga thinks he be! So ya better start tellin' me where the fuckin' money be, mutherfucker, or I'm gonna start carvin' ya, yer daughter, and this fancy place right the fuck up."

Coughing, Basil pointed to his desk across the living room. "Top…drawer."

Billy pulled the drawer out of the desk and dumped its contents onto the coffee table. Along with stamps, stationary, and several grease pencils, a wad of cash in a silver money clip fell out. Billy didn't even pick it up. "You want I should take it that a high class nigga, livin' in digs like these, only got this much money to 'is name? You thinkin' I'm a fool, Basil Starks! You thinkin' I'm a fool!"

Basil tried to lift himself onto the couch. Blood ran from his mouth and he wheezed noisily. Billy flipped the coffee table over, kicked off one of the legs, and started beating Basil with it. Despite the knife at her neck, Victoria screamed, "Stop! Stop! Please! He ain't lyin'! The money's in the bank. We can get it for you Monday! Please!"

Billy paused, looking Victoria in the eye. He swung the leg of the coffee table into her temple. Her world collapsed into blackness.

She regained consciousness in bits and pieces. The ticking of the cuckoo clock was the first thing she would consciously remember later. Then it was the throbbing pains. Her head. Her neck. Between her legs. A half hour passed before she could open her eyes. As she did so, the world rotated into focus. The first thing she saw was the mantle that had been installed around the fireplace a few months ago. She threw up on the Victorian rug. The pain in her head spiked as she heaved. When she finished, she pulled herself to her hands and knees and cast about for her father. He was sprawled amidst a pile of broken furniture, his eyes wide open, the kitchen knife jutting up from his chest. Her underwear was draped over the handle of the blade. Blood covered almost all of him, slick in the dim light, as if he had swam in a pool of the stuff.

How could he have so much blood on him? she thought. She crawled to him and laid her head on his chest, her eyes an inch from the blade of the knife. Victoria unleashed a guttural moan that shook every bone in her body. She took his hand and clutched it against her face. The smell of his blood was overpowering but she breathed it in deeply. A few moments later she fell asleep. That's how she was found by the cleaning woman who always came on Saturday mornings.

Victoria's feet were tucked beneath her buttocks as she lay back flat. Her arms were extended to either side. Her breathing was slowing now. Her eyes were still blank, but tears streamed from either side of each of them. *Now*, she thought, *the hardest part*. The cards around her were a forked path. Circles inside circles inside circles…She had to choose again. And she was scared to death of that. *Back, back, back…*

As soon as the police released her, Victoria fled to Mam-maw's cabin outside of Pikeville. She did not tell them who had done this. She claimed she could remember nothing. The enormous bump on her temple made that believable.

She stumbled from the pickup truck into Mam-maw's arms, sobbing. Mam-maw stroked her hair and walked her onto the porch of the cabin. There she rocked the girl until she slept. Several neighbors stopped by, but Mam-maw waved them away.

Other than letters to the lawyers and bankers in Knoxville, Victoria communicated with no one for the first two weeks following her return to Pikeville. Mam-maw said little to her granddaughter. She held her every night until she slept. She posted the letters Victoria wrote to put her father's estate in order. She cooked her meals and cleaned her clothes. Silently, she cared for the girl.

After several weeks, Victoria broke from her catatonic state at dinner time. Mam-maw had prepared cooter stew. The shell of the turtle sat by the washtub. Victoria had been staring at it since Mam-maw killed the creature.

"Why did you carve that circle into the inside of the turtle's shell, Mam-maw?" she asked.

Mam-maw smiled, which caused her smooth face to fracture into thousands of crevices. "I lets out the soul a' the beast," she replied.

Victoria nodded and fell silent for another ten minutes. She did not touch the stew before her. "What do you keep in the root cellar?"

Mam-maw frowned. The lines on her face rearranged themselves into an entirely different pattern. She could have been a different woman. "Nuthin', chile. Juss tha roots an' spices an' picklins."

"They say in town you can talk to the dead," Victoria pressed. "That you're a hoodoo who can conjure. I want you to show me how."

Mam-maw's face smoothed. She had not expected this. Victoria had always been so practical, like her father. She'd shown no interest in roots or stones, let alone spirits or hoodoo. She even slept through Sunday School most of the time. This sudden interest in Mam-maw's secret business was disturbing in the wake of her father's death. Still, there was no harm in showing the girl how to make root potions and heal the sick. The main thrust of conjure was simply in knowing how the world worked. For a moment, Mam-maw stood on the precipice of a vast decision she could not possibly understand. "Surely, chile," she said. "We kin start tamorra."

That night after Victoria was asleep, Mam-maw took two brass keys from the hanger by the stove. One's head was the shape of a square. The other's was a spiral like a sea shell. She flipped them back and forth with her fingers. Other than their heads, they were identical. Even their teeth. Mam-maw stopped flipping the keys and selected the spiral headed one. She had never been able to make this key work in the lock that it was meant for. Perhaps she should remove it from the ring. But, then, what did it matter? She hung the keys back up and went to bed.

The next morning, Mam-maw and Victoria descended the stairs leading to the root cellar, a cramped space lined with shelving and packed with bail lid jars. Until a few weeks ago, Victoria never noticed that Mam-maw vanished into this recess for hours at a time. There was barely room to stand up. She had no notion how both of them were supposed to fit down there. The ceiling was nothing more than the slat boards and joists of the kitchen floor.

"Stay close, chile," Mam-maw said.

"How are we going..." Victoria began. Mam-maw released a hidden latch and an entire section of shelving swung inward.

"This way," Mam-maw said. She lit an oil lamp and descended into the darkness. Once both were inside, Mam-maw secured the shelf behind them. "Nobody kin know a' this place 'cept you an' me, chile."

Eyes wide in the flickering lamplight, Victoria nodded.

Victoria stayed close as they walked through an unfinished tunnel. The roots of trees burst through the soil of the walls and ceiling. The floor was strewn with stones to allay washout. As they traveled the temperature dropped. Victoria shivered. Several minutes later, they came upon a fork in the path. Without comment, Mam-maw took the right path. A rickety door with a steel and brass padlock emerged from the tunnel's gloom. Mam-maw pulled two keys from her dress, selected one of them, and unlocked the door.

The flame of the lamp was not enough to light the chamber beyond the door. Mam-maw lit candles and oil lamps throughout the room. Victoria wondered where she got the tallow for so many candles. What emerged from the flames' light was a large circular cavern filled with odd things. More bail lid jars containing strange objects lined a series of shelves built into the rock of the walls. An entire section contained jarred pig fetuses. Piles of dried herbs occupied two shelves next to a stack of earthen pots, each labeled with a rune. Improbably, a cast-iron box stove stood in a corner. Pots, pans, and glassware hung around it from a railing system built into the wall. The stove's chimney climbed into the root covered ceiling. Several gallons of water sat on the floor nearby.

Victoria was shocked. Her mouth was open, her eyes wide.

"Mam-maw," she said, "you're a witch!"

Victoria never saw the hand that slapped her, but suddenly the dim room was a white flash of pain.

"Nevva you use that kinda word wi' me, chile, lest I slap ya head right offa yer neck."

Victoria put her hand to her inflamed jaw. She could feel the outline of Mam-maw's fingers pulsing on her cheek. Anger and a sense of shame flickered in her belly. Her tongue moved to tell the old woman what a horrible hag she was, but Mam-maw turned away and started a fire in the box stove. The numbers 124 stood out on its door. It was a very nice, very expensive stove, made by Atlantic. It also weighed a ton. How did Mam-maw get that thing down here?

Victoria explored the room. Cellars like this were often musty and moldy smelling. This one smelled like a clean kitchen. While the walls and ceiling were unfinished, the floor was cobbled with smooth river rocks, each placed to interlock with the next. Victoria knew very little of water tables, but this entire room should have been geologically impossible. There was a lift in one corner that could be raised and lowered via a geared pulley system. Firewood was neatly stacked beside it. Twenty feet up, a trap door created a jarring square against the organic root structures of the ceiling. This gave Victoria a sense of how deep the room lay, but not what was above them.

"That goes ta the floor a' the huntin' shed," Mam-maw said, gesturing up.

Victoria's eyebrows rose. That shed was located on a hill about half a mile from the house. She and her friends had often played in that shed. She'd never noticed any irregularity to the floor. Her world lurched. What else hid beneath the common moments of her life?

"Ther ain't much magics ta hoodoo," Mam-maw said as the fire roared to life. The temperature of the room leapt up. "Mos'ly, it's jus' the knowin' a' things. I know some. My momma knew more 'an I, but she passed afore she could teach it all. I figured out a bunch on my own, though, and I reckon I kin teach ya how things is done. I call this place the Kitchen."

Victoria approached the inviting warmth of the stove. "I'm sorry for calling you a witch, Mam-maw," she said, lowering her eyes.

Mam-maw nodded and said, "Good." She took down a pot and handed it to Victoria. "Besse Jackson's boy got a fever from a animal bite- prolly a possum, but nobody sure. I reckon 'e's infected. Mebbe loose 'is arm. We're gonna try to save tha arm. Chile, ther ain't nutthin' 'bout what I do what's got the devil in it. You understand?"

Victoria stared at the pot and thought of little Benjamin. Her heart sunk. He'd been bitten? When? That was always big news. Could be rabies. She didn't know. She couldn't remember a single detail of her life in the last month, except that circle carved into the turtle shell. The words in the letters she wrote to the lawyers and bankers swam in her memory, but they were unattached. Like she herself had been this entire time. Well, perhaps she could help Benjamin.

"Yes, Mam-maw. I understand," she said.

The two women worked in the firelight for the rest of the morning. Mam-maw kept up a stream of instructions, hints, stories, and admonishments. Victoria took to the new information, clinging to it and absorbing it. A singular purpose to her life emerged, as if a window opened with daylight streaming through. She leapt through that window, immersing herself in her grandmother's instructions. At the end of the morning they had created a green, lumpy paste and two vials of a rust colored broth. They brought these things to Benjamin that afternoon and by the next day his fever broke.

Victoria was astonished. She pestered her grandmother for more instructions and spent hours alone in the Kitchen. She kept a log book of her activities so she could cross reference them. She recorded dates and times for everything she did. When they had their first failure and George Tannen died of consumption she spent an entire day going over every detail of what had been done to save him. Mam-maw became exasperated.

"Chile, he 'uz sixty an' seven yers old! Ya canna save tha' which God's thought ta take."

After a few weeks, Victoria asked where the left fork in the underground path went. Mam-maw told her that hoodoo was complicated, and for now she needed to focus on the herbs and healing. That had been enough for Victoria. However, events took an unpleasant turn a month after their first journey into the earth.

Victoria woke up an hour earlier than usual with horrible stomach cramps. She fell out of bed, crawled to the kitchen, and retched into a large pan. Little but bile and saliva came up. She collapsed on the kitchen floor, thinking that she'd be sick for the week. However, an hour later, she felt fine. *Must have been something I ate yesterday*, she thought.

The next morning the same thing happened. Rather than collapsing on the kitchen floor, she dragged herself into Mam-maw's room. The old woman already up and sitting on the edge of her bed. She wore a cotton button up nightgown printed with pink poppies that she'd had as long as Victoria could remember. Despite being threadbare, it still looked as soft as it had when she'd been a child. Victoria stumbled into her grandmother's arms.

"I'm sick again this morning," she said. "Mam-maw, what's wrong with me?"

The older woman stroked her hair and rocked her. "We'll find out, chile..."

That afternoon, Mam-maw stopped over at Joe Stether's farm and brought home a doe rabbit.

"What are we going to do with that rabbit?" Victoria asked. She put her hand into the wire cage and stroked the creature. Its fur was black except for a white ring around its left eye.

Mam-maw grunted, which she often did when Victoria asked questions to which the answer would soon be self-evident. "Bring 'er whin we go ta tha Kitchen," she said.

Later in the Kitchen, Mam-maw handed Victoria a jar and said, "Make water."

By this time, Victoria had overcome the shock of dealing with body fluids. She had been astounded to learn that the human body's unpleasant places and functions were the cause of so many of its problems. She did as she was asked. Mam-maw took out her syringe kit. She screwed the needle into the stainless steel barrel and clicked the finger rings on top of the plunger. The last time Victoria had seen her assemble the device, she had used it to lance a boil in Katie Livingwell's arm pit. The thought of what she was going to do with the rabbit was disturbing.

"Put on tha gloves, chile, and pull tha rabbit out tha cage."

Mam-maw opened the jar containing Victoria's urine. Victoria pulled on a pair of thick leather work gloves and extracted the rabbit from the cage. Mam-maw placed the needle into the urine and pulled the plunger until half the barrel was full. She replaced the lid of the jar and turned to Victoria.

"Hol' the beast tight, an' keep 'er mout' away. Understand?"

Victoria frowned but nodded. She took hold of the rabbit by its hind legs and around its neck. The rabbit relaxed in her grip. It had obviously been domesticated before being called into service here.

With a deft motion, Mam-maw hooked the needle under the rabbit's skin and depressed the plunger. Victoria understood this would happen, but found the actual act sickening. The rabbit thrashed for a moment, but Mam-maw had the needle out before it could damage itself. Victoria placed the kicking animal back in its cage. Mam-maw disassembled and cleaned her syringe. The rabbit settled down and regarded Victoria with black, unblinking eyes.

"Now what's going to happen?" she asked.

"Nuthin' fer the moment. Tamorra answers'll come."

The next afternoon, Mam-maw slit the rabbit's throat. Once she'd drained the blood into a hammered copper bowl, she opened the rabbit's abdomen and pushed its guts onto the table.

"Here," she said, motioning to the rabbit's ovaries with a knife. "This 'ere's what we're afta."

The small, round organs were marbled with dark red dots.

"What does it mean?" Victoria asked.

Mam-maw sighed. "It means you's wi' chile."

Victoria blinked and her knees gave out. She fell straight down, landing with her legs tucked. A distant part of her bemoaned the dirt that would stain the white cotton of the dress beneath her knees. Somehow the possibility of pregnancy had not occurred to her. Her mind blanked right back to the moment the maid woke her up, her dead father a pillow beneath her head. The edge of the knife that killed him was razor sharp and hyper-focused just inches from her face.

Mam-maw tossed the rabbit into a garbage bin to give to the hogs. She said, "Baby'll come by tha end a summer."

Victoria pulled herself up from the floor. She said, "Oh," and busied herself cleaning the Kitchen. Mam-maw stayed silent and the pair worked the rest of the afternoon as if nothing was amiss.

But something was very amiss. A kernel of hate had been planted in Victoria and she was not capable of digging it out. Over the course of the next few months, the kernel grew into a small shrub that had the future makings of a large tree. There was a thing living inside her. Feeding off of her. A thing she hadn't asked for and a thing given to her by the very man who had taken away her father with a kitchen knife. As the pregnancy progressed and the signs of this thing in her became more apparent, her hate for it grew as well. Every time it kicked, she felt the knife plunge into her father. Every time it turned inside her, her own mind turned back to what she could remember of that night.

She hid these thoughts and feelings from Mam-maw. She was ashamed of the hate more than she was ashamed of being pregnant. Common knowledge of the county knew that Mam-maw had been raped by the sheriff right after the man hanged her husband. Hence Victoria's mother, Tabby. Mam-maw loved Tabby very much, despite the circumstances of her birth. The feelings of hatred Victoria bore toward her unborn child could not be anything Mam-maw would understand. So Victoria acted as if she had accepted the pregnancy and made peace with it. She took all the precautions a woman in her condition should take. She allowed herself to enjoy the glowing month. She remained externally positive. She sewed clothing for the coming child and hummed songs while she did it. Mam-maw could never know how she felt. When Mam-maw asked if she'd like to know the gender of the child, Victoria laughed and said, "I think it should be a surprise."

After the fifth month, Victoria refused to leave the cabin. Her belly started to show and she had no desire to hear the noise everyone would make about it. She even forsook going to church on Sunday mornings, something she had done without fail since returning to Pikeville. She acted as if nothing was amiss other than the physical demands of pregnancy. Mam-maw did not make a fuss about any of this, which angered Victoria. Irrationally, she hated Mam-maw as much as she hated the baby and hated the shame that came with hating the baby. She wanted the woman to fight with her. To tell her that she was being selfish for the way she felt. But she continued to hide her feelings and Mam-maw never asked her about them. It was while Mam-maw was at church one Sunday morning that Victoria decided to take the left fork in the path and see what was there. By this time, Mam-maw trusted her with the keys. Victoria stood in the upstairs kitchen and flipped the keys between her fingers. The square headed key to the spiral key. Back and forth. A small grin lit her face.

When she arrived at the fork in the path, she paused for a

moment. She tapped her index and middle finger against her lips before she dove into the darkness. This path descended from the fork, whereas the other path had been a steady incline. The air chilled and the smell of mold became pervasive. The path narrowed and the ceiling crept lower as she progressed. By the time Victoria reached the second door, she was crouched. The door was only four feet tall. It was a rough square made of decaying but sturdy oak boards. The metal bolts that held it together were rusted, as was the lock. The lock popped apart easily, though, when she inserted the spiral-headed key. Victoria's breath sharpened as she pulled the door open. The hinges groaned and squealed. No one had opened this door in a very long time. Gingerly, Victoria thrust her lantern into the pitch black room.

Light crawled into the space, illuminating a small, circular chamber packed with a variety of objects. She recognized some of them—globes, a glass distillery (an exact copy of which could be found in the Kitchen), and an entire shelf of hidebound books. But the space was mostly filled with various apparatus that Victoria couldn't begin to imagine the function of.

Once inside, she could stand up fully, but only six inches separated her bunned hair from the roots on the ceiling. She wasn't sure why she had come here, and now that she was here, she had no idea what to do. This seemed to be a storage space for antiquarian devices and rubbish. She turned to go. As the light from her lantern dragged across the room, it illuminated a green jewelry box tucked into the bottom of a shelf otherwise filled with animal bones. The bright green flash made her pause. She set the lantern down on the floor, which she noticed was brick and mortar, and crept over to the shelf. The box was carved from jade with a relief of a cornucopia etched onto its top. A gold latch held it closed. Crouching, she slid the box from the shelf, swung the latch, and lifted the lid. At first, she thought it was empty. But the bottom of the box appeared to be an inky black void. Victoria reached inside with her right hand. It vanished up to her wrist. She jerked her hand out, snapped the box closed, and thrust it back onto the shelf.

Eyes glued to the box, she scooted backwards on the floor. Her back hit the leg of a table, whose contents rustled. With a shaking hand, she reached over and picked up the lantern. The bottomless box had to have been a trick of the light. It was probably like one of those illusions she'd seen at the county fair. Her knees were still not trustworthy, so she scooted back to the box, this time with the lantern held firmly before her. The skull of a deer regarded her from the shelf above where she'd found the box. She ignored it and pulled the box from its cubby, set it on the floor, and opened the lid. From this angle, the light of the lantern penetrated the entire inside of the box.

The green sides glowed, but the bottom of the box was stubbornly black. Not black with local color. Rather, black with the complete absence of reflected light. Though it trembled, she put her finger into the blackness. It vanished. She jerked her finger back out. The next few moments were blurry and panicked. She stuffed the box back onto the shelf and scrambled from the room, slamming the door and fumbling the lock back into place before scurrying down the tunnel. Her hair snagged on the roots of the low ceiling. She didn't notice. When she'd clamored out of the cellar into the bright sun of late spring, her breathing calmed and her mind cleared.

It had to have been an illusion, she thought. In the face of a blue sky with puffy clouds, the thought of a bottomless green box seemed silly. She had simply lost control before she figured out its trick. Her brain had become sluggish the deeper she got into her pregnancy. Mam-maw said this was normal and her mind would return once the child came.

Still, she wasn't going back into that room. She was spooked all the way to her toes. Mam-maw would be home soon and they had to work out something to help Jessa Benson's acne, which covered the poor girl's back in a blanket of puss and infection. She turned her mind to preparing an astringent and perhaps something to help pull out the swelling. The inside skin of an eggshell worked well to draw out boils…Her mind continued down that path, but she waited until Mam-maw got home before descending once more into the earth.

She did not mention her journey to the other room to Mam-maw. While there was no official ban on that area, prudence cautioned her to remain discreet concerning the events. The other woman didn't seem to have any inkling that it had happened. Not that there was any reason she should have. Still, Victoria was relieved when they finished their work and nothing amiss had passed between them. Mam-maw was the kind of woman who often knew things she shouldn't. The rest of the afternoon and evening passed with no incident. Usually, Victoria would have stayed up several hours past dinner reading. She had recently received a comprehensive book called Health Knowledge, which featured color plate inserts with die-cuts in the shape of the human body. *Every* organ was described with shocking clarity. Nothing like it had been available in Tennessee before. She had waited weeks for the book to arrive and within a week had read it through twice. She was halfway through it for the third time. Tonight, though, she felt exhausted and retired early.

Once in bed, she lay wide awake beneath the light blue comforter one of the ladies at church had quilted for her. Her exhaustion had evaporated. She was not prone to insomnia. Even after her father's death, she had slept every night. If anything, she tended to sleep too hard and too long. But that night she could not quiet her mind or close her eyes. Every time her eyelids descended, the black bottom of the jade box appeared before her. Her heart heaved and her eyes popped open. Just after midnight, however, when her eyes closed and the blackness appeared before her, she did not leap back to wakefulness. Instead, she fell forward into that blackness.

As she did so, her body peeled away from her awareness. Only her thoughts and the darkness remained. She found this to be a calming experience. A pleasant reduction. After a few minutes, however, another presence made itself known. Fathomless power oozed into the void. This power could do more than kill her. With no effort at all, it could erase her. Terror struck her formless mind. Without a physical body, she could not move. She floated, frozen in thought as whatever else was with her moved in the black. While it had no true form, it felt like a predator. A hungry predator.

"Hello, Victoria," it said. Its voice was genderless and shattered the paralysis of her mind. It was the only real thing in the sea of black. A real voice that she heard with her ears, even if it sounded nothing like any voice she'd ever heard before.

"Who are you?" she stammered back, elated that she could feel the words form in her throat and mouth.

"I'm the one who lives in the box, Victoria. You visited me today, and you touched me so that I might visit you. Thank you for that, Victoria. Thank you."

"Uh, uh. What do you—um, what can I—Can I help you?"

"I like to think, Victoria, that we can help each other."

The predatory danger of this thing in the blackness seemed to grow as it spoke. Victoria cast about with what senses were available to her. The thing seemed to be everywhere.

"Let's make a bargain. I know what's happened to you. I know how you really feel. I can help you with that."

For a moment Victoria was lost. Then she understood.

"There's nothing to do about that," she said weakly.

"I helped your Mam-maw when it happened to her," the voice purred. "Tell me, Victoria, what happened to that sheriff? Hmmm...?"

Victoria's panic turned to a dull horror. The sheriff had been killed by his own son, who had before that day been his loyal deputy. His son then turned the gun on himself. This had happened five years after Mam-maw had been raped, though.

"What's that got to do with me?" she asked.

The thing in the black whispered, "She found me years after she'd been hurt, Victoria, and I took her revenge for her. You have found me now, when you are ripe and we can cut while the wounds are fresh. The sheriff never understood why he had to pay. But Billy Dillon... He'll know. Nelly Brown... She'll know."

For a moment, Victoria rejected the reality of this entire situation. The sheriff had raped Mam-maw all those years before as an act of revenge himself. He claimed that Mam-maw's husband killed his wife. There wasn't enough evidence for even an arrest, but the sheriff assembled a lynch mob with the bare accusation. In the end, he hanged the man and raped his woman in what was seen as a fair act among the white authorities. Mam-maw herself never spoke of it. The story was local legend and coupled with the son's murder-suicide, it was burned into the collective consciousness of everyone in the county. After turning the situation over in her mind, though, Victoria began to see her Mam-maw in a different way. The do-gooding old lady became tinged with the blood of the sheriff and his son. That made her a witch, despite her vociferous protests otherwise. Victoria's heart hardened toward the old woman.

"What do you want from me?" she asked.

"Victoria, I want something from you that you don't even want. I want your unborn child. Give him to me and I will give you revenge."

If Victoria had a face, it would have creased with a frown. Him. To hear the baby's sex named should have sparked some empathy in her. However, she found that knowing the baby was male did not generate an ounce of human interest. In fact, her hatred grew. Especially in light of the fact that Mam-maw had made a deal like this before. That woman was no better than Victoria. She'd lashed out the same way. That slap across the face had not been in righteous indignation, but in guilty anger.

Victoria felt cold. Her mind began to click and her fear evaporated. "So what will you give me for the child?"

The presence wobbled, but responded smoothly, "The lives of those who have hurt you."

"That's not good enough," Victoria said. Her own voice was flat and unyielding. Her anger had become something so confident that she was at ease negotiating with the predator. "I want to destroy them myself. I want the power to do that. Give me that power and you can have my unborn child."

"No, foolish girl. I will kill your enemies. You will give me the child."

Victoria shook the head she didn't have. "Do with me what you will. You can destroy me utterly right now. But you cannot have my baby."

There was no response for an indeterminate period of time. The presence in the blackness seemed absent. Finally, the smooth voice said, "Take your weapons from the jade box. Place your child within it. Do it tonight. Our business is finished."

Victoria burst awake, as if breaking through the surface of water one second before drowning. She was soaked in sweat and trembling. Her hair, which had been neatly braided when she went to bed, was spread around her head in all directions. Without hesitation, she got up, toweled herself dry, and changed clothing by the light of the moon through her window. She poked her head into Mam-maw's room before leaving. The old woman was snoring like she always did. Victoria hesitated, staring at the face of her grandmother above the patchwork quilt. That lying face. The woman seemed at peace, though. All those lines that appeared every time she smiled were smooth and quiet. Victoria squelched further thought and crept from the house.

A few minutes later she crouched before the small oak door, tapping her lips with her index and middle fingers. Perhaps it had all been a dream. Perhaps she was being foolish. There was a disconnect between the events of her dream and this door. This solid door with a heavy lock. She inserted the key and the lock popped open. Her lantern's light spilled into the room and she found the jade box. Looking at it, she became certain that this entire situation was nothing more than an overreaction to the wild dreams of a pregnant woman. Mam-maw had warned her about that and she'd been very correct. Dreams, no matter how realistic, were only dreams. Slowly, Victoria entered the room. She set the lantern on the floor beside a table to shed as much light as possible on the shelf. She pulled the green box from the bottom and opened it. Rather than the black non-bottom, she found a large, ornate deck of what appeared to be gypsy fortune telling cards. She pulled them out, set them next to the lantern, and closed the box. What on earth were those doing in there? The box had been empty before. Was she still dreaming? She reopened the box. A small glass vial lay inside. A note was tied around the lid like a seal. In cursive script it read, "Drink this. It will give you the power you asked for."

Victoria felt the world as she knew it slide away. That had been no pregnancy dream. She or some part of herself had been in this box with whatever thing lived inside. She was now expected to seal the deal she made. If she drank the contents of this vial, that would be her signature on the dotted line. She opened the vial. The liquid inside smelled musky, like the sweat of a horse. She drank it. It tasted like liquorice and crawled actively down her throat. Once in her belly, it spread. She gasped as it moved through her like a living thing, digging into her guts. It slithered through her muscles, skin, eyeballs, fingernails, and even the hairs on her head. She knew from this moment forward that she was more than human. She was not invincible. But she was close. And she was very strong. That was fortuitous, because she could not have otherwise survived what happened next.

She held the open box in one hand as the last shivers of her transformation took place. The black non-bottom returned. She began to close the lid, but it snapped open in her hand. She dropped the box and backed away. Tendrils of black gas spilled from it and crawled along the floor. She reached down for the lantern, but never quite grasped it. An obsidian hand shot from the box. It grabbed her around the waist and pinned her to the floor. She screamed and struggled as another hand slithered from the box. The second hand shredded her clothing and pried apart her legs. Despite her new strength, despite her feelings of near invulnerability, Victoria was helpless. She began to cry and begged the hands, "Stop! Please, stop!" But the hands did not stop. A third, smaller hand emerged from the box and dug into her crotch. It sunk into her, grabbed ahold of something inside and began pulling.

"No! No! No!" she screamed. "Not like this!"

The hand continued to pull. Blood fountained from between her legs. The hand emerged with a sac connected to a cord leading back into Victoria. The hand jerked. Victoria screamed so loudly that objects fell from shelves. Once the cord was free, the hand retreated to the box. Victoria struggled onto her elbows. She saw a fetus en caul, hands pressed against the sac, eyes wide open and mouth agape in a scream frozen forever in amniotic fluid. Then everything was sucked into the box. The lid snapped shut and the gold latch flipped back into place.

Grunting with effort and twisting herself around to use undamaged muscles, Victoria pulled herself to her feet. The amount of blood on the floor was more than she should have been able to lose without passing out. Her abdomen and crotch were twitching and spasming, but she could already feel them knitting themselves back together. Her clothing was reduced to rags. She tied it over her body as best she could. The deck of cards still lay by the lantern. After a moment of consideration, she gathered up both. She left the jade box on the floor where it had fallen, turned, and fled the room.

She stumbled through the passage. Every few steps, blood or a wad of something would drip from between her legs, causing her to stop until it passed. She reached the panel leading to the root cellar. Just as her fingers brushed the lever, the door swung open. She pitched backwards to avoid being struck. Her lantern extinguished as it hit the ground. She looked up and there stood Mam-maw, every line on her face deeply etched.

"Chile, what—oh, sweet Jesus, chile!"

"Mam-maw," Victoria said from the floor of the root cellar, "I've done a terrible thing."

Back in Minnesota, Victoria Starks cried. Tears rolled out the sides of her eyes, dripped down her temples, and pooled on the hardwood by her ears. Once the sobbing ceased, Victoria sat up and looked into the zig-zag pattern of cards before her. Circles. Circles. Circles. She had to go back to the Twin Cities. She couldn't just run away from this mess. Not if she planned to keep the baby that had been planted in her tonight. How that happened was still mysterious to her, since much of what was necessary to make a baby had been damaged all those years ago. She was caught up in powers beyond her considerable understanding. Despite the improbability, she planned to keep this baby. To do that, she'd need to know what it was.

Chapter 4
Party Going

Andre poured salt from a two quart carafe into a salt shaker without spilling a single grain. He spun the lid back onto the shaker and dropped it into the chrome plated condiment rack. He stuffed sugar packets into the rack so that not one more would fit. Before replacing the condiment rack, he scrubbed the table where it sat to remove built up grime. Servers were rarely detail oriented enough to satisfy his cleanliness standards.

The lunch rush at the Pit Stop had subsided, leaving the dining room clear of guests except for Paul, the homeless coffee drinker. He was mumbling to himself in a corner booth beneath a print of Archibald Motley's *Blues 1929* that Andre had talked Brenda into hanging.

Jose cleaned the kitchen noisily, while Stacey, the lone remaining waitress, wiped desert shelves in the server station. Rather than listen to her endless blabber about current and past boyfriends, he'd banished her to menial work. That would keep her away from him until he could retreat to the back office to process the bookwork for breakfast and lunch.

Andre's legs felt leaden. He had a low grade headache that could only be cured by hours of solid sleep. Going out last night had been a mistake. It was a mistake he'd made often in recent weeks as Craig used drugs and alcohol to cope with Kevin's death. A party lifestyle was one thing. Getting wasted every night another. Sooner or later, Craig was either going to have to chill out or seek professional help. It was even odds on which way it would go.

The bell above the front door rang. He gathered his side work paraphernalia and headed for the host stand. Brenda, carrying Amber, came around the corner as he got there.

"Hey, Andre," she said, "How's it going?"

Amber squealed, "And-ay!"

Andre winked at the little girl, which sent her into a giggling fit. "Well, good," he said, nodding to the register. "We had an $1800 breakfast/lunch. You'll get a bonus this week."

She snorted and said, "We had that wrapped yesterday. Did Gina make it in on time?"

"I assume so. Jose didn't call to narc her out if she didn't. What are you doing here? This is your day off."

Brenda waved her hand and said, "Are you doing bookwork soon?"

"Yeah, actually, I just finished cleaning the dining room."

"Good. And Stacey is working this afternoon?"

"Yup."

"I've got Mai coming in at two. Let's go back to the office."

Andre nodded and fetched Stacey. Brenda was already in the office before Stacey took up her position at the host stand.

"I'll be in back doing books," he told her. "Let me know if you need me."

He counted down the till and bagged the money. The

office was a cramped room by the cooler that housed a desk, two chairs, and a safe. OSHA posters lined the walls, as well as framed newspaper articles citing the Pit Stop as "Best of Twin Cities—Diner" for three consecutive years. A computer with a cathode ray monitor sat on the desk. Amber was on the floor coloring a kid's menu with broken crayons while Brenda stared at the screen. A laser printer shot out reports. Andre dropped the morning deposit into the safe and sat down.

"Let me see the numbers," Brenda said. Andre handed her the register Z slip and money count. They were off by $50.28, which, Andre suspected, was the reason for Brenda's visit on her day off. It had been off by about $50 every Thursday for the last two months.

When the printer stopped shooting out paper, Brenda pulled out the stack and set it on the desk.

"As you know, we've had a pretty bad shortage problem recently." She waited until Andre nodded before continuing. "Well, I narrowed it down to Stacey or Michael, based on patterns of who was working when the shortages happened."

"Michael?" Andre said. "That guy's a devout Mormon. I've never even heard him cuss. He was telling Gina the other day that every time she slept with someone, she gave a piece of her heart away."

"Yeah," Brenda said, "I thought the same thing. And, as it turns out, it wasn't him. I revoked his access to the register two weeks ago. I told him it was a computer glitch we were working on. But the shortages, in very similar amounts, kept happening. It's got to be Stacey."

Andre frowned. He had wondered why Michael wasn't allowed on the register. He didn't like Stacey, but he hated situations like this. That girl was in a continual financial bind.

"You want me to break it to her?" he asked.

Amber chose that moment to stop coloring and start pulling binders from a shelf. Brenda casually slapped her hand away and told her in a voice that Andre loathed to "stop that and go back to coloring." It was a voice she never used at work and it seemed very out of character. It was a "mom" voice.

Brenda sighed. "No, I'll do it. Mai will be here shortly. If you'll watch Amber for a few minutes when she gets here, I'll take care of it."

Mai arrived at 2:00 p.m. Her apron was thrown over her shoulder, but otherwise she was already in uniform. Stacey asked her why she was here, since she wasn't scheduled until 5:00 p.m. Mai just shrugged and said, "Brenda asked me to come in early."

Andre approached the host stand and said, "Hi, Mai. Go ahead and punch in and watch the front, OK? Stacey, please come with me."

Brenda sat in the office for the five minutes it took Mai to arrive and brooded. She hired Stacey eight months ago and was happy she'd done it. While Stacey had a wreck of a personal life, she was punctual and quickly developed a loyal following among the regulars. Replacing her would be difficult.

A knock on the door broke her train of thought.

"Come in," she said.

Andre opened the door and said, "Hey, Amber, you wanna see the hamburger?"

Amber jumped up from the floor.

"Meat! Meat! Meat!" she shouted. For some reason, she

was fascinated by the ground beef they used to make hamburger patties. She took Andre's hand and drug him to the prep station.

"Hello, Stacey," Brenda said. "Please come in, shut the door, and have a seat."

Stacey's blonde hair was curled, dyed, and gracefully held off her shoulders with chop-sticks. Her eyes were wide and already trembling.

Brenda firmed her voice and said, "Stacey, I've reviewed your performance on the register over the course of the last few months. It seems we're always short on your shifts by about fifty dollars. In light of this evidence—" she held up the stack of reports "—I don't really have much choice. I have to let you go."

Stacey's face crumpled and she began sobbing. "I—I—I'm so sorry, Brenda!" She covered her face with her hands. "I—I didn't want to do it, but Keith hasn't given me a check in two months, and I have rent...and Brad got another DWI and lost his job at the pizza place..."

Stacey rocked on her chair with her fingers curled in front of her face, which was now a mess of running green mascara. Brenda waited until she finished her litany of excuses for the theft. The confession was unexpected. Few accused of stealing ever confessed, let alone apologized.

Brenda said, "My hands are tied, Stacey. You know that. If you leave me the apron you have on, I won't back charge you for the other one. You can drop it off any time."

Stacey sniffled several times. "OK, I will."

Brenda handed her two tissues. Together they left the office. Brenda cashed her out, took her apron, and wished her luck. Unexpectedly, Stacey grabbed her in a hug as they approached the front door.

"I really am sorry, Brenda," she said. "I hope one day I can be as strong as you are."

Brenda watched her drive away. She went back to the office, shut the door, and collapsed into her chair. Every fiber of her body wanted to cry. But she could not. In a way this feeling was a horrible tension, but in another it was welcome. She'd cried so much in the last two months that it was nice not to for once. She took three deep breaths and left the office to collect Amber for their daily trip to the park. *Thank God the weather is holding this year,* she thought. She didn't know what she'd do with herself and her daughter when the temperature became too cold to go the park.

Just after 9:00 p.m., Craig's party was in full swing. He'd sent a flurry of text messages before his phone battery died. His charger was on the fritz, so this would be a mystery night. Nine people had already shown up, including Stacey from the Pit Stop. She'd brought whatever boyfriend was most current and a black girl with a red stripe dyed through her bangs named Angela. With or without boyfriends and other friends, Stacey was a problem. Andre didn't have many strict rules. However, he made it clear that mixing work drama and personal drama was absolutely prohibited. Craig had no idea that Stacey had been fired mere hours before he sent her a text that read "party 2nite mi casa". He should have diffused the situation by moving the whole thing to the neighbors' apartment. Those guys were already drunk in his kitchen and would have gone for it. However, his judgment was stilted by a day spent drinking.

His own work life was a total wreck since Kevin died. The guy who'd replaced Kevin was a fuck-stick who spent all day in the office playing online games. The owner had always been an idiot, but Kevin made it work despite him.

Between the owner and the new manager, the future of Rick's Tire and Battery was deteriorating. So when Stacey cornered him in the hallway and confided that she'd been fired from the Pit Stop, he smiled widely and said, "Well, we can't win 'em all, can we?" Andre could deal with it.

The two girls from First Avenue the night before also showed up. Craig was pretty certain that Andre had slept with the blonde one and that he had not slept with the hipster chick, Galina. Otherwise, last night was as blurry as this one was turning out to be. His lab partner from BioChem, a pudgy, half Korean/half white guy named Winton, was nursing a beer in the recliner. His shoulder length hair was tucked behind his ears and his leg bounced in time to the hip hop music blaring from the stereo. Craig and Andre had known Winton since high school. He always looked like a caged animal at parties, but he was handy to have around for a sober cab. Tonight, Craig made it a point to get him wasted.

As Craig tried to rekindle a conversation with Galina, Stacey's boyfriend caught him by the arm, leaned in to his ear, and said, "Hey, bro, I brought some blow."

Craig tilted his head so the guy's lips and cologne weren't so close and said, "I don't do that with my shirt on. Let me know." He pushed past the guy and announced, "I've got a Crystal Skull full of vodka! Who wants a shot!"

An hour later, Craig's shirt was off and he was pontificating about how scraping cow brains into test tubes could cure cancer. With the exception of Winton, everyone was huddled around the coffee table, occupying furniture in a way that only cocaine could make comfortable. Winton watched them like they were a pack of rabid rodents.

An 8x10 black-and-white photograph of Tupac laid on the center of the table in front of Craig. The space on the wall where the picture had been hanging moments before was several shades whiter than the paint around it. A fat line was cut neatly on the picture glass, next to a tidy pile of cocaine and a razor blade.

"Nigga, hit that shit!" Stacey's boyfriend shouted, interrupting Craig just as he espoused the virtues of lyophilization.

Craig smirked and snorted the line with the McDonald's straw he'd been using as a pointer.

Andre's dinner shift was a wreck at the Pit Stop. As soon as Mai learned that she was there to cover Stacey, she said, "Well, I guess this is the last time I have to clean up after that bitch." Andre thought Brenda's choice for a replacement for the shift had been clever. Mai would be happy that Stacey was gone. He and Brenda were proven wrong. Andre fielded more complaints about Mai's service tonight than he had in the two years he'd worked with her.

Michael came in sick, so Andre sent him home and ran one short. Mai had no love for that guy either. She became more annoyed as what should have been a routine Thursday night deteriorated. Complaint after complaint slid off of Andre's smooth exterior. He averted several disasters through table touching and extra work on the back end. The thought that kept him going through the whole mess was his bed. It was big. It was empty. And it waited for him with high thread count sheets and an expensive comforter that his grandmother had given him for Christmas last year.

When he got home he stood at the door of his apartment, listening to the raucous party going on behind it. He almost turned around and drove to his parents' house. When Craig was on a raging bender, there was no stopping him until it was over. Since Kevin died, Andre found himself in his old bed several times a week, under the same thread bare covers that had been on it since he was fourteen years old. He glared at the door. A resolve hardened within him.

"Fuck it, Craig," he said. "This shit has gotta stop."

He opened the door and marched in.

When he saw Stacey, her most current boyfriend (his name was Brad but he annoyingly tried to get everyone to call him Boo Yah), the girl he'd not-quite had sex with the night before, and various other people snorting cocaine off the picture of Tupac his brother had given him, Andre's sudden resolve evaporated. He wished he'd gone to his parents' house.

Craig finished a line of cocaine and stared at him with a wide, loose grin. Craig's eyes, though, were terrible things. They were black and blank.

Andre sighed, closed the door, and said, "Hey, everybody. What's up?"

Two hours later, Andre was smoking a joint and staring at the electronic compass reading "SE" on the dashboard of Craig's dad's Caravan. The van was tucked behind a shed in Minnehaha Park. As a teenager, Andre had worked for Minneapolis Parks and Rec, so he knew all the hidden spots of every park in the city. The radio was bumping the latest release by P.O.S. Brad was sitting in the front passenger seat and five other people were crammed into the back. Andre wasn't certain who had come and who had stayed behind. Another joint was floating around back there somewhere. So was Debra, who Andre avoided in fear that she might end up back in his bed when this was all over. He needed that bed to himself.

Brad was elaborating on his love for the local rap scene. He had attached himself to Andre and hadn't left his side except to take a piss. The guy had done the same thing last time they'd hung out. He was desperately trying to look cool to a black guy. He called Andre "brotha" every chance he got. The first time they'd met, Andre made it clear that Brad was not allowed to use the "n-word" in any capacity. While Brad was annoying and culturally confused, he could at least be trained.

Andre handed the joint to Brad in the hopes that for the five seconds it took him to hit it his voice would stop. Brad took the joint but didn't shut up. Craig was in the back bench seat, doing much better with the art chick from the night before. Cocaine had that effect on girls. Even girls like her. Stacey and her black friend with the red stripe in her hair were in the middle bucket seats discussing hair stylists on Selby Avenue in St Paul.

Andre had turned down the blow, but allowed himself to get tangled into this entire mess anyway. He wasn't sure how that happened. He suspected that Craig's dad had not "lent" the van to his son. This whole situation was a social powder keg. And maybe that's why Andre was there. He was so good at smoothing things over. Covering blemishes. Making sure shit didn't get any more fucked up than it had to. So he'd made his own bed and now he was high in it. None of his annoyance with the situation or himself showed externally.

"Yeah, so, like, when Astronautilus moved here a couple months ago, brotha, this rap scene got a fuckin' money dude! I mean, he's white and shit, but he's fuckin' stylin'. Blazin' hot. Dope. I heard him do this freestyle and ni—brotha, he just made up the maddest shit outta whatever the crowd yelled at him. He's good friends with Stef, you know, and..."

Andre did know. He knew all those guys. The whole Doomtree clan. Listening to Brad talk about them was getting to be more than he could handle. As soon as Brad hit the joint, Andre said, "OK, folks, let's go down to the Falls. You can get behind them if you know how. It's pimp shit."

Crouched in the doorway of a nearby bathroom, Number 9 watched smoke leak from the cracked windows of the minivan. He'd shadowed the party in Kimm's car since they left the apartment. In a funny turn of events, his Datsun blew a head gasket yesterday, so he'd returned to this very park and taken the Lexus. Kimm had no use for it now.

Craig and Andre were now the focus of his attention. The direct route to nabbing the child was not working, so it was time to change up his strategy. His perspective had altered since his reading with Victoria the night before.

Number 9 hated how that ended. Very messy. A big loose end he'd have to tie up. But not now. Now he needed to figure out the puzzle in the reading. Though he'd been drugged nearly to death, he could still remember every second of the reading with eidetic clarity. His stomach rumbled as he pictured Victoria in his mind. Though she had satisfied his sexual urges, his appetite would not be quenched until he'd stripped her down to her bones and crunched through each of them. He rubbed his crotch with a clawed hand. There were girls in the van, too. He had become a hedonist in the last week.

His refocused on Victoria's reading. "All is not what it seems." That had been an unnecessary statement. All was never as it seemed. "Death is reversed." He couldn't figure out what that meant. Death was a one way door. Perhaps the child carried her father's genes in some way that the cards saw as his life coming back. Certainly possible, since her father wasn't supposed to be able to pass on any of his genetic material. "You are watched. Home is no longer a safe haven." Someone from The Elpis Foundation was watching him. Probably not Clarence or any of the other Térata, considering what he'd done to Number 4 when she interfered with him. He was the best of his father's children. Above reproach. The politics among the Awakened were thick. Perhaps one of them was making a move. "The Dead" had been Victoria's answer when he'd asked who it was. That made no sense, but probably tied into the "death reversed" business. He should not have asked that question.

The final question had been the most important. Its answer dictated how he would go about collecting the child. Amber had what Clarence was looking for, making her extraction process critical. She must be taken whole and alive. His instincts had kept him from taking her thus far and he was happy they had. Her value would interest all sorts of people at The Foundation, who were probably watching her, and him, too. He could leave no tracks. No traces.

In a fog of marijuana smoke, the group of kids emerged from the van. They were all wasted, except Andre. Number 9 would have to be careful with him. At first he'd followed the two kids due to Craig's connection with his brother and Andre's with Brenda. A Confluence of spiritual energy swirled around them, binding them together. Their lives were intertwined in ways that seemed incidental, but had been guided by larger, mysterious forces. As he watched the Confluence flow back and forth, he could see that it was amplified. Each possessed untapped gifts, though none were Awake. Brenda was causing animalistic urges in him, without even knowing it. She must have affected his brother in a similar manner. She had some kind of psychoactive chemical abilities. The boys' gifts were buried, though the black one had an incredible sense of detail.

Number 9 had decided on a course of action earlier today. Andre was close to Brenda. Craig had been close to Number 1, who thought of himself as Kevin. All four had shared a special bond. If something happened to the boys, it would unhinge Brenda. In the wake of Kevin's death, further disruption of the Confluence shared by these individuals would be catastrophic. If what happened to Andre was horrible enough, it would push Brenda over the edge. Up to this point, she'd been distracted by her husband's death, but it had not overwhelmed her. If she went right off the tracks, the ensuing chaos should provide him the opportunity he had not yet seen.

The fact that these stupid kids had landed right in his most comfortable zone, Minnehaha Park, was delightful. The fact that they'd brought a few extra snacks along was an added perk. This job had gone poorly so far, but the course of events was shifting in his favor. Patience always paid off.

As the party moved from the van into the park, Craig felt marvelous. His eyes tingled and his skin melded with the cool air around it. Brad's cocaine was top shelf stuff. Galina warmed up to him once she'd snorted a line. They had been laughing together and talking nonstop since then. He'd score tonight for sure. If he played his cards right, the act might go down in the recess behind Minnehaha Falls. That would be a story for the legends. A condom was tucked into his back pocket.

Stacey's boyfriend was still pestering Andre, who acted cool and charming. Considering the circumstances, that meant he was enraged. Craig didn't care. Right now all he cared about was making tonight the crown jewel on a week of debauchery. Andre would get over it. He always did.

Stacey, Angela, and Debra were still chatting nonstop. There wasn't much difference between a sober Stacey and the current version. The trick would be to get Galina separated from the group. He clamped down his mouth by force of will and managed to pretend to listen to her babbling—something about Mary Timony or PJ Harvey or Dessa. Whatever. Female musicians. As they climbed down the stone steps leading to the Falls, he slowed his pace while nodding and smiling at all the right times, creating a comfortable distance between the pair and the others. Galina either didn't notice or didn't care. She was passionate about the use of synthesizers and acoustic guitars. When she paused for a moment to collect her thoughts, Craig made his move. He leaned in, meaning to kiss her. She jerked back.

"Hey," she said, "I know we're all fucked up and stuff, Craig, but, you know, I'm gay."

For a few seconds Craig stared at her. Anger boiled up from his chest and the pleasant tingling in his eyes turned to a fiery burning. He choked and said, "Oh, right. Nice to tell me now."

She frowned at him and said, "Every girl that talks to you doesn't want to sleep with you." She pivoted on her platform shoes and hurried down the stairs to rejoin the rest of the party. Craig's mouth was suddenly dry and its numbness bothered him.

"Fuck it," he muttered, hopping the railing on the stairs and stalking off into the woods.

Shit, Andre thought as he watched Craig jump the railing.

The party had arrived at the landing overlooking Minnehaha Falls. The water sparkled in the autumn moonlight, falling fifty feet into a wide pool that fed a stream running under a bridge further down the trail. No one present besides Andre had been here before. They were entranced.

"Look," he said, pointing to a ledge that ran halfway up the Falls from the gorge below. "If you follow that path there—ignore the sign—and get on the ledge, you can actually get behind the Falls. I'm going to go get Craig before he falls in the creek. Take a look."

The others milled about uncertainly, but Brad said in a take-charge voice, "Cool! We'll spark a blunt back there. Meet us when you get Craig."

Andre smiled and said, "Word."

He sprinted up the stairs and hopped the railing where Craig had vanished into the woods.

Craig sat on a rock by the stream, staring into the glittering reflections on the water's surface. He had stomped through the trails that crisscrossed the gorge for about ten minutes before choosing this roost to sulk. Along the way he'd picked up a thin stick which he broke into fragments and arranged in a geometric pattern on the rock beside him. He heard someone approaching and said, "Hey, Andre."

"Hey, man, what's up?" Andre said, sitting on the rock beside him.

"Galina's a lesbian," Craig replied, tossing the rest of the stick into the water. He stood up. "Let's walk. The coke's got me all jazzed up."

"All right," Andre said.

They walked along the bank of the stream until they encountered a bridge. Craig marched onto the wooden planks.

"I thought you'd figured that out already and were going for broke on it, man," Andre said from behind him as they crossed the bridge.

Craig barked a laugh and said, "Well, it doesn't matter now."

They followed the trail deeper into the woods. The trees blocked out the ambient city light, but their eyes adjusted.

Craig laughed again. "I know I pissed you off with Stacey, man. I didn't know she got fired until after she showed up."

"Yeah, well, it is what it is," Andre said. "She's been giggling all night, so I figure she ain't too broke up about it. At least her boyfriend's around. That keeps her off of me. I foreswore white girls for the rest of the year."

"Yeah, I know," Craig said. "I'm not always as passed out as I seem to be. Too bad her boyfriend don't leave you alone."

Andre laughed. A tension inside Craig relaxed. Andre's laugh was infectious.

"Man, I'm wiped," Andre said. "I worked a double today after you drug my ass out last night. You wanna head back soon? You need to sleep, too."

"Soon," Craig said. "I wanna stare at the river for a minute. It should be just up here somewhere. I can hear it."

They followed the trail for another five minutes in silence. Andre kept peering into the woods, almost tripping several times. Craig followed his gaze, but couldn't see anything through the dark underbrush. The trail ended at the bank of the Mississippi, which roiled twenty feet below. A lone picnic table sat in a grassy clearing. They sat on its top with their feet on the bench, staring at the river and downtown Minneapolis. Craig's knees shook uncontrollably, but he figured that was better than his mouth running constantly.

"I gotta slow down a notch, man," Craig said.

Andre was looking past Craig into the shadows of the bushes. "Yeah," he mumbled. "That's probably a good idea."

Craig looked where Andre was staring and didn't see anything. After a minute, Andre shook his head and said, "Nights like this are what weed was made for, eh?"

"Yeah," Craig agreed. "I shoulda stuck with that. We gotta get that minivan back tonight, too. Once we drop off the party patrol, you wanna follow me out to my dad's place so I can dump it in the driveway?"

"No," Andre said, irritation showing in his voice for the first time since he got home. "I don't. You didn't tell him you took it, did you?"

Craig jumped down from the table and turned to face Andre. "So what if I didn't? Fuck that guy. He can live without his van for one night."

Andre's eyebrows came together and his lips peeled away from his teeth. Craig had never seen that expression on his face before.

"You're stirring up the hornet's nest to make this a big fucking mess, man," Andre said. "None of this shit is gonna bring Kevin back, you know? Pissing your dad off every chance you get ain't helping anything. And I just want to go home and go to bed."

Craig didn't know how to respond. Andre never made outbursts like that, even when he was angry. The words stung, but coming from Andre they were devastating. Craig was about to punch his friend in the face when he noticed movement over Andre's shoulder... Then time slowed down.

A large, blackish shape emerged from the darkness. At first, Craig didn't realize that time had lagged, so the shape seemed to hover in space, moving forward in perspective incrementally. Craig had done enough drugs to know a hallucination when he saw one and this was not a hallucination. This was insane. He glanced at Andre, whose face was frozen, eyebrows furrowed and lips drawn into a tight line. Frozen. When he glanced back the black shape was closer. At this range, he could see details. Big teeth, big claws, black skin and fur, pink (*pink?*) horns on its back. Its trajectory was aimed squarely at Andre's back.

Shit! Shit! Shit! he thought. He leapt onto the table. When he did that, time sped back up. The black shape blurred forward. Craig turned his body to catch the creature's left wrist and moved his legs in a sweeping pattern that was ingrained in him from years of Aikido practice. The weight and momentum of the monster was immense. Craig exerted all of his energy into three pivots before flinging himself to the ground in a tucked roll. The creature flew over Andre's head, one of its claws grazing his afro. Craig came out of the roll and sprung into the air with excess energy. At the peak of his arc, he watched whatever-that-scary-fucking-thing-was fly thirty feet past the bank of the Mississippi and splash into the water below. He fell back to the earth like a crumpled bolt of cloth.

"What in the living fuck just happened!" Andre exclaimed as Craig hit the ground. Andre had only managed to turn his head halfway around during the fight. What he saw in that instant was a snapshot his mind could not accept. Some large, black beast with pink horns had been locked in what looked like a graceful dance with Craig. *Pink?* Everything after that was a blur of motion.

Andre jumped from the table and ran over to his friend, who had landed near the edge of the precipice that fell into the river.

Craig lay on his back, breathing in large gulps. His wide open eyes rolled back and forth. Spit sprayed out of his mouth with each exhale.

"Craig! Craig!" Andre shouted. He didn't know what to do. He knew CPR. He knew to call 911 in emergencies. He knew all sorts of things that were useless right now. Craig kept wheezing and his eyes kept rolling. In lieu of anything else to do, Andre grabbed Craig's shoulders and tried to pull him up. As he lifted him off the ground, Craig screamed. Startled, Andre dropped him. Craig screamed several more times and relaxed. His eyes stopped running around in their sockets. His breathing became a pant rather than a struggle. Andre sat down next to him, frightened and confounded.

After a few minutes, Craig's breathing evened and he blinked his eyes. Andre leaned over him. Craig's eyes locked onto his.

"Did I... just throw... a fucking big black monster... into the river?"

"I think you did, man, and I don't know what the fuck to think about that."

"We should... probably get... the fuck... out of here... then."

Andre's vision destabilized and panic welled up inside him. His brain couldn't make any sense of what had happened and that was causing his mind to unravel.

"Andre," Craig croaked. "It... might... come back."

Andre's paralysis broke and he nodded. "Yeah," he said, "We should get the fuck outta here."

Andre helped Craig get to his feet, but Craig could not walk unassisted for more than a step. Andre slung an arm around his friend's shoulders and together they returned to the Falls. Craig swam in and out of consciousness. Andre kept his eyes on all the shadows of the woods at once. This park used to be one of his fondest childhood memories. Now it was a threatening miasma. As he peered into the shadows, he remembered the shapes he had seen as they had approached the river. Always the same shapes. Two triangles that weren't quite leaves. The ears of the monster. He had seen them several times before that thing had attacked. Were there more monsters? At least now he knew the sign. His eyes scanned the tangled shadows of the dying underbrush. As each shape emerged from the darkness, he fought back panic until he could tell that it was a stubborn leaf, broken branch, or the bark of a tree. This dedicated search kept him from dragging Craig in a terrorized sprint all the way back. It kept him from dropping Craig and sprinting all the way back alone.

When they reached the Falls with no incident, Andre's fear receded. It flared to life again when they reached the overlook platform. He expected to hear the sound of voices through the falling water. There was none. Andre leaned Craig against the railing and studied the Falls. Perhaps they'd gone back to the van. Perhaps they were elsewhere in the park. He pulled his phone out of his pocket. No text messages. No voicemails. He looked at the Falls. Just as he began to put Craig's arm back over his shoulder, the water fell at just the right angle, allowing him to catch sight of what could only be a hand.

"Oh, shit," he said. His knees weakened and he felt like someone punched him just beneath his navel. The terror that had taken up residency there leaked into the rest of his body. "Oh, man, I hope that isn't what I saw."

Craig rolled his head toward the Falls. "What?"

"Behind the falls..." Andre said.

"You gotta check it out, man. You gotta."

Andre shook his head "no", but his feet moved on their own. He had to know. He sprung over the railing of the platform and worked his way down the gorge. Upon reaching the falling sheets of water, he slipped behind them and threw up.

The scene was lit by a pair of small flashlights laying on the stone ground. Pieces. That was all that remained. Stacey's torso sat on Brad's legs. Galina's head was upside down in a pool of blood that nearly reached her open, vacant eyes. The others were too much of a mess to make out. Blood splattered the rock walls. The smell was coppery and sharp. When he finished retching, Andre put his hand into the falling water, brought it back to his face, and washed his mouth out. He could not stop staring at the massacre.

Craig broke his trance by yelling, "Hey, what's... going on back there?"

Andre ran back up the gorge to the platform. "You don't wanna fuckin' know, man," he said as he wrapped Craig's arm around his shoulder. "You don't—ah, *shit!*"

Andre saw two triangles that weren't leaves, deep in the shadows on the other side of the creek. They weren't exactly the same, but the shape was unmistakable. Another monster had arrived. He and Craig were as good as dead. His entire body shivered and he began to shake. Andre whipped Craig's arm over his shoulder.

"What?" Craig said as they stumbled up the stairs.

"The monster has a friend," Andre hissed. He missed a step and they pitched forward.

"Oh," Craig grunted as he hit the concrete. "That's bad."

They scrambled back to their feet. Craig was trying to walk, but Andre still had to hold most of his weight. As they reached the top of the stairs, Andre saw the two triangles again, this time in the gorge. He clamped both his arms under Craig's shoulders and dragged him backwards toward the van. Adrenaline threatened to overpower his senses, but it also gave him a burst of speed that helped keep him from losing his mind. It wouldn't be enough, he knew, but he was moving as fast as he could.

When they got to the van, Andre dropped Craig to the ground and fumbled the key out of his pocket. His fingers shook so bad he could hardly get the automatic side door to open. He glanced back over his shoulder and spotted the triangles again, this time in a thicket on the other side of the parking lot. His thread of hope snapped, but he kept moving anyway. He pushed Craig onto the floorboard of the van and leapt into the driver's seat. The entire time he wondered why in the hell they weren't in as many pieces as their friends behind the water fall.

Tires screeching, the van burst from behind the shed, into the parking lot, and onto 46th Street.

Number 9 hit the cold water of the Mississippi in a limp state. He wasn't sure what had just happened. The icy water enveloped him, sinking into his fur, his eyes, and his mouth. He floated in the cold void until his lungs tugged at him. He swam back to the surface and sprayed water from his snout.

What in the world had that kid done? How had he done it? His biological systems were clouded with multiple drugs and enough alcohol to kill a normal person. Even if he were Awake to his capabilities, he should not have been able to access them at that point. And he wasn't Awake! Number 9 could smell it. Craig was just a normal, depressed twenty-one-year-old kid on a drinking bender. Nothing more.

Well, obviously something more. Number 9 swam back to the shore. He estimated he'd floated a couple miles downstream. He crawled onto the bank and shook himself like a dog. Water flew in thousands of shimmering drops. He stalked over to a log and sat down. His mind picked over every detail of the failed attack. Andre had spotted him several times, but that wasn't surprising. He'd expected that and moved out of his view. Craig was obviously a skilled martial artist of some variety, but that didn't matter except that he could move so fast. Number 9 hadn't been ready for that. Had he suspected that Craig could move like that, he could have overpowered him and killed Andre, anyway. Instead he was sitting on a log. Soaking wet. Bewildered.

Worst of all, he was exposed. Both of those kids had seen him. Now both would need to die. But not tonight. Tonight he'd go back and finish his meal behind the Falls. Tomorrow, he'd retrieve his guns from his hotel room and just shoot the pair. No more fooling around. No more risk of exposure. He could shoot them from far enough away that if Craig managed to move like that again he'd still be dead. No matter how fast a guy could move, bullets always moved faster.

In no particular hurry, Number 9 made his way back to Minnehaha Falls. He went through the last month in his mind over and over again. Something about this entire experience didn't make sense. He knew he'd been out of control in many ways. His mind seemed sharp and focused, but his successive failures indicated that what he thought were minor distractions could no longer be ignored. His carnal appetites were increasing. His continual hesitation to grab the child was unfounded. The Confluence around Brenda was uncommonly powerful. As he processed through each event, he decided that he was compromised in some way. Probably by whatever chemical magic Brenda exuded, but at this point he couldn't be sure of even that.

There was also the mess of Victoria's reading to consider. How convenient that he should so easily find her, of all people, here now. Something wasn't right here. He wasn't right here.

He considered calling The Foundation for backup. Such a thought was a staggering blow to his ego, but if he kept finding himself drugged and thrown over cliffs, he was going to end up dead. Especially with three people running around who had seen him for what he truly was. If he didn't let his ego lie, things would continue to spiral out of control. This was new territory for him. Even when things got messy in the past, he had always turned that to his advantage. He never lost. Ever.

Then again, maybe this line of thought was corrupted, too. Call home for help? Such a thought was alien to him. Eating people was also something he didn't do. Sex was not a need for him. He'd only engaged in it before to manipulate people. Now he was acting like an incompetent, horny, flesh-eating monster. With that realization, a new sensation took hold of him. It stopped him dead in his tracks.

Fear.

He was learning what fear felt like.

He growled and knocked over a nearby birch tree with the back of his hand. He picked it up and beat the other trees around him. Once he'd destroyed the birch and a chunk of forest around him, he sat down on what was left of it. He put his clawed fingers on his temples and stared into empty space. A plan. He needed a plan.

First, kill the kids. Second, grab the child and deliver her to his father. Third, find and kill Victoria Starks. Do the first two things tomorrow. No nonsense. No more sex. No more eating people. No more self-doubt. Just movement and discipline. He would have to clean up the mess he made behind Minnehaha Falls tonight, but he'd do it by dumping the bodies into the river. No more eating people. Confident in his plan, Number 9 sprung to his feet and stalked through the woods.

When he got back to the Falls, something was wrong. He couldn't smell the dead kids behind the water. He leapt from the cover of the trees, across the pool, and onto the ledge. They were gone. All the blood had been cleaned up. He put his nose to the air. No scents. None. His mind raced. He kept sniffing. He circled the Falls, sniffing the air, the dirt, the trees, everything. After an hour, he had counted the exact number of animals living in the park, the number of visitors the park had over the course of the last week, and how many people had made love there in the last six months. He kept sniffing.

At the edge of the parking lot, he stopped and snarled. Finally, the barest hint of a familiar scent reached his nose. It was his brother's odor. Number 1. He had covered himself well, but a sliver of his smell remained on the curb near the shed where the minivan had been parked. He wasn't dead. This thought stunned Number 9, but the pieces started to come together. Death was reversed. Who watched him? The dead. A low, heated growl rumbled from his chest. His anger was white hot, but he calmed his mind. No more emotional mistakes. His brother would pay for this. They would all pay for this. Now he knew exactly where to strike.

Andre was killing it. The crowd roared with laughter. Craig laughed so hard it hurt and he couldn't stop.

He watched Andre walked across the stage, paused for a moment, and put on his best serious face. The crowd quieted. Craig's laughter bounced around the barroom. He twisted in his chair to laugh away from the stage.

This isn't how it happens! he thought.

Thankfully, no one noticed and Andre went on with his routine.

"So," Andre intoned, "do you see how I'm lit from the left and right?"

Red lights shone from Andre's right side and blue from his left. This was the standard stage lighting for the Top Hat in downtown St Paul on Comedy Open Mic Sundays. The crowd went into that neutral/safe zone where they expected to be entertained but didn't know where the boundaries were. Craig grabbed a drink from the table beside him and poured it into his mouth. His laughter continued despite the beer in his throat. He was laughing while choking, which didn't make any sense at all.

What the fuck! he thought. *I can't fuck this up for Andre! I didn't fuck this up for Andre!*

Andre said, "It's OK. I couldn't tell I was black with the red shining on one side and the blue shining from the other, either. Hell, I thought I was a Barack Obama poster."

The house erupted in laughter, covering Craig's maniacal cackling. He lurched toward the bathrooms at the back of the bar.

Andre continued, "Now, if you turned those lights off, you'd see I was white, so you'd already know I was voting for Mitt Romney." He walked across the stage in a reproduction of a Cab Calloway dance, arms swinging and legs stomping. The crowd went quiet again. He ripped into a dance move that stilled the audience even further. When he spun to a stop, his face was again lit by both red and blue from opposing sides. Once the motion of his body had come to a full and complete stop, Andre dipped his head and said, "Oh, sorry… I meant Newt Gingrich, or whoever it was the

Republicans nominated."

"*No!!*" Craig thought as he kept laughing. His hand covered his mouth and he ran from the room.

This wasn't how it happened at all. That dance/joke combination had bombed. No one had laughed, even Craig. The audience had sat there with a few spattered murmurs while Andre smiled and spread his hands. When they got home later that night, Andre had blamed weed for his idea to combine politics and dated dance routines into bad jokes.

As he ran, Craig's own laughter swelled. He tripped over the threshold between the seating area of the bar and the thin hall leading to the bathrooms. His face smacked the floor but he kept laughing. A jangling ring floated from down the hallway. At first Craig thought the concussive hit had resulted in temporary tinnitus. But the ring became more persistent and recognizable. It was a telephone.

I lost my phone earlier tonight! he tried to say, but laughter clogged his mouth.

He banged his head against the tiled floor several times and laughed as blood oozed down his forehead. Big band music blasted from the barroom, joining the laughter and ringing. Andre had researched 1930s scat dances on YouTube looking for material for his routine. Craig recognized the tune as a Benny Goodman song called "Sing, Sing, Sing". The ring of the telephone penetrated the music dissonantly and his laugh compounded the auditory turmoil.

Still laughing, he peeled his face off the floor and looked back. There was Andre, awash in failure but marching on. The scene in the bar transformed into a 1930s tableau. A pianist, bassist, and entire horn section were seated impossibly on the small stage around Andre, smoking cigarettes and leaning forward on the off beats. They had on bright blue tuxedos. The trumpet blared an unbridled jazz solo. The small crowd multiplied into a full house of high society white people politely tapping their feet and smiling. Andre was swinging his arms and legs, scatting in a parody of himself. Through all of this, Craig kept laughing and laughing and fucking laughing and the phone kept ringing.

He hit his head on the tile over and over, knocking a tooth loose before he recognized the ringing. A pay phone. He hadn't heard that kind of ring since he was a kid in Pennsylvania. The memory was jolting and clear. Fourteen years ago. He had been sitting in the back seat of his mom's Impala, which was parked by the pay phone at the 7-11 while she waited for a call from her boyfriend, whom she had paid a quarter to page. Their phone service had been cut. His half-brother was sick, whimpering in the car seat beside him. A winter storm raged outside the car. The heater in the car didn't work. The phone rang two hours after she'd sent the page for the third time. His mother had fought off pimps and drug dealers to take that call.

Craig scrambled to his feet and stumbled to the phone at the end of the hall. He reached to answer it, but the hand set was missing. The cord had been tucked into the coin box, which was locked closed. Through the sudden burst of a trombone solo, Craig remembered that the pay phone had been shut down when the company that owned it went out of business. The bartender, Margaret, had been happy to see it go, since it was only used by a seedier element.

Craig pulled on the corrugated steel cord. It didn't budge, but the ringing kept on. So did his laughter. He cast about for some way to break into the locked coin box. His laughter started to fuse with the music from the other room, as if he were an instrument that was out of tune and poorly played. Deep within him, a scream welled up. It poured out with the laughter and eclipsed it.

"*Katalambano!*"

His mind and mouth translated his feelings into Greek, though he'd never studied the language beyond the roots, prefixes, and suffixes necessary for biology. His half-sisters went to a private, nondenominational religious school and a speaker at one of their incremental graduations had used this term to express how it felt to be "seized" by the love of Christ.

Screaming, "*Katalambano,*" Craig rushed back into the main room of the Top Hat and searched for some way to get into the locked box on the pay phone. For the first time, everyone noticed him. Andre looked at him with a WTF expression. The anachronistic audience leaned back in their chairs as if assaulted. The pianist started running through scales at high speed. The trombone player swung his slide up and down. The drummer slapped a symbol every time "*Katalambano*" reverberated through the room.

Craig felt embarrassed, but he just kept running around looking for something, anything. A series of dart boards hung on the wall behind oak cases. On Thursdays, the Top Hat moved the tables for league darts play. Without knowing why, Craig leapt onto a table and tore the doors off of the first case. "*Katalambano!*" A camel hair dart board with green, red, and white numbers hung in the case. He stared at the number 20 as the drummer tapped his high hat expectantly. Nothing. "*Katalambano!*" He jumped to the next table, sending glasses and ashtrays flying in his wake. He tore the doors off of the second dart board. 20. Nothing. "*Katalambano!*" The high hat kept tapping. He leapt to the next table, shattering glass once again.

Someone in the background yelled, "Call 911!"

Did 911 exist in 1930? he wondered.

He tore the doors off the next dart board. 20. Bull's eye. A key was thumbtacked into the bull's eye. It was a brass skeleton key with a head in the shape of the Fibonacci sequence. It couldn't possibly fit into the pay phone, but Craig grabbed it and jumped back to the floor. Aping the moves that Andre had spent a week perfecting, he danced back to the pay phone.

"Katalambano!" he screamed with each bass drum kick, arms flailing, legs taking exaggerated steps, head jerking back and forth. In cruel appreciation of his dance, the audience started clapping and hollering. When he got back to the hallway he paused with his back to the room. He could feel everyone staring at him. The musicians were playing a fanfare. The audience clapped in unison and shouted, "Go white boy! Go white boy! Go!" Andre stood on stage. Without looking at him, Craig knew Andre felt confused, annoyed, and deeply hurt. Craig stared at the key clutched in his hand. Its spiral drew him in and he screamed, *"Katalambano!"*

He raced to the ringing phone and crammed the key into the coin box. Its face flipped down, ejecting a mass of quarters onto his feet. A sudden, terrifying choice lay inside that phone. The handset at the end of the cord was miniaturized and crammed into the coin box. He knew if he pulled it out that it would be the right size and he could answer the insistent ringing. Somehow, this would stop his screaming and laughing. Behind the handset, though, was absolute blackness. This blackness housed something dangerous and powerful. Something whose insistent call muffled the music, the clapping, the hollering, and even Craig's laughing. The blackness beckoned and Craig knew with absolute certainty that if he didn't answer the phone, the blackness would come out. When it did, that blackness would give him whatever he wanted. Anything.

Craig grabbed the handset and said, "Hello?"

Chapter 5
Two Dead Return

Brenda sat on her couch, stirring her fingers through a bowl of microwave popcorn. The last few minutes of the movie *Harvey* played out on her TV. James Stewart exited the gate of the nuthouse alone, having just taken leave of his large, invisible friend. This had been her favorite movie since childhood. She and her father had watched it on VHS every Saturday night the summer before she entered kindergarten. She would tuck herself into his side, the top of her head in his armpit, and ask questions to make him laugh.

"How many drinks does it take to get drunk?"

"Does Mommy see Pookas, too?"

"Can I be a bartender when I grow up?"

Her father always smoked cigarettes and finished several beers during the movie, answering her questions in a conspiratorial way.

"As many as it takes."

"I have no doubt she sees Pookas and all manner of other strange things."

"Honey, you can be anything you want when you grow

up. Except a dentist. I just hate dentists."

He and her mother had split up in the spring, so Brenda only saw him on the weekends and some holidays. *Harvey* was the only movie he owned. His one bedroom apartment was spartan and as far across Kansas City as he could get from her mother while remaining in the metro area. Sometimes they would stop at the video rental shop on the way back from her mother's place, but Brenda didn't like grownup movies and her father didn't like cartoons. *Harvey* was their compromise and it was a good one. She loved to be near him. She loved the smell of his sweat, the cigarette smoke curling lazily around the room, and the rumble of his beer burps. The couch had a sprung spring in the middle, so they always sat off to the side. She was still small enough that when she slept on it, the spring was at her feet and didn't disturb her.

These memories were vivid. She supposed that was because less than a year later his chest had become riddled with lung cancer. He died so suddenly that her recollection of that period was etched in sharp detail. Tonight as she watched the credits of the movie roll, all those memories seemed bleached and unreal. The warm sensations of nostalgic paternity that followed the shock of his death were no longer accessible. She had played the movie in a moment of desperation, hoping that perhaps it would help alleviate the continual sense that her life was not her own. On the contrary, the memories of her father now seemed tainted by Kevin's death.

"At least I'm not bawling," she mumbled, clicking the TV off with the remote control.

As she got up from the couch, the bowl of popcorn tumbled to the floor. "Great," she muttered.

She pulled the vacuum out of the hallway closet. Amber

was asleep in her bedroom, but Brenda decided that it wouldn't be such a bad thing if the vacuum woke her up and flipped it on.

Andre pulled the van into the parking lot of the apartment he shared with Craig in Dinkytown. He flipped the key off and rubbed his eyes with the palms of his hands. The pressure felt good, dispersing the exhaustion in his tightened face. Red flowers bloomed and receded behind his eyelids. The flowers resolved into blood stains on rock. He snapped his eyes open.

Craig was unconscious on the floor of the van, but his breathing was steady.

I should take him to the hospital, Andre thought, but the idea seemed illusory. How would he explain what had happened? Craig would be treated as an OD or bad trip case. And what about their dead friends? They'd probably both end up in jail.

"Fucking fuck!" he shouted, slamming his fist into the steering wheel. The horn gave a sharp beep, causing Craig to groan. Andre's wrist flared with pain. He frowned at it and ground his teeth.

Andre got out of the van and opened the side door. Craig was deathly white and tucked into a tight ball between the bucket seats, his knees against his chest and his hands folded under his chin. The hospital seemed more reasonable now, but Andre pulled him from the van. Craig unfolded like a ladder. He could stand as long as Andre propped him up. He did not, however, recover full consciousness.

Andre walked him into the apartment complex. Once inside, he propped Craig against the wall and hit the button to call the elevator. When the doors slid open, two drunk, laughing guys tumbled out, nearly knocking Andre down.

"Whoa, dude! Sorry 'bout that!" one of them said as the other stumbled sideways and knocked over a fake plant in the corner. "Shit, brah, wha's up with your roommate?"

They were the neighbors, who hadn't fit into the minivan and stayed behind. Lucky them.

"Bad fucking night, man," Andre replied, peeling Craig off the wall and pushing him into the elevator. He hit the button for the third floor. The pair stared into the elevator with open mouths. As the doors slid closed, Andre shrugged and said, "Like *Weekend At Bernie's*." They didn't laugh, but he didn't expect them to. They probably hadn't seen the movie.

The hallway on the third floor was empty. Andre slid his key into the deadbolt of their door, but it was already unlocked. He *never* forgot to lock the door. He swallowed hard and his heartbeat accelerated. Then he remembered that they had left Winton passed out on the couch. Winton probably woke and left, leaving the door unlocked behind him. Andre propped Craig against the wall and nudged the door inward with this foot, peeking inside as it swung. His kitchen and living room were exactly like he had left them, including a snoring Winton on the couch. He craned his head into the apartment as panic rose in his chest. At least Winton was in one piece.

"I'm quite harmless," a female voice called from a portion of the living room hidden by the kitchen wall.

Andre let out a throaty scream and threw himself backwards, arms extended in a defensive crouch.

"Who's in there?" he sputtered.

A light-skinned black woman appeared from behind the kitchen wall. Her age was hard to pinpoint, but he figured she was in her thirties. She wore a black sports jumper and black sneakers. Her hair was pulled into a tight bun. She was the picture of serenity, but Andre almost growled when she approached. He put a hand on Craig's shoulder, intending to drag him to the stairway and back to the van. Strangers who broke into his apartment were not something he could handle just now.

"Your friend Winton let me in," the woman said, gesturing to the couch. "He went back to sleep. He seems to have had too much to drink. My name is Victoria. You must be Andre. Where is your roommate, Andre?"

He didn't have time to answer before she saw Craig. Her serenity broke in a rush. She pushed Andre out of the way as if he weighed nothing, picked Craig up, and hauled him into the apartment. Andre scrambled to his feet and lunged after her. Her voice stopped him like a palm on his chest.

"How long has he been like this?" she demanded as she lay him down on the carpet.

Andre blinked. "I'm not sure. Thirty minutes? Who the fuck *are* you?"

"Victoria Starks," she said. "I'm here to help you."

She peeled back one of Craig's eyelids and blew into the white socket. The eye rolled down and snapped back up. She relaxed.

"Craig is on a journey, Andre. He may not come back from this journey and if he does, he may not be your friend anymore. There isn't much we can do for him right now, though. His decisions are his own...." She leaned forward, whispered something into his ear, and wiped his blonde hair away from his forehead.

Andre drifted into the kitchen and eyed the knife block on the counter by the microwave.

Victoria sighed. "Why don't you close the door and lock it, Andre? I'll make some tea and you can tell me what happened tonight."

Kevin Jones, formerly known as Number 1, watched Andre and Craig's apartment complex from behind a thick row of arborvitae growing along the neighboring privacy fence. From this vantage point he could see the entire parking lot and back of the building. The back door was the only entrance unlocked at this time of night.

Victoria Starks was upstairs. He wondered what she was doing here, but didn't consider her a threat to the boys. In fact, she was probably an asset in this situation considering Craig's condition. Number 9 had changed tactics. His behavior was erratic, which made keeping up with him more difficult. His choice of identity, Daniel, was also notable. He'd used it five years ago on a job they did together. His brother was not sentimental and the Térata rarely reused an identity that had been so exposed. Something was wrong with Number 9.

By the time Kevin tracked down Craig and Andre at the park, his brother had already made his move. Somehow, Craig had defeated Number 9. But at some terrible, unclear cost. *He might be Waking Up*, Kevin thought, though that seemed like a far stretch. Craig hadn't shown any signs before tonight.

The kids behind Minnehaha Falls were a sad situation. He'd cleaned that mess up because he knew it would enrage his brother. And draw him into this trap. Though all the Térata were supposedly emotionless, Number 9 had a mean and violent streak. When he felt insulted or undercut, he could fly off the handle. Kevin hadn't been prepared to face Number 9 in the park tonight, just as he hadn't been prepared any time in the last two months. The pair had stalemated. Number 9 hadn't made a move big enough to expose any vulnerability and Kevin had stayed in the shadows, using his supposed death as a cover. Number 9 was the more powerful of the two. He was eight "models" newer. The only way to defeat him would be through wits, which was itself a formidable challenge.

If Kevin gauged his brother correctly, tonight he would follow the boys back here and kill them both. This afforded Kevin the opportunity to strike while his brother was distracted and psychologically compromised. The tricky part would be to take him alive. He needed information. Per a prearranged agreement, Number 7 had tipped Kevin off that he'd been located. She hadn't given him an ounce more information and he could not risk contacting her now. He needed to know much more about what was going on at The Elpis Foundation.

So he lurked in the trees with a breech loading pistol and four rounds of etorphine darts. He exuded a pheromone that masked all traces of himself. One of those darts could take down an elephant. Kevin planned to use all four. He also had a packet of syringes containing enough etorphine to keep Number 9 down long enough to get him to his cabin near Brainerd. There he could contain and question him. It was a simple plan, suggesting few potential problems. This was how he liked to operate. However, if any part of the plan went wrong, the consequences would be severe. Blowing his cover at this point required complete success.

After twenty minutes, Kevin began to fidget. His brother should be here soon. It wouldn't take him long to get out of the river and back to the Falls. Once there, his rage should carry him straight here. Kevin's nerves were not what they used to be. Precious little about him was what it used to be, but his training was still good enough to keep him planted in place and alert. Another fifteen minutes ticked by. He eyed each car that drove by longer than necessary. Every movement in the parking lot caused his head to jerk.

His brother would move. No matter how odd his behavior had become, he *would* move. By cleaning up the mess with the kids, Kevin had upped the ante. Number 9 considered himself to be the best of the Térata and probably wasn't wrong about that. Why wasn't he here yet? Unless…

Kevin's heart was made of a carbon-titanium interstitial mesh and did not respond to emotions. It was impervious to adrenaline and psychological reactions. Even so he felt it miss a beat.

…Unless his brother had somehow figured out that he was still alive. In that case, his immediate targets would be Brenda and Amber.

Kevin flew from the cover of the trees, nearly tore the door off of the Suburban he'd been driving for the last two months, and peeled out of the parking lot so fast he almost hit a pair of drunk college kids walking down the middle of the street.

"Oh, God," he prayed as he laid on the horn, "Oh, God, please let me not be too late!"

Daniel stood in the hallway outside of the door to Brenda's condo and listened with some interest as the last few scenes of *Harvey* played out on the other side of the door. He liked that movie. He was dressed in light blue coveralls and wore a baseball cap that read St Paul Plumbing and Mechanicals. He had a toolbox in his right hand and a 20 inch pipe wrench in his left. His first impulse upon arriving at the condo complex was to break the glass on the security door, smash in Brenda's door, kill her, grab the child, and leave. That would have been a fine plan, but a plumber had shown up just as he arrived. No sense in making an unnecessary mess at that point. The plumber—Fred, according to the patch on the coveralls—had a security fob. He also wore a size XXL, which was convenient.

Once the movie ended, Daniel rapped on the door. However, Brenda turned on the vacuum at the same time and didn't hear. He tried the door handle in mild frustration. To his surprise it opened as he turned the knob. Brenda was about five paces away, running the vacuum in front of the couch in the living room. Her back was to him. She had no idea he was there. He took a step into the apartment and raised the pipe wrench. His mouth watered, but he focused to keep Daniel's facial features firmly in place. No more eating human flesh.

Inexplicably, Brenda turned around and saw him. She did not, as he thought she would, begin to scream. Instead, she flipped off the vacuum and demanded, "What are you doing here?"

For a split second Daniel hesitated, which was the biggest mistake he'd made in a long string of them. She hit him full force with whatever chemical magic she unwittingly used. Entire parts of his mind came unhinged and floated away.

"Uh, oh, I, uh, guess I have the wrong place," he stammered, backing out of the condo. He needed to get away as fast as he could. His identity was dissolving, his memories fragmenting. "Sorry. Sorry about that."

Brenda's glare froze him in place and an entire section of his childhood evaporated like it had never happened. She strode towards him and said, "Is it protocol to just barge into places? Who are you with? Oh, I see on your cap. St Paul Plumbing and Mechanicals. I'll be giving your boss a call in the morning, *Fred*. Now leave." She pointed at the hallway.

Daniel fled the condo. He dropped the toolbox in the stairwell and stripped off the coveralls and cap in the parking lot. He stumbled to the Lexus, triggering the car alarm before managing to get the door unlocked. Once inside, he began sobbing into his hands. His memories roiled inside his head, crashing into one another, recombining, and evaporating faster than he could track them. His will was rubble. He had to move or he was going to die in a puddle of mental confusion. He stared at the key to the Lexus for a moment, trying to figure out how to insert it into the steering column. Other keys dangled from the key ring. One of them opened the front door of the used car dealership Kimm had owned. Daniel's mind reformulated around that key. He'd go to the car dealership. He'd go there and hide until he could get himself back together. Kimm's Auto World. That was a safe place. He needed a safe place.

Several minutes after the Lexus pulled out of the parking lot, Kevin's Suburban bounced into it. He drove to the back door and parked haphazardly across two handicap spaces. The door flew off its hinges as he sprung from the still-running SUV. He had the door fob in his hand as he leaped both sets of stairs. With his last ounce of restraint, he allowed the little light above the sensor on the door handle to turn green before bursting inside. Seconds later he was standing in front of Brenda's doorway.

His brother's stink was all over the hallway and extended into the condo. He'd also killed someone on the way up, probably in the parking lot. However, Kevin could smell both Brenda and Amber inside. Both were alive. He stared at the door. What had happened? Why was Brenda still alive and Amber still here? Suspicions began to form in his mind.

The implications of what Brenda could have done to his brother were disturbing. He needed to see her. He needed to *know* she was still alive, that his brother hadn't left a false trail of scents and sounds. He retreated back to the Suburban. Along the way, he picked up the toolbox and Fred's overalls. These must have belonged to whoever his brother had killed. A plumber's van sat in the service bay. A sniff told Kevin that a dead body lay inside.

Kevin held the door of the Suburban in place as he parked it behind a dumpster. The "door open" light on the dash blinked maniacally, reflecting his state of mind. The door would need to be reattached. He'd do that now and think about the situation while he worked. However, he'd need to shift identities. Too many people here knew Kevin Jones. Despite faking his death, he had maintained Kevin's form this entire time, using pheromones to remain unnoticed. Four years had passed since he had taken on any form beyond his true self and Kevin. He wasn't sure he could be anyone else at this point.

Using a screwdriver from the toolbox he assumed belonged to Fred, he jimmied the door shut and crawled into the back seat. After removing his clothes, he shifted to his true form. It was similar to his brother's, but his features were blunter and his fur grew in thicker, covering his body in an ashy grey pelt. Black lines radiated from his eye-sockets, traveling down his neck, shoulders, and flanks. They converged at the small of his back. Neither horns nor bony protrusions grew from his bones and joints. His snout was less pronounced and his form less canine. He could stand fully erect on his heels, while his brother's true from required a continual crouch for balance. Like his brother, he had immense teeth and his fingers ended with retractable claws. This form was not as dense as Kevin's body, so he was now squished into the back seat of the Suburban like a pile of throw rugs.

After three protracted breaths, he began to change again. All his joints popped. His fur, claws, ears, and snout slipped into his skin. He gasped for breath, groaning with the effort. When he was done, sweat soaked the leather seats. He sat up and flipped open the mirror on the back of the seat in front of him. A sigh of relief slid from his mouth. It had been a long time since he'd looked at Matt Kurac: sandy blonde hair, a wide mouth, and glazed blue eyes. This was his least memorable persona and his most disposable. Unlike when he was Kevin, a severe tension existed inside him, as if a bolt had been tightened too far somewhere in his chest. Holding identities other than his true, monstrous form had always been difficult until he had encountered Brenda as Kevin. He'd been comfortable in that form ever since.

Unfortunately, he still thought of himself as Kevin. He usually had no problem taking on an entire identity when he changed forms. Matt Kurac's name and physical attributes were accessible, but his history and memories were gone. At least he only needed the identity to fix the door on the Suburban and check on Brenda.

The door was more damaged than he'd thought. The hinge was bent and the actuator for the automatic door lock was smashed. He could hear it rattling around inside the door. He took the interior panel off and began removing broken pieces. As he worked he tried to get back his identity as Matt Kurac, but failed. The details of Matt's life were erased. Brenda's brand of chemical magic was potent stuff.

When Kevin first encountered Brenda, he was eating at a chain diner near the U of M campus and she had been his server. At the time, he thought of himself as Number 1 or whatever identity he wore while outside The Elpis

Foundation. He was in town to do a job for his father: find Victoria Starks, which he'd already done, and bring her back to Des Moines in mint condition. Basic nab and go.

The moment Brenda walked up, welcomed him to the restaurant, and asked him if he wanted to start off with an iced tea, or maybe a soda, he had sensed something extraordinary. The hair all over his body rose. Her voice penetrated into his ears with an odd ringing. He hadn't thought much about it at the time, but when he got back to his hotel room after lunch, she was all he could think about. He even missed a golden opportunity to snatch Victoria from her favorite coffee shop later that day. He'd been thinking about Brenda's face and voice instead of watching the front of the goddamn building he'd staked out for a week. For some reason, he could not follow Victoria's red truck to her house. Such tricks were common for witchy people like her. With that setback, the job would take a few extra days while he staked out the Grey Owl again.

So the next day he went back to the diner and asked Brenda to go to dinner with him after her shift. He was prepared to use persuasive pheromonal techniques. That wasn't necessary. She played coy, but relented. As far as Kevin knew, love was neither genetically nor bio-mechanically programmed into himself or any of his siblings. He understood love, like all emotional reactions, as a tool and used its consequences often while working. The actual feelings it produced, though, were foreign. He suspected that she was causing something like it in him. He planned to grab her and bring her back with Victoria. Somebody needed to know this sort of shit could happen. It was dangerous.

But things didn't go that way at all. He took her to Fogo De Chao just to impress her. They had a wonderful time. He spoke more over the course of those three hours than he had in the previous month. After he dropped her off at her apartment that night, he realized the tension inside of him had vanished. Holding Kevin's form no longer took any effort. In addition, all of Kevin's fabricated memories and invented backstory became more real than his actual life. He sat in his hotel room, staring at the mirror on the wall. His cell phone was on the bed beside him. He almost dialed home a hundred times, but something in his chest always stopped him. He cast about for reasonable explanations. Did Victoria have anything to do with this? She was a person of interest to The Foundation and had helped them more than once, though she didn't know that. She was difficult to find and possessed uncanny abilities, but there was no way she could know he was after her. Even if she did somehow know, her history suggested flight over fight. Why would she tangle him into an emotional conundrum? Could she even do that? Nothing in her dossier suggested so. If she knew he was after her, she would have vanished like she did every other time things got hot around her. Like DC. Like Chicago. She had a solid pattern. Playing cupid didn't fit it at all.

So, then, something about Brenda was at work on him. Something powerful and native to her. Something about the way her physical presence affected him. This was random, he decided. And fascinating. He would hold off one more day to study her before grabbing both her and Victoria and driving straight back to Des Moines. Instead of dialing home on his phone, he dialed Brenda's number, despite the fact that it was midnight. Also despite the time, she answered and didn't seem at all displeased to talk to him.

The few weeks following that first date were a blur. Kevin forgot about Victoria Starks. He rented a room down the street from Brenda's apartment from a guy he found on Craigslist named Bert. He invented a back story about losing his parents in a house fire last year somewhere in Washington State. He intertwined that with Kevin's prebuilt back story, claiming he was in town for a couple of job interviews as a vehicle mechanic. He needed to start over in a new place. Lying to Brenda and Bert was easy, because as he invented these stories, they seemed very real to him. He knew they were fabrications, but when he talked about his life, his words created memories indistinguishable from his own real ones. His ability to differentiate his identities became unstable.

None of this mattered very much to him, because he and Brenda had fallen in love. He got a job at Rick's Tire and Battery as the Service Manager and was running the entire shop in less than a month. He and Brenda spent every spare second with one another, almost collapsing her college career in its last semester. For only one moment in that entire period did he doubt what he was doing.

Two months into his relationship with Brenda, Kevin realized he hadn't taken on his true form since meeting her. Alarm bells sounded in his head in ways they had not when he had destroyed his cell phone, shipped his car to Kansas City, and cut out the tracking chip in his neck. Like his brothers and sisters, he kept most of his identities secret from his organization. Kevin Jones was unknown to them. They had no way to find him short of sending a search party to the Twin Cities to sniff him out. He assumed they would do that, so he habitually hid all traces of himself with pheromones, something that seemed much easier than it should have been. There was less to hide. The fact that he had not been *himself* for two months finally made him pause and think about just what in the fuck he was doing.

This realization hit him in the shower after he got home from work at Rick's. His roommate was working the late shift at UPS and wouldn't be home until after 3:00 a.m. the next morning. Kevin and Brenda had plans for later that evening. With an hour or so of privacy, he could shift between his forms, just to stifle that nagging feeling. He stepped out of the shower and willed himself to become himself. For a few seconds, nothing happened. His brain could not process that, so he willed harder. With an audible *pop*, he slid into his true form. A cataclysmic flood of mental anguish followed, as if a spring had been released in his mind, launching everything into chaos. And hunger. Hunger so overpowering it was compulsive.

He burst out of the bathroom and bounded into the living room of the apartment. For some reason, Bert was not at work. He was standing in front of the TV with a DVD in one hand and a Pabst Blue Ribbon in the other. Bert barely noticed Kevin's monstrous form before his entire mid-section was torn out and stuffed down the monster's throat. Kevin ate him in less time than it would have taken to eat a hamburger. He licked and sucked at the carpet until every trace of blood was gone. An immense thrill shivered across his pelt and into his muscles. He had to have more. More blood. More meat. He turned to the door, planning to leap into the street. He could kill and stuff himself until there was no one left in the Twin Cities. Just before kicking the door from its hinges, he stumbled to a halt. Kevin was supposed to meet Brenda for dinner in an hour and a half.

Kevin's stomach heaved and he began to vomit on the kitchen floor. Bert came up in large chunks, piece by piece. He took considerably longer to come out than he had going in. At one point, Kevin thrashed on the floor with a thigh lodged in his throat. When he'd finished throwing up his roommate, Kevin found himself crumpled on the kitchen floor, spraying blood through the nostrils of his snout. Once his mind stopped spinning, he calculated how to get the mess cleaned up before Brenda arrived. Kevin's form came back to him with no effort. He bagged Bert in multiple trash bags and took him to the dumpster outside. He cleaned the kitchen floor and carpet in the living room with bleach. He made plans to dispose of all of Bert's things and pretend he'd just moved out. Brenda could never know this had happened. Never.

He felt horrible about killing Bert, which was almost as out-of-character as the love he felt for Brenda. Killing was ingrained in his nature. For death to mean anything more than a simple stoppage was an immense idea. Bert had been a slob with a drinking problem, but he had never done anything to warrant being consumed and then vomited up. A new emotion blossomed in Kevin's heart. Guilt. After he tossed Bert's regurgitated remains into the dumpster, Kevin stared at the logo printed on its side. It was a maple leaf, stenciled with a thin green line. He traced the line with his finger.

He said, "I will never eat human flesh again. I will never take my true form in anger. I will protect."

His emotional core seemed to settle into place as he spoke those words. Certainty returned to him for the first time since he had met Brenda.

After that, Kevin went deep into the north woods of the Boundary Waters to experiment with shifting shapes. The first few attempts were catastrophes, but he regained his senses before finding any people to devour. The local wildlife did not fare so well. Over time, he mastered being both Kevin and the monster. By his fifth month of knowing Brenda, Kevin Jones was as human as he could be. The monster was relegated to an occasional hunt for animals in the wilds of northern Minnesota. Kevin made peace with the monster, who in turn simply stopped being so monstrous. There was no going back from his decisions at the dumpster. As time went on, his hunting trips up north became less frequent. The past he had programmed into his own head, not the one he had lived, became his reference point. He transformed into a very competent manager at Rick's Tire and Battery, a husband, and, though he had thought it impossible, a father. The life he'd led before became a hazy series of events belonging to another being.

As Kevin finished fitting the door back into place, he muttered to himself, "I cannot escape who I was... I was a fool to try." Those words felt correct to him, but they also felt like a great lie.

The door's power would not work until he had a chance to get it into a shop, but he managed to reattach the hinges and stop the blinking light on the dash. He put on Fred's overalls, grabbed his toolbox, and headed upstairs.

Outside the door to the condo, he paused for a few moments, listening and smelling. Brenda was still awake and moving about inside. Amber was sleeping in the master bedroom. Without his adrenaline pumping, Kevin experienced another, more poignant, feeling. Sadness. He knocked on the door.

Even if he hadn't been able to hear her movements, he would have known that Brenda was looking through the peephole. She enjoyed having it on the door. She said it reminded her of Alice and the Looking-Glass. The deadbolt clicked, but she left the chain latch in place. Half of her face showed in the crack of the door. Seeing that face alive and well gave him half of what he wanted.

With an impatient frown, she demanded, "Can I help you?"

Being this close to her was difficult, but he replied, "It seems that we've got a leak upstairs, ma'am, and I'm so sorry to wake you up, but we really need to get into your utility closet to make sure there was no water intrusion."

Brenda frowned deeper and said, "So you're Fred, too, huh? Your other guy just barged in without knocking, you know."

Kevin nodded and said, "We're really sorry about that mix-up. Fred—the other one—he feels awful about it. He thought the unit was empty. He thought it was one of the foreclosed ones."

Brenda relaxed and said, "OK, do what you need to do. Be quiet, though. My daughter is sleeping." She closed the door, released the chain latch, and let him in.

Kevin went to the kitchen sink and pretended to check underneath. He checked the bathroom in the hallway and the utility closet, which housed the water heater.

"No water here," he said. "I just need to inspect the master bath and I'll be out of your hair."

Brenda said, "I just used that bathroom. There wasn't any water on the floor or cabinet."

He shrugged and said, "I still gotta see it. My job's on the line if anything goes wrong and I don't catch it. The association is picky about these things."

Brenda snorted. She had more than one disagreement with the association. Since he had been designed to be sterile, Kevin told Brenda he could not father children. She claimed she had no intention of having children, anyway. The eventuality had not been a concern when they bought the condo. The association's representative implied that the "lifestyle" of this building was not designed with children in mind. Children weren't banned by the building's charter, but Amber was the only one in the entire place. This caused a few unpleasant moments with the neighbors and a flurry of letters from the front office. He knew the association would be a soft spot with Brenda and he needed to see his daughter.

"OK. Follow me. But be quiet. My daughter is asleep and I don't want her to wake up."

Amber slept like a rock at this point in her life, but Kevin respected Brenda for remaining in control of the situation. She led him through the bedroom, where Amber had thrown the covers off the bed and was spread eagle in the middle. Pillows were under both her head and feet. Her face was serene and her breathing even. Kevin stared at her until Brenda made an impatient waving motion and pointed at the bathroom. He went in, flipped on the light, and saw himself in the mirror. A huge smile was spread across his face. He dropped it. He opened and closed the cabinet under the sink, switched the light back off, and left the bathroom. Brenda kept herself between him and Amber on his way out. When they got back to the living room, she said, "Was everything OK?"

He turned to the door and said, "Yup. Dandy. Thanks for your time. Again, we're sorry for the late night intrusion."

The doorknob to the master bedroom rattled as Amber worked to get it open. Despite himself, Kevin turned to look just as it opened. His daughter stepped into the hall. For a moment, she was a groggy two-year-old. But as soon as she saw Kevin, her eyes lit up and she dashed toward him. She dodged her mother's hands and jumped into his arms.

"Daddy! Daddy! Daddy!" she squealed.

Kevin dropped his toolbox and caught her. Before he could stop himself he had enveloped her in a hug. She giggled and squirmed against him. He felt tears begin to stream down his face. *No!* he thought, even as he crushed her tight to him. *They cannot know!*

Brenda stared, obviously confused and jolted. She narrowed her eyes and walked towards them. Kevin looked up from Amber and was frozen in place.

Oh, no, Brenda, don't do this... he thought. It was too late. She had him and she wasn't going to let him go.

"Amber, please come here," she said in her most firm "mom" voice.

Still smiling, Amber disengaged from Kevin and backed toward her mother.

She cocked her head to the side and said, "Daddy has masks!"

Brenda gathered Amber into her arms and continued to stare at Kevin, who could not move or speak.

"Who are you?" she demanded.

The change came upon him unbidden, forcing him to shift forms outside his own control. He collapsed in a twisting, thrashing mess. His vision blurred as his body contorted. This was the wrong way to change. He should have shifted into his true form, then into Kevin's form. Brenda was making him change directly into Kevin. No pain in his past was even close to what he was experiencing now. He stifled screams and the tears in his eyes ran with blood. He coughed and gagged. His lungs froze and his blurred vision became a tunnel.

She's killing me, he thought in a panic. He could not die. He would explode, killing Brenda and Amber. He fought to breathe. He fought the encroaching blackness in his vision. It was no use, though. He tumbled into unconsciousness, fighting and snarling curses in his mind.

Brenda gasped as the plumber went into convulsions on the floor. Amber perched in her arms, head cocked to the side, still smiling. The plumber's convulsions led to more traumatic physical alterations. His face collapsed, his hair fell out of his head, and his spine crackled as he twisted into sickening shapes. Blood oozed from his mouth, eyes, and ears. After a few minutes, the thrashing stopped. All that remained of the plumber was a man-shaped blob of putty. His clothing lay in tatters around him. With liquid slowness, the putty began to take shape. The hair on its head grew back, rich and black. The muscles in its arms and torso took shape. Its fingers and toes reformed. The body was beginning to look familiar to her. A face emerged, drawn forth from the glob of flesh.

Amber smiled at her mother and said, "See! Daddy take off mask!"

Craig emerged from his dream in stages, first becoming aware of the smells around him. Stale sweat. Cheap incense. He was in his own bed. He peeled his eyelids open, rubbing layers of crust from them with his fingers. His muscles felt as if they'd been beaten with sticks. All his joints popped as he moved. His mouth felt like cardboard. He had never been so thirsty.

"Good, grief," he muttered. "What did I drink last night?"

He stumbled to the bathroom, stuck his face under the sink faucet, and sucked in water. He looked in the mirror. Dark, black circles encased both of his eyes. His skin was bleached of all color. Blood stained his chapped lips and nose. A scraggly stubble sprouted from his face, but it was all white.

This is not good, he thought.

He shaved the white stubble from his face with an electric razor. There was nothing to do about the black eyes. He prodded his front teeth and cried out in pain. They were loose. Touching them felt like biting a flaming stick. He must have gotten into a fight. A bad one. The fact that he was in his apartment and not the hospital or jail was a good sign, he supposed.

After taking a shower as hot as he could stand it, he went back to his room and dressed in jeans and a t-shirt that read, "Do You Want To See My Beaker?" He noticed the shirt he wore last night, torn apart and lying on the floor by his bed. That had to be an interesting story.

"Time to face the music," Craig said to his dresser mirror. Andre always woke up hours before he did and was always ready to either give him good natured shit or bitch him out for his drunken antics. Today, he doubted there would be anything good natured about what Andre would say. Craig hated fights.

To his surprise, Andre was not sitting in the living room playing video games. Instead, Winton was splayed out on the couch. His hair was tangled over his face and his hand was tucked embarrassingly down the front of his pants. More notably, a black woman was sitting in Craig's recliner drinking tea and reading the latest issue of *Playboy*, which he assumed she'd taken from his bedroom.

"Good morning, Craig," she said, watching him over the cover of the magazine.

Her voice triggered his memories from the night before. Suddenly dizzy, he knelt down and put his hand on his forehead.

"Oh, God," he said. "It was your voice. It was your voice

136

that said, '*Katalambano*'."

"No," she said, shaking her head, "that was your voice. I simply lent it the strength it needed to speak. I don't speak Greek. Tell me, Craig, what did the creature in the dark do for you?"

Craig shook his head, "I don't know. Nothing, I guess. I answered the phone."

She prompted, "The phone?"

"Yeah, the phone. It was answer the phone or talk to the thing in the dark. One of those 'this or that' options. Like the hamster car commercials. I answered the phone."

The woman put the magazine on the coffee table, revealing a gun on her lap. Craig could not tell one gun from another, but this one looked big for a handgun. "My name is Victoria, Craig, and I'm going to need you to answer a lot of questions for me. Then I'm going to do a card reading for you. If you do anything besides what I tell you, I will shoot you between the eyes." She spread her hands over the gun in her lap. "Do you understand?"

Craig didn't hesitate. "Yes, ma'am."

"Now, please come and sit on the floor in front of the coffee table."

He obeyed.

"Winton!" she said.

Winton snapped awake, pushed matted hair out of his face, and looked at her.

"Please leave, Winton," she said. "Thank you for your help. Remember what I told you."

"Yeah, sure thing," he said blankly and walked out the door.

"Where's Andre?" Craig asked.

"Sleeping," she replied. "Now, please describe in detail everything about your dream last night. Don't leave anything out."

At first, Craig couldn't call up most of the dream, but it began to come back to him as he spoke. He ended up telling her everything. He even told Andre's bad joke, which he had wanted to hold back. She seemed to know he was trying to hide something, so he figured Andre's ban on mentioning the joke didn't apply in this scenario. The dream was insane, but she seemed to believe that it had all actually happened, which is how he felt. She prodded him with questions. What did the key look like? Who was playing piano? Did Craig put any part of his hand into the dark space at the back of the pay phone? How were his teeth this morning?

When he told her everything, she smiled and tucked the gun into a gym bag on the floor beside the chair. She pulled a porcelain box out of the bag and spread a silk blanket over the coffee table. Lions and ribbons danced in a pattern across it. She opened the box and removed a deck of tarot cards, which had the same pattern on their backs. She shuffled them. His eyes blurred before she finished and set the deck down. He had to shake his head to make them focus again.

"Take the top card and turn it over," she instructed. The inflection of her voice was deep and commanding.

He did so. It was a picture of a skull with its top removed. Written at the bottom of the card were the words The Hollow Skull.

Giving no hint as to what this meant, she reshuffled the cards and set them before him.

"Take the top card and set it next to your first."

The Anchor.

Again she reshuffled.

"Take the top card and set it perpendicular above the other two cards."

The Tower.

For several minutes, Victoria did not move. Craig had never seen a card reading before. Hocus pocus stuff didn't excite him. After last night, though, hocus pocus seemed much more plausible and therefore much more interesting. He looked at the cards. The artwork was stunning in its detail, like mannerist carvings he'd seen at an art museum. The rope tethering the Anchor twisted around the card like a snake. The perspective in the drawing of The Hollow Skull caused it to stare directly into his eyes as he looked into its empty head. The Tower, if he looked at it right, seemed to be an immense structure, spiraling upward forever, despite the fact that it was a drawing on a card no bigger than six by four inches.

Victoria's voice jerked him away from the cards. It was booming, resonant, and filled with danger. "Your choice has not been finalized. Your second trial will come. Resist the temptation once more, or forfeit your mind as a consequence."

She blinked several times and nodded as if satisfied. "Please go wake Andre up. I've ordered breakfast and it will be here shortly. In the meantime, I'll brew some tea."

"Does this mean you aren't going to shoot me?" Craig asked.

"It means I don't have to shoot you at this time and you have been armed with the knowledge necessary to prevent me from ever having to. Now wake up your roommate."

She gathered the cards into their box and tucked it into her gym bag.

"We don't have any tea here," he said.

"I brought my own, thank you," she replied.

The remnants of Number 9 sat behind a large oak desk in

Kimm Peter's office. Daniel Clark was no longer recognizable. His face was caved in from the eyes down, missing nose, lips, and a lower jaw. His lidless eyes were bloodshot and sat at the bottom of their sockets like deflated balloons.

Kimm had not been a tidy or tasteful man. Stacks of papers in manila folders lay on every flat surface. The filing cabinets were unsorted. Perhaps half of the keys to the inventory were hanging in the key cabinet behind the desk. In a corner drooped a dusty fake fern. A motivational poster hung on one wall, reading "Life Is Good" beneath a picture of a mountain trail at sunset. A cheap katana, the kind sold at dodgy import stores, was mounted on the wall behind the desk.

Number 9 read the sales ledger from last month, his flaccid eyes creeping back and forth. Drool dribbled from the cavern of his mouth, dotting the pages. When he finished reading, he grabbed a folder labeled Current Inventory. He read it, stacked it, and grabbed the next folder. When he finished reading that, he opened the bottom desk drawer. A bottle of cheap vodka rolled forward. He set it on the desk. A manila envelope labeled Family was nestled in the drawer. Inside were tuition payment stubs, various personal records, and a stack of pictures rubber-banded together. Number 9 popped the rubber band, sending it flying across the room. The pictures were snapshots of Kimm's kids and other relatives. On the back of each picture was written the date it was taken, the location, and who was in it. Ashlyn and Phoebe were Kimm's daughters. Oren was his son. There had been two wives. The first was Jennifer, from whom he was divorced. The second, Layla, died in a car accident, according to her death certificate. The children were from his first marriage.

Number 9 stared at each picture, front and back, before tenderly stacking each on the desk. When he'd seen them all, he rooted around the office for more. In a closet full of suits still in their bags from the cleaners, he found a stash of Kimm's personal effects, including his college diploma, passport, a stack of yellowing pictures from his childhood, and an old driver's license. He set the driver's license aside. When he'd exhausted the room of anything that told a personal story about Kimm, Number 9 picked the driver's license back up and stared at it. It was from six years ago. Kimm Donald Peters. Height: 5' 10". Hair: Blonde. Eyes: Blue. Weight: 175. The picture had worn away, so he rummaged back through the stack of snapshots until he found one from about that time. Kimm was standing with his children on a beach somewhere south of the US border, smiling broadly and making a peace sign with both hands. He wore a pair of thick rimmed glasses.

I have to be someone, Number 9 thought. *Right now, I'm no one. I'm gone.*

There was no way he could fit into the form described by that driver's license. He turned to stare at the katana hanging on the wall. The metal was bright, but the edge was dull. Number 9 ran his palm across it. Blood trickled down the blade and dropped to the floor. Dull, but sharp enough. He pulled it from the wall. With a precise movement, he swung the sword back at himself. His left arm flew off at the shoulder socket. Blood sprayed the wall. Careful to keep the fountain away from the desk and its pile of precious artifacts, he swung the sword again. His left leg fell away below the knee. He dropped into Kimm's swivel chair and hacked off his other leg at the knee, too.

That should be enough, he thought. He removed his blood soaked clothes.

Number 9 shifted into his true form. As he did so, his limbs regrew, twisting out of the bleeding holes, robbing mass from the rest of his body. He was the same monster he'd always been, but smaller. He lay down on the floor and closed his eyes. The monster folded into itself. Kimm Peters from six years ago, with a tan, six-pack abs, and a gaudy smile, replaced him.

Kimm stood up and looked around the office. The excited smile on his face never wavered.

"What a mess!" he exclaimed.

He busied himself cleaning up. There was so much to do. If he was going to get his life back together, he was going to need to get organized. In a gleeful whirlwind of action, Kimm began cleaning the office. By the time he opened the doors of the car dealership for business, no trace of blood remained. All the keys were located and put in their box. The floors of the small showroom were swept and mopped. The leaves were blown off the cars and out of the lot.

Kimm was dressed in a sharp blue suit with a yellow and white checkered tie.

"What a day to sell cars!" he said as he walked the property. "Life is good."

Chapter 6
The Art Dealer

Octavio pounded a speed bag at The Elpis Foundation's gym. Sweat glistened across his skin, soaking his sleeveless t-shirt and headband. He slid from stance to stance without slowing the motion of his fists. His mind drifted, lost in the cadence that echoed through the empty gym. The faces of the boys who'd died in Minnesota appeared and dissolved. The affidavits he'd signed about the "boating accident" rippled around them. Number 10's burning eyes opened and closed. His mother's broken heart became the Sacred Heart, pierced by thorns and burning with love.

A chirping phone interrupted the fluidity of his thoughts. He eyed it on the floor by his gym bag. That ring tone indicated something was wrong with the Térata. He disengaged from the bag, feeling a twinge of remorse as the steady pounding stopped. The message on his phone read: "Number 9 Status Offline." He frowned and picked up his gym bag. A shower would have been nice, but if Number 9 was "Offline", Octavio needed to know why. He toweled off and jogged through empty hallways to his small, private office. Ensconced at his desk, he watched a red light blink on his computer screen.

"What are you up to, Number 9?" he asked the computer, leaning back in his chair. He tried phoning him and wasn't surprised to end up in voicemail. Flashing red lights on user profiles in the Elipsis System meant that someone's tracking device had failed or been removed. Or they were dead. If 9 was dead, news of a freak explosion in NE Minneapolis would reach him through tapped police lines very soon.

A timer started in Octavio's head, tracking how long it would be before he received a phone call from Clarence. Since Clarence's health had interrupted his ability to control both The Foundation and Elpis Enterprises, his inner circle had decayed. Octavio was the only Awakened human Clarence could turn to in a crisis. He favored odds before 06:15.

Octavio picked up a small rock carving of the Aztec god Quetzalcoatl and turned it over in his fingers. It had been a gift from his youngest sister. The surface of the feathered serpent was smooth from the oil of his skin. After a few moments, he set the figurine back on his desk and tapped the space bar on his keyboard twice. The computer's speakers made an aquatic sound before a cold, feminine voice answered, "Hello, Octavio."

"Hello, Number 7," Octavio replied, "I think you'll be going to the Twin Cities today."

"Is this about Number 9 going red?" she asked.

"Yes," he said, stifling surprise. Her clearance level had increased. Clarence was getting desperate if the Térata were watching each other. "You're the only one close enough. Clarence wants 11 and 12 out on their own, but I'm not ready to unleash that on Number 9 just yet. Could be ugly. He's worse than they are in many ways."

"Got it," she replied. "I'll be ready."

"Thanks," he said and hit the space bar again.

Octavio disliked his new job as a coordinator for the Térata. He felt like a zookeeper. While they were monstrous in their true forms, sophisticated hardware slithered through their nervous and circulatory systems, regulating their response to stimulation. In theory, they should have been cool and clinical at all times. In practice, Octavio found that they all showed signs of emotional and rational weakness.

Number 1 had vanished before Octavio had been recruited into the Elpis Foundation. No one was telling the story there. He resurfaced with a wife and child, only to die later. Children weren't even supposed to be possible. Number 9 was sociopathic and cruel. Number 8 was arrogant. Number 4 was vicious but she kept a pet salamander in a terrarium. Number 10 had gone right off the rails in Minnesota and Clarence's explanation of "bad wiring" was thin. Number 7 was the only one for whom Octavio felt affection, and he suspected that was only because she had a sexy phone voice. When he saw her in her true form, though, he certainly didn't find her attractive or empathetic. She was a monster, just like the rest.

All the Térata demonstrated crevices of personality except Numbers 11 and 12. Elpis had gotten what he wanted with them. There were minor politics between the first 10, but 11 and 12 spent all their time eating, sleeping, and training. They were the only ones who used the gym more than Octavio. Always together. Always silent. And, so far, always obedient. Though they could change shapes at will, they did not revert to a true form like their brothers and sisters. They could be anyone at any time.

He leaned back in his chair, pushing it all the way to the edge of tipping. The back of his head bumped into something cold and hard. He froze and said, *"¿Qué demonios?"*

"Sorry, Octavio," said the voice of Tim Shelton, Clarence's chief executive assistant, "but you're being laid off."

It was stupid of him to talk, Octavio thought as he tipped the chair past its balancing point. *I'm glad he never liked me.*

The gun went off, clapping with the sound of a silencer. But Octavio rolled as the chair flew out from under him and the bullet only grazed the top of his skull. Blood splashed forward. The bullet shattered the glass covering a photo of an Aztec pyramid. Octavio grabbed Tim's wrist and spun, breaking the man's arm in the process. Tim cried out in pain as the gun tumbled from his hand. Octavio stood, twisting the arm further out of shape.

"What's this all about, Tim?" Octavio asked. "And who do I send a bill to for my picture? That's an original photograph I got in Tenochtitlan. Number 4 of 200. Signed by the photographer."

Tim looked at his mangled arm. His eyes rolled back into his head and his body went limp.

Octavio pursed his lips and dropped Tim. He grabbed a towel from his gym bag and wiped the blood off of his face and head. Small tentacles knit the shallow wound on his scalp back together. He dabbed blood off his desk and computer monitor.

"Fuck you, Tim," Octavio said, tossing the towel at his bag.

He flipped Tim's crooked arm out of the way, grabbed the lapels of his sport jacket, and pulled him to a standing position.

"Wake up, Tim. Now!" Octavio said.

Tim's eyes fluttered for a moment before opening and filling with panic.

"Oh, Christ, Octavio," he stammered.

"I don't suppose you'd like to tell me what that was all about, hmm?" Octavio said.

Tim thrashed in an attempt to free himself.

Guess we'll do it por las malas, Octavio thought.

Two tentacles swallowed Octavio's eyes from behind and shot forward from the sockets. Tim's mouth opened, but his scream withered in his throat as the tentacles shattered his optic foramen and dug into his brain. With peristaltic action, they sucked in Tim's grey matter. Information flashed through Octavio's mind in torn fragments. Most of it was useless, but the tentacles were looking for specific events. They located Tim's most recent memories. Octavio allowed his brain to meld with Tim's thoughts. A phone call from an unidentified, unknown voice. Plan 8 TF had been approved. Adrenaline surge. Feelings of giddiness. Plotting exactly what to say before pulling the trigger. The walk down the hall. Drawing the gun…

Octavio threw Tim's body to the ground, where it twitched and jerked. The tentacles receded into his skull and regurgitated his eyes. That was not enough information. Tim's memories were locked and codified to such a degree that even Tim wasn't fully aware of what he was doing. Someone had tampered with his mind.

Octavio's computer speakers resonated with an aquatic sound. He turned around and tapped the space bar.

"Hello, Clarence," he said. 06:14.

"Hello, Octavio," Clarence replied, his voice smooth despite its age. "I assume you're aware of the situation with Number 9."

"Yes," Octavio said. "I've already contacted Number 7. Should I send her out to recon and report?"

"I think that might be good, though I would like you to use 11 and 12 if possible."

"I'll hold them in backup position. I'd like her input on this. She knows Number 9 well."

"That will be fine. Let me know what she finds out. Things in the Twin Cities have become very complicated."

"I will. Good-bye."

"Good-bye, Octavio," Clarence said. The speakers made a clicking sound.

Octavio righted his chair and sat down. This was the second attempt on his life in two months. He had hoped to get a smoking gun from Tim's brain. No such luck. He suspected that Tim was tied to Number 10 in some way, despite the fact that Clarence defended the Térata as unfailingly loyal. Where was the connection? Octavio put his elbows on his knees and scowled at Tim's body. Politics had never been of any interest to him. Now he was swimming in them.

Four tentacles slid from Octavio's armpits and dug into Tim's flesh. Octavio exhaled as they chewed the man up and sucked him in. Human flesh was by far the most thrilling of meals. When all traces of the body were gone, Octavio gathered the empty suit. He took it to Tim's office and tossed it on his desk. If he was to be surrounded by mysteries, he would create a few of his own.

As he rounded a corner in the hallway, he nearly bumped into Aaron Black.

"Whoa," Aaron said, recoiling. When he recognized Octavio, his eyes widened and his hand slid into his jacket. He relaxed quickly, though, and said, "Slow your roll, man. You're short, but I think you outweigh me by fifty pounds."

Octavio said, "Sorry. My mind was somewhere else."

Aaron nodded and said, "Yeah, I could tell. You looked like you were going to kill me. So you think about that beer..."

"Sorry," Octavio interrupted. "I've gotta get back to my office. Crisis with Clarence's pets."

"Sure," Aaron said. "Call anytime."

Octavio nodded and stalked away.

Why did Aaron reach for his gun? he thought. He shook his head. He'd worked with Aaron since joining The Foundation. Aaron didn't like Clarence, but he had always been a solid friend to Octavio. Paranoia was creeping up on him.

When he got back to his office, he phoned Number 7 and told her to head to the Twin Cities. Then he grabbed his bag and returned to the gym to shower.

"You still smell like vodka," Andre complained as Craig shook him awake.

"Yeah, well, I think I'm still drunk," Craig replied. "And there's some crazy black chick with a big fucking gun in the living room."

Andre bolted upright, threw off his covers, and said, "Shit! Not a fucking dream!"

"No shit, Sherlock," Craig said. "Not a dream for anybody. Except maybe Winton. He seems to have slept through everything that happened last night. Also, you're naked. You didn't bang her, did you?"

"I think she drugged me with some tea," Andre said, pulling a towel from his dresser and wrapping it around his waist. "Now that I think about it, I'm sure she drugged me and I'm glad she did. I don't think I'll ever sleep without drugs again."

Craig shrugged, "What? Monsters killing a bunch of our friends isn't cool with you?"

Andre scowled at him.

"Sorry, man," Craig said. "I *am* still drunk. Breakfast is on the way, apparently. I didn't know anybody delivered breakfast. You've got blood on you."

Andre didn't stop scowling.

"What, man? I said I was sorry," Craig grumbled.

"Dude, you look like you've been dead for a week."

"Oh. Yeah, I know. I was, um, hoping that would just wear off when the hangover set in."

Andre nodded. "It's not a good look for you. I'm taking a shower. This is your blood. Tell that woman I'll be out shortly. And no, I didn't bang her."

After showering, Andre stood in front of the sink and stared at his face in the mirror. The condensation made his reflection distant and blurry, which was how he felt. Opium. She'd drugged him with opium. That was good. Feeling distant and blurry was what he needed right now, since the only other available feelings were anxiety and confusion.

He prodded the crosses hanging by his mirror, making them swing back and forth. He had been a Catholic his entire life, attending weekly mass throughout his childhood. Since leaving his parents' house, his attendance dwindled to Christmas, Easter, weddings, and funerals. Despite his sagging attendance, he had never wavered in his faith until this moment. He laughed at his reflection. Looking in the mirror was like looking at someone else. Someone who did all the things he'd ever done but wasn't going to do many of them again. His faith wasn't the only piece of himself that now seemed to exist elsewhere, but it was the most poignant. What did Jesus think of this sort of thing? He selected the gold cross and put it around his neck.

Therapy, he thought. *I'm going to need years of therapy. Therapy jokes always go over well. I can come up with some great shit in the loony bin.*

In the kitchen, he found Craig and Victoria sitting at the table eating waffles, bacon, and eggs. Craig put food into the side of his mouth and chewed with caution. He lifted a plastic fork and said, "This is great! Who knew you could get breakfast delivered?"

Andre said, "Some website asked the Pit Stop if we were interested in being part of their delivery system, so I guess I did. Welcome to the brave new world we all live in."

He sat down at the table but didn't touch the food.

Victoria said, "Did you sleep well?"

Andre grinned at her. "Yes. Thank you for drugging me. I'd still be schizing out, otherwise."

She didn't smile back. "Do you have to work today?"

Craig waived his fork again and interrupted, "I just quit my job over the phone. Dad'll be thrilled. So much for two week notice, huh?"

Andre grimaced. "Not until five. I assume you have all sorts of weird plans for us. Should I call in?"

"Yes, you should. Call in for the next few days. Unlike your roommate, you probably don't need to quit and burn bridges when you do it. A week should get this sorted out one way or the other."

Andre stared at a waffle, watching the syrup slide across its checkerboard surface. Like Catholicism, his job seemed distant and questionably important. Still, he couldn't leave Brenda hanging, so he retrieved his phone from his room and called the Pit Stop.

"Pit Stop Diner, how can I help you?" Gina answered. Her voice could have been a radio commercial for perky stupidity.

"Hey, Gina, it's Andre. Can you let Brenda know I'm not going to make it in today? There's been... a death. Anyway, I'm going to need some time off. Have Brenda give me a call when she gets in."

The inflection of Gina's voice never changed. She piped, "Well, I'll let her know, but I don't think she'll be happy, since she called in with an emergency this morning, too. She told me you were in charge. Who died, Andre?"

Andre didn't answer. Brenda's only absence from work had been when Kevin died. If she called in this morning, something was wrong. "Did she say what happened, Gina?"

"Well, no, but she sounded really messed up, you know? Kinda like she'd been drinking, but, you know, she hardly drinks, so I think she was just upset. Like, you know, about Kevin and stuff? Anyway, let me have you to talk to Mai, OK?"

She didn't give Andre time to decline before Mai was on the line. "Andre, what's going on? Are you guys OK?"

"Not really, Mai. I don't know about Brenda, but I can't come to work today. There have been some..." He didn't know what to say to her. He regretted using the word "death" with Gina. "Look, some people have died and I can't make it in for a few days. I'll talk to Brenda. Can you guys handle it for today?"

"Yeah," Mai said. "I'll clock on as assistant and work a double. Michael was looking for extra hours, so I'll call him in." She paused for a second and said, "You sound bad, Andre. Call me if you need... anything. OK?"

"Yeah," he said. "Thanks."

He hung up the phone and looked at Victoria. "What the fuck is going on here?"

Victoria tilted her head back. "Do not curse at me, Andre. Do you understand?"

Her tone made him feel small and helpless. Anger surged in his chest. He just nodded, though. Losing his cool was an alien notion. She could be a bitch if she wanted, just like the occasional crazy customer at the Pit Stop.

"Good. Now, as I was telling you last night before you nodded off, you boys are mixed up in something that is beyond anything you've ever experienced. The less you do know, the safer you will be. For now, we need to find this monster that attacked you and kill it. Once he is dead, you should be safe. I will need you both to help me find him."

Craig's mouth was full of eggs, but he spoke anyway. "What're we s'posed ta do ta 'elp you?"

Victoria pursed her lips. "Draw him to me."

Craig choked.

Andre said, "We're bait?"

Victoria nodded. "I had anticipated the monster would show up here last night, but things have gotten more complicated than I imagined." She seemed vexed for a moment before regaining her serenity.

Craig hacked eggs from his lungs.

"You were unbelievably lucky to have escaped," she continued. "He will come for you again, though. You've seen him. Creatures like him cannot tolerate being seen. While everything that will happen next will be confusing, understand this: there are rules. We all abide by them, because if we do not we are destroyed. This monster is confused right now. He is lashing out. He is making mistakes. But he knows the rules and the rules say you must die."

Andre leaned back in his chair. "Do you play by his rules?"

A slight smile crossed her face. "You are ever so observant, Andre. Not exactly. I have my own rules. You are safe with me."

Craig cleared his throat and mumbled, "I didn't feel very safe with you this morning. Anyway, what are you gonna do? Stick us on a hook and hope he bites?" He made a casting motion with his fork.

"No. I plan to expedite the process. I plan to bring you to where he is likely to be."

"Like he—" Andre began, but curbed himself. "No. I saw that thing. If we get close enough for you to do something to it, we're dead. You might not kill us, but something tells me your heart won't break if we die."

"He can be defeated and I can defeat him," she replied. "I will protect you. Yes, you may die as a result of this plan, but without me your death is certain."

"Well," Craig said, "Let's do another plan, then. Something with less possible death in it, please."

Andre nodded in agreement.

"There is no plan with 'less possible death in it'. You are already past that point."

"Why don't you just go there by yourself?" Andre demanded. "Why not get some of your witchy friends together and cast a spell on him or something like that? Why do you need us?"

"Confluence," Victoria said. "You two have a... relationship that makes you stronger together. It makes me stronger when I am with you. It is what I assume attracted that monster to you in the first place. I believe our chances are better together, and I believe they are better if we act first rather than wait for the monster to make another move."

Andre scowled. "Confluence? That sounds like total bullsh—that sounds ridiculous."

"Is it so hard to believe that there are forces in this world acting on us without our total understanding, Andre?" She gestured to the cross hanging around his neck.

Andre frowned and tucked the cross into his shirt.

Craig shook his head. "Well, what about that super-fast

thing I did last night? I tried to do it again, but it's like trying to use the Force when you were a kid, you know? I could never get the toy light saber to move. I can't go fast again. What's that all about?"

"Doing that again would probably kill you, Craig. You, like Andre, possess a set of gifts. These gifts lie beneath the surface of you who are. They are not accessible to you directly. What you did last night was an anomaly. Something very powerful has taken an interest in you. I do not know what you did to attract its attention. Your card reading made it clear that this thing will try one more time to tempt you. You must not make any agreements with it."

Craig narrowed his eyes. "The thing in the payphone? What, it can make me super-fast?"

Victoria shook her head. "Yes and no. It can unlock what is inside you, but that was yours to begin with. If you take the shortcut that thing offers, you will pay a terrible price."

"So how do I do it without that thing in the phone?" he asked.

"I don't know, Craig," she said. "You live in a world that doesn't want such abilities to manifest, so the path to it has been lost. If we survive this, you can devote your life to finding that path. Others have done so with varying degrees of success. For now, though, don't dwell on it. You cannot rely on it happening again. You should hope it does not."

Andre leaned forward, his eyes locked on Victoria's, and said, "You did it. You got this phone thing to make you strong."

She met his gaze. "Yes, Andre, I did. And I can tell you, the price I paid was not worth it." Her eyes glistened. "When you pay a price like that, you are not the only one to pay."

Andre did not like this woman at all, but he believed that

statement. He fiddled with the cross through his shirt.

"I need to talk to Brenda," he said.

Victoria's eyebrows rose and she said, "If she is involved in this, I find it unlikely that she is still alive, Andre."

"According to one of the servers at work, she called in this morning in bad shape," he replied.

"Call her," Victoria said.

Andre looked at her sideways, holding the phone in his hand. "I won't cuss at you," he said, "if you don't act like my mother."

Victoria nodded and said, "Call her, please."

He hit the "call" icon on his smart phone, but the connection went to voice mail without ringing. He hung up.

"She's got her phone off," he said. "What now?"

Victoria pulled a leather wallet out of her gym bag. From this she took a folded up piece of paper and set it on the table among the Styrofoam takeout containers.

"My last encounter with the monster did not go well, but like you I managed to escape," she said. "This is the monster's wallet. He can take the form of a man when he wishes. Your names and address are on this piece of paper."

She produced a plastic card that read "Small Comforts Hotel." The number 324 was written with black marker above its magnetic strip. "This is a room key. We can assume that the monster stays here in his human form. He goes by the name Daniel Clark. Let's see if he is still checked in."

Craig picked up the piece of paper. "Creepy," he said.

Andre glanced at it. "Why us?" he asked.

Victoria said, "I'm not sure, Andre. If everything goes well, you'll never have to find out."

Brenda stood in the doorway of her bedroom and stared at

the man in her bed. His face was ashen but he looked peaceful. He looked just like Kevin always looked when he slept. Her right hand rested against her cheek while her left was tucked across her chest. She mumbled, "What the fuck…" several times without noticing she spoke.

In the living room, Amber was watching *The Lion King* for the third time in a row. The child was thrilled that her mother was allowing so much TV.

Why are we still here? Brenda asked herself.

Because that guy in your bed could be Kevin, she answered.

He weighed much more than his frame suggested, which was just like Kevin. She had barely managed to roll him into the bedroom and hoist him onto the bed. His entire body, down to the scar on his knee, looked like Kevin. But Kevin was dead.

After Kevin's death, one of her servers gave her a bottle of Xanax. She'd pulled the bottle from the top of her medicine cabinet twice this morning, but replaced it unopened each time. She had no idea what Xanax would do to her, and her daughter was here, and there was this guy who looked just like Kevin, but had also been a plumber and then a blob, in her bed. She and her daughter could be in very real danger. That last thought came in Zazu's voice. Did transforming plumber blobs kill people? There really wasn't any precedence she could refer to for that question. Maybe the Xanax would help her calm down and think. Or maybe it would make her even crazier. Or put her to sleep.

Amber joined her at the door and grinned.

"Shhhh!!" she whispered. "Daddy still sleeping." She bounced back to the TV to listen to Jeremy Irons sing the Boy Scout motto.

What's the motto with you? Brenda asked herself.

"You'd better wake up soon," Brenda whispered, "or I'm

going to lose my mind."

As if to satisfy her request, the man opened his eyes and sat up. He looked down at his body and put his hands on his face. In a crushing moment, he turned his eyes to her and said, "I'm so very sorry."

Brenda's knees gave out and she fell. He launched himself from the bed and caught her. Tears streamed from her eyes, which she couldn't focus. She lost track of where she was. When she swam back to full consciousness, he held her in his arms and he was crying, too. It was him. It was Kevin. Her emotions were split into so many pieces she didn't know what to do, so she just grabbed ahold of him and cried.

Ten minutes later Kevin sat at the kitchen table eating a bowl of cereal. He wore her bathrobe since, on advice from a friend, she had donated all his clothes to charity a month ago. Amber sat at the table next to him drawing on a piece of junk mail that promised to lower their mortgage payment by half if they acted in the next week. Like most of the junk mail, Kevin's name was still on it. Brenda washed dishes. Since disengaging from Kevin, she had not spoken a word. Kevin and Amber were talking like they always did. Amber accepted his reappearance naturally, as if he'd come back from the grocery store.

Brenda's impulses were a stack of conflicting options. She wanted to grab him and hug him and never let him go. She wanted to slap him. She wanted to scream and pull her hair out. The last two months of her life were blasted apart. Once she opened her mouth, she wasn't sure what was going to come out, so she kept it shut. Amber didn't need to see her mother be a raving lunatic.

"That's a great sheep," Kevin said when Amber pushed the page at him. The drawing looked like a purple, crayon

Rorschach test.

"Shaun the Sheep!" Amber squealed.

"Honey," Kevin said to her, "I think it's about your nap time, isn't it?"

Brenda frowned. It was only 10:00 a.m. Amber didn't nap until 1:00 p.m. Amber, however, yawned and said, "I can sleep in my own bed."

Kevin smiled, gathered her up, and agreed, "Yes. You can sleep in your own bed."

Brenda watched him take Amber to her bedroom. She fell into a chair at the table. Shortly, her mouth was going to open and she had no idea what would come out of it.

Kevin disliked using pheromonal techniques to make his daughter sleep. He'd never allowed himself to do it before. He laid her on her bed and pulled covers decorated with dancing princesses up to her chin. She smacked her mouth and curled into a ball.

"Sleep tight," he said. "I love you."

Brenda hunkered at the kitchen table, her elbows on her knees. Her face was turned up, her eyes on him. Taking the chair beside her, he reached for her hands. She pulled them away and crossed her arms over her chest.

"I'm sorry—" he began.

"You already said that," she muttered. Her voice became stronger as she continued, "You said that when you woke up. You said you were sorry, but I don't know why you're sorry. You're sorry for what? Dying and coming back to life? Doing... something with the way you look and trying to invade our house without me knowing? For drugging our daughter just now? You know, Kevin, I don't think saying you're sorry means very fucking much right now."

Her eyes shifted back and forth between each of his as she spoke. He focused on a point directly above her nose and braced himself for a longer tirade. To his surprise she relaxed, stood up, and went to the fridge.

"You want a beer?" she asked.

He nodded. She pulled out two bottles of Summit, popped their caps off on the bar with the palm of her hand, and set them on the kitchen table. She sat back down. Her eyes were sharp and focused in a way they hadn't been a few moments ago.

"So," she said, "why don't you tell me something that makes more sense than 'I'm sorry' because frankly I don't fucking care if you're sorry."

Kevin took a drink of the beer and stared at the label. He felt a chasm open around him. What he said to her now would determine the entire nature of their relationship going forward. When he'd decided to remove himself from her life before, the decision was all his. This time, the choices would all be hers. Did he want her to throw him out? Did he want her to forgive him and restore their family? Was that even possible?

"Well?" she said, slapping her hand on the table. "Are you going to talk to me or stare at that bottle until it gets warm?"

He almost apologized again. Instead he said, "I am a monster."

She sniffed and said, "I'm not looking for metaphorical—"

He willed his face to take its true shape while keeping the rest of his body stable. Partial transformations were tricky. She gasped, but did not leave her chair.

"Oh," she said and took a long drink of her beer.

Kevin restored his face and continued, "I was engineered by a man named Clarence Elpis in the early 1960s. I consider this man my father, though I doubt we're actually related.

My body is partly flesh and bone, and partly metal and computer components. My heart contains a titanium nanotube lithium ion cell which powers a computer that is integrated into my spinal column and brain. The battery recharges via aspiration and food. The nucleotides of my DNA are a recombinant sequence that integrate several animals and about five distinct human strands. However, they are spliced together with some kind of magic that allows me to restructure them at will. I have been "upgraded" several times. In my first incarnation, I was so large and immobile that I was more or less a talking piece of furniture."

Kevin took a drink of his beer and scratched at his beard. Brenda stared at him with level, expressionless eyes, so he continued, "My father thought I would die, but I didn't, so he kept working on me until he arrived at the form you saw just a few moments ago. That was in the mid '70s. Once he had perfected me, he bred others like me, each one better than the last. He calls us Térata. He uses us to advance his agendas, which I confess I know little about. He holds several patents that have made him very wealthy. His company, Elpis Enterprises, is a world leader in biotechnology. I am a monster."

He spread his hands and shrugged his shoulders. Brenda went to the fridge for another beer. When she got back to the table she stood, staring at him.

"Show me," she said.

He frowned at her.

"Show me!" she demanded. "Show me all of it. Show me the entire monster."

He could feel the chemical magic begin to roll out of her, so he threw up his hands and said, "OK! Please relax. You have no idea how much it hurts when you make me change, or how dangerous I can become when I'm not in control of the change."

Brenda's eyebrows furrowed, but the chemical magic receded. Kevin sighed in relief. He stood, dropped the robe on the floor, and shifted into his true form.

Her eyes widened and she set her beer on the table. Some of it spilled. She reached out to touch him, but paused and looked at his face as if asking permission. He nodded. She touched his belly and ran her fingers through the fur on his chest. Standing on her tiptoes, she poked his nose, which was damp like a dog's. She pushed his lips aside and ran her fingers along the side of his teeth. She walked all the way around him. He stood still for the entire process, allowing her to prod and inspect him.

"Can you talk?" she asked.

"Yes," he replied.

"Why doesn't your mouth move?"

"My external lips cannot form human sounds, so I have another mouth in my throat. Would you like to see it?"

"Yes," she said.

He opened his jaws. He knew what she would be seeing past the rows of razor sharp teeth and the enormous tongue. Tucked into the right side of his throat was a human mouth. The lips were connected to a separate trachea and larynx leading to his right lung. He said, "Pretty crazy, huh?"

Brenda laughed and said, "That might be the grossest thing I've ever seen."

Kevin became concerned. Humor was not the response he expected. Something was wrong. He shifted back to Kevin's form, put the robe on, and sat down.

She sat and they stared at each other for several minutes. He took another drink of his beer.

"Why didn't you ever tell me about this?" Brenda asked.

"The same reason I faked my death," he replied. "You aren't safe knowing this about me. Beings like me live by a strict set of rules. No one is allowed to see us and live. These aren't just my father's rules. There are rules that go deep into who we are that don't really have a, uh, direct source. Once I fell in love with you, I buried my past..." He shook his head. Anger was sparking to life in her eyes. There was no helping it. "I thought I could escape who I was. I thought I could just walk away from everything and start a new life with you. That's what I'm sorry for, Brenda. I'm sorry I ever put you into this situation. It was a horrible mistake."

"Fuck you," Brenda spat. She grabbed the edge of the table so hard her fingers turned white. "You don't get it at all, do you? Four years of my life are gone, Kevin. Four good—no, four *great* years are gone. And then, for the last two months, I've been a pile of *shit*. *Shit*, Kevin! And you call that a fucking mistake?"

She grabbed her beer bottle and threw it at him. He let it bounce off his forehead and spin into the living room. She laughed with an edge of mania.

"I never knew you," she said, putting her hands to either side of her face and shaking them. "All this time. *Four years!* I never knew you. What is wrong with me? We had a fucking funeral for you! My mom sent a card! A fucking card! You're fucking dead, Kevin, and I'm not even ready to accept that... but now you're back, and you're telling me that this whole mess is a *mistake* and that you're *sorry*? Tell me this, then, Kevin, why in the fuck did you ever make that first mistake? What in the fuck were you thinking when you started doing so many things you'd be sorry for later?"

Her face was beet red. She was sobbing and began to hiccup. Kevin had never seen her in this condition before. He chose his words carefully.

"I was not made to fall in love. I was designed unable to feel love. You made me feel it, Brenda. You have some kind of magic in you that changed me. I was swept away by you. From the moment I met you, Brenda, you became my life. I wasn't thinking then, Brenda. I was feeling. For the first time in my life. I was feeling."

She stared at him for several seconds and smiled. "That is—*hic*—the most romantic thing I have ever—*hic*—heard in my life. Say it—*hic*—again."

Kevin repeated himself as best he could. She nodded when he finished.

"OK. I need to—*hic*—go to sleep now. Please—*hic*—be here when I wake up. Promise—*hic*—me that. Promise me you will be here when I wake up."

"I promise I will be here when you wake up," he said. He gathered her in his arms and squeezed her to his chest. She melted into him. After a few minutes she stopped hiccupping and began snoring. He carried her to their bedroom and tucked her into bed.

"You are right," he said, moving her hair out of her face and tucking it behind her ears. "I am not sorry. I'm not sorry at all."

The Small Comforts Motel was squeezed onto a corner lot north of downtown St Paul, across the street from St Joseph's Hospital. Its entire front façade was covered by a parking garage. Salmon paint peeled from the cinderblocks and small piles of trash gathered in the corners. Victoria pulled into the only entrance. At the far end of the garage, a neon vacancy light flashed above a plate glass window. The desk on the other side was empty. An out-of-order sign hung on the doors to the elevator beside the window. The door to the stairway was propped open with a planter. She spotted another elevator across the garage and parked near it.

"Classy place," Andre remarked from the bench seat beside her.

Craig was passed out, his face pressed against the glass of the window.

Victoria nodded and turned the truck off. The stereo cut off in the middle of a Benny Goodman song playing from a cassette tape.

"Wake up, Craig," Andre said, elbowing his friend. "Alice has arrived in Wonderland."

Craig blinked and complained, "Fucking light."

As Craig fumbled with his door handle, the radio squawked back on. A news reporter from a public radio station announced, "The bodies of five people were found in a dumpster in South Minneapolis this morning. Unconfirmed sources report that the bodies have been badly mutilated. The police have not commented, but a press conference has been scheduled for later this afternoon pending an initial crime scene investigation... The U of M men's hockey team has—" The radio bleeped off.

"What the fuck?" Craig said, pointing at the radio.

Victoria pursed her lips. "My radio has been altered to inform me when Minnesota Public Radio mentions something that is of direct interest to me. I assume those were your friends. The police will eventually be looking for you, I suspect."

Andre rubbed his forehead and laughed.

"What's so fucking funny about that?" Craig asked.

"I have an app on my phone that does that," Andre said. "It aggregates news stories about people from the web. Right now I get news stories about Barack Obama, Will Smith, and Britney Spears. My phone dings when one is posted."

"That's lame," Craig said. "Britney Spears?"

"Bitch been off her rocker, man. It's funny shit," Andre said.

"Still lame," Craig said. He looked at Victoria. "What do we do about that? All those people have a text from me on their phones telling them to come to our place last night."

Victoria shook her head. "That's a problem for later. Right now we need to concern ourselves with the monster that wants to kill us all. The police will take time to get to you about this."

"What exactly did you have in mind?" Andre asked.

"I will know when he is close. We will wait in his hotel room until he returns. When he comes into the room, I will capture him and Craig will shoot him. Once he's dead, you can leave and I'll get the information I need."

Craig had been shaking his head since the word "shoot". "Look," he said, "I don't know a goddamn thing about guns. One of my mom's boyfriends liked to terrorize me with his when I was a kid, and since then I think the right to bear arms involves chopping off yours and transplanting Paddington's in their place. I can't shoot shit."

"Relax, Craig," Andre said. He turned to Victoria. "What kind of piece do you have?"

She pulled the gun from her bag and handed it to Andre.

"I thought you said she had a big gun," he said to Craig, who snorted. "This is a Taurus 9mm. Like a Berretta, but cheaper, last time I checked. He released the clip, checked to be sure it was loaded, and slapped it back into place. He flipped the safety off with his thumb. "How many times do you think I'll need to shoot that thing to kill it?"

Victoria said, "As many as it takes." She handed him another clip.

"This is going to be extremely loud," he said. "Somebody

will call the cops. They're usually slow to show, but the state capital is five blocks away, so we'll probably have heat pretty quick. What do you plan to do about that?"

Victoria said, "It is impossible to follow me if I don't wish to be followed. I can get what I need quickly once he is dead. As long as we get back to the truck before the police arrive, we won't have any problems."

Craig stared at Andre as if he'd never seen him before.

Kimm Peters sat across the street in his Lexus and peered into the gloom of the parking garage. Victoria Starks. The last person on earth he expected to see today when he returned to destroy the artifacts of his previous life. She was not the type of person to remain on the scene of a direct conflict. His memories were fragmented, but Victoria was a pillar of clarity. She was back to confront Daniel about what he'd done to her after the reading. She'd brought two boys. Memories of anger and water surfaced when he saw the white one, but they drifted in the jumbled pile of his past.

He weighed his options. He didn't need anything in the hotel room. It was all part of a life he had abandoned and mostly forgotten. But Victoria was a dangerous enemy and there was information in that room that could lead her to Kimm. To be fair, raping her and attempting to murder her were things he would pay for eventually. His past was his past, even if he couldn't remember it well and didn't know why he had done the things he had done.

He tapped his fingers on the car steering wheel. What to do about Victoria? Confront her now? Send her a message asking for forgiveness? An apology card wouldn't cut it with her. The conundrum nearly caused him to pull out of the parking lot and retreat back to his car dealership to think.

Then he saw a black SUV pull into the Small Comforts parking lot. Memories surfaced in his mind as if dredged up, half rotten, from a muddy lagoon.

"Oh, shit," he said. His fingers drummed the steering wheel like little hammers. That SUV had his sister in it. Not Kimm's sister. His previous self's sister. Number 7.

Perhaps his sister would solve his problem by taking Victoria out of the picture. He rejected that notion, since evidence in the room might lead Number 7 to Kimm. Also, a dark debt bound him to Victoria. Letting his sister kill her was unacceptable to his new identity. He had to get involved. Perhaps get himself killed.

That would be a pity, he thought, *I've got a meeting with my bank in two hours and then dinner with Oren at Mayslack's tonight. Hate to disappoint my son.*

Daniel's motel room was tidy and clean, but Andre doubted that had anything to do with maid service. The carpets were orange shag and smelled like cigarette smoke. A laptop sat on a small, wobbly desk beside a king bed. At the back of a cramped closet full of clothes, a safe was bolted to the wall. Three suitcases sat beside the safe.

Craig went into the bathroom and closed the door.

Andre clenched the gun in his right hand and peered out the window. "How will you know when he's here?" he asked.

"He's in the hospital parking lot watching us right now," Victoria replied. "He pulled in while you were waking up Craig."

"Shit!" he said, backing away from the window. "First of all, how do you know that? Second, does he know we're here?"

"I used some of his... bodily fluids to construct what I suppose you could call a 'spell' that allows me to feel when he nears me. Yes, he knows we're here. But he doesn't know that we know he's here. This is going better than I hoped."

The sound of retching came from the bathroom.

"So what's he doing over there?" Andre asked.

"Sitting in his car. When he moves, I'll feel it."

Andre's heart pounded. His direct experience with firearms was limited to the classes he had taken as a teenager with his father. If he could shoot this monster as well as he could shoot paper targets, things would go well. If not, he'd end up dead.

"He's moving," Victoria said. "We've got about three minutes before he gets here." She pulled a series of ribbons out of her gym bag and arranged them on the bed. "When he comes in the door, which I expect will be a dramatic moment, do not attempt to shoot him. He will be too fast. Stand in that corner. I will trap him and tie him to the bed. Once he is tied, shoot him in the head until he stops moving."

Andre moved to the corner. He swallowed. His mouth tasted like metal dust. "I get it. You can't kill him yourself, so you have—"

The door to the hotel room blew off its hinges and slammed into the wall. A blackish blur followed the door. It swung Victoria onto the bed, where the ribbons snapped around her body, wrapping her in a cocoon. Andre began to raise the gun, but he might as well have been moving through waffle syrup. The blur knocked the gun from his hand and paused long enough for him to see enormous green teeth closing around his face.

Fuck, he thought.

The door to the bathroom flew across the room and

plowed into the monster as its teeth snapped shut. Three bloody gashes erupted on Andre's left cheek. Craig shot from the bathroom, too fast for Andre's eye to follow.

Two blurs engaged in a high speed dance that lasted less than five seconds. The monster ended the fandango by throwing Craig across the room. He hit the wall so hard the drywall collapsed. The monster turned its attention back to Andre. Green steam oozed from its eyes, black fur covered it except where green discs dotted its torso. It lifted a hand which was tipped with green claws. Andre was pressed into the corner, casting about in an attempt to locate his gun. He would never reach it in time, but at least he had something to do before he died.

A third blur punched into the room, slamming into the black and green monster with such force that it flew out the window, across the street, and onto the roof of the hospital. A blonde man wearing a blue suit looked at Andre and said, "If you want to live, do exactly as I say."

Andre nodded.

"Gather your friend and get him to the truck." He grabbed Victoria's gym bag and threw it at Andre. "The keys should be in here. You will be safe in the truck. I need a moment with Victoria."

Andre caught the bag. Craig was unconscious, so Andre drug him from the room much the same way he'd drug him to the van last night. He passed a pile of women's clothing in the hallway.

Where the fuck did those come from? he thought. *Nevermind. Who cares? The next time a monster attacks us and Craig turns into the Flash, I'm going to be the one who passes out.*

Victoria stared at the monster who had taken Kimm

Peters' form.

He said, "I have a third reading, right?"

She frowned. He glared at her.

"A third reading," he demanded. "You told me three and we've only done two."

The monster was mistaken. She'd done Kimm's third reading without him. And the monster only got one. However, her bargaining position was compromised, so she replied, "I can give you a reading."

The monster nodded with relief. He grabbed the ribbons and tore them apart with his hands.

"You have my number at the car dealership," he said as he worked. "When you're ready, please give me a call and we'll schedule a time."

As he pulled the last of the ribbons from her, Victoria sprung forward and grabbed his hand. A current of energy passed between them. She narrowed her eyes. "I will call on you, Kimm Peters," she said. "Be sure of it."

For a moment, Kimm seemed dazed. He recovered, nodded, and jumped out of the window. Victoria grabbed the laptop, which had miraculously survived the fight. She also grabbed her shredded ribbons and the 9mm. There were other objects she wanted, but time was not on her side. She considered the window, rejected the idea of jumping, and ran from the room. She grabbed a pair of pantyhose from the pile of clothes in the hallway. The door to the stairway was open, but she opted for the elevator. The other monster would be back soon, and she guessed it—or her, judging from the hose—would take the stairs.

Andre felt the tick of a manic, invisible clock as he fumbled the truck's passenger door open and piled Craig inside. He climbed in over his friend and slammed the door. Craig mumbled in his sleep.

"Be quiet!" Andre whispered.

Craig groaned, so Andre clamped his hand over his mouth.

A black blur appeared in the parking lot and shot straight toward the truck. It stopped by the passenger window. Saliva dripped off its green teeth. Andre's breath came in short gasps. The guy in the blue suit said they would be safe in the truck, but that seemed like the stupidest thing Andre had ever heard right now. His blood was all over the door handle. The monster sniffed the door before blurring to the stairway at the other side of the parking lot. Andre regained control of his breathing. A few seconds after the monster vanished into the stairway, Victoria emerged from the elevator. Andre fumbled the pin lock up and opened the driver door. She ran to the truck, snatched the keys out of his hand, and peeled out of the parking lot.

When they were several blocks away, Victoria said, "We've got bigger problems than I thought."

"No fucking shit!" Andre yelled.

"Language, Andre," she replied. "I'll not have it from you."

Andre shook with fury. "Sorry," he said, "It isn't every day monsters try to kill me! Oh, wait, it's happened two days in a row, so maybe a pattern is developing. I guess I should get used to this and just chill."

"Perhaps you should," she said.

He stared at her. She was the most colossal bitch he had ever met.

"Right," he said, twirling his hand. "I'm in a magic truck, after all. Nothing to be worried about. Nothing at all. It's like a Steppenwolf song!"

Number 7 picked her clothes up from the floor, walked into the hotel room, and propped the door back into place. She slid the desk against the door to keep it shut. After sniffing the air, she lay on the bed and warped into her current identity. Sheila was a tall, beautiful woman in her late twenties with porcelain skin and light green eyes. Her blonde hair reached the middle of her back. She put on a silk blouse and skirt, annoyed by her missing panty hose. She guessed Victoria had taken them, but she couldn't imagine why.

Once dressed, she gathered the luggage and clothing from the closet. A spiral bound notebook and manila envelope were in the safe, which she opened by tearing the door off with her hands. She loaded the contents of the room into her Suburban. As she drove west on University Avenue, she affixed a Bluetooth earpiece and said, "Call home."

"Hello, Number 7," a male voice said.

"Hello, Octavio. Work order number TC13822 requires assistance. Send backup. Number 9 has removed his tracker. He's hostile. Also get a crew to take care of the damage to room 324 at the Small Comforts Motel in St Paul. Make sure to confiscate any video footage. There are other players involved, including Victoria Starks and two unknowns."

"Sure thing, 7," Octavio responded. "Any new information on Amber?"

"No," Sheila said.

"Backup will arrive from Des Moines in four hours. I just sent their work order. Call me if anything changes. Clarence is very concerned about this operation."

"Will do," she replied.

She removed the earpiece and dropped it into her console.

Upon arriving in Minneapolis, she expected to find Number 9 in the midst of one of his complicated schemes. After two months in the field with no results he needed help, whether he wanted it or not. She had not expected to find Victoria Starks laying a trap in his hotel room. She had also not expected Starks to have a fully Awake human being with her and a Sleeper with a gun. None of those people were in the itinerary. More disturbing was Number 9's hostility. Why did he defend Victoria? Why was he so much smaller than he had been? Why was his tracker out?

She pulled up to the valet ramp in front of Le Méridien Chambers in downtown Minneapolis.

"Please bring the contents of the back seat to my room," she instructed the valet, handing him her keys.

This was an ostentatious choice for lodging, but it fit her current identity. Sheila Barnstock was a contemporary art dealer who was known to The Elpis Foundation. Since she wouldn't be working alone, a known identity was the best choice. Before she returned to Des Moines, she would buy one of the pieces in the Burnet Gallery on Le Méridien's first floor and have it shipped to Christi's Auction House in New York. She kept all her identities active and in character.

Her room was simple and elegant, in keeping with the style of the hotel. The curtains and furnishing were white. A Damien Hirst print featuring pill bottles hung above the king bed, providing the only colors.

A bellman arrived with the luggage she'd taken from the Small Comforts. She thanked him and handed him a ten dollar bill. She spread the contents onto the bed. Clothes. A rifle. An MP3 player, e-reader, and tablet computer. $2,000 in cash. A digital camera. Her younger brother was spartan compared to her.

The notebook she'd taken from the safe was a trove of

information. It contained the names and addresses of everyone Number 9 found of interest, as well as detailed reports including dates, times, locations, and activities. She admired his thorough investigation practices. The exception to his meticulous notations was Victoria Starks, of course. Her name was nowhere in the notebook. He certainly had some contact with her, or she would not have been trying to trap him. Sheila guessed that if she tried to write that woman's name down, something would happen and she would simply forget to do it. The phone would ring. A siren would go off. She'd get a stomach cramp. Victoria was slippery.

Victoria had been blamed for Number 1's disappearance four years ago, since he'd been on her trail when he vanished. Sheila knew better. She knew her brother purposefully abandoned The Foundation for, of all things, love. She was fascinated by the development, since it was unprecedented. Sheila and her brother had reached an agreement after his disappearance. She would tip him off if The Foundation ever located him. In return, he gave her tantalizing descriptions of his condition. The fact that one of the Térata could be twisted in such a way held a dizzying number of possibilities for her.

When word of Amber reached Clarence via Number 4, she'd sent Number 1 a message through their secret channel. A few days later he was dead. That was obviously faked, though she kept that information to herself. She admired the move as a clever tactic. Unfortunately, she may have to kill him for real. Love did not act logically, but it did have patterns. He would protect Brenda and Amber at all costs, even his own life.

Her own feelings, like the feelings of all her siblings, were little more than instincts, much like weather vanes to show

how social winds were blowing. Sometimes, though, they broke through. Number 1 had known of her fascination with love, which is why he chose her as his lone contact. He had somehow found a path to those feelings. She would find him and take it from him. Then she would vanish, too. Only she'd do a better job than he'd done. She would never be found.

She snapped the notebook shut. Backup would arrive in three hours. She had time to get her nails done and do some shopping. A great little boutique had opened a few blocks from the hotel since her last visit to the Twin Cities. She could use some new nail polish.

Craig held the handset of the payphone again. There was no ringing. No jazz music. No Greek words. In fact, there was no Top Hat around him. No floor. No walls. Just him, the phone, and the black, empty space inside it. In his mind, he could see the three cards he had turned during Victoria's reading with new clarity. The Hollow Skull. The Anchor. The Tower. Behind each card was information about the journey he was about to take. He took a deep breath and dove into the phone. His body became elastic, flattening and reshaping itself to make its entry into the small space possible. The cards revealed much of what was about to happen, but not everything. He was terrified.

On the other side of the blackness was a scientific laboratory. The Hollow Skull. It housed a full set of contemporary machinery, which he had seen before at the U of M. Most of the surfaces were stainless steel. A row of chillers with glass doors lined one wall. Touch screen computers occupied a variety of work stations, each displaying the same aquarium screensaver his father had used for most of his high school years. At the nearest one of these stations, a bald man in a white lab coat sat with his back to Craig. The Anchor.

"Welcome," the man said. "I'm occupied just now, but I'll be with you momentarily."

Mustering all the courage he could find, Craig replied, "Take your time. I'm not in a hurry."

The man laughed and turned around in his swivel chair. His skin was albino white, but his facial features were those of a black man. His eyes were pink. This man, The Anchor, was something Craig expected to find here. He had not expected his albinism or his striking resemblance to Victoria. He could have been her grandfather. Or, upon closer inspection, maybe her great grandfather. His skin was sagging. His eyes were sunken. He moved with care, as if afraid of breaking himself.

"What do you think of my lab?" the man asked.

"It's nice," Craig replied. "You didn't spare any expenses. I'm more curious about who you are and why I'm here than I am about your equipment, though."

"My name is Clarence Elpis," the man said. "I'm a scientist." He extended his hand.

Craig looked at it and crossed his arms. Under no circumstances was he going to touch that person.

Clarence Elpis shrugged. "Would you like to know what I'm working on, Craig?"

"Sure," Craig said. The Tower. "I have a feeling you'll tell me anyway, Dr. Elpis."

"Call me Clarence, if you would. I've never been to college and I don't think honorifics are necessary."

"OK," Craig said. "So what are you working on?"

"Bdelloids," Clarence replied. "Are you familiar with them?"

"Yeah," Craig said. "Asexually reproducing microorganisms that incorporate DNA from other beings to continue their existence. Very resilient. Can withstand complete dehydration by repairing themselves with the DNA of whatever is nearby when they rehydrate. This allows them to mutate somewhat like a sexually reproducing organism. Been around 80 million years, give or take a millennium."

"Exactly," Clarence said. "I discovered their abilities fifty years ago and have been working with them since then. Come look at this."

Clarence motioned to what he had been working on. A petri dish was placed on the stage of a microscope, though Craig had never seen a microscope quite like this. It had a single ocular lens, revolving nose piece, and four objective lenses. However, a clear tube ran from the nosepiece to the ocular lens. Yellow, grainy gas flowed up its length.

Craig pointed at the tube. "What's that?"

"Are you familiar with Paracelsus?" Clarence asked.

Craig frowned at him. More of the Tower. "Yeah. Father of modern medicine and all that."

"Did you know that Paracelsus found a way to grow a human being outside the womb?"

Craig laughed. "You mean by squirting jizz into horse shit and heating it until it started moving, then feeding it human blood until it grew into a tiny man? Yeah, I took a philosophy course a few semesters back. I liked how Paracelsus told us that we should educate the little guy. He was ahead of his time."

Clarence said, "The alchemists spoke in riddles seldom understood in today's clinical parlance. To quote Paracelsus, 'For as putrefaction in the bowels transmits and reduces all foods into dung, so also, without the belly, putrefaction in glass transmutes all things from one form to another, from one essence to another... For putrefaction is the change and death of all things, and the destruction of the first essence of all natural objects, from whence there issues forth for us regeneration and new birth ten thousand times better than before.' Look into the microscope."

Craig hesitated. Most of the happenings in this dream were predicted by the cards, an amalgamation of his own past and Clarence's weird world. The screensaver. The microbiology report he'd done on bdelloid rotifers last semester. The four page paper he'd written on Paracelsus. The lab and equipment. From this point forward, he knew that he would be experiencing things that weren't his. These things would change him. Transmute him. Fear made a tight knot in his throat as he considered the lens of the microscope.

Clarence slid his chair sideways, making space.

Craig leaned forward and peered into the microscope. Inside the circle of the lens, human embryos swam about, reminding him of the brine shrimp he'd grown as a fourth grader in Pennsylvania. Sea monkeys. With a practiced hand, he moved the stage of the microscope to isolate several areas of the petri dish. It was densely populated. He roughly estimated the embryos were in stage 18 of development. The magnification of the objective lens was 10X. That meant there could be fifty of them in that petri dish. Craig's stomach lurched. He put a hand down on the table to steady himself, but was unable to tear his eye away. Those embryos were doing impossible things for their stage of development. As he watched, they flitted about one another, completely unconnected to an umbilical cord.

Steeling himself, Craig leaned away from the microscope and turned to Clarence. "So that's neat but I still don't know what that yellow stuff is on the side of the microscope."

"*Venter equinus,*" Clarence replied with a wave of his emaciated hand.

"I thought that the homunculus *lived* in shit," Craig replied. "And I don't think they had microscopes in the sixteenth century, though if they did, I'm sure horse shit would have been involved."

For the first time, Clarence's calm rippled. "Riddles, boy," he said. "The alchemists spoke in riddles. Perception is the key to knowledge. You can't transmute what you cannot see!"

"Great," Craig said. "So, then, what do you want from me?"

"Don't you see, Craig?" Clarence asked. "*This* is the future. If you help me, we can reform the entire world. All of it!"

Craig regarded him coldly. "I'm not interested in some Bond villain future, Dr. Elpis. I like to drink vodka, snort cocaine, and fuck hard-to-get girls. My dad wants me to be a scientist, so I keep up the charade for him. I figure I owe him one for saving me from a fucked up situation when I was a kid. At this point, though, I just don't give a shit anymore. You're going to have to do better than this." He swung his hand toward the microscope.

Clarence stared at him for a few moments and said, "I can give you the power you've seen. The power you've used to save your friends twice."

"That's lovely," Craig said. "Then do it."

"Everything has a price, young man," Clarence remarked.

"Name it."

"I need a child. Specifically, I need Kevin's child."

"I can give you someone else's kid?" Craig asked, shaking his head.

"You can give me whatever comes into your possession. And all I need right now is your promise. You can awake from this dream with the power to move and act hundreds of times faster than any normal human being. When you get the opportunity, you just have to bring me the child. And—this is the best part—I am already making a large effort with my other resources to take the child. If I succeed in getting her before you have a chance to, you are released from our bargain. You are an insurance policy. My agents probably have Kevin's child already. You've seen how effective they are. Brenda doesn't have anything like the power you have and without Kevin to protect her..." Elpis shrugged.

"And if I reject this bargain?" Craig asked.

"You will never wake up," Elpis replied. "It's surprising you survived your first Awakening. You will not survive your second without my help."

"Why bother with all the theatrics, then?" Craig motioned to the lab around them. "You could have just told me you'd kill me if I didn't do what you wanted."

"You have more gifts than you can imagine," Clarence said. "I hoped you would join me now." He stood up. "But you will join me later. I can wait. If you want the power I have promised, drink the petri dish. That will seal our bargain. Good night, Craig Miller Jr." He ambled to a door on the far side of the lab.

After Clarence Elpis was gone, Craig collapsed into the chair. He rolled it forward and stared at the petri dish. Up close, he could see movement inside with his bare eye. He released it from the stage clips. Victoria's warning about making deals to Wake Up didn't mention that he'd die in a dream if he didn't do it. He spun the chair around and lifted the petri dish.

"Bottoms up!" he called to the empty lab.

Like a shot of vodka, Craig swallowed its contents in a single gulp.

Chapter 7
Showdown at Phalen Park

"You've lost weight," Oren said after the waitress departed with their order. "And you're pretty tan for October. Did you go on vacation or something?"

Kimm smiled. "Yeah, I've decided to turn over a new leaf."

Oren grimaced. Kimm knew he'd heard those exact words before.

"Well," Oren admitted, "you look better than you have in years, anyway. Even in that blue suit. And where are your glasses?"

"Thank you," Kimm said. He tipped his beer forward and took a drink. "I finally got Lasik."

Oren watched him from across the table, mistrust etched across his freckled forehead. He ran his hands through his short, reddish blonde hair.

"I wanted to talk to you first, Oren, before I spoke with your sisters," Kimm said. "You're the oldest." He placed his palms face up on the table. "I've had a pretty rough time in the last few years and I wanted to apologize for my, uh, absences during this period."

Oren lifted an eyebrow and frowned. "Just the last few years?" he asked.

Kimm was on treacherous footing here. He'd ransacked his house looking for clues about the past of his new identity. Just because he had become Kimm Peters didn't mean he had any knowledge of the intimate details of his life. He found more pictures, a few letters, and, the treasure trove, e-mail. He was working from piecemeal information gathered in haste. Haste was important, however. His inherited life was crumbling and, as the events earlier today illustrated, Number 9's life may not be so easily left behind.

Kimm sighed and said, "Honestly, Oren, I'm trying my best to put the past behind me and start over. There just isn't a good starting or stopping place. Do you understand?"

"Not really," Oren said. "I mean, don't get me wrong. I always like it when you try to make up for stuff, but..." he shrugged, "... you, you know, promise lots of things. I got another letter from Hamline. They're going to drop my schedule if you don't pay them. I don't know how you talked them into this payment thing in the first place."

"You remember your twenty-first birthday?" Kimm asked.

Oren smiled. "Yeah. That was a riot. My friends still think you're the coolest dad ever for that. I think you bought this entire bar a round of drinks."

"I was looking through the pictures of that night on my phone," Kimm said, "and I thought about how it's always been like this. I show up and make a big splash, but then I don't see you for a long time. I don't want it to be that way anymore, Oren. I've really been thinking about this stuff and I've missed too much of your life... and your sisters'."

Oren leaned back in his seat. "Look, Dad, are you sober right now?"

Kimm held up his beer. "Well, this is the first drink I've had in ages."

"You seem different," Oren said. "Did you go to one of those New Age camps or something? Get on some prescription? I mean, you never used to look at me like that. And you aren't smiling all the time."

"I've done some, uh, therapy. Things like that. I'm a very different person now," Kimm said. He'd known that he couldn't ape Kimm's demeanor, so he wasn't bothering to try. Instead, he opted for heartfelt sincerity. Considering the kind of used car salesman, and monster, he had been, people like Oren were unlikely to buy into it. He hoped he would have time to convince them.

The waitress arrived with the food. Both ordered the same enormous roast beef sandwiches they had on Oren's twenty-first birthday, six months ago. Pictures of the sandwiches were still on Kimm's phone. They ate in silence. Oren's phone rang, but he sent the call to voicemail.

"I spoke to Hamline and made arrangements to get your tuition taken care of," Kimm said, wiping the last of the sandwich's bread across his plate to soak up errant juice.

Oren stared at him. His own sandwich was only a third gone and he hadn't touched the waffle fries yet. "Jesus, Dad," he said, "I can't believe you ate all that so fast."

"Oh, uh, yeah. Haven't eaten yet today." He could have eaten three more sandwiches just like it. When he got home tonight, he'd eat everything in the refrigerator. His appetite was razor sharp.

"Anyway, don't worry about Hamline. That's taken care of."

Oren went back to eating. The waitress returned to ask how the food tasted. She laughed when she saw Kimm's plate and said, "Well, I guess you're satisfied. Need another beer?"

Kimm smiled at her and said, "Yeah, and can you bring me a side salad with ranch, too, please?"

She shook her head and said, "OK," before turning to Oren and asking if he needed anything else.

"No, I'm fine," he said. When the waitress left, he said, "You *have* changed. I've never seen you be polite to a waitress without hitting on her before."

"What did Arnold say when he was running for governor a few years back?" Kimm asked. "Something like, 'I've behaved badly with women,' I think. Well, I suppose I feel like him these days."

Oren laughed. "Yeah, well, Mom would agree about your history with women. She's also pissed about paying my rent these days. The new husband thinks I should get a job and pay it myself."

"How is Jack?" Kimm asked.

Oren said, "Still a douche. But he tries."

They shared a moment of silent agreement. According to a string of e-mails Kimm found on his phone, Oren despised his stepfather.

The waitress returned with the salad, which Kimm ate with buckled restraint. He still finished before Oren pushed his plate to the side of the table. He eyed the remaining quarter of a sandwich and smattering of fries. Oren waved his hand and said, "You can eat it. I'm not going to take it home."

Kimm did. When he finished, he said, "Well, I have a plan that might make your mother a bit happier."

Oren's eyes became slits.

"I had to let Gary go today, down at the dealership, and I could use some help on Fridays and Saturdays. Things are really tight right now and if I can't get them turned around..." He spread his hands. "Would you like a job at Kimm's Auto World? I can pay you enough so you can pay your own rent."

Oren leaned forward and peered at Kimm. Then he sat back in his seat. "You mean, like, selling cars?" He leaned forward again. "I dunno, Dad."

"Well, mostly I'll need help with the books and keeping the place clean. It's hard work, Oren, but I'd really like to have you come be a part of the business. You don't have to answer now. Just think about it."

Oren's eyebrows drew together. "Uh, yeah. I'll think about it."

Kimm excused himself to use the restroom. As he stood up, Oren's phone rang. He answered the call as Kimm walked away. Kimm tuned his ears to track the conversation as he made his way to the bathroom.

"Hey, Ashlyn," Oren said.

"What's up with sending me to voicemail?" his sister demanded.

"I'm at Mayslack's with Dad," Oren said. "He just went to the bathroom."

"Oh, gawd," Ashlyn said. "You aren't going to end up tagging him in pictures dancing with the Coors Light Girls again, are you?"

"No," Oren said. "He just asked me if I wanted a job at the car dealership."

"What?" she exclaimed. "Seriously?"

"Yeah, crazy, huh?" he said.

"I'd say. Is he on drugs?"

"Maybe. He's acting really weird. Look, he'll be back in a minute, so I'll call you later."

"If Dad's asking you to work at the car dealership, some big shit's going down. Oh, before you go, Phoebe wants to know if you can make it to dinner at Mom's tonight. They're doing some salmon thing 'cuz Jack-off saw it on the Food Network. She begged me not to abandon her tonight."

"Uh huh. I'll be there," Oren said. "Later."

Kimm flushed the urinal and returned to the table.

Oren stared at him as if he'd grown fangs, fur, and started howling at the moon.

"So I gotta go," Kimm said. He dropped two twenties on the table. "Tell your sisters I said 'Hi' and think about the job. I'll call you tonight."

"OK," Oren said. "See you later, Dad."

Kimm touched his son's shoulder. "See you later, Son."

Brenda awoke to a room dark except for the LCD screen of the alarm clock and the sliver of light beneath the bedroom door. The clock read 8:12 p.m. Her mouth was dry and she needed to urinate. Voices drifted from the living room. Kevin really was alive. She stayed in bed for a few minutes trying to wrap her mind around that fact, but her bladder overcame her confusion and she stumbled to the bathroom.

What am I going to tell people? She thought, leaning forward on the toilet with her elbows on her knees. *What can I tell them? How am I going to go back to work? What about the life insurance settlement? Can I give it back? Thank God I didn't spend it. And he's a monster. What the fuck am I supposed to do with that?*

She was reminded of her best friend in high school. The woman married her boyfriend instead of going to college, but divorced him two years later. Their wedding cost obscene amounts of money. Last year, she remarried him in a courthouse. Brenda stood as a bridesmaid both times. The whole affair seemed like a confusing and embarrassing waste of fiscal and emotional currency. It paled in contrast to what she was now trying to deal with.

She brushed her teeth and drank two glasses of water. Her reflection showed a fatigued woman with wild hair, so she washed her face and pulled her hair back into a pony tail. She crept to the living room, pausing at the end of the hallway.

Kevin sat on the couch in audience for one of Amber's stories. This was a typical bedtime routine for their family before Kevin had died. Or, not died, apparently. She didn't know how to think about that event—the singular most important event of her life until today.

Amber held a stuffed unicorn in one hand and a toy car in the other. She said, "Once 'pon time was ho'se!" She thrust the unicorn into the air and smiled at Kevin, who nodded in appreciation. "And wed caw!" She displayed a Matchbox Fiero Kevin bought at a thrift shop. "And...wed caw... wides ho'se." She put the car on top of the unicorn and danced around the living room.

"Then what happened?" Kevin prompted.

Amber grinned. She dropped the car, which landed upside down on the carpet. "Caw fall. Down come baby... cwadle an' all! The end!"

Kevin laughed and she jumped into his arms. "Tell sto'y! Tell sto'y! Tell sto'y!" she squealed.

"OK, OK," Kevin said. He took a deep breath as she settled into his lap. "Once upon a time there was a beautiful queen and a powerful king and a pretty, pretty princess. They lived happily together in a big castle. Then one day, an evil wizard came to the castle and turned the king into a terrible monster."

Amber interrupted, "A d'agon? A d'agon!"

Kevin nodded and tweaked her nose. "Yes. The evil

wizard turned the king into a dragon. The king didn't want to hurt his queen or the princess, so he flew away to the far mountains. The queen didn't know the wizard had turned her husband into a dragon, so she thought the dragon had eaten the king. She sent her best warriors to find the dragon in the mountains. After months, the warriors found the dragon in a cave. He had been eating sheep and had grown even bigger as time passed."

Amber began to nod off, but Kevin didn't slow the narrative.

"They sent a message to the queen that they had found the dragon. She was a warrior queen, so she came to the cave without fear. A terrible battle raged between the queen and her warriors and the dragon, but the queen overpowered the beast. She plunged her sword into the dragon's belly and killed it. As the dragon died, the wizard's spell was broken and the dragon changed back into the king."

Amber's eyes closed and her breathing steadied. Kevin continued.

"Realizing she had killed her husband, the queen wept. She and her warriors carried his body back to the castle. The princess saw her dead father and wept over his body. As her tears fell onto his face, his eyes fluttered and he sprung back to life! He found the evil wizard and burned him at the stake. The king, queen, and princess lived happily ever after. The end."

Tears welled in Brenda's eyes as she walked into the living room. She sat down on the couch next to Kevin and put her arms around him and their daughter. He leaned into her. After a moment he looked into her eyes and said, "We have to leave. Now. Gather up what you need."

She nodded, got up, and started packing.

Victoria pressed the gun against Craig's throat and pulled back the hammer. Andre neared hysteria, but he clung to his cool as he continued a one sided argument with her.

"You can't fucking shoot him!" he said for the fourth time. "You don't know what's going on! You can't know! And even if you did, you promised us we were safe with you!"

Victoria ignored Andre's pleas. She crouched above Craig with her hand on his chest and the gun tucked under his chin.

The three of them had returned to the apartment following the debacle at the hotel. Andre wasn't convinced they should have done that, but Victoria assured him that it was safe for the moment, like her truck. That unnerved him further. They carried Craig into the building between them as if he were passed out. As soon as they'd locked the door, Victoria tore Craig's shirt off and pressed her hand against his chest. She recoiled as if struck and grabbed the gun from her bag.

Beads of sweat ran down Victoria's face and she mouthed unspoken words. Craig's hand twitched. His eyes fluttered. Victoria snapped back to the moment. Her forearm flexed. She was going to shoot him.

Andre screamed, "No!" and lunged at her.

Craig's eyes flew open and a gunshot rang out. The following seconds were impossible for Andre to track. Craig vanished from beneath Victoria, who slapped Andre in midair, sending him rolling into the kitchen.

He hit the dishwasher with his upper back and scrambled to his feet. Craig stood in front of the TV in the living room, holding the gun in one hand and a bullet in the other. Something was very wrong with him. His chest and head jerked sideways spasmodically while his legs vibrated and his torso remained stable. Looking at him upset Andre's stomach.

Craig's flickering head regarded the bullet. He said, "You can't put it back in. It's all smashed up. Single use items, I guess." He tossed the bullet and the gun onto the couch.

Victoria stood up.

Craig said, "I need a reading. Right now."

Victoria frowned at him. "You have no right—"

"Right fucking now!" Craig said. His body blurred in different directions, reforming and breaking apart like a kaleidoscope.

Victoria inhaled sharply. She said, "You shall have a reading."

She pulled out a porcelain box from her gym bag. Craig sat down in front of the coffee table. His body tore itself apart and put itself back together in flashes. He looked like the best 3D video game ever made while it malfunctioned. Andre stayed in the kitchen, watching what was happening from behind the bar separating it from the living room. If those two got into a fight, he would be collateral damage.

Victoria shuffled the cards. The ritualistic grace with which she handled them was impressive. As he watched her, a shimmering blue spiral radiated from her hands. She finished shuffling and sat the cards down. Andre blinked and the spiral vanished. He rubbed his forehead with his palm. *What was that?* he thought.

Craig pulled the top card before she had a chance to say anything. He turned it over on top the deck. The Hollow Skull.

"Again," he said.

Victoria pursed her lips and shuffled the cards. When she set them down, he pulled the top card. The Hollow Skull.

"Again," he said.

Victoria reshuffled the cards. As Craig pulled the Hollow Skull for the third time, Andre's vision became a tunnel and the card leapt forward in perspective. The room around him dimmed. He knew what that card meant. It showed the only path that Craig could take without fulfilling the bargain he'd made with a madman. His tunnel vision receded and the room shifted back into focus. Victoria and Craig were staring at him. Craig's body was no longer flickering.

"What did you say?" Craig asked.

"I didn't say anything," Andre said. "But I know what that card means. You have to..." He could not remember what that card meant. Just moments ago, he could have written an essay about it. Now the card was nothing more than a cleverly drawn skull on a piece of thin cardboard. "Shit!" he said. "I knew! But I can't remember."

Victoria said, "He said, 'Free the hag into the child. Beg for the trust you'll need from the one you planned to harm the most. Trust the number eight, but seek not the first.' It's a prophetic admonition."

Craig frowned.

Andre threw his arms in the air and said, "I'm sick of this shit. Anybody want a drink?"

Craig murmured, "I don't think I should ever drink again."

To Andre's surprise, Victoria said, "Yes, please." She turned her attention to Craig. "Obviously, I would prefer you were dead. Whatever deal you made has yet to be sealed. This makes you dangerous. Very dangerous. Do you feel the tug yet? Do you feel compelled to act?"

Craig shook his head. "Not really. I know he's tied to me. I know he can watch me if he wants to. I know he can make me, um, do things if he really tries. But I think he's very weak right now. I'm pretty sure he's dying of cancer. He looks just like my uncle did at the end. Well, except he's an African American albino who could be your great-grandfather. My uncle didn't look like that at all."

Andre came into the living room with two beers. Victoria took hers and drained half of it before gathering her cards and tucking them away. She collapsed into the recliner.

Andre sat down on the couch between her and the gun. "Is he a relative of yours?" he asked.

She didn't answer. Her eyes were watery and distant. After several minutes she asked Craig, "Is he watching you now?"

"No," Craig said. "I think he's a pretty busy guy."

She drank the rest of her beer and asked Andre, "Do you have anything harder than this?"

Andre smiled and said, "Why yes, I do, and I'm so glad you asked."

He drained the rest of his beer and took both bottles to the kitchen. A few minutes later, he returned with two mixed drinks. "I felt like screwdrivers were appropriate."

Victoria nodded and the right side of her mouth twitched. She drank half the glass. Andre was impressed. Her screwdriver was more vodka than orange juice.

"I need you to tell me exactly what happened again, Craig," she said. "Just like you did with the other dream. Once you do that, I'll tell you who I am and how I am... related... to that man."

Craig regarded her carefully. "Promise me you won't try to kill me again."

She waved her hand. "I don't have to. If I could kill you, you'd already be dead. I tried to pull that trigger. The gun went off was because Andre lunged at me and I jerked it up as you moved. I surely wish I could have killed you, Craig. If it makes you feel better, I promise not to kill you. But that promise is just a fact. It's part of the rules that govern me. I can't kill anyone."

"Well, that's a great relief," Andre said.

Craig smiled at his friend and said, "Then I guess it's story time."

He recounted exactly what had happened from the moment he found himself before the pay phone to the moment he woke up with a gun in his face. Andre was disgusted by the entire scenario, but he kept his mouth shut. Craig finished, "So, basically, I've got to give Amber to this Clarence guy. It has to happen. I know that like I know my name. What I need to figure out is how I can do that and then get her back, I think. I dunno."

"Why didn't you just die?" Victoria asked.

"Why didn't you?" Craig countered.

"I didn't have that choice," she replied.

"Well, look," Craig said, "not everything about that dream was a prop. He's doing this shit. He's making little people in petri dishes out of horseshit and magic, which until yesterday I thought were the same thing. I don't consider myself an expert on ethics, but I have spent the last three years of my life studying biology. What he's doing… is wrong. I know that the same way I know I have to give Amber to him. If I hadn't accepted his bargain, he'd just go ahead with this mad scheme and probably kill everyone on the planet. I don't know how to describe this right, but I was somehow chosen." He paused and shook his head. "No, that's not close enough. I'm the guy in the right place at the right time. I dunno. Since you did my reading this morning, something changed in me. It's like I'm watching what I'm doing because I'm part of something bigger than me. So I knew I couldn't die or he'd just do all this crazy shit and the world would get overrun by his madness."

"Glad you didn't shoot him, now, huh?" Andre said to Victoria.

"Maybe," she said. "Will you make me another drink?"

She was going to tell her story and it appeared she needed some grease to get started.

Victoria drank the second screwdriver with reservation. Andre mixed it more potently than the first. Alcohol helped relax her and took some of the shock out of what Craig had said. The implications of Clarence Elpis were staggering. His face still floated in her mind, imprinted there when she turned the third Hollow Skull for Craig. Only after the second drink did she allow herself to acknowledge the fact that he was probably her son. Having recognized the worst case scenario, she could press forward. For a moment she regretted not retreating from the entire situation, as she had done at the end of other periods in her life. Pikeville in 1939. Chicago in 1952. Washington D.C. in 1984. This time was different, though. This time she didn't want to run away.

"I am over ninety years old," she began.

"You've aged well," Andre said.

She smiled at him. "Yes, I have. And I will continue to do so. Perhaps indefinitely, provided I'm not killed in a violent manner. I don't really know. Recently, I was raped by the monster that attacked you in the park."

Andre dropped his drink and Craig grunted.

"What?" Andre exclaimed as he picked his glass up from the floor. He went to the kitchen and returned with a towel and a full glass.

"He was in human form at the time," she said. "I don't know what that monster is, but he came to me as a man and demanded a card reading. His questions were about his father, his brother, and his father's interests in a child. I believe this child is Amber. I believe the monster's brother is Amber's father. I believe the monster's father is Clarence Elpis."

Andre shook his head as he dabbed the floor with the towel. "This is fucked up, you know? This Elpis guy may be related to you somehow. His son *raped* you?"

"They are not genetically related. I would know if they were. I think he created this monster and he plans to create many more." She sighed. "Clarence Elpis may be my son."

Craig and Andre looked at each other. She could see sick fascination in their eyes and she didn't blame them.

Andre said, "Amber's father's name is Kevin. And he's dead. Died in a car crash two months ago."

Craig nodded. "How did you know about Amber?"

"The Confluence I told you about," Victoria said. "It encompasses all of you, including Brenda and Amber. It is like a map I can read."

"So what about Kevin?" Craig said.

"I don't believe he's dead," Victoria said. "I did not give that monster all the information I could have. I did not lie to him, but I left out as much as I could. When he pulled the first card, he asked, 'Who killed my brother?' The cards don't tell whole stories, but they give a series of clues that I can read. I usually encrypt these clues into codes that will help my clients understand themselves better. In this case, I made it very difficult for him to understand. The cards implied that his brother was still alive. I told him, 'Death has been reversed' because the cards also implied that the monster himself would soon be dead. There was little chance he could untangle that knot. So Kevin probably faked his death. Maybe to set a trap. The cards weren't clear on that."

Craig's mouth was hanging open.

Andre said, "Well, that would be nice, I guess. What else do you know about this monster? He scares the shit out of me."

"He is no longer a threat," she said.

"How do you know that? He raped you!" Andre insisted. "You can't just let that go."

"He is no longer a threat," she repeated. "We have much bigger problems right now. I'm going to tell you both something I've told only one other person in my life, and she didn't believe me. Perhaps—"

Craig put his hand up. "Hold on, hold on," he said. "Kevin is still alive?"

"Yes, Craig, I think he is," Victoria answered.

"Oh, wow. We have to find him. I've got to start begging, right?" He looked at Andre.

"Don't look at me," Andre said. "I don't remember saying that at all."

Victoria nodded. "We do need to find Kevin. But first, you need to know what you're facing."

"Right," Craig said. His eyes were like platters.

Victoria said, "When I was seventeen years old, a man murdered my father…"

She told the story matter-of-factly, leaving out much of the emotional turmoil. Still, she could see empathy welling in both boys. When she described how the thing in the box took the child from her womb, an unnoticed tear slid down Andre's cheek. She stopped the story there. "So you can see we're dealing with something very old and very powerful. I don't believe my son inhabits the body of Clarence Elpis. I believe the thing in the box does. What I did to my son is worse than anything I can imagine."

Andre coughed, cleared his throat, and asked, "What

happened to the box?"

"The box?" Victoria said.

"Yeah, the box," Andre said. "Did you ever go back and look in there?"

Victoria paused for a moment, collecting her thoughts. She said, "No. When Mam-maw saw me after all that had happened, she thought I had aborted the child myself. I took her to the second door, but the key would not open the lock. She told me that the key had never opened that lock. She thought I'd gone hysterical. Our relationship... didn't survive long after that. I left the area and have never returned."

"We're going to need the box," Andre said. "It contained this thing once. It will again."

"Why do you think that, Andre?" Victoria asked.

"It's weird," he said. "I can see the box in your eyes when I look. It's like when I looked at the card and knew what Craig had to do, only not as strong. The world around me goes kinda dark except for your eyes, and there's a green box floating in them. It's the box you described in that underground room."

"You're Waking Up, Andre," Victoria said. She had hoped that this wouldn't happen.

Andre considered his glass for a moment. "Yeah, I know," he said. "It's been going on since Craig started going all fast forward. I just started seeing more and more. I didn't really notice it until you started shuffling the cards just now. It doesn't happen because I want it to. It just kinda happens."

Craig frowned and asked Victoria, "Why is this happening to us?"

"You said it best yourself, Craig," Victoria replied. "You were in the right place at the right time. You had hidden gifts to begin with. As the Confluence has strengthened around you, it's drawing them out."

"But, like, you know, is God doing all this?" Andre asked. He fingered the crucifix beneath his shirt. Craig snorted.

"Perhaps it is," Victoria said. "I think so. I need someone who can forgive me for what I did to my son. So I believe that God set the events into motion. But, just like with everyone else, God doesn't come out and tell people like us what He is doing. We have to choose. And I chose poorly."

"Dandy," Craig said. "Well, theology aside, I'd just as soon have been hit by a bus. Instead of asking why, I guess I should have asked if it was ever going to stop."

"No," Victoria said. "It will never stop. You can't go back to sleep. This is your life now."

"That's going to complicate things," Andre said. "My future as a professional stoner and video game connoisseur is shot. How do you think that makes me feel?"

Both Craig and Victoria laughed. For the first time since Victoria met him, Andre relaxed. He sat back on the couch, his signature smile wide and genuine, and took a long drink from his screwdriver.

When Sheila answered the knock at her hotel room door, Numbers 11 and 12 stood in the hallway. Both were tall, broad men wearing khakis and polo shirts. Other than their size, they were nondescript. Sheila didn't bother greeting them. The latest generations of Térata were almost autistic in their focus. If a motion didn't need to be made, they didn't make it. Small talk was something they did only when necessary. She didn't like them at all, but they were effective tools.

They were also dangerous tools. The technology fused to their central nervous system allowed their brains to connect to the Elipsis Network via wireless signals, so they could communicate with one another without speaking. When they worked in tandem they seemed to be part of a choreographed dance.

They also didn't have a true form like their older brothers and sisters. This was the part that unnerved Sheila the most. She was a monster. When Elpis melded biological DNA with technology and magic, he had chosen a monstrous form that his creations should inhabit. Her identity was grounded in the fact that she was a nightmare to the humans around her. Numbers 11 and 12 were in no way connected to the monster mythology that had inspired their predecessors. They were machines melded with flesh that could change form at whim. They were, in Sheila's estimation, too perfect. They had no style.

Sheila handed one of them a notecard with a series of locations and addresses written on it.

"I assume you've already seen all the photos I sent," she said. "We need to find the child and her mother first. Then, we'll need to clean up some loose ends."

Number 11 read the card and handed it back to her.

She said, "I'll take the condo. One of you stake out the diner. If Brenda's not there, find out when she'll be back. She's the general manger so pretend you're a vendor or something. The other one should check on the addresses on the card. Eventually, we'll find them. Call me if you spot them first. Do not engage until we have all arrived on the scene. There are extra players involved and it appears that Number 9 has gone rogue. I want a smooth grab with as many survivors as possible. Is that understood?"

They both nodded and left.

Sheila went into the bathroom and opened her makeup case. Changing forms obliterated the stuff. She drew a tasteful shade of brown around each eye and applied caramel lipstick. She chose a simple gold choker and earrings to compliment her beige blouse, dark tan skirt, and matching jacket. When she didn't know what to expect, she liked to look good. At the moment she looked smashing.

Kevin pulled his SUV into the parking lot of the Pit Stop Diner. He knew this was a tactical error, but Brenda insisted on coming here before they left town. Their conversation on the way had been short and tense. While she hadn't demanded to know his entire plan, she fidgeted with her hair like she did when she was mad or distracted.

"I obviously can't go in," Kevin said as he parked by the front door. His windows were tinted, so no one would recognize him if they glanced at the vehicle.

"That's fine," Brenda said. "I just need ten minutes with Mai and Andre. My job probably won't survive this fiasco, but I don't have to leave a pile of shit for Jerry and Mac."

As Brenda got out, Amber began kicking at the back of Kevin's seat.

"Kick Daddy! Kick Daddy! Kick Daddy!" she chanted.

Amber always sat behind Kevin so that she was easier to reach from the passenger seat. Kicking the back of his seat and getting him to tell her to cut it out was a tradition she had not forgotten during his absence. The Suburban put his seat just out of her foot's reach.

Funny how such small things mean so much to kids and they just go with the big stuff, Kevin thought. He dropped his seat back so she could reach it. She whooped in delight and drummed it with her feet.

Kevin scanned the parking lot and nearby streets. A tall man in khaki pants stood at the bus stop fiddling with his phone. Kevin caught his scent when Brenda opened the door. Nothing was amiss with him and he was gone the next time Kevin looked at the bus stop. Nothing else warranted his attention.

A few minutes later, Brenda emerged from the diner with a deep frown on her face. She got into the SUV and said, "Andre called in this morning. God, I wish I hadn't turned my phone off. Anyway, he said something about people getting killed to Gina when he called. I'm going to call him back now and figure out what's going on."

Kevin had not mentioned what happened at Minnehaha Park last night. He saw no reason to do so now. Clarence and his minions would only be interested in Amber. Once she was out of the picture, the boys should be safe. Victoria Starks had taken an interest in them and she was slippery. Based on what he knew about her, he was certain she would help protect them. They would be fine.

"Andre?" Brenda said into the phone. Kevin could hear Andre's voice.

"Yeah! Brenda!" Andre said. "Are you OK? Is Amber OK? Is Kevin there?"

Kevin grimaced.

"Yes," Brenda replied, "We're all fine—wait a minute. You know Kevin is still alive?"

She turned to Kevin with a frown.

Andre whistled. "Well, I wasn't sure until just now. Look, some crazy, crazy shit is going down. We need to get together ASAP. Hold on."

Kevin could still hear him talking, even though he had taken the phone away from his face. He also heard Victoria Starks's voice. They were discussing where to meet.

"OK, Brenda?" Andre said when he was done talking to Victoria.

"Yeah," she said.

"Can you meet us at that park you always take Amber to over off Phalen?" he asked.

"Hold on," she said. She put her thumb over the bottom of the phone and turned to Kevin. "Andre wants to meet us at Phalen Park. Why does he know you're alive?"

Kevin shrugged. "He's with a witch. She knows things. We should meet them at the park. That's a good idea. Wide open space."

For a moment Brenda just stared at him, her expression blank. She put the phone back to her ear and said, "OK. We'll be there in ten minutes or so. Are you guys in Dinkytown?"

"Yeah," Andre said. "It'll take us probably twenty or so to get there."

"OK, see you then," she said.

"'K," Andre said.

As she hung up, she looked out the front window and said, "How much more of this kind of stuff is going to happen?" The strain it took her to sound reasonable in front of Amber was apparent.

"A lot," he said. "Do you see why I didn't want to involve you in all this?"

Brenda took a deep breath and closed her eyes. When she opened them, they were blazing but she kept her voice cool. "All right. Well, I want you to tell me as much as you can about what's going on before we meet the boys and this witch. I feel like I'm floating on a raft in the middle of the ocean right now and I don't like it."

"That's understandable," he said.

As he pulled out of the parking lot, he noticed the guy who had been standing at the bus stop leaning against the brick wall of the diner, still fiddling with his phone. He must have missed his bus.

As they drove to Phalen Park, Kevin explained everything that had happened last night at Minnehaha Falls. He also described the physical and mental effect she had on him and, subsequently, his brother when she encountered him as Fred last night. When they reached the park, they sat in the SUV while he described Victoria Starks. Amber had fallen asleep on the drive.

Brenda stared out the windshield at Lake Phalen, which reflected streetlamps in the darkness several hundred yards away. When Kevin stopped talking, she said, "So the witch you were hunting when you found me is now hanging out with Craig and Andre. Your brother is messed up because I can make...Térata...feel things and...have babies?" She shook her head. "What did you plan to do about Craig and Andre? Leave them here to fend for themselves?"

Kevin said, "You'll understand more when you meet Victoria. I think they're pulling in now. That red truck is pretty unmistakable if you actually notice it."

"What red truck?" Brenda asked.

Kevin pointed three parking stalls over, where Victoria was pulling in.

"Oh, wow. How did I miss that?" Brenda asked.

"Be careful with Victoria, Brenda," Kevin said. "She's a powerful woman."

Kevin left the vehicle running as he and Brenda got out. The boys and Victoria piled out the truck. Victoria looked the same way she did the first time he'd seen her, almost thirty years ago. Andre looked rattled and he smelled drunk. Three fresh cuts ran along his face, but they weren't serious. Craig's skin and tangled hair were white. Purple circles encased his eyes. He seemed jittery. Something was very wrong with the way he smelled, but Kevin couldn't pinpoint what.

"Kevin!" Craig exclaimed. He threw himself into Kevin's arms. Kevin caught him and hugged him. Craig's skin felt cold and, again, somehow wrong.

"Kevin, you have to trust me," Craig said into his chest, squeezing him around the waist.

Kevin frowned and pushed him away, but kept ahold of his shoulders. "What?"

"I'm begging you, Kevin," Craig said, his arms falling to his sides. His face was crumpled and his right eye was ticking. "Trust me. Please. It's the only way we're gonna get out of this alive."

Kevin turned to Victoria. "What did you do to him?"

Victoria said, "He did that to himself. I told him not to, but he didn't listen to me. He's Awake. The hard way."

Brenda and Andre regarded the exchange silently.

Kevin looked back at Craig. "You're Awake? How?"

Craig looked small, sad, and weak. "I—I made a deal with Clarence Elpis—" he began.

Victoria put up a hand and interrupted. "This will have to wait. The creature we ran into earlier today is nearby. She will be here in a minute. We need to leave. Now."

"What did she look like?" Kevin asked, releasing Craig.

Andre answered. "Oh, you know...black fur, green glowing eyes, weird green discs all over. If it was a she, I really couldn't tell."

"Number 7," Kevin said. "Let her come. We will wait."

Victoria arched an eyebrow and said, "Are you certain you want to engage this monster?"

"We have an arrangement," Kevin said. "She should not be hostile."

Andre laughed. "Well, take a look at my face, man. She's hostile."

"Is this Number 7 your sister?" Brenda asked.

"Yes," Kevin said. "It will be safer for you in the car, Brenda. Take the driver's seat. If anything goes wrong, leave. I will catch up with you. Boys, get in the back."

Craig shook his head and said, "No. I'll stay out here."

Andre nodded in agreement. "I want to see this."

Kevin began to argue with them as Brenda got into the vehicle, but another black Suburban pulled into the parking lot.

"Do all of you drive those things?" Andre asked. Kevin ignored him.

The Suburban parked in the adjacent row. The driver's door opened and Number 7 stepped out. She tossed her blonde hair as she strode toward them.

Andre mumbled, "She got a lot hotter in the last few hours. Maybelline should do a before and after commercial with that bitch."

"Hello, Sheila," Kevin said. "Interesting choice for an identity."

"Hello, Number 1," she replied. "I suppose you prefer Kevin these days."

"Why are you here?" Kevin asked.

Sheila shrugged and winked at Andre. "The same reason Number 9 was here. You've somehow managed to reproduce and that's of great interest to our father. We can make this really easy if you all want to just come with me. I didn't expect to find you all together. My lucky day."

"You know I won't do that," Kevin said. "You sold me out."

"No, I didn't. I have no idea how they found you. And I figured you wouldn't just hop on board. So I brought some of our younger brothers. You haven't met them since they were in puberty, but I'm sure you remember Numbers 11 and 12."

Kevin crossed his arms as two men materialized beside Sheila. He recognized one of them as the man in khakis at the Pit Stop.

"They could have killed us all before you ever got here," Kevin said.

"Yeah, but I find such methods distasteful," she said. "You're a very clever man, Kevin, and I thought I could count on your ability to do math. Victoria, your wife, and the kids die in the first ten seconds. You and the child come anyway. Or we can all go home peacefully." She smiled and spread her hands.

Victoria said, "What does your father want with me and the boys?"

Sheila laughed. "You've been on the wanted list for a long time, my dear. Number 1, or rather, Kevin, was supposed to bring you in before he vanished four years ago. Don't ask me why. As for the boys, I don't really think it's such a great idea to leave Awake humans just lying around. The Elpis Foundation is the right place for them." She snapped her finger. "Enough talk. What's it going to be Kevin? I say one word and this goes from pleasant chat to slaughter house."

"We'll come," Kevin said.

Victoria grunted.

The door to Kevin's Suburban opened and Brenda got out. She walked up to Kevin and stared at Sheila and the two men. Kevin turned to her, but she spoke before he had a chance to say anything.

"Stay where you are," she commanded. Kevin felt a wave of energy pour out of her.

Sheila froze and her eyes rolled upward. The other two began to quake, but they did not stay still. They lurched forward, each step faster than the last.

"Shit!" Kevin said, pushing Brenda back toward the car. "It's not gonna work on them for long. They're not the same as us. Get back to the car."

Brenda ran toward the car. Andre pulled a gun from his jacket and Victoria backed up. Craig seemed to have vanished.

"Get out of here," Kevin told Andre and Victoria.

Kevin was probably going to die, but if he could delay things long enough for the others to get away, it would be worth it. With a roar, he exploded into his true form, tearing his clothes away as he did so.

Numbers 11 and 12, even impeded by Brenda's command, blurred forward. 11 swept Kevin's legs while 12 jabbed at his throat, forcing him to dance backwards. He pivoted, ducked, and avoided them until a small opening gave him the chance to grab 11 under his arm with a clawed hand and tear away a chunk of his triceps. Kevin's left kidney exploded in pain as 12 flanked him with a kick. He flailed forward. Air exploded from his lungs as 11 punched his chest. Blood gushed blood from 11's armpit, but that did not slow him down.

Kevin heard gunshots as Andre unloaded the clip of the 9mm. His attackers took hits alternately with each bang, buying him precious seconds to get his breath back. He grabbed 11 and swung him toward 12. Like an eel, 11 turned in his hand and grabbed his throat. He felt 12 jump onto his back. His vision blurred as blood flow to his brain stopped.

Brenda backed the Suburban up, tires squealing. She slammed on the breaks, rolled the window down, and screamed at Number 7, "Help him!"

Number 7 surged forward, taking on her true form in midair. Her clothing and Sheila's identity flew away in tatters. Kevin's knees buckled, but he snarled and flailed to keep their attention on him. Number 7 grabbed 12 by the throat, pulling him from Kevin's back. Most of 12's neck splattered onto the concrete.

Number 7 flipped, using her motion to twist 12's head backward. Blood cascaded onto Kevin's shoulders. With an immense heave, she lobbed 12 toward the lake. Halfway through his arched projection, his body caught fire, blazing a red smoke trail across the night sky. As he hit the water, a white explosion sent waves crashing onto the beach.

Kevin managed to push 11 away from him in the confusion. Surprisingly, Victoria waited behind 11 with what looked like a sliver of fishing line. She laid it gently on 11's shoulder. The line spun to life and encased him in a cocoon. 11 struggled and hissed. The lines began to snap and unravel, splaying in all directions. Kevin shoved his claws into 11's throat and ripped out his esophagus and carotid artery. He sidestepped a fountain of blood and twisted 11's head backwards. For good measure, he turned it all the way around. 11's eyes were still intensely alive, but a slow heat built from his chest. Kevin grabbed him by the shoulders and lobbed him toward the lake. Like his brother, he caught fire in the air and exploded when he hit the water. The surface of the lake roiled.

Kevin rubbed his throat with a clawed hand and surveyed the scene. The concrete was awash with blood. Victoria stood near the Suburban, looking into the back window and tapping her lips with an index finger. Andre had the gun pointed at Number 7, who stood still as a statue. He could not see where Craig had ended up.

Kevin approached Number 7. She locked her eyes to his and with unmoving lips said, "What is happening to me?"

Kevin glanced back at the Suburban. Brenda was hanging out of the window, gaping at the scene in disbelief. Kevin said to her, "Brenda, please tell Sheila that she is free."

Brenda blinked twice. With a trembling voice she said, "Sheila, you are free."

Number 7 dropped to the ground as if invisible lines holding her in place had snapped. She grunted through the transformation process back to Sheila's body. Tears streamed down her face. She stood and put her hand on Kevin's furry cheek. His upper lip twitched, revealing his teeth.

"Thank you," she said. She gathered up the pieces of her clothing, got into her vehicle, and drove way.

Kevin exhaled and asked, "Where's Craig?"

Victoria said, "He's in the back of the Suburban with Amber."

Craig was blipping backward again. He had coined the term himself and he was very satisfied with how accurately it captured the negative side effects brought about by moving in fast forward, which he thought of as blipping forward. His body felt overloaded, flooded with more energy than it could process. Different parts of him moved at different speeds, tearing him apart but putting him back together faster than his nerves could send signals to his brain. He knew it should have been painful. He had once seen a movie in which a paraplegic was stabbed in the leg with a pen knife. He imaged that he felt like the paraplegic would have felt. Damaged but unable to sense it.

Lying on the floorboard of Kevin's SUV, he blipped backward and fought with Clarence Elpis. Elpis wanted Amber, whose shoes were the only thing Craig could see. The girl was giggling as he blipped, amused by his contortions. She had been sleeping when he opened the door with the intention of grabbing her and running full speed all the way to Des Moines, a feat that would have killed him as surely as the marathon killed its founder. She woke up as he unfastened her seatbelt, which he had slowed down to do. Some things didn't work very well when he blipped forward. Objects, especially plastic ones, tended to disintegrate if he didn't slow down before touching them. She opened her eyes as he finished unfastening her and said sleepily, "Hi, C'aig." Her voice had shattered Elpis's hold on his mind, and he collapsed onto the floorboard. Now, he held onto conscious thought with a thin string and he didn't know how much longer he'd be able to do so. As he fought, he began to hear voices.

"He's doing that thing again," said Andre. "Like he's malfunctioning."

Victoria said, "He is malfunctioning, but he's also locked in battle with Clarence Elpis. He's trying to resist taking Amber."

"Taking Amber?" Brenda exclaimed from the front seat. Craig could see her begin to climb between the bucket seats above him.

Andre said, "Hold on, Brenda. I've got to do something. Then maybe we can figure this out."

She stopped, but she was poised to move again.

Craig felt Andre's hands grasp his temple. His head stopped blipping. That was disturbing because as his body blipped his head was disconnected and floating in space. Andre's fingers felt as if they were sinking into his temples. Clarence Elpis vanished from his mind. He stopped blipping.

Andre pulled his hands away and said, "Clarence is gone for now. He'll be back."

Victoria said, "He's touched you now, Andre."

"I know," Andre said, "But unlike the two of you, I'm not making any fucking deals with that devil. I blocked him out."

Craig sat up and rubbed the skin around his neck and chest. It felt like every pore on his body was erupting in tiny, volcanic fury. Kevin, Andre, and Victoria were gathered around the door of the SUV, their faces a mixture of concern and apprehension. Seeing Kevin standing there stark naked, covered in blood, with an unsure look on his face made Craig angry, but he didn't know why.

"How did you do that?" he demanded from Andre. He immediately felt ashamed for the harsh tone of his voice.

Andre pulled the cross out his shirt and said, "I just thought of this and repeated the Lord's Prayer in my head until Elpis went away. I made a choice before he ever touched me. I decided I would not deal with him. That kinda settled into me. I'm not sure why, but he can't get in unless I ask him, which I am not gonna do."

Kevin said, "That's amazing, Andre. Most of us have to make that kind of choice after the damage is already done."

Victoria nodded.

Craig sighed. It was too late for him. Way too late.

Brenda said, "Can I talk now?"

Kevin looked at her and nodded.

She glared at Craig and asked, "Are you trying to kidnap my daughter?"

"I have to," he said. He tried to explain why he had to make the deal with Clarence Elpis. Explaining to a mother why he planned to steal her child made the logic behind his decision seem flimsy. Humanity be damned. Brenda's face was an illustration of maternal fear. For the first time, he regretted not just sitting in that dream until he died. He finished by saying, "I'm stuck on this one. I'm sorry. Please forgive me."

Brenda looked past him, into some dark space at the back of the Suburban. After a few seconds of silence she said, "We need to get out of here before the cops show up." She looked at Craig, "Is this Elpis person going to make you steal my daughter in the next few hours?"

Craig shook his head and said, "No. I can't go fast right now. I'm broken. Pretty badly. I doubt I can even walk. I think I'll heal, but I don't know how long it'll take. Days, probably. He won't bother me until I'm useful again."

Brenda pursed her lips and addressed everyone, seeming to speak to each one individually. "There's a truck stop on I-35 East just north of Shoreview. Let's all go there and figure out what to do next. I'm starving and I can smell Amber's diaper from here."

Victoria said, "That sounds fine to me." There was a whiff of disdain in her voice. She was clearly not used to being herded. She better get used to it if she was going to spend any time with Brenda.

Andre helped Craig up from the floorboard and into the bench seat.

"Thanks," Craig said. "Sorry about snapping at you..."

Andre laughed and said, "You've got the devil inside you, man. It's tough. Like that INXS song." He snapped Craig's seatbelt into place for him, since Craig didn't have enough strength in his hands to manage it.

Craig shook his head and said, "Your dad ruined your taste in music." He became serious and said quietly, "He's not the devil, though. In Greek, the word 'elpis' means 'hope'. Katalambano. I've been seized by Hope."

Victoria's jaw dropped.

Andre looked at Craig like he'd just explained the theory of relativity with a stick figure drawing.

"The last thing in Pandora's Box," Andre breathed. "The green box…"

Octavio opened the door to Number 7's motel room at Le Méridien with a key he'd finagled out of the receptionist. He'd already knocked and waited, merely as a formality. He doubted she was in the room. Her light in the Elipsis system had been blinking red for four hours. On top of this, both 11 and 12 were dead at the bottom of a lake. If she was dead like them, this entire hotel would be cinders. So far what should have been a simple extraction of a child had become a staggering loss. Clarence wasn't happy at all.

Octavio was not accustomed to this kind of field work. His job was behind a desk or dealing with economically challenged kids. He felt like a fraud, pretending to be a detective. But sending any more of Clarence's numbered pets would have been categorically stupid. Other Awake humans with much better qualifications could have done this if any of them could be trusted. After Timothy Shelton's attempt to murder him, Octavio no longer trusted any of them.

Number 7's room was a mess. The bed was off kilter, clothes littered the floor, and paperwork was scattered everywhere. Not good. Number 7 was a neat freak.

"Hello?" Octavio said. He thought the room was empty, but as he took a step inside, he heard soft whining sounds from the bathroom.

"Number 7?" he asked.

A small voice from the bathroom responded, "My name is Sheila."

Octavio stepped through the debris on the floor and pushed the bathroom door open. Inside, a strikingly beautiful woman with blonde hair lay curled up on the floor. She was nude. Her skin was covered with lipstick, eyeliner, and rouge. She looked just like one of his toddler nieces had when she got ahold of her mother's makeup case. A tracking chip was crushed in a puddle of blood by the toilet.

"Number 7?" Octavio asked again.

The woman stared at him and said, "My name is Sheila. Sheila Barnstock. I'm an art dealer. I've got a plush apartment on the Lower East Side. I have an appointment at Christie's in a week to look at something for...I may have to cancel that. I'm free now. And I'm in love with you, Octavio."

Octavio shook his head and said, "What happened?"

"She set me free. The woman—Kevin's wife—she set me free." Her eyes spun into focus and she put her hand against the toilet to help her stand. "Oh," she said, "I seem to have made a mess. How odd. I looked so beautiful in the mirror... like art." She stood up and considered herself in the full length mirror on the wall. "Well, I guess... I guess I should probably get cleaned up. Go make yourself a drink, Octavio. I'll be out in a minute."

She turned away from him and switched on the shower. He spent a moment staring at the curves of her back.

"Uh, OK," he stammered.

There were no windows in the bathroom for her to climb out of, so Octavio backed out and shut the door. The hotel room was as cluttered as his mind, so he tidied the mess. He found her phone and purse and placed them on the night stand by the crooked bed, which he straightened. The sheets were torn but the pillows and comforter survived. He made the bed as neatly as possible. Papers and documents were strewn everywhere. He gathered them into a large pile on the bed.

The sound of the shower drifted from the bathroom and with it images of Sheila Barnstock cleaning herself. She was humming the tune of a pop song. Images of her supple curves invaded his mind and drove a spike into his crotch that made his stomach flutter. Like her other siblings, Number 7 was capable of controlling a person's physical reactions through pheromonal secretions. But he knew she hadn't done that. He was having this reaction on his own. He hadn't slept with a woman since before his deployment to Afghanistan. Had she really said she was in love with him? That was impossible. For some reason, though, her nakedness and those words made his heart beat as if he'd just spent thirty minutes sprinting on a treadmill.

To suppress the urges boiling inside him, he read through the stacks of paper on the bed. The picture of what was happening here in the Twin Cities formed around this information as he stacked it back into piles on the bed. Why hadn't Number 9 acquired the child? Who was Kimm Peters and why was he so important? So much information… He found a notation that made him stop and say, "*¿Qué?*" Number 1 was still alive. That was news. Big news.

"Thank you for tidying up, Octavio," Number 7 said from the bathroom door. She was wearing a red, silk bathrobe and her hair was wrapped in a white towel.

Octavio held up the piece of paper he'd been reading. "Number 1 is still alive? And you've known that the entire time? What are you up to, Number 7?"

She shrugged. "We all keep secrets. My name is Sheila. I won't tell you that again."

She walked toward him, hips rolling. Octavio took a step back. His dick was at attention and his throat was tight, but he was frightened out of his mind.

"Look," he said, "I need to bring you back to Des Moines.

You've been compromised."

Sheila smiled. "What if I don't want to come back? What if I *like* being compromised?"

Octavio swallowed and said, "I'm supposed to—I'm supposed to bring you back or kill you."

Sheila arched an eyebrow and said, "I'm not Number 10. I don't think you can kill me. You can't really kill anyone unless you have to. I think that's why I'm in love with you. Have you ever noticed that all The Foundation really does is bring death? Everywhere we go. Death. Clarence talks about hope for the future, but, really, we're just killers with a cause. You're not like us, Octavio. You bring life. It oozes out of you like sunshine." Her bathrobe fell open.

Octavio shook his head. He could not think properly. What was she talking about?

"Are you going to try to kill me?" he stammered.

Sheila shook her head. "No, Octavio. I'm going to try to make love to you. And from what I can tell..." she inclined her head and sniffed the air "...you're going to let me do it."

She slipped the towel off her head and let the robe slither to the floor.

Octavio unbuttoned his shirt and pulled it apart to reveal his chest. Several tentacles squirmed beneath the skin of his pectoral muscles, excited by his lust and fear.

"You know what I am," he said to her. "Are you sure you want me to—"

Sheila crossed the span between them and locked her mouth over his. They collapsed onto the bed, pushing papers off as they grabbed one another. Octavio had no idea what the mass of tentacles that inhabited his body would do, but he was pleasantly surprised to find that they receded deeper inside as Sheila removed his clothing. Her fingers played across the skin of his back as he slid his thumbs across her nipples. She licked his face, neck, and ears. His fear evaporated as she guided him into her.

If she means to kill me, he thought, *then she can kill me. It will be worth it.*

Chapter 8
Oren's Choice

The yellow and red neon lights of the truck stop infiltrated every space of the parking lot. Minnesota's autumnal darkness, Victoria thought for the twenty-sixth time, was such an oppressive thing that even chemically manufactured lights were reassuring beacons. Andre sat beside her in silence. His eyes had blanked and refocused in rhythm with the signs on the road. He muttered to himself every few minutes.

"We're here," she said.

"Here..." he mumbled. "God, it's bright here."

Brenda pulled the Suburban into the space beside Victoria and climbed out, clutching a wad of bloody baby wipes. She stuffed them into a trash can and walked over to Victoria's truck.

Victoria rolled her window down.

"I've gotta get Kevin some clothes," Brenda said with an apologetic laugh. "His are all somewhere else. He's sitting in the front passenger seat with Amber's blanket spread over his junk."

Victoria didn't think she'd ever enjoy the changing

parlance of the English language, but she forced herself to smile and said, "OK, we'll go inside and get a table for six."

Brenda replied, "Tell them five and a half. Amber still needs a booster."

Suppressing an urge to glare at Brenda, Victoria turned to Andre. He stared at her with black eyes. The truck's cabin darkened and he intoned, "You'll have yours, but you must choose how much others pay for it."

The light snapped back.

"What are you staring at?" Andre asked.

Victoria shook her head and said, "Nothing. Let's go in and get the table. Brenda is getting Kevin some clothes."

"Oh, right," Andre said with a quick laugh. "He is kinda naked, huh?"

Brenda stood in front of a retail tandem loaded with various personal effects a truck driver might need. She had a Duck Dynasty t-shirt, a pair of sweat pants, and a package of socks in her hands already, but she was stuck at the underwear. Kevin wore boxers, but white briefs were the only thing available in the correct size. Brenda sighed and grabbed a three pack. She also bought a highly overpriced U of M hoodie and returned to the Suburban.

She nodded as she passed Victoria, Andre, and Craig on their way in. Craig looked like he'd been on a methamphetamine bender. Andre's eyes were dazed, despite his earlier gunslinger antics, which had been sharp and flawless. Tight bandages covered his left cheek. Victoria, the picture of calm self-possession, directed them toward the restaurant portion of the truck stop. Brenda's maternal instincts could not help blaming Victoria for what was happening to those kids, even though Kevin had insisted she had little to do with it.

When she got back to the Suburban she tossed the bag of clothes to Kevin and said, "The boys look awful."

"Yeah," Kevin replied as he tore open plastic bags. "They do."

Kevin grumbled about "tighty whiteys" as he struggled to dress in the front seat of the vehicle.

Amber chanted, "Tighty whitey! Tighty whitey!" until Brenda told her to hush. Kevin laughed at his daughter, which at once annoyed and thrilled Brenda. Laughter in the face of the current situation seemed inappropriate. But it was *his* laughter, something she had missed sorely over the last two months.

"Can we trust her?" Brenda asked as Kevin pulled the t-shirt over his head.

"Probably," he said, yanking the tag from the hoodie. "She can't lie when she's doing one of her readings, but she can otherwise. Still, from what I remember about her, she's a bit of a stuck up prude with an unreasonable sense of right and wrong."

"Readings?" Brenda asked. She enjoyed hearing Victoria described as a "stuck up prude".

"Yeah. Among other things, she's a fortune teller," he said. "The best. I got a reading from her in Washington, DC in 1984. I could quote you every line she said during the reading and it was very accurate."

Brenda frowned. "I was born in 1984."

"You know the first plumber guy from the other night?" Kevin asked as he tugged on his socks.

Brenda nodded.

"Like I said, that's my younger brother. We were in DC gathering information on some politician. Victoria is a high priority person to my father, so we knew she was in DC at the time. We booked a reading with her hoping she'd give us some leads. She lived in a huge house in Georgetown. Very tastefully decorated with contemporary paintings, except for this tacky lamp shaped like a cat. For whatever reason, I think of that cat whenever I think of her."

He waved his hand, as if dispelling the image of the lamp. "Anyway, she gave us the information we wanted and I tried to kill her to cover our tracks. I'll never forget it. I pulled a gun from my jacket and shot her point blank. When the bullet hit her, she exploded into glass shards. Somehow, right in front of us, she'd managed to replace herself with a mirror. We tore the house apart looking for her. Never found her. Nobody knew where she went until she surfaced in the Twin Cities four years ago."

He took her hand. "Brenda, for people like us, things always happen for a reason. Usually someone's reason, but sometimes for reasons that don't have any clear source. We call this a Confluence. You're Awake now. You're going to have to start seeing patterns and trying to connect them. I can see this pattern, and it points at Victoria. Trusting her is less important than finding out why she's at the center of this Confluence."

Brenda shook her head. Patterns in events. Confluence. This all seemed like a religious experience. The only time she'd ever gone to church was when her father died. The week after his funeral, her mother tried to take her back to that church. She'd thrown an enormous temper tantrum. As far as Brenda was concerned, churches were places you went when you died. She'd have to ask Andre how all this seemed to him. He was a Catholic.

"OK," she said. "I'll keep an eye out for patterns. I don't have to like Victoria, do I?"

Kevin laughed and released her hand. "No. You don't.

She's not a very likable person from what I can tell. To be fair to her, if you know the future, it's difficult to make human connections. Imagine if you knew when your daughter would die. That can't be a pleasant life to live." He pointed behind him with his thumb. "I have to get my shoes. I've got a pair in the back of the car."

Brenda felt a sudden sense of submersion, as if she were thrust backward in time. She and Kevin had conversations like this on a daily basis before he faked his death. They rarely fought. They just discussed problems out of existence. She missed those conversations more than she realized.

Kevin opened the back door to retrieve Amber. Brenda jerked her head around to make sure it was him.

Amber explained her toy, a small stuffed pig, to Kevin as he extracted her. "Pig has teef! And a mouf!"

Kevin said, "And ears and a nose."

"Uh huh," Amber said. "Like Daddy!"

Brenda stifled a surge of emotion and got out of the Suburban.

Victoria watched Brenda and her family come into the restaurant. Kevin was wearing navy sweat pants that clashed with his maroon hoodie and a pair of tan leather oxford shoes. She took a deep breath and a drink of hot tea. The alcohol had worn off, leaving a mild headache in its wake. She was exhausted.

Craig mumbled, "I can't believe he's really alive."

Andre turned to his friend and said, "Yeah. Pretty crazy."

Both were drinking coffee with more cream than was ethically acceptable.

Once she returned from the bathroom with a freshly diapered Amber, Brenda made a fuss of arranging the chairs around the circular table to accommodate her reach and control of the child. Victoria sipped her tea and used meditation techniques to achieve patience.

Kevin said, "Well. I guess I was wrong about Sheila. Sorry about that. She shouldn't be a problem anymore."

Victoria eyed the rest of the dining room. It was populated with solitary truck drivers, all of whom were glued to their smart phones or laptops. She set her cup down and said, "I assume her fate and that of the other one of your kind that attacked me are the same."

Brenda looked at her and frowned.

"Yeah," Kevin said, picking up a menu. "So… you had a personal run in with Number 9?"

"He called himself Daniel," Victoria replied. "Now, I believe he's become a person named Kimm Peters."

Kevin nodded and said, "Brenda can make us do what she wants, but it isn't exact. Somehow, she interferes with the way our genes interact with our programming. We're creatures of flux. Whatever she does twists the way we change. I don't understand it, to be honest."

Victoria touched the back of Kevin's hand with her fingertips. He was prepared for this, so the amount of information she could pull from him was limited. She would only get what he wanted her to know. So. DC. That was an interesting connection. He wasn't sorry for what he'd done then, any more than he was sorry for anything he'd ever done. But he was a different creature now. Like his brother when she'd grabbed his arm in the hotel room. Totally different beings. This was a moral train wreck. She released his hand.

Brenda leaned forward, eyeing the exchange with a flat facial expression. Victoria turned to her and said, "This must be very troubling for you."

Brenda only nodded. The woman was vexing, but she was neither stupid nor weak.

Craig and Andre held their cups of coffee in both hands like shields against the rest of the table. Amber was busy scribbling on the kid's menu with broken red crayons.

Victoria felt that she was supposed to take the lead here, but she waited until the server had come and gone with their order to do so.

"I have a vested interest in Clarence Elpis," she began. "I believe that his corporeal body is that of my son."

Kevin dropped his menu.

She continued, "My son is lost, but Craig claims that the creature inside him, this Elpis, has plans to breed a new race of... creatures."

Craig nodded behind his coffee cup.

"Perhaps, Kevin," Victoria said, "you can enlighten us."

Kevin cleared his throat and bunched his thick eyebrows together. He said, "Well, I've been out of the loop for four years, but I was never aware of anything like that. Clarence is the kind of man who has an enormous, ambitious vision. The inner workings of Elpis Enterprises' management team are very secretive. The charity arm of things, The Elpis Foundation, is even more cloaked. I did most of my work under that organization. Still, even when I was doing horrible things, I always thought he did what he did for some broader good. I wasn't really made to consider moral implications. Whatever he's doing, he believes in it."

Craig said, "I think he wants to replace humanity. At least those of us who aren't Awake yet. He thinks it's the only hope for our species, but there's something else, too. It's not all altruistic."

"But why does he want Amber?" Brenda demanded.

Craig retreated behind his coffee cup and said, "I don't

know. I didn't ask him."

"He is dying," Victoria said. "I believe he needs a new body. If I understand your kind, Kevin, and I think I'm beginning to, you cannot reproduce. Amber is an anomaly. Something that should not happen. She would be of great value to a creature looking for a new host. Are you certain Amber is your daughter?"

Kevin grimaced and said, "At first I doubted it." He shrugged apologetically to Brenda and continued, "But yes, she is definitely my daughter. I don't even have the correct genes to make a heart, or the occipital lobe of a brain. Also, I was made sterile. I have no idea how this happened, except that Brenda wanted to have a child so much that she changed me to make it possible."

"Well," Victoria said, "I don't know exactly what Elpis could want from Amber, but I will say that your brother suffered the same fate as you as far as becoming reproductive goes."

Andre exclaimed, "It's too soon! How do you know?"

She smiled at him. "I know."

Craig, who blinked several times before realizing the implication, said, "Oh, God. You know, he could do it to you again, Victoria. Elpis could—"

Victoria dismissed this with a wave of her hand. "No. No he couldn't. You have to make bargains with creatures like him. There is no bargain, not even the fate of the entire world, that would convince me to make that deal again."

"What about this 'Hope' thing?" Brenda asked Craig. "What did you mean by that?"

Craig looked into his coffee cup. He said, "Well, I was thinking about this box that Andre saw in some vision, and about the Greek words I kept yelling in my dream—that's how Elpis got into me—and then I thought about Pandora.

Hope was the last thing in the box of evil the gods gave her. So this Elpis person thinks he's Hope, even though that deity was female in the original Greek. He may even be Hope. I dunno. Ask Victoria about that stuff. I'm just remembering what I read in junior high, mostly."

"Andre has visions," Brenda whispered, looking at him.

Andre withered under her stare and raised his eyebrows as if to say, "Sure, why not?"

"I have no idea what that box is," Victoria sad. "I'm not prone to believing in grand mythological tales. Most events have much simpler sources. However, Craig's logic is admirable. We'll find out more when we go back and retrieve the box, providing it is still where I left it in 1937."

"It is," Andre said.

Their food arrived. The server, carrying a large tray, tried to be friendly and congenial. Amber gave him some satisfaction, but the rest of the table ignored him. He refilled everyone's drinks and brought Victoria a fresh pot of hot water and new tea bags. She made a mental note to tip him well as he said, "Well, I'll be back in a few to check on you guys. Enjoy your meal!"

After they finished eating, Craig and Andre excused themselves to the parking lot. Andre didn't usually smoke cigarettes, but he'd left his dugout at home. Smoking something was better than smoking nothing at the moment. Craig leaned heavily on the brick wall of the truck stop's dumpster enclosure.

"You know," Andre said after lighting the cigarette, "it feels like two days ago was years ago."

"Yeah," Craig said. He took a deep drag and exhaled it. The air was chilly, so the condensation from his breath coupled with the smoke to form an impressive cloud. "I need to sleep soon. Like, really sleep. For maybe a week."

"Good luck with that, man," Andre said. "This is like that time we went to Bemidji and got wasted at Winton's grandparent's cabin for three days. I think I slept two hours that whole time."

Craig barked a laugh. "Yeah, you kept going all paranoid. 'The locals are gonna get me! I'm black in the heart of KKK country!' I think the neighbor's daughter would've fucked you if you hadn't gone all Malcom X on her."

Andre smiled. He'd eaten half a bag of mushrooms and drank half a bottle of whiskey the first night. He said, "Winton still hasn't forgiven you for peeing on the neighbor's propane tank. The wife was so pissed when she caught you, and you just turned around mid-stream all like 'What?' "

They joked about rednecks and dicks for a few minutes. Then Craig got very quiet and lit another cigarette.

"Look," Craig said. "I gotta figure this out. The next time Elpis takes ahold of my mind, I won't be able to stop him. I made a deal. I can delay things, but I can't stop them."

Andre folded into himself. He didn't have the foggiest notion about what Craig should do. He suspected that if he wasn't "Waking Up" himself, he'd have abandoned the entire situation. He hated himself a little bit for thinking that. Kevin had called what he'd done in the park heroic, but thinking about shooting at those men made him nauseous. "I dunno," he said. "Maybe Victoria and Kevin and Brenda can figure it out. I feel like a tourist in Japan right now."

Craig nodded and handed him another cigarette. "It's on me, you know," he said. "Even if they figure it out. It's on me."

Andre lit the cigarette and looked Craig in the eyes, which

was much harder than he thought it would be. "Yeah," he said. "I know."

When they got back inside, Victoria had the laptop she'd grabbed from the hotel room open on the table. Kevin stared at it with a stumped expression. Andre glanced at the screen, which was black except for a small white box that asked for a password.

"I have no idea what password he might be using," Kevin said. "And I know nothing about what my brother might have locked up in this thing. This is a dead end right now."

He closed the laptop.

Andre and Craig looked at each other. Andre turned to Victoria. "You know," he said. "Winton's a computer nerd of the highest order. We could call him."

Victoria tapped her lips with her fingers. "We may do that. Tomorrow. Right now, we all need to sleep. I have a cabin north of Pine City that should be safe for the night."

"Sleep!" Craig said with unfeigned enthusiasm.

"Sleep!" Amber mimicked, holding aloft a fork, her face covered in soft serve ice cream.

Kevin was propped up by pillows in the bed he, Brenda, and Amber had been assigned in one of the two bedrooms of Victoria's cabin. His face glowed in the light of his smart phone. Brenda was asleep and Amber snored between them. He and Brenda would have preferred to have this night to themselves, but the situation hardly called for it. Victoria had taken the other bedroom and the boys were upstairs in the loft.

The cabin was situated on Chill Lake, ten minutes northeast of Pine City. There was something odd about the lake. Kevin could sense a presence there, but couldn't discern any details. Witches often located themselves with strategic purpose, so whatever it was must serve Victoria in some capacity. It wasn't powerful enough to cause him great concern.

The cabin was built from notched pine logs. Four windows took up most of the wall facing the lake, and even in the darkness they provided a spectacular view. The interior décor could have been transplanted directly from the 1920s. Handmade quilts hung on the pine walls next to tastefully framed, authentic period posters from stage shows in Chicago, New York, and Paris. The only disturbing feature was the cat lamp, which stood on an oak desk in the living room. It was as jarring in the context of the cabin as it had been in the Georgetown mansion.

Kevin scrolled through his contact list to the entry assigned to Number 7. He changed the contact name to "Sheila Barnstock". Both he and The Elpis Foundation were familiar with that identity. Bad luck for her on that account. Vanishing would be very hard for her to do. But did she really want to vanish anymore? He wasn't sure. Her changes would not follow the same pattern as his own. Brenda had been a continual presence in his life while he underwent the physical, emotional, and mental transformation that solidified Kevin Jones. Sheila was alone. He had no idea how she'd handle it.

More importantly, Kevin wondered if she could be of some help in this situation. She was a trove of information about Clarence and the Elpis organizations. Craig's description of Clarence's plans was disturbing. For all his ruthless ambition, Clarence had always maintained a strong sense of humanity. To want to destroy and replace people did not fit with the man Kevin knew.

Kevin pursed his lips and stared at the phone's screen

until it went dark. He sunk down into the blankets and put his arm around his daughter, who moaned but didn't wake. He kept the phone in his other hand.

Octavio stared at the ceiling of the hotel room at Le Méridien. Light from the window passed through the shades, casting fuzzy, orange shadows on the ceiling. Sheila slept with her head on his chest and a hand on his belly. Her breathing was steady and endearing. Occasionally, one of his tentacles would reach up and tap the subsurface of his skin where her face or fingers lay, then recede. She didn't notice.

He was exhilarated. He'd always been attracted to Number 7's icy personality, but he'd seen her in her true form more often than in a human one, so the attraction remained muted. Right now, he was a school boy in love or lust with her, which was about the most dangerous thing on earth to be. She was mentally unstable. She may wake up and eat him. She may also wake up and kiss him, which was why he was still in bed with her.

From the table beside the bed came the sharp, repeated chirp of a smart phone. Sheila didn't move and her breathing remained steady. He picked up the phone and looked at the screen. It said, "Incoming: One."

Octavio answered the phone but did not speak.

"Hello?" someone whispered. "Sheila? We need to talk. Sheila?"

Octavio hung up the phone and replaced it on the night stand.

He considered the implications of the phone call. She had Number 1's phone number in her contact list, which meant they kept up some kind of regular communication. That phone was not a Foundation issued device. What, he wondered, had happened to Number 1? Something similar to what had happened to Sheila today. She'd mentioned something about Number 1's wife doing it. Maybe his wife was like Victoria, a witch of some sort. Perhaps Sheila could clarify this mess when she woke up. If she didn't kill him first. He'd already sent a status report back to Clarence with his phone, leaving out any contact with Sheila. That should buy him enough time to figure out what was going on.

Like it had every time he tried to sleep for the last two years, his mind drifted back to Tulsa and his childhood. He hadn't had any contact with his family since coming back from Afghanistan. They thought he was dead, according to Clarence. His death had surely hurt them, but he didn't feel like the Octavio that they knew was alive anymore, anyway.

His father had died in a farm accident when he was thirteen. He was a first generation immigrant with a brilliant knack for repairing expensive farming equipment. Octavio's first thirteen years on the planet were happy ones. He attended a private Catholic school with his older sisters. Both of them excelled academically and socially, which paved a path for him. The only significant mar he could recall from this period was his mother's miscarriage when he was seven. The procedure that saved her life and ended the prenatal life of his brother left her barren. A sadness descended on her.

That sadness deepened into a full scale emotional retreat when a tractor jack failed and Octavio's father was crushed. It happened the week after Octavio's thirteenth birthday. His own reaction had been confusion and anger, but it was directionless. His father worked seventy hours a week, so he had not been a central figure in Octavio's life the way his mother had been. In retrospect, he believed he had been hurt more by his mother's emotional distance than the death of his father.

After his father's death, he decided to become a Marine, modeling himself after his maternal uncle, a decorated veteran from the first Gulf War. His mother disapproved, citing the horror of war and his role as the last man in the family. To make her happy, he'd gone to Rogers State University for two years after high school. He earned an associate's degree in criminal justice. However, instead of furthering his studies or getting a job with a police department, he enlisted with the Marines and found himself in Afghanistan six months later.

The two years he spent in Afghanistan were sealed inside him in a place he was not prepared to open tonight. Why was he alive when so many others who'd been mutilated did not have the opportunity to just "Wake Up"? It was an impossible question to answer.

As he thought before, perhaps he'd made the wrong choice when given that opportunity. There was a price. His promise to Elpis was only the beginning. When the dormant part of his body had burst from his burned chest in Elpis's lab, the fine print of their deal grew large. Flesh eating tentacles were not what Octavio considered a restoration to "better than before," though he had grown accustomed to them.

Elpis had been a brilliant guide through the process of his Awakening, giving him a purpose and a reason to exist. He felt good about the work he'd done with the kids at The Foundation. But the nagging feeling that he should have died would not abate. Like tonight, it kept him from sleep, gnawing at the sides of his mind.

Then there was the promise itself. The clarity of the moment he had made that promise would not leave him. It had been a beacon in his life until he'd stared at the stars over that lake in northern Minnesota last month. His course away from that promise was set, even if he was still tied to it.

'Help me defeat the cancer that is killing me,' Elpis had said.

It had been an easy promise to make, and he found it difficult to fault the promise itself. The fact that he'd been able to help Elpis stall the cancer had been one of the main points of his continued existence. So why then did he want out of the arrangement so badly? How could he resolve this promise with the decision he'd made at the side of the lake a month ago?

Octavio struggled with his internal dilemma for another thirty minutes before drifting off. As soon as his breathing steadied and his muscles relaxed, Sheila's eyes snapped open. A sharp, lean smile spread across her face.

Kevin waited at the table in the breakfast nook for Andre to finish in the bathroom. He had to urinate so bad that he considered the Maple tree in the yard.

"What is that cat lamp all about, Victoria?" he asked.

Victoria looked up from the eggs she was beating in a large bowl near the oven. She and Brenda were doing their best to bond over cooking, a passion they both shared.

"It was a gift from my mother," she said.

"Where do you keep the garlic powder?" Brenda asked.

"Third cabinet past the sink," Victoria replied.

"It seems out of place," Kevin said. "I thought so in DC, too. Where did your mother get it?"

"Wow," Brenda said, examining a glass jar. "You grind your own garlic powder. Is there anything in this kitchen you didn't grow yourself?"

"Very little," Victoria said. She turned to Kevin, "I have no idea. She worked for a carnival for several years before she died. That cat was the carnival's mascot. They painted it on the trucks that carried the equipment and made stuffed animals of it for midway prizes. The lamp was part of that kitsch. I've never liked it, but I can't bring myself to part with it." She shrugged. "It was a gift."

Amber brought her stuffed pig over to Kevin and handed it to him. "He b'oke," she declared.

"I see," Kevin said, turning the pig over in his hand. "Looks like his bones are broken."

"Fix them! Fix them!" Amber shouted.

"Keep your voice down," Brenda said.

"Please," Amber whispered.

Kevin shook the toy and smashed it between both hands. "There," he said, handing it back to her. "It's all better, now."

Amber smiled, hugged the pig, and bounded back into the living room, where she had been watching a video on her mother's tablet computer.

Craig slogged down the stairs of the loft.

"'Mornin', everyone," he said. He flopped onto the bench across from Kevin.

"You look like a ghost," Kevin said.

"Yeah, I feel like one, too," Craig said.

"Well, get in line for the bathroom. I'm after Andre, if he ever gets done."

Craig barked a short laugh. "You might as well start reading *War and Peace* or something. He's worse than a girl."

Brenda shot him an exasperated look, which he didn't notice.

Andre stepped out of the bathroom. "All yours," he said

to Kevin.

"Thanks," Kevin said.

As he stood, the TV in the living room clicked on with a static squeal.

A female voice reported over images of the Minneapolis skyline. "Sources at CNN have confirmed that there were five bodies found in a dumpster in Minneapolis yesterday morning. Police are not releasing an official statement and there is no word yet on the identities of the victims. A press conference is planned for 3:00 p.m. today…" The camera switched to a shot of an alleyway dumpster which was quarantined by police tape. Several police cars were visible in the shot.

"Oh, shit," Craig said. "How in the hell did they end up in the dumpster?"

Andre looked right at Kevin, but didn't say anything.

Kevin asked, "Why did the TV just come on?"

"Victoria has a bunch of stuff like this," Craig said, waving his hand.

Victoria said, "I like to remain informed of events that concern me. It looks like Craig and Andre's friends have made national news."

"Police are calling for footage from nearby security cameras and anyone who might have information about this crime is asked to call…" the TV continued.

Kevin sighed. He'd been very careful in the disposal of the bodies, so nothing should trace back to him. The same couldn't be said of Craig and Andre, who had both been with the group before they were murdered. In retrospect, he should have dumped the bodies in the river. However, he'd wanted them to be found, for the sake of those kids' families. Such sentimental actions always came with a price. He hoped that Craig and Andre wouldn't pay the price for this one.

"I wouldn't worry about this too much," Victoria said to the boys, who were frowning at the TV. "The police may link you to the murders, but you didn't kill them and it will be very difficult to prove that you did."

Andre snorted, "At least it's the white kid's number on their cell phones. If it was mine, I don't think my innocence would be quite enough."

Craig's voice was shaky and he said, "I feel like, you know, if I hadn't called them, they'd still be alive. God, I've fucked up everything."

Andre said, "Well, you saved my ass that night, so you aren't all bad."

Kevin reached out and took ahold of Craig's shoulder. He pulled him up to a standing a position. "Craig, I need you to hold it together right now. Look at me."

Craig lifted his eyes from the floor.

"You can handle this, Craig. Relax. Breathe. Let go of your friends. You can mourn them later and you can cry if you need to, but you're going to have to stay strong right now. We need you to stay strong."

Tears leaked down Craig's face, but he kept his eyes on Kevin's. "OK," he said, his voice breaking. "I—I'll get my shit together."

"Good," Kevin said and pulled Craig into a hug. Craig sobbed into his chest. Kevin patted his back, the same way he did with Amber when she was injured or having a meltdown.

When Kevin released Craig, he slumped back into the bench seat of the nook. He stared at the TV screen, which had turned itself off once the report ended.

"Breakfast will be ready in about fifteen," Brenda said. "These omelets are going to be phenomenal."

"I may not be done peeing by then," Kevin said.

"TMI, honey," she said.

After finishing with the toilet, Kevin spent a few minutes in front of the sink scrubbing flecks of blood out of his hair and beard. He was dressed in the same clothing he'd been wearing the night before and it smelled of stale sweat. He needed to go by the studio apartment he'd rented in Frogtown to gather his clothes and a few other things.

Breakfast was indeed phenomenal. Brenda had gone to the grocery store and bought eggs, fresh vegetables, and bacon. She and Victoria made omelets that could have been on a cooking show. After breakfast, the mood in the cabin improved. Good food was, apparently, a morale booster.

As Andre began loading the dishwasher, Kevin's phone rang. He fumbled it out of the pocket of his hoodie. Sheila Barnstock. He looked around the room. Everyone was staring at him. None of their phones worked here. He considered taking the call in the bedroom, but instead answered it.

"Hello," he said.

"Hello, big brother," Sheila replied. "I noticed I missed a call from you last night. And you didn't leave a message..."

"Yeah," Kevin said. "I was concerned about you. I've been through, uh, the kind of change... you know, that you're probably having right now."

"Oh, I'm fine," she said. "How sweet of you to care. I actually have a favor to ask of you."

"A favor?" he said.

"Yeah," she replied. "I need to know what in the hell is going on with Number 9. I think he's off his rocker and like you, I'm concerned for him." She laughed. "We are, after all, family. Aren't we?"

"Who answered your phone last night, Sheila?" he asked,

ignoring her request for the moment.

"Oh, you don't know him. After your time. A very nice boy, though. I think you'd like him. What's left of him, anyway." Her tone of voice was playful, teasing. She had never, ever been like this before. She was definitely not fine.

"Look," he said, "I don't know what's going on with Number 9 right now. It's the same as you and me. Brenda hit him hard. Really hard."

"Well," Sheila said, "I bet Victoria knows."

Kevin didn't like the direction this conversation was going, so he changed it. "Sheila, what's Clarence up to right now? From what I've heard, he's gone a bit off the rails."

Sheila laughed again. "Oh, he's been off the rails for about two years. It's a miracle the place hasn't fallen down around him. He has an acute case of leukemia and it's killing him. I'll tell you what, *Kevin*, I'd be happy to tell you all about Clarence, but I really need to talk to Number 9. So give the phone to Victoria for a few minutes and then we'll gossip about Dad as long as you want."

Kevin turned to Victoria and said, "She wants to talk to you."

Victoria nodded, so he handed her the phone.

"Hello, Sheila," Victoria said.

"Oh, hi, Vicky," Sheila said. "I was just wondering who my brother had recently become. I figured you might have a line on that, since you were trying to kill him and all."

"Why do you need to know that, Sheila?" Victoria asked.

"It's family business, dear, and I'm not all that interested in gossiping with *you*. I will say this, though, since you seem to have developed a fondness for him, despite what he did to you—I could smell his stink on you even past the lavender soap, sweetheart—I don't plan on hurting him. This is a family matter now that Kevin's wife has us all feeling real feelings and acting irrationally. Just tell me who he is. I can figure the rest out for myself."

"Kimm Peters," Victoria replied.

"Ah, that makes sense. Perfect, darling. Thank you so much. I owe you a favor someday."

Victoria said, "I will be in touch about that." She handed the phone back to Kevin.

Kevin said, "So what's Clarence up to? Why does he want Amber?"

"You already know why he wants Amber. Someone, specifically your wife, although he doesn't know that yet, has fiddled with one of his creations, and now you've gone all reproductive. You know how he likes happy accidents. Hmmm. I wonder if I'll do the same... Number 9 certainly has. Anyway, Clarence has been sequestered in the R&D labs for the last couple of years trying to beat cancer. He can almost generate life from scratch, but this disease is beyond him. He's not handling it well. He's gone a bit loopy and the organization is more chaotic than you'd remember. Some of the Awakened have been eyeing his spot at the top and the politics are thickening. Number 10 is dead. Investors are starting to pry into The Foundation, which we all know leads to bad places. Typical supernatural corporate drama, I'm sure."

For a few moments after Sheila's monologue, Kevin stared out the windows of the cabin and deep into the blue space of the cloudless sky. He said, "Are they sending anyone else after us?"

"Oh, probably," she said. "I would, if I were them. I'd send people after all of us. That's one of the things I want to talk to Number 9 about. I suppose I should call him Kimm. I'm pretty sure he's absorbed that identity, just like I'm Sheila and you're Kevin. Stay in touch, Kevin. We're going to need each other soon."

"We should meet now," Kevin said.

Sheila laughed again. "No. Not now. Have Victoria do a card reading for you. Maybe she'll be able to work out the Confluence. Now I've got to go. I've eaten more than my own body weight today and I'm still starving."

"Be careful about that," Kevin warned.

"Oh, you know me, big brother," she said and hung up the phone.

That wasn't true at all. He had no idea who she was anymore.

Kimm sat in his office, satisfied with the balance sheets he just finished calculating. An adding machine sat on his right and spat out a ribbon of paper that curled across his desk and cascaded over the other side. This ledger book contained records going back to the opening day of Kimm's Auto World. The numerals he wrote on the pages today were distinctly neater than those in previous entries. What entries existed were haphazard, sloppy, and didn't balance out. Entire weeks were missing. The overall picture was still as red as a ripe tomato, but at least now it was becoming an organized financial disaster. He looked up at Oren, who was sorting sales documentation at the filing cabinet.

"How's it going over there?" he said cheerily.

"Bad," Oren said. "You don't have any of the reconciliations for April. None. May is better. You really need to get all this into Quickbooks or Excel or something. I don't know how your accountant does your taxes."

Kimm didn't know either. His accountant, whose information he'd found on one of the cards in the rolodex on his desk, was a shady man in Apple Valley who worked out of his attic. The IRS would throw Kimm in jail if it ever audited him. Saving this business was probably not possible, but Kimm felt compelled to try. Oren was majoring in finance and had taken to the paperwork instinctively. He'd already pieced together the backup from Quarter 1 of this year and was deep into Quarter 2.

Kimm took the last piece of pizza from the box on his desk and stuffed it into his mouth. They'd ordered an extra-large meat-lovers for lunch. Oren had eaten only one piece. Kimm was becoming concerned about his appetite. It was growing sharper. Almost painful.

Foot traffic in the dealership was slow for a Saturday. From what Kimm could tell, this had been the case for some time. He hadn't been keeping regular hours and the inventory hadn't been updated in almost a month. The vehicles sitting on the lot were all leveraged and didn't have much consumer value. There was an auto auction in Hastings on Tuesday that he planned to attend to spruce up inventory. He had a pile of cash from his blurry previous life that he could use to buy the new inventory outright. If he handled that correctly, he might be able to limp through Quarter 4 and still pay the electric bills.

"Aha!" Oren said, holding up a manila folder. "Most of April was filed with August. 'A' confusion, I suppose..." He buried his head back in the cabinet, apparently energized by the idea that there may be more missing links hidden in the wrong place.

As Oren leaned forward, Kimm couldn't help but notice the slab of his latissimus dorsi muscle. Oren was in great shape and there was a huge hunk of meat stretching from his deltoid to his lower back. In fact, his entire body was quite muscular. Very little fat, but he was still young. Supple.

Saliva began to drip from Kimm's mouth and he felt a familiar release. Something was wrong, but something was so very right, too. He was hungry, and there was this meal crouched across the room, oblivious and exposed. His teeth moved forward, tingling as they sharpened. His muscles expanded, tearing at the fabric of his suit. His fingernails lengthened, sharpening into perfect carving knives. He crawled onto his desk, careful not to disturb the prey. He just needed to position himself for a leap and he could tear out that boy's throat with—

"Kimm!" a commanding female voice shouted from the door of the office.

Kimm snarled and turned his attention to the door, where a blond woman and a one-armed Hispanic man stood. Where had they come from? No matter. More meat. The boy was on his back now, screaming and pointing at him, so the element of surprise was lost. That didn't matter, either. Now he had three meals. Saliva pooled on the desk beneath him. He lunged toward the woman, since she would be the weakest.

As he flew forward, she burst into a black furred, monstrous form. She caught his arm and threw him sideways. He landed on all fours and growled. Her sudden change and unexpected strength enraged him. He swung his claws in blind anger, but they slid off of green discs that spotted her flesh. She handled him like a child, twisting both his arms behind him and pointing his snapping jaws into the air. He growled in rage. How could this be happening?

"Kimm," she said. "Kimm. Look at him, Kimm. Look at him."

The blind rage subsided as she spoke and he realized he was face to face with the boy who should have been his meal. The Hispanic man held the boy with his one arm so that his face was just out of reach. That boy should have been inside him. That boy, all that meat, all those bones, that boy was... that boy was crying. That boy was his son.

"Oh, God, Oren!" Kimm cried, his body shrinking and folding into itself. "I'm so sorry."

The monster woman released his arms.

Oren's terrified eyes were wide and streaming. A ribbon of snot hung from his nose and clung to his upper lip.

Kimm reached out and grabbed his face with both hands. "Oren, I promise I'll never hurt you!"

A calm, powerful feeling surged through him. Kimm wiped the snot away from his son's nose and the tears from his eyes. "I will never, ever hurt you. I love you, Oren. I love you."

Oren blinked. Confusion was writ large upon his face, but he said, "I love you too, Dad."

The Hispanic man released Oren and he fell into Kimm's arms. Kimm clutched his son. The only thing holding him to the earth was Oren. His hunger was gone. In its place was the solid understanding that he would do anything—*anything*—to protect his son.

Octavio leaned against the closed door of the office as Sheila and Number 9 discussed what had just happened. Sheila had warned him on the way over that Number 9 was unstable and that they'd find a mess or a very dangerous situation when they arrived. He was still stunned by the timing. Had they arrived seconds later that kid would be dead. Had they chosen to go to Kimm's house instead of the car dealership, that kid would be dead. Such slim margins made him queasy, but he kept his exterior calm.

Oren was sorting through the paperwork he had thrown

when Number 9 attacked. He cast confused glances towards the man he thought was his father. He was just a normal kid. Why in the hell did Number 9 bring him into the situation? Becoming Kimm Peters must have scuttled his judgment.

"What if it happens again?" Kimm said to Sheila. He sat on his desk, slumped forward with his hands dangling between his knees. He hadn't gone through a full transformation, so his clothing was torn at the seams but not destroyed.

"It shouldn't," Sheila answered. She was pacing the room, repairing her torn clothing. She tied the tattered garments to look like they were supposed to be that way. Her spandex sports underwear had survived the transformation. She'd fit right in at a punk rock concert. "The same thing happened to me this morning," she continued, "and I suspect something similar happened to Kevin. If you choose wisely when the opportunity presents itself, the hunger just goes away. I'm starting to get the hang of what Brenda did to us."

She smiled at Octavio, who nodded. The same thing had indeed happened to her. She managed to eat his entire right arm before coming to her senses. She wouldn't have stopped if he hadn't punctured her left side with his tentacles, breaking her hunger rage. He'd almost killed her in confusion and pain. Self-control was not high on his priority list when he awoke with his arm lodged in a monster's jaws. He was lucky she hadn't started with something more vital, although he was sick of having his arm torn off. That seemed to be happening every time he came to Minnesota.

Kimm stared at Octavio for a moment. "I know I know you, but I can't remember who you are."

Octavio said, "Well, I'm glad you don't remember me. We didn't get on well."

Oren said, "Uh, Dad, I've got Quarter 3 wrapped up.

What should I do next?" He stood with a stack of folders in his trembling hands.

"Sit down, Oren," Kimm said, gesturing to the rolling chair in front of his desk. "I didn't think you'd get involved in all this... but now you are. By the way, this is Sheila, my sister. I have no idea who the Hispanic guy is, but I apparently don't like him."

Octavio laughed and said, "My name is Octavio. Sorry for handling you so rough, but it was necessary."

Sheila beamed at Oren and said, "You know, that makes me your aunt. I *love* the idea of being an aunt."

Oren sat down and stared at her like she was a rattlesnake.

"You'll probably want to avoid any further contact with me," Kimm said with a hollow voice. "I may or may not be as dangerous as I just was anymore, but my past is. I'm sorry I ever got you involved. I'm not thinking very clearly right now."

He looked at Sheila and said, "Sheila, can you, you know, take care of him. If he sleeps hard enough, he'll think it was all a dream. I seem to have forgotten how to use many of my abilities at the moment."

Oren cleared his throat and stood up. "You aren't my dad at all, are you?"

Sheila stopped pacing.

Kimm took a deep breath. "I suppose not," he said.

"I knew this was too good to be true," Oren said. He set the stack of folders on the desk next to Kimm. "When I told Mom that you were giving me a job, she said, 'Don't get your hopes up. A tiger doesn't change his stripes.' I really wanted..." His voice broke and he cleared his throat again. "I really wanted it to be true. Now I feel like a fool. Who are you, then?"

Kimm pursed his lips and sighed. "I'm Kimm Peters. I

can't be anything else anymore. I'm not your father, though. He's dead. I just picked up where he left off."

Oren fell back into the rolling chair and stared into space.

"I thought—" Kimm began.

"Can you do it?" Oren interrupted.

"Can I do what?" Kimm asked.

"Can you be my dad?" he said.

Kimm's eyes widened. "I don't know, Oren. I thought I could. I really wanted to."

"Well, that makes you better than my dad, then. He never wanted to be my dad. I don't know what he ever wanted. He was a prick. I'm glad he's dead. I'm glad you killed him. I know you did. I can tell." Oren's voice began shaking. "You can't just kick me out, now. You can't just kill my dad and turn into him and then tell me to get lost, or go to sleep and think it was all a dream, or whatever. OK? Do you get it? You have to tell me about this." He gestured wildly at Sheila and Octavio. "I wanna know who my aunt is. I wanna know who that guy is. I want to know! I want *you* to be my dad." He was crying again, but he kept talking. "I—I—You *are* my dad! OK? Dad?"

Kimm started to climb off the desk, but Sheila put her hand up. She walked over to Oren and ran her fingers through his short hair.

"He can do it, Oren," she said. "I promise. And I'm going to show you and your dad what I showed Octavio this morning. It's the way we can all be free. It's a long shot, but we can do it. You're part of it now. You're part of our family." She took his hand in hers, pulled him out of the chair, and led him to the desk.

Octavio locked the door and joined them. This situation caused a dull ache in his chest. His own family had been the center of his universe until two years ago. His throat was tight and he knew that if he blinked tears would fall from both of his eyes. Thoughts of his mother and sisters swam through his mind, along with precious memories of his nieces and nephews. They would be so much bigger now…

There was a tear-away calendar on the desk. The month showing was June. Sheila ripped the top sheet off and flipped it over. She pulled a tube of lipstick out of her purse and twisted it until half an inch protruded from the base. She began drawing, her hand moving with confident strokes. She spoke as she worked.

"Last night, after Kevin's wife hit me with whatever magic she has, I came back to the hotel room and drew all over myself with makeup. At first I thought I'd just lost my mind, but when I looked at myself in the mirror afterwards, I understood. It's a Confluence."

She had drawn a spiral, like a sea shell, but impossibly complicated. Various lines intersected and overlapped, pulling the eye to the center of the spiral and out again. The drawing was an optical illusion. She had drawn the same shape on notebook paper with a pen this morning. Octavio had no idea how Sheila managed to make lipstick replicate it on the back of the calendar sheet. Her artistic talent was impressive. He hadn't seen anything like it on her naked body last night, but he had been looking at other things at the time.

"Each line," Sheila continued, "is one of us." She pointed out a short, squiggled line. "This is you, Oren. This one is me. This is your dad. This is Octavio. These lines are others that are involved." She looked at Kimm. "Victoria, Kevin, Brenda, Amber, the boys from yesterday. There are others, but I don't know who they are yet."

Octavio's line was the straightest in the drawing, spanning its far edge and running to the center. He was familiar with magical Confluences that bound events and people together for periods of time. According to Clarence, a Confluence had brought him and Octavio together so that neither would die. Octavio had never before seen anything like this used to describe them, though.

Sheila looked at each of them in turn. "The center is Clarence Elpis. There is a lot of space for him. I don't have any clue what happens in that space, but everything else is lined out well. If we can follow this pattern, we can get out of this." She looked at Oren. "Kimm can be your dad. Amber can grow up. I can be free. It's all here. But we have to follow this closely from now on. Are you ready for something like this Oren? If you aren't, I can make you sleep and forget everything that just happened. Your line will vanish from this drawing and the others will move to fill the void."

Oren looked at Kimm and back at the drawing. "I can see it," he said. "If that line is me, and that line is Dad, then I have to go almost to the center with him, right?"

Sheila nodded. "Yes, you do."

"And then I'm with some other people for a short time, and then I'm back with him?"

Sheila nodded.

"OK," he said. "Well, I'm going to need to know what's really going on then, huh?"

Sheila smiled at him. "You're going to be a great nephew," she said.

Kimm smiled with such intensity that Octavio found himself smiling, too.

Loco, he thought. *Loco*.

Chapter 9
The Reading

"So," Victoria said, crossing her hands on the table of the breakfast nook, "Sheila thinks I should do a reading…"

"Yeah," Kevin said. He sat across from her, staring at the cat lamp. Victoria wondered about his fascination with it.

"I think she's figured out the Confluence," he said, "but she seems to think you can unravel more. I'm not sure why."

Amber played a make believe game in the living room with Craig and Andre. The boys were princesses locked in a tower and she was either a dragon or a knight, depending on the moment.

Victoria tapped her lips with her fingers. "A reading might be the best way to map a way forward, unless you know what we should do next. My plans were inadequate for this situation."

Kevin barked a laugh. "I have no idea what to do. My plans were even worse than yours."

Brenda sat down in the nook next to Kevin. "What can you learn from these… readings, Victoria?"

"I never know until the cards turn," she replied. "I'm often not happy with the information I gather when it relates to myself. And we're in the middle of a powerful Confluence. This reading will be difficult. I'll need time to prepare."

"Anything I can do to help?" Brenda asked.

"No," Victoria said.

Victoria spent the rest of the day preparing the cabin for the reading. She melted new candles from hog tallow, burned incense, rearranged furniture, and brewed multiple pots of tea.

Brenda and Kevin went to St Paul early in the afternoon to retrieve necessities from his Frogtown apartment. Victoria was surprised when Brenda asked her to watch Amber while they were away. For most of her life, Victoria had avoided children. But Amber was adorably inquisitive, asking Victoria questions like "How does you' lamp wo'k?" and "Whe'e do you keep magic?" Brenda mentioned that Amber was not this way with everyone, so Victoria agreed to watch her. The girl fell asleep on the couch, clutching her stuffed pig, an hour after her parents left.

The boys spent the day walking around the lake and smoking too many cigarettes. Andre complained about his mobile phone's lack of signal. Both here and at her house in Minneapolis, Victoria maintained a magical buffer that disabled recording technology and wireless transmission. At Kevin's request, she had allowed his phone to work. Exposure to the world at large was the most prominent danger facing the boys. Victoria had not been party to many Awakenings, but most had ended with the death of the Awakened. The rules were the rules, whether one understood them or not. Despite her warnings, the boys did not appreciate how delicate their existence had become.

As Victoria arranged mats on the floor of the living room, Andre and Craig opened the glass sliding door. The smell of cigarette smoke and autumn followed them in.

"There's a dead body in your lake," Andre said to Victoria. He smiled at Amber, who was smacking her lips in her sleep.

"Yes," she said. "And it will stay there."

Andre looked at Craig, who shrugged, took his jacket off, and fell onto the couch.

"She's not happy about it," Andre ventured. "She'd like to be exhumed and buried."

"I'm sure she would," Victoria replied as she placed pillows on each mat. "I'm also sure that if we exhumed her, she would go on to haunt and torture those she feels are responsible for putting her in the lake in the first place."

"According to her, they'd deserve it," Andre said.

"And that may be the case," Victoria said. "It may also be the case that she is mad and would haunt and torture anyone she came into contact with. The lake holds her prisoner because her bones remain at its bottom. If freed from the lake, she would become something quite powerful and terrible. She's been there for over one hundred years. Who would still be around for her to torture?"

Andre nodded.

Craig said, "So are there ghosts like her everywhere?"

"No," Victoria replied. "They are rare. It is old magic that holds such beings in this world. The contemporary world has little tolerance for such aberrations."

"She's not happy with you, either," Andre said to Victoria.

"I doubt she would be. I could free her. Instead, I steal the magic that her presence generates and use it for my own purposes. I built this cabin because she was here. She doesn't like me at all."

"I could free her, too," Andre said.

Victoria glared at him. He pursed his lips and bowed his

head. He knew as well as she did that the spirit in that lake was malevolent. The boundaries of his new abilities held hard lessons for him, but she wasn't going to let him do anything ridiculous while she was around.

"Craig, please go take a shower," Victoria said. "You smell like a wet dog and we all have to sit near you to do this reading. Andre, I want you to watch how I position the reading. It is a five point star. I, as the reader, will be seated in the North position. You should be on my right, since you have Sight. I expect this to be a very difficult reading. You will learn much from it."

Craig said, "I hope we all do," and sulked to the bathroom.

"We should get back to the cabin," Brenda said.

Kevin nodded, but continued to comb his fingers through her hair. They were in the back seat of the Suburban, naked and tangled together. The car seat was in the floor board. They'd already spent an hour having sex in Kevin's Frogtown apartment, but that hadn't satisfied either of them. Kevin pulled off of I-35 and parked behind a foreclosed farm house. He had been considering going for round three before she'd spoken. She was right, however. They should be getting back. Brenda sighed and curled her fingers through his chest hair.

"We could do one more quickie, though," she said.

They did, though it went longer than the word "quickie" implied. Kevin hadn't felt so buoyant in two months. In Brenda's arms, he floated above the nonsense of their predicament.

When they were dressed and back on the highway, he said, "Victoria's reading should clarify the situation. At least, it will help us make the right decisions to get out of this mess. Honestly, I have no idea what to do at this point."

Brenda stared into the sky, which was turning deep blue with the onset of dusk. "You know," she said, "I don't really expect you to know what to do. I just expect you to do something." She pulled her hair back into a pony tail with a purple hair tie. "I realized last night that nothing was going to be the same ever again. And I'm OK with that, I guess. There's nothing to do about it, you know? I want my job back. I want our life together back. But I can't have both. We're together now and we'll figure it out. I trust you."

Kevin's throat constricted. He swallowed and said, "I... Yeah. Yeah, we'll figure it out."

She reached across the seat and ran her fingers along his bearded jawline.

Craig and Andre were standing outside the cabin smoking when Kevin pulled into the driveway. Craig waved and flicked his cigarette into the yard. Andre glanced at them and returned to staring at the lake.

Kevin followed his gaze. Andre felt the presence in the lake as well. That boy had always been able to see details with extraordinary clarity. Waking Up was probably sharpening the focus on all sorts of things he had been unaware of before. He looked like a paranoid fugitive. Finding out the visible world was merely a slick surface concealing a bottomless pit never sat well in the beginning.

Brenda smiled at Kevin and squeezed his hand before gathering their things out of the back of the Suburban and going into the cabin. Kevin joined the boys and asked Craig for a cigarette. Craig handed him one with a quizzical look. Kevin had never smoked in front of him before.

"Got a light?" he asked.

Craig passed him a lighter. Kevin lit the cigarette, took a

long drag, and considered the lake.

"What's out there?" he asked Andre, passing the lighter back to Craig.

"Oh, just some crazy ghost lady who wants me to dig her bones out of the bottom of the lake," Andre replied, using one of his theatrical, casual voices. That kid should have been on a TV comedy show.

Kevin laughed. "I'd leave her there if I were you."

"Yeah, yeah, don't worry," Andre said. "Victoria already gave me the lecture."

"Andre says she's hot and naked," Craig said. "Why does he get to see hot naked chicks and I get to blip and malfunction?"

Kevin grimaced. "Why do I turn into an oversized dog and tear my clothes off?"

Andre and Craig laughed. Andre said, "You should totally wear spandex all the time. You could be a super hero." He cleared his throat and took on the voice of a newscaster. "Super Dog Man has saved the life of every orphan in the tri-state area. Details at ten."

"Yeah," Craig said, "and it would be a lot less embarrassing for us. Your dong is huge when you're all wolfed out. Makes us all feel inferior."

Andre doubled over laughing.

Kevin smiled and said, "I don't really do spandex. Chafes the hair."

"Why don't you have a tail?" Andre asked.

Kevin hadn't considered the idea before. "Not sure. I was made the way I am. I didn't choose it. Maybe I'd have gone for a tail if I could've."

Craig shook his head. "Naw, man, it would look dumb. You should get a cape if you wear spandex, though. Capes are awesome."

Andre flicked his cigarette butt into the yard and said, "We should all get capes. We're a bunch of superheroes now, aren't we?"

Kevin's smile faded. He shook his head. "We're not really superheroes, Andre. We're anomalies. There are rules for people like us. Rules that aren't written down anywhere, but still bind us. If we go around wearing red tights and saving the day, we'll get killed. There's only so much exposure to us that the world tolerates. That's why Victoria operates the way she does. Tarot card readers fit into the world in a way that doesn't expose her." He took a final drag from his cigarette, field stripped it, and put the butt in his pocket. "We don't have to hide, exactly, but we can't be out in the open, either. I don't think it was always like this, but I know it is now. I've watched several Awake humans burn themselves out through exposure. It's like the world just corrects itself around them and they end up dead. Be careful as you Awaken."

Andre sighed and said, "There goes my career as the next David Blaine. My options are getting more limited by the day."

Craig said, "And there goes my career as the fastest delivery service on earth."

Kevin narrowed his eyes and stared at Craig. "How are you feeling?"

"Terrible," Craig said. "I can walk around for a while, but I have to sit down every twenty minutes. My muscles are always on the verge of cramping. I won't be doing any super-heroic shit any time soon."

Kevin nodded. "Good, he said, then entered the cabin.

Inside, Brenda was changing Amber on the sofa. "Did she nap?" he asked the room in general after he'd hung his jacket on the rack by the sliding door.

Victoria replied, "Yes. She woke up an hour and a half ago."

Brenda said, "She actually asked Victoria to use the potty. Unfortunately, it was a little late for that." She nodded to Amber's bare bottom as she wrapped it in a fresh diaper.

"I'm not Mary Poppins," Victoria said. "When I checked her diaper, I thought it best to wait for you to return."

Kevin smiled at his daughter, who giggled in delight.

"She is," Victoria continued, "a very well behaved child."

"What else do have to say about her?" Kevin asked.

"Nothing, yet," Victoria said.

Kevin scowled at her.

Brenda said, "She's been through all the wellness checks and doctor's appointments. If there was anything missing in her, I think we'd know by now."

"It's not what might be missing that I wonder about," Kevin said.

Victoria touched her belly. "Trust me," she said. "I am as interested in her development as you are. I will tell you if anything becomes apparent to me. In the meantime, dinner is almost ready. Kevin, will you please call in the boys before they develop lung cancer."

I'm pretty sure that was a joke, Kevin thought.

Sitting at the dining room table with his family, Victoria, and the boys, Kevin could feel the Confluence surrounding them. The same Confluence twisted through them at the diner last night, but now it was much more powerful. Pulsing bands of invisible energy ebbed and flowed in intricate patterns, moving into and out of each one of them. Even Amber was wrapped in their coils.

The conversation was muted, except for Amber, who babbled away about how the ham she was eating had once been a pig, but not her toy pig, and the carrots had once been buried in the ground. Brenda told her to "hush and eat" several times.

No one mentioned Victoria's impending reading. Kevin hoped that the cards would provide a path that could get them all out of this mess. Victoria was impeccable at her craft. Perhaps she could tease out some unexpected piece of information that would help. They desperately needed it.

Andre stared into the fire place, watching the flames consume a pine log that wasn't quite seasoned. It hissed and popped, launching embers against the chain curtain. At least the fire didn't want to talk to him. As long as he focused on the flame, the rest of the room left him alone.

"Is Amber sleeping?" Victoria asked.

Brenda went to the bedroom door, peeked inside, and closed it. "Yeah. She's out."

"Well, then, we should start," Victoria said.

Andre's pulse quickened with her words. He could tell that she was nervous about the reading, despite her calm exterior. Her unease doubled his own. Crazy, crazy things were going on around him. Everywhere he looked, information leaked from the environment.

First, the woman in Chill Lake had appeared out of nowhere, begging him to free her from her watery prison. Inanimate objects began speaking after that. When he happened to glance at the cat lamp on Victoria's shelf, it laughed and told him that Victoria had slept with the same man who'd stolen her mother from her father.

When he told Victoria what was happening, she said, "You'll learn to control it with time, Andre, but you will just have to accept some of this." He had not been happy to hear that, so he told her what the cat lamp said. She replied,

"Objects can lie as easily as people. Especially if they have an agenda. That lamp has quite an agenda. You will need to start discerning truth from nonsense when using the Sight. Those objects are not alive. They are being used as conduits by forces you might think of as spirits." He noticed that she hadn't outright denied what the cat lamp had said.

Everyone gathered to their assigned positions on the living room floor. Victoria sat at the point of the pentacle. Andre sat to her right and Craig to his right. Kevin sat on Victoria's left and Brenda to his left. A Persian blanket sporting lions and ribbons was placed in the center. Candles burned on copper stands behind each of them. Victoria removed the cards from their box and began shuffling. As happened with Craig's reading, a mystical energy seeped out of her.

The air around Andre became oppressive and his sight dimmed. The cabin faded, leaving himself and the others seated in a black void. Pathways of golden energy materialized in the air around them. *This must be the Confluence that Kevin and Victoria were talking about,* he thought in amazement. It was a beautiful, knotted river that moved in hundreds of directions at once. No one else noticed. Their eyes were on Victoria's hands as she shuffled. Andre reached out to touch one of the flows. As his fingers brushed its surface, his consciousness dislodged from his body and spun upward. His mind floated through the energy of the Confluence with a distinct absence of weight. The sensation was as close to bliss as he'd ever known. He looked down. The others, including his physical body, were still seated in nothingness, watching Victoria. The Persian blanket remained between them. She began to sweat as she shuffled and a deep frown bent her mouth and forehead.

Andre swirled in the currents of the Confluence, the

others receding into space below him. He found that he was riding the energy of the Confluence back to its source, wherever that was. Instinctively, he knew that he could allow himself to be absorbed into the energy flows. His being would disintegrate and merge with the pathways of the Confluence forever. That was a peaceful thought. However, it was also a cowardly one. With a concerted effort of will, he repositioned himself into a flow that moved the other direction. He was jerked downward. This flow moved through everyone seated below, starting with Victoria. He tried to change flows again, but couldn't reposition himself or fight against the current.

Oh, I hope this isn't going to fuck anything up, he thought before crashing into Victoria's chest.

Victoria watched Andre raise his hand into the air as she shuffled. *He can* see *the Confluence*, she thought. Even she could not see it, only sense its presence. His Sight was extraordinary. As his fingers brushed the edges of the Confluence's boundary, the pupils and irises of his eyes lifted out of their sockets and vanished into the flow of energy, leaving just the whites behind. Victoria tried to stop shuffling the cards, but to her horror she found that her arms and the cards were spinning of their own accord. Nothing like this had ever happened before. The reading was no longer within her control.

She tried to speak, but instead of the words she formulated, she said, "The Herald."

A card flew from her hands into the air where it remained suspended. The drawing was a nude man holding an unfurled scroll that read, "Proclamation." Small wings grew from his ankles. He wore a helmet and carried a golden scepter entwined with two snakes. She had never seen that card before. More disturbingly, the figure's eyes were Andre's. A moment later, she felt Andre slam into her chest, go through her, and exit the other side. The world around her dissolved except for those seated in the circle, replaced by a black void. Kevin jerked forward, followed by Brenda and Craig. The eyes on the card blinked each time this happened. The Herald fell onto the blanket, face up.

Kevin recovered from the shock first and said, "Where are we?"

Victoria continued shuffling because she could not stop. There was literally floating in *nothing*. "We are in the Confluence, I think," she said. "I believe that Andre brought us here."

Andre himself was not present in the circle.

Craig said, "How are we not falling through the—"

He stopped talking as The Herald peeled himself from the card and stood up. He spoke in Andre's voice, "I will do my best to guide you through what comes next, but I am only The Herald. How you react to my news is your choice."

As he finished speaking, Victoria threw another card. "The Scales," she intoned. The card enlarged and rotated into a window as it spun through the air.

Andre, as The Herald, said, "This card is for Kevin." He motioned for Kevin to go into the window.

Kevin frowned, "I'm not sure I'll fit into—"

A flash of light burst from the card and sucked Kevin inside. The window collapsed and the The Scales card fell, face up, on the blanket next to The Herald.

Brenda exclaimed, "Where did he go?"

Victoria tossed another card and said, "The Queen of Swords."

The Queen rotated into a window, pulled Brenda inside,

and fell next to the Scales.

"I guess I know what's going to happen next," Craig said.

"The Hollow Skull," Victoria said as another card spun from her fingers.

"Yeah, I figured," Craig said before being pulled into the window of the card.

The Herald turned to Victoria and said, "Stay strong for them or they will perish here. They are not made for this place." He sunk back into the card.

Victoria continued to shuffle the cards. She knew the moment she stopped the spell would be broken. A sense of relief flooded her when she realized that she could stop if she wanted. If she stopped too soon, though, those inside the cards would never return from them. There were still cards that needed to be thrown.

Kevin sat in his cramped office at Rick's Tire and Battery. Sales reports were piled on his desk in a chaotic jumble. A family picture of himself, Brenda, and Amber sat behind him on a large filing cabinet stuffed with client records. Several comic strips cut from newspapers were taped to the wall, yellowing and curling with time. His old roommate, Bert, sat in the half-broken chair on the other side of the desk, smoking a cigarette and drinking a Pabst Blue Ribbon.

"You know, Kevin," Bert said after blowing two perfect smoke rings into the air, "being dead isn't all that bad. I mean, really, what did I have to live for anyway, huh?" He took a swig of beer. "I get all the beer and cigarettes I want! And you can't die of cancer when you're already dead. What else could heaven be, huh?"

Kevin pushed himself back from the desk and said, "Bert, I'm very sorry for what happened."

"Oh, don't worry about it," Bert said, waving his hand. "Shit happens, man. Guys get eaten every day."

Kevin opened the bottom drawer of his desk and retrieved the pack of menthol cigarettes he kept hidden there. Bert smiled and proffered a lighter.

"No thanks," Kevin said, sliding a book of matches from the cellophane of the pack. He lit one and said, "I wish I could undo what I did then, Bert. I honestly do."

Bert laughed. "I bet you do, don't you, buddy?" He waved the beer can around the room. "I bet you'd like to have all this back, too?"

Kevin shook his head. "No. It's gone, Bert, just like you."

Bert frowned at him and said, "You take loss really well, you know? It's kinda annoying. I never liked you—except I conned you into paying the whole rent on the apartment. I liked that. But, Kevin, buddy, you don't get it, do you? Stupid fucker." He took a drink of beer. A smile began playing on his lips again. "It's OK, though, because you're about to get taught."

Kevin took a drag of his cigarette and sat back in his chair. After exhaling he said, "Bert, I'd honestly like to know what you have to teach me."

Bert's frown returned. He stood up and pointed at Kevin with his cigarette. "Not this time, buddy. This time you're going to learn what it's like to be on the other end of your bullshit. You've been walkin' free, but now you're going to pay!" He chucked his beer can at the family portrait. The glass cracked and beer splashed over the picture, the file cabinet, and the wall.

Kevin watched the beer dribble for a few moments. He stood up, pulled the picture from the frame, and wiped the beer off on his shirt. He folded it and tucked it into the back pocket of his pants.

Bert smiled. He said, "You remember that girl I started dating right before you ate me? Debbie? Well, the reason I didn't go to work that night was because I was going on a date with her. If you hadn't eaten me, I'd have married her. Had three kids. Lived a fulfilling and happy life. One of my kids would've been Governor of Minnesota. You don't feel guilty about all the death you've caused, because you don't feel like it was you who did it. Well, it *was* you who did it, buddy. You changed the fate of the world one snuffed life at a time. Don't kid yourself, killer. You're culpable for all this. You're evil to the core and all this bullshit about being a dad and a husband is an illusion you've got going to hide yourself from yourself. You don't have to take my word for it. I've got everyone you ever killed lined up outside this office, and every one of them has a story to tell about what would've happened if you hadn't killed them. You want me to get you something from the pop machine in the lobby? This is gonna take a while."

Kevin pushed past Bert and opened the door to the office. A line of people ran down the hallway, past the service bays, and out the overhead door at the far side of the shop. Hundreds of them. Men. Women. Children. Too many to count. The first person in line was Emily Castor, a stout woman who had been a security guard at a parking garage in Kansas City. He'd killed her when she accidentally ran into him on his way out of the building. Her eyes were pleading and teary. She said, "You know, I had three kids. Their dad died just the year before you killed me..."

Kevin closed the door and turned back to Bert. "So I have to sit behind that desk and hear the story behind every person I ever killed?"

"Oh, not just that," Bert replied. "You have to hear how things would have turned out if you hadn't killed them."

Bert cackled. "It's going to take a really, really long time. You might want to take a piss before we get this show on the road."

Kevin took a long drag from his cigarette and blew the smoke up to the ceiling. He turned back to Bert, who grinned with malicious glee. Kevin grinned back and shifted into his true form. Bert's eyes widened and he backed up against the door. With a clawed hand, Kevin picked Bert up by the neck.

"What!" Bert sputtered.

Kevin closed his fist around his former roommate's throat. Bert flailed, eyes bulging, blood pouring from his mouth.

"You have vastly underestimated the monster I really am," growled Kevin, shaking Bert back and forth until he stopped moving. Kevin dropped the body to the floor and opened the door.

Emily Castor looked up at him and he took her head off with a flick of his hand. He moved on to the older man behind her, Bill Phillips, who'd been a salesman for a biotech company that had stolen secrets from Elpis Enterprises. Kevin pulled his heart out and tossed it over his shoulder. He kicked two small children, collateral damage in an explosion he'd caused at a restaurant, so hard they split in half. With mechanical motions, he proceeded to kill his way through the line of his past victims. They all opened their mouths to speak just before dying. None had the chance to utter a word before he split their heads, disemboweled them, or tore their throats out with his teeth. Blood saturated his fur as he rounded the last bay, exited the building, and smashed skull after skull against the brick facade. Sometimes he remembered their names as he slaughtered them. Sometimes he'd never known them. It didn't matter. He killed until he reached the end of the line. When the last one—a nurse named Wilma Hartford—had been strangled, he stood before the tarot card that Victoria had thrown to bring him here. The Scales. The card enlarged, becoming a window once again. The scales wobbled in that window, tipping back and forth. Kevin leapt into the card, making sure to backhand The Scales as he jumped. They crashed to the ground and a blinding whiteness enveloped him.

Craig tumbled through the Hollow Skull and landed back on the floor of the cabin. Andre sat alone, his hand raised up as if to pluck fruit from a tree. His eyes were open, but their irises and pupils were missing.

"Oh, shit!" Craig yelped. The fall through the card hadn't been far, but the landing sent spasms through his sore muscles.

"Craig," Andre said in a voice that echoed as if he stood on the far side of a vast canyon.

Craig crawled over to the circle and took up his previous spot. All the cards that had been thrown so far were lying on the Persian blanket. "Yeah," he said. "I'm here. What did I do to win the 'get out of vision free' card?"

Andre's unblinking, white eyes stared straight ahead. "You have a choice now, Craig. I can see it in the Confluence."

Suddenly, Victoria appeared in the living room. She looked surprised to be back, but she never paused in her shuffling. She threw another card and said, "The Twins." The card landed on the blanket and Victoria vanished.

Craig studied the card. It showed two identical little girls holding hands. They both wore purple dresses with white flowers stitched onto the hems. One smiled brightly, awash in innocence. The other grinned deviously, her eyes full of hate. Both drawings were of Amber.

"What does that mean?" Craig asked Andre.

"Retrieve the bones from the bottom of Chill Lake," Andre intoned.

Craig shook his head. "What? How am I supposed to do that? I can barely walk. I can't swim right now! That would probably kill me."

Andre said, "You have a choice. Retrieve the bones or do not. The Twins card will vanish and you may remain here if you so choose."

Craig stared at the card. His heart pounded in his chest. He was really getting sick of making decisions. There was never a simple right or wrong. Just a judgment call. He would probably die if he jumped into that lake. He had no idea where the bones of that woman were. He had no idea how deep the lake was. It was forty degrees outside, meaning he might suffer hypothermia from the effort alone. On top of everything else, he didn't even know what to do if he managed to find the bones.

"Why do I need the bones?" he asked.

Andre's white eyes stared straight ahead and he remained silent.

"Well, shit," Craig said, pulling himself up from the floor.

He looked around the cabin for something that might be useful for digging up bones from the bottom of a lake in October in Minnesota. There was not, he noted, a wet-suit anywhere here. He went into the bathroom and grabbed a towel, with the optimistic view that he'd need it to dry off after getting the bones out of the lake. He also noticed a gardening spade lying on the patio by the back door. He opened the sliding door, picked it up, and made his way down to the edge of the lake.

The shoreline near the cabin was neatly kept. All the

aquatic plants had been removed and a pebbled beach hugged the shore. Craig dropped the spade and stripped off his clothing. The acts of pulling his shirt over his head and bending down to remove his shoes hurt. He hoped swimming would be easier than undressing. A stiff breeze bit his bare skin when he'd stripped down to his boxers.

He walked into the water, the spade clutched in his right hand. The chill of the water jolted his toes and ankles. When it reached his calves, the muscles began to tighten.

"Oh, no, you don't," Craig said, grimacing. He bent over and stretched his calves until they stopped quivering. After walking a few more feet, he said, "Aw, fuck it," and dove into the water.

An electric shock hit his entire body. Every muscle began to twitch and protest. Craig did his best to ignore his screaming nerves and pushed himself to the bottom of the lake. There he found dead plants rooted in loose and muddy rock. With no light and no goggles, he was forced to use his hands to do all the searching. He surfaced after ten seconds, gulped air, and regretted being such an avid smoker. Steam rose from his skin and hair. He dove again. His extremities began to lose their sense of feeling. This was great in the sense that pain began to recede, but it made searching the bottom of the lake difficult. He began grabbing wads of mud, rocks, and plants, rubbing them against his chest to discern their shape. Nothing bone-like yet. He surfaced and dove again. As he clawed at the muddy bottom, his fingers began to ignore his requests. He knew that his forearms had cramped up even though he couldn't feel them. He didn't notice when the spade slid from his fingers and sunk. Soon, he would be unable to work his limbs, at which point he'd sink to the bottom and drown.

Craig swam back toward the shoreline, continuing his

fruitless search as he went. A severe stomach cramp flipped him forward into waist high water. He thrashed until the cramp gave way, allowing him to stick his head above the water and suck in air. Had that cramp not receded, he'd have drowned.

"Fuck!" he shouted into the air. Steam rose from the water around him. "Hey, Lady of Lake, some help would be nice right about now, eh? I'm not out here working on my triathlon times. I'm trying to retrieve your bones!"

He floated for several minutes, scared to move again because his muscles were all near cramping. He stared up at the cloudy sky and realized he was probably going to die. That was really too bad. A great many people would be disappointed in him. At least one of those people was Clarence Elpis. Fuck that guy. Kevin would also be disappointed and that hurt. But Craig felt a keener sense of disappointment from his father, of all people. He'd been on the outs with the man for years, but as he gulped air to keep himself from slipping beneath the surface, it was his father's frowning face that floated in the eye of his mind.

Craig's plan was to time his breaths to make his body like a bobber. When he sank, he kicked against the bottom, steering himself toward shore. After several cycles of this procedure, his foot slipped off a rock and he was unable to resurface. He lost the sense of up and down until his shoulder sank into mud. Panic reared in his belly as he struggled against the bottom of the lake. He managed to surface, sputtering for a single breath before sinking again.

Gritting his teeth, Craig straightened his legs and attempted to stand up. Lightning bolts of pain shot up from his calves as both cramped at once, pulling his feet up to his buttocks.

Well, that was a bad idea, he thought.

He pushed his arms out. Or, rather, he imagined he did. He could no longer feel anything past his elbows. Thrashing, Craig tried to push forward with his arms, hoping that they would engage the bottom of the lake and allow him to push himself up to the surface. Nothing happened. In a rage, he expelled his last breath. Drowning was not, he reflected, a peaceful way to die.

Brenda sat on her gilded throne and surveyed her court, which congregated around an oval table that stretched across the great hall of her castle. The kingdom's administrators were arguing with each other about what to do since the King had gone missing the night before. The wizards dithered about changes in the wind. The regional governors swore at one another about border disputes. The tax collectors bemoaned lack of revenue. Generals clanged their gauntlets and demanded war with the neighboring kingdom. The trade masters, with the notable exception of the blacksmith, griped at the generals about how war would ruin their trading routes. As the cacophony reached a fever pitch, Brenda sat forward, drew the Swan Hilted Sword, and said, "Silence!"

The court fell quiet. A general released the lapels of the Head of Agriculture, who tumbled to the floor noisily.

"I have been told," Brenda said, lowering her sword, "that a dragon was spotted fleeing the castle last night. I believe it has kidnapped or eaten the King. Either way, we will pursue the dragon and destroy it. Until then, all else in the kingdom must get by as best it can."

Plans were drawn up to follow the beast. Within a fortnight, an army of five hundred men with the Queen at its head was ready to pursue the dragon. It had been spotted in the far western province decimating the local sheep population. Before departing, Brenda entered the nursery to say good-bye to her daughter.

"Mommy goes on t'ip to see Daddy!" Amber said after Brenda explained that she would be gone for several weeks.

"Yes, darling," Brenda said, combing her fingers through the child's thin black hair.

As the army marched to the western province, the Queen minded the kingdom's business as best she could. She sent and received missives. She signed decrees after scanning their contents with half an eye. But only one thing could hold her attention for more than a few minutes: the dragon. She must destroy the dragon. She read every book available on the beasts and consulted with wizards daily to learn the creatures' every weakness. She dreamed about dragons at night and wrote countless pages of notes about them. Soon, her preoccupation allowed her highest advisors to stop asking for her permission before making decisions. They began running the kingdom how they saw fit. The generals declared war on the neighboring kingdom. Taxes were tripled. Several of the outlying provinces declared their independence. Trade ground to a halt and people began to starve. By the time the Queen's Army reached the cave where the dragon was reported to live, the entire kingdom had fallen into chaos. Brenda barely noticed and didn't care.

As she stood at the mouth of the cave, her hand resting on the Swan Hilted Sword, a heightened sense of excitement coursed through her. She would finally face the dragon. Sunlight glinted off her golden armor and that of the army behind her. A strong breeze stretched her banners out like the wings of a hundred colorful birds.

Brenda drew her sword and raised it. "Foul beast!" she yelled. "Come out and show yourself!"

Her voice rang into the cave and echoed back, bringing a chill with it. Brenda steeled herself and said to her men, "Prepare to enter the cave! The beast is a coward, so we must dig it out!"

The men cheered, lit torches, and one hundred of them descended with Brenda into the cave. Hours later, they tumbled into a vast cavern. An underground lake halted their march, but an island was apparent in the distance. Smoke rose from the island and rolled across the top of the cave.

"The dragon is there on the island," said one of the wizards. "He slumbers."

Supplies were sent for and soon the army built twelve rafts to cross the lake. Once they arrived on the island, Brenda marched them to the center, where the dragon lay curled under a vast ledge. It was an immense male, spanning one hundred yards from tail to snout. His wings were tucked down as he slept. Red and orange scales glistened metallically in the army's torchlight.

"Strike now," the wizard hissed into Brenda's ear, "while he sleeps!"

Brenda nodded and raised the Swan Hilted Sword.

"Charge!" she screamed.

The army surged toward the sleeping dragon. His eyes popped open, two huge orbs each the size of a man. He lunged from beneath the ledge, snorted, and blew fire from his mouth and nose. Brenda held forward the Swan Hilted Sword and the flames passed harmlessly around her. The rest of her army vaporized in a swirl of fire. The smell of their roasted flesh burned Brenda's nose, but she pushed into the flames with her sword. She knew of a chink in the beast's scaly armor—a spot on his belly where his genitals retreated after mating. This area would be soft and vulnerable.

Brenda pushed against the fire, the blade of the sword glowing white hot. It couldn't take much more of this heat, she realized, but she was close enough to risk it. She leapt forward, swinging the blade at the dragon's face. As she hoped, he reared back, exposing his belly. Fire scorched the ceiling of the cave. She darted in and thrust the blade into the telltale diamond in the scales near the bottom of his stomach. The Swan Hitled Sword sunk into soft flesh and the dragon screamed in agony. Pressing forward, Brenda dragged the sword upward until she reached his heart. With a final, agonizing moan, the dragon fell backward. Brenda held onto the hilt of the sword until the beast came to rest on his back, wings stretched out and tongue hanging limply from his mouth.

She stood upon his chest and pulled the sword free. The blade was blackened. She held it aloft and cried, "I have defeated you!"

The body of the dragon shrank beneath her feet. She frowned and jumped off. The body continued to shrink until it was the size of man. Then it began to change shape. When it finished changing, Brenda cried out, "Oh, Kevin!"

She dropped the Swan Hilted Sword and fell to her knees by the body of the King. He was naked and split from his crotch to his heart. His eyes stared off into nothing. Brenda gathered his body onto a raft, rowed back across the lake, and carried him to her encampment.

"I have found the King!" she announced to the remainder of her army. "And he is dead!"

The body of the King was wrapped in gauze and felt. The Queen's Army returned to the castle, crestfallen and defeated.

Craig's brain shut down in phases. First his sight went, which he thought was fine since he couldn't see anything in the water, anyway. Next his hearing faded to a high pitched ring. The last physical thing he could remember was the gritty taste of the lake's water on his tongue. As even that sensation faded, he felt something tugging on his hand. Except that wasn't right. He couldn't feel his hand. Something was tugging *through* his hand. It pulled him out of himself, leaving his body behind as if it were an orange peel. He floated up through blackness until breaking through the surface of the water. Holding his hand was a beautiful, nude woman. She was, like himself, an opaque, blue specter. She smiled at him and said, "Welcome to my lake. My name is Loretta." Her voice was light and pleasant. She spoke in an accent that reminded Craig of the movie *Fargo*.

He said, "Hi, Loretta. I'm Craig. Sorry, but I have no intention of staying here. I'm not sure what happens when you die, but I royally screwed up in life and if I've got to hang around all mystical-like, I'm doing it somewhere else."

She nodded in understanding. "Oh, I know how you feel. But you can't leave, you know." She motioned to the edge of the lake. "Go ahead. Try."

Craig didn't know how to move, so he just looked at the edge of the lake and sighed. "I wish I'd have found your bones," he said.

"What did you want with my bones?" she asked.

"I was going to take them out of the lake," he said. "My friend Andre said you wanted to be free."

She wrapped a finger through her long hair and twirled it. "Oh, but you're friends with the witch who holds me here," she said.

Craig laughed, which caused the world around him to briefly triple. *Being dead is complicated,* he thought. "Friends? Hardly. I wish I'd never met her. I thought if I could grab your bones, you could help me be free of her. She holds me prisoner as surely as she holds you."

Loretta said, "She is a horrible, horrible woman... if I put you back into your body, will you promise to dig me up and take me out of the lake?"

Craig blinked. "I thought I was dead."

"You're not all the way dead, yet," she said. "I don't have the power I did before she showed up, but I can make it so that your body does not die while you find me. But you must promise to take me out of the lake."

Craig said, "I promise to take you out of the lake."

Loretta's face disfigured into a snarl and Craig felt a current of energy latch onto his neck like a dog chain. It was the same feeling he had when Clarence Elpis was watching him.

How many chains will I have to break? he thought.

Loretta's face smoothed and she took his hand again. They descended to the bottom of the lake. A blue glow emanated from Loretta, illuminating Craig's body, which lay tangled in brown plants. His open eyes stared into the murky water. A small fish pecked at his lips. Loretta grabbed Craig's specter by the shoulders and stuffed him back into his body. The blue glow transferred from her to him and she faded. Before disappearing, she pointed to a spot several feet away.

Craig floated for a moment, noting that he felt quite comfortable in the freezing cold water. He had no urge to breath and a blue sphere surrounded him, giving off a soft light. His spade lay near where Loretta had pointed before disappearing. Craig swam over and picked up the spade.

His muscles felt great. In fact, he thought he may even be able to blip forward again, but decided against it. Now wasn't the time for experimentation.

Craig moved several large rocks away from the area and began to dig. Mud clouds sprung up, but the blue light pushed them away, leaving a clear working area. After digging for only a few seconds, he hit something solid. Using his fingers, he pulled a child's skull from the mud. He sat the skull down and began digging again. Small human bones surfaced, as well as more skulls. The blue light held the mud back as he dug. Soon, twenty tiny skulls watched him work. When the hole had descended six feet beneath the bottom of the lake, his spade struck a skull much larger than the others. He cleared muck away, revealing an entire skeleton. The bones clung to one another as he pried them from the bottom of the lake.

That's nice, Craig thought. *At least I don't have to find every single piece individually.*

He swam back toward shore, clutching the skeleton by a collar bone. When he surfaced, the sphere around him popped in an oily spray of blue light. He coughed and water spewed from his mouth. Fatigue returned to his muscles, though they did not cramp up. A card appeared above the pile of his clothes on the shore. It rotated, enlarging into a window. The Twins.

As he took his first step onto the shore, the skeleton jerked and spasmed.

Craig dropped it and yelped, "Shit!"

Like an unstrung marionette, the skeleton rose. Water, mud, and brown plants slid from its bones.

"That's just fu…" Craig began.

The skeleton grabbed him by the throat. Its bony fingers sunk deep into his neck, cutting blood flow to his brain.

Goddammit, he thought, *how many ways can I die tonight?*

He pivoted on his right foot, aimed his body toward The Twins card, and blipped forward. In slow motion, the effects of strangulation became much less pressing. Craig and the skeleton clutching his throat crashed into the Twins card, causing an explosion of kaleidoscopic colors. The bones of the skeleton merged with the maliciously smiling drawing of Amber, which expanded into three dimensions. A child's delicate hand now gripped Craig's trachea. Craig twisted the child's wrist into a joint lock and wrapped his other arm around her waist. Once he was certain she was secure, he turned the blip off and braced himself for the rest of the fall through the card.

Instead of tumbling onto the floor of the cabin as Craig hoped they would, the card spat them out in what appeared to be a medieval mausoleum. The floor, walls, and ceiling were made of large granite blocks. A gauze wrapped body was laid out on a black marble slab. Candles on sconces illuminated the room with flickering, orange light. Craig recognized Kevin's face on the body.

How real is this? he wondered. *I don't think I can handle Kevin dying again.*

The girl in his hands squirmed, so he applied more pressure to the joint lock. She squeaked in pain and relaxed.

"Look, Loretta," he hissed, "you're not going anywhere I don't want you to go, so settle down."

"You tricked me!" she shouted in Amber's most petulant, snotty voice, though with clear enunciation.

"You tried to kill me," he said. "Fair's fair. Now hush up while I figure out where we are and what we're supposed to be doing here."

"You don't know?" she gasped, relaxing.

He ignored her and looked about the room as a trickle of

water ran from his boxers, down his leg, and to the stone floor. There were no windows, but a large oak door stood on the far side of the room. Tapestries hung from the walls, depicting battle scenes, dragons, and swans. One of them was the card they had fallen out of, but it no longer contained two girls. Only the happy version of Amber remained and the name of the card had changed to The Twin. He drug Loretta to the tapestry and tapped it with his foot. It swung back against the wall.

"Not going back that way," he muttered. "I guess we go to the door."

He paused to consider Kevin, whose eyes were sunken. The skin of his face was a yellowish green color. He smelled like rancid meat.

The oak door was unlocked. He hooked his foot into the handle and turned on his heal, catching the door with his butt and pushing it open. As he finished the move, quite satisfied with himself, he found the tip of a blackened sword pointed at his nose.

"Put my daughter down and explain why you violate my husband's tomb!" commanded a regal woman clad in a red and gold dress. A crown of two swans with touching wings rested on her head.

"Brenda!" Craig exclaimed. "Brenda, it's me, Craig!"

"I did not ask your identity," Brenda replied coldly. "Answer me or die right now." She moved the sword so that its blade came to rest against his cheek.

Craig choked and said, "Brenda, please! I just came from the cabin. We need to get back there. Please, Brenda, this isn't your daughter! You have to trust me!"

Brenda's features hardened and she pushed the sword forward. Blood spilled from Craig's cheek as she did so. Loretta squirmed in his arms again and cried, "Mama!

Mama!"

"You've got to believe me, Brenda," Craig begged. "If I let go of her, she'll kill your daughter and take her place. We've got to get out of here! Please, trust me!"

Brenda pushed the sword deeper into his cheek. Tears sprung from his eyes, rolling down to the blade.

"I have no concern for your begging," Brenda said. "I warned you. Now I will kill…"

Where Craig's tears touched the blade, the blackness receded, leaving the gleam of polished steel. Brenda frowned and pulled the sword away from his face. She watched as the blackness faded along the entire blade. It looked newly forged.

Sheathing the sword, she said, "Let us test you. If my daughter remains in her nursery, I'll know what you say is true. If not, you die upon the spot."

Craig expelled his breath and said, "Good. Good. Fine."

They marched to the nursery, through miles of labyrinthine passageways above the mausoleum where Kevin lay. Loretta cried the entire way and pain sparked from Craig's heels to his neck. At least he didn't start blipping backward, as he feared he would. Holding onto Loretta would have been impossible if parts of him dematerialized around her. People dressed in antiquarian clothing gave them strange glances, but Brenda ignored them and allayed any interruption with a wave of her hand. She was, Craig figured, in charge around here. That wasn't too surprising. He felt ridiculous in soaking wet boxers, traipsing about a medieval castle, leaving wet foot prints in his wake. He figured it was time to reconsider the word ridiculous.

Finally, they stood before a door painted pink and blue. Brenda opened it and gasped. Inside, Amber played with her nursemaid. The nursemaid took one look at Craig's captive and fainted.

"Well," Brenda said. "You were not lying."

Amber ran to her mother, peering around her legs at the child in Craig's arms.

"Bad me!" Amber cried, pointing. "Bad me!"

"We have to get out of here," Craig said. He looked down at Loretta. "Do you know how to get out of here?" he asked.

The little girl sneered. "No. You brought *me* here, remember?"

Brenda gasped again. Amber screamed and began crying.

"That thing is unholy," Brenda said, clutching her daughter to her chest.

"Yeah, I know," Craig said. "But I need it." He thought for a moment. "Can we all go back down to the mausoleum? There has to be a way out there. Something I missed. Maybe with you and Amber…"

"My daughter will go nowhere near that room," Brenda said.

Craig shook his head. "I think she has to, Brenda, or she'll be trapped here forever."

"This is her home," Brenda said. "She is not trapped."

Craig implored, "Please trust me, Brenda. Something has gone very, very wrong, or I wouldn't be here. You need to follow me. I promise it will all make sense soon. I promise."

Brenda's fingers played over the hilt of her sword. She gathered Amber in her arms and said, "Follow me."

They traced their way back to the mausoleum. Craig felt a tightening sense of panic setting in. It was similar to the feeling he had while drowning. Fatigue was also becoming a problem. Holding Loretta in place for so long burned the muscles of his arms and chest. When Brenda opened the door to mausoleum, Craig asked her to take Loretta. She put

Amber down and grabbed Loretta, deftly avoiding both kicks and biting teeth.

Her motherly instincts are impressive, Craig thought as he stumbled toward the tapestry.

"Shhh!" Amber admonished. She whispered, "Daddy sleeping. Daddy need bath! Stinky Daddy."

Brenda said, "Yes, he does." Tears glisten in her eyes.

Craig realized that Brenda hadn't told her daughter of her father's death yet. What a mess.

He studied the tapestry. The Twin. There was Amber, standing in the same purple flower print dress that Loretta now wore. The flesh and blood Amber behind him wore the same dress. Behind her in the tapestry stood a river that lead to a castle. The space previously occupied by her twin was blank, leaving a white silhouette.

"I've never seen that tapestry before in my life," Brenda said. "I chose every one hanging in this room."

Craig nodded and traced his finger along the stitching on its surface. "C'mon, Andre," he said. "I need a little help here."

To his surprise, Victoria's voice rang out in the mausoleum. "The Broken Scales," she intoned.

The image on the tapestry melted. It was replaced by a picture of a set of torsion scales, bent and laying on the ground. The iron counterweights were scattered, as were several bars of gold. Craig found if he pushed against the surface of the tapestry, his fingers sank into it, becoming part of the image.

"Huh," he said, and stepped forward. His body flattened into two dimensions, but he could still move across the surface of the tapestry. More importantly, he could touch the objects therein. He righted the scales and bent the fulcrum into its correct shape. He then replaced the counterweights and gold bars. The scales swung for a moment, but came to rest in perfect balance. He stepped backwards and fell to the floor of the mausoleum.

"Wizardry," Brenda hissed.

"Yeah," Craig said. "It pisses me off, too. But we should be able to go through now."

When he pushed his hand against the surface of the tapestry, it just swung back against the wall.

"Oh, what now?" he said. Frustration built within him, as well as the impending sense that he was running out of air to breath. Why had Victoria thrown the Scales card again? That had been Kevin's card. Kevin was dead. How were they supposed to get home through a card meant for a dead man?

Craig turned around and stared at Kevin's body. "Well," he said. "It's worth a try."

He slogged over to the marble slab, grabbed Kevin's heels, and dragged him toward the tapestry. The effort took the last of his energy and caused his muscles to tighten again. Kevin was heavier than he looked.

"What are you doing?" yelled Brenda.

Amber giggled and pointed.

"I'm not sure," Craig said, "but I think Kevin needs to go first, dead or alive. This is his card, after all."

Craig stuffed Kevin's feet into the tapestry. To his relief the familiar rotation of a window took shape.

"Let's get the fuck out of here," he called, waiving for the others to join him as he dragged Kevin's body into the white light. He prayed that this window led back to the cabin near Pine City.

Floating alone in the void, shuffling cards, Victoria felt a tension snap inside her. She smiled and set down the cards. The reading was done. Blackness faded and the shape of the cabin formed around her. She hadn't been sure that would happen, so relief bordering on joy swept through her. It died quickly, though. The living room was in a state of chaos.

Amber sat on the couch, wailing and crying. Craig sat next her in his underwear, covered in mud. He was trying to comfort the child, but every time he touched her she screamed with renewed energy. Kevin, in his monstrous form, lay on the floor, soaked in blood. He clutched a photo in one clawed hand. Brenda, wearing a ridiculous outfit that looked like something from a Renaissance Fair with an enormous sword strapped to her waist, chased *another* Amber about the kitchen. That Amber had a kitchen knife and slashed at her mother, cursing in perfectly pronounced words. Beside Victoria, Andre sat with his hands covering his face. She reached out and touched his arm.

"What happened?" she asked.

Andre pulled his hands away from his face, revealing white eyeballs. "I've gone blind," he said. He reached out and took ahold of her hand. "I can only see—"

A loud crash came from the kitchen. The pan rack was tipped over. Brenda had disarmed and subdued the second Amber, but was bleeding from several cuts on her forearms. She used duct tape to hog tie the child.

Andre continued, "I can only see in the 'spirit world' or whatever you call it. It's mostly black. Sometimes visions pop up, sometimes strange shapes try to talk to me. It's—It's like being in two places at once. It *hurts*."

"Close your eyes, Andre," Victoria instructed.

Andre seemed startled and did so.

"Is that better?" she asked.

"Yeah," he said. "Now I'm just regular blind. Why didn't I

think of that?"

"That place has many names, Andre," Victoria said. "But let's just call it the 'spirit world' for now."

"OK, whatever," Andre said, running his fingers across his eyelids.

Brenda tossed the bound child into a bedroom and slammed the door. She grabbed a towel from the kitchen, soaked it in the sink, and ran to Kevin. She scrubbed his fur, ruining the towel in seconds. Kevin groaned under her attention, but did not regain consciousness.

At least he is alive, Victoria thought. She'd thought the blood was his. It ran from him in rivulets, pooling around his body.

"Take him to the bathroom," Victoria said to Brenda.

Brenda looked at Victoria for a moment as if she had no idea who she was, blinked several times, and said, "Right. OK." She hooked her arms under Kevin's shoulders and dragged him across the floor, leaving a smear of blood in her wake. She tripped over the sword as she entered the hallway, so she removed the sword's scabbard and propped it against the wall. Where in the world had that sword come from? Victoria could feel strange energy pulsing inside it.

Craig had managed to calm Amber. She was snuggled in the crook of his arm, staring sleepily into space. Craig hummed an out of tune lullaby, but it was working.

"Andre," Victoria said, squeezing his hand, "can you tell me what happened?"

Andre expelled a breath that he didn't seem to know he'd been holding. Eyes closed, he composed himself and said, "I slipped into the Confluence when you started doing the reading. I didn't mean to. I had no idea it would happen. It just did. Then I brought all of you in, too. That's when things went south. I could see it all. I could see the whole reading from start to finish. I just... I just did what I thought was right. I went into the deck and became The Herald. It seemed like I could use the Confluence to guide things. Get everyone back out. I think it veered off course when Kevin knocked over The Scales on the way back from his card. It was like some kind of fabric tore when he did that. He didn't follow the rules or something. I don't know. But the cards got mixed up. The Confluence pushed everyone together in ways that weren't supposed to happen. Everything became *real!*"

Victoria tapped her finger against her lips. She knew of no precedent for any of this. She had encountered powerful Confluences before. She had encountered Awake humans and other supernatural creatures before. But never had anyone else she'd ever known shifted from one plane of existence to another. She wanted to fleece Andre for information, but she knew that now was not the time. His mind was reeling. He was staggered by the loss of his vision. He needed guidance now. He needed to believe that she knew how to untangle this mess.

"You did an amazing thing," she said. "This Confluence was stronger than any I've ever seen. You saved us all, Andre."

"Really?" he muttered. "I saved you all from myself after I put you through hell. The things that happened in those 'visions' actually happened, Victoria. Kevin killed everyone he ever killed before again. Brenda killed Kevin. I'm still not sure why he came back like he did and not split in half and rotten. It has something to do with that photograph... Craig *died*, Victoria. That ghost in the lake is the only reason he came back. And now that psychotic bitch is Amber's twin. Victoria, if this is what saving people looks like, I'm scared shitless of when I actually fuck something up."

"Andre, you need to rest now. You are not at fault for these things. I take most of that blame. I knew something was wrong with this reading, but I pushed forward with it anyway." She squeezed his hand hard and said, "And we can restore your eyesight, Andre. I promise we can do that." She had no idea if that was true, but he needed to believe it.

Craig called from the couch, "Hey, Andre, come here."

Victoria guided Andre across the room. Amber snored against Craig's chest. Craig raised a shaking, muddy hand. Victoria caught it and brought it to Andre's.

"Look, man, you saved me tonight," Craig said. "I can take Loretta to that Elpis fucker, dump her off, and be done with this. Might get us all off the hook. I ain't mad at you, man. The others will be OK, too. Shit all worked out. Don't beat yourself up. OK?"

Andre reached out his free hand and touched Craig's face. "You really did die, you know," he said. "Loretta was lying. She brought you back to life. To do it, she used the souls of all those little boys she lured into the lake over the years. Craig, what happened is so much worse…"

"Shut it, Andre," Craig said, his voice cracking with strain. "I don't care if she ate a school bus full of orphans to bring me back at this point. None of us had good choices, and I'm sick of feeling like shit for making the best choice I could make in a fucked up situation. That's all you did, man. It's fine. Now, would one of you drag me somewhere I can sleep for about two days, please? I'm worse off than that night I chugged three bottles of Night Train in a row."

A short, bitter laugh slipped out of Andre's mouth. Victoria smiled and guided him to a chair.

"I'll take care of Craig," she said. "Then, we'll get you ready for bed, too. Rest will help you. We can sort all of this out in the morning."

Andre's shoulders slumped. "OK. I wonder what my dreams will be like…"

Victoria put her hand on his cheek. "You won't have any," she said. "I'll make sure of it."

Chapter 10
Blank Canvas

I am a sinner in the hands of an angry god, thought Clarence Elpis as he stared at the array of LED monitors in his production laboratory at Elpis Enterprises. He leaned forward with his back hunched and planted his elbows on the black desk. This position minimized the continuous pain that throbbed through his body.

On one of the screens, a green dot flashed reassuringly. Octavio was still alive and in the Twin Cities. As comforting as Octavio's whereabouts and well-being were, Craig C. Miller Jr's approach through Iowa was more important. Computers and screens were not necessary for Clarence to track that trajectory. When he focused, Clarence could see through Craig's eyes. Amber was sleeping in his arms. Craig was "blipping" along I-35 in controlled bursts. Clarence wrested that term and little else from Craig's mind, cobbling together information through their unstable mental connection. Craig was not only learning how to control his abilities. He was also learning how to block Clarence out of his mind. He would be a useful addition to The Elpis Foundation if Clarence could survive long enough to exploit him.

The most important piece of information Clarence gleaned from Craig was that Number 1 was still alive. Assuming Number 1 knew where Craig was heading with his daughter, there could be no doubt that he'd follow. Numbers 4 and 8 had been activated to corral him if he arrived. Clarence would have liked to use several of the Awakened in this situation, but they, like his god, had lost faith in him. They were destroying Elpis Enterprises as surely as his god was destroying his body.

A chime rang from one of the speakers on his desk. Clarence smiled and pushed a button on his keyboard. "Hello, Octavio," he said.

"Hello, Clarence," Octavio said through the speaker. "I've located Number 7 and Number 9. They are coming back with me. I think they were drugged or something. They're fine now. I have crucial intelligence about Number 1. I'll give a full report when I get back."

"That is wonderful news!" Clarence said. "Even better than I dared hope."

"We should be arriving at the Foundation in about four hours," said Octavio.

"That will be fine," Clarence said. "When you return, I will need you to report to me immediately. Number 7 and Number 9 can get settled before reporting."

"Yes, sir," said Octavio.

"Good-bye, Octavio," said Clarence.

The speakers made a static click.

Clarence resumed his hunched position and considered the implications. He had hated to send Octavio to the Twin Cities. That was an enormous risk. Octavio was not involved in the political storm sweeping through both Elpis Enterprises and The Elpis Foundation. Other than the Térata, Octavio was Clarence's last loyal man. After the losses of 11 and 12, sending another Térata would have been madness.

Clarence waved his hand, wincing as pain flashed through his wrist. The array of monitors in front of him rearranged themselves. A larger screen faced him, displaying the progress of his latest project in charts, graphs, and video. His only hope for continued life hinged upon this project. He clicked his mouse to activate a camera in the production laboratory behind him. The camera panned across seven hundred glass tubes, each containing a genderless humanoid figure suspended in amniotic fluid.

Blank canvas, he thought.

The organisms in the tubes were growing at the predicated rates. Progress reports showed fully developed organs. Tissue samples from each one were identical. Only one more piece of the puzzle remained and Craig was bringing that to him now. Science brought Clarence to the brink of success, but magic was the only way to bridge the final gap. He was certain that Number 1's child held such magic. There was no other way she could exist.

Clarence bowed his head. "I had to trap you inside me," he recited to his god, as he had hundreds of times before. "You need to give me just a little longer."

He imagined the god locked into his bones grumbling angrily. By all his calculations, the matrix of magic that held that god captive should have been an impervious seal. But the leukemia leaking out of Clarence's bones was not natural. Somehow, the god that had held Clarence in the womb, raised him, and been the source of his powers was killing him.

"I have another plan," he continued. "This time, it will work. You can walk among mankind once again. You just have to give me more time." Clarence said all these words as a prayer from one who has fallen from grace.

When Numbers 11 and 12 had not proven immune to the rules that govern supernatural creatures, the god that had lived symbiotically inside Clarence decided his time was up. The Rattlesnake Prophecy was nearing its culmination. In a few short months, the greatest Confluence in twenty one hundred years would begin. Without an army, the god was dissatisfied.

Though Clarence believed in his life's work, he was a careful and calculating man. He had foreseen the possibility that his patron would turn on him. When it happened, he trapped the god in a magical prison fused to his bones. This was not meant to be a permanent solution, but Clarence had expected it to work better than it had.

"I am so close," he muttered, returning his attention to the screen showing his blank canvases.

Kevin sat on the sofa in the living room of Victoria's cabin with Amber on his lap. He was in his true form and could not shift back to Kevin's body. When he willed the change, a bottomless abyss appeared around him. When he tried harder, he felt the world spiral into oblivion. Though he wasn't certain what was happening, he was sure that if he continued to push, he would die. He tried to shift into another human form, but that didn't work, either. All his other identities were gone.

His daughter was giddy with delight. She found his hair and canine features amusing. He'd woken up on the floor of the bedroom with her straddling his chest, poking her finger into his nose and giggling.

"Daddy a dog!" she'd squealed when he opened his eyes. After failing to shift forms, he picked her up and wandered into the living room, where Victoria and Brenda sat at the table in the nook studying a large sword with swans on its hilt. He'd plopped down on the couch with Amber and watched them.

Amber twisted her fingers into Kevin's chest hair and pulled as hard as she could.

He said, "Please stop that."

She obeyed.

"When Andre entered the Confluence," Victoria said to Brenda, "the reading reacted in some way I do not understand. He created some kind of bubble in the reading that penetrated into the spirit world. This bubble splintered into each individual's reading, making what should have been metaphorical visions that only I could see into very real worlds. On top of that, the Confluence merged the bubbles into one another."

Brenda expelled a breath and ran her fingers along the hilt of the sword.

"It was definitely real," she said. "I can still remember every detail. I know the name of the head cook in the castle. I can tell you how many bushels of wheat were to be shipped to a neighboring kingdom tomorrow. It's like I've lived two lives for the last several months. One here and another there. When I was there, though, I had no memory of my life here…"

"So," Kevin interjected from the couch, "you remember killing me?"

Brenda's forehead creased. She said, "I remember it very clearly. It was the saddest moment of my life."

"I think," Victoria said to Kevin, "that a part of you *is* dead. I touched you while you slept. You are not whole."

"Dead is fo'ever!" Amber said. Kevin wondered where she'd picked that up. He stroked her hair with a clawed hand that engulfed her entire head. She leaned into him and rubbed her face into his fur.

"Apparently not, honey," Kevin said to her. To Victoria he said, "I cannot change back into Kevin's form. I still have all his memories and emotions, though."

Victoria nodded and picked up a tarot card from the table. It showed a detailed drawing of his true form with the number 1 in the corner and a golden, swan encircled crown on his head. Celtic knots ran along the borders. The title of the card was The Dog King.

"This card fell out of my deck when I put it away. It is yours."

Kevin stood up and carried Amber over to the table. He took the card from Victoria. "What does it mean?" he asked.

Brenda answered, "We have to go back, Kevin. We have to go back to Tir Naomh."

"Tir Naomh," Kevin repeated. "I don't have the kind of memories you do there. I walked from... from my card into the body of a dragon. I didn't really have my own mind anymore. I moved on instinct until you showed up and killed me. I don't remember anything after that except waking up this morning." He adjusted Amber, who was squirming in an attempt to climb onto his shoulder. "That name sounds Irish."

Brenda nodded, "Yeah. According to Victoria, my card was supposed to be a symbolic journey into the fairytale stories we tell Amber at bedtime. You know that book my mom sent Amber? The one about Irish folklore?"

Kevin nodded. He'd told many variations of those stories to Amber when he'd tired of reading it directly.

"Well, I think a lot of that ended up there. And other stuff, too." She shook her head. "It's hard to distinguish what comes from the stories and what is just there, now. It's all blurred together in my head."

"So this place really exists?" Kevin asked.

Victoria pursed her lips. "Yes. It did not until last night, but now it does. It exists as a bubble in the spirit world. I have no idea how long it will last. It may last forever. It may fade with time. It is a piece of human imagination come to life. I've never encountered anything like this before. My abilities allow me to glimpse snippets of information from the spirit world. I cannot travel there. I did not think that was possible."

A voice from the hallway intoned, "It will remain if the Dog King plants his heart in the Hearth of Souls. This is his path to freedom and resurrection."

Andre stood against the wall, his fingers clinging to the doorframe of the bedroom. His eyes were open, but they were completely white.

"What happened to your eyes?" Kevin asked.

Andre closed his eyes and sighed. "They're in the spirit world now. When I open them, I can see the world beneath and above and in us." He smiled like a salesman on TV. "It's actually pretty cool in a 1960s psychedelic sort of way."

Victoria took Andre's hand and led him to the table. "Thanks," he said, maneuvering into the bench seat. "Being blind is a lot more difficult that I thought it'd be. My shins are not adapting well and I almost killed myself trying to take a piss. You know, I'm going to miss doing that standing up."

Kevin shook his head. "Where is Craig?"

Victoria said, "I sent him to Elpis this morning. His cards turned a double of Amber which he managed to bring back from the bubble of his reading. I don't know if that will satisfy Elpis or not, but Craig was certain it was what needed to happen."

"A double of Amber?" Kevin gasped. "And you're giving

her to Clarence?"

Brenda said, "That creature is nothing like Amber. Craig somehow put the evil spirit from the lake into a body just like Amber's. She's a wicked thing. A dangerous thing."

"Bad me," Amber whispered.

"I put her to sleep with morphine," Victoria said. "Craig should have no trouble getting her to Elpis. I also helped him learn to block Elpis out of his mind, though I'm sure he lets things slip. As long as he's moving in the right direction, Elpis won't push too hard on him."

Kevin frowned. "But what will happen to Craig after he gives Clarence this other Amber."

"I'm working on that," Victoria said. "Your sister will be of great help to us if she returns the favor she owes me. We've been talking. She wants to talk to you, too. She has an agenda for something called the Térata. You and Brenda are part of her schemes. She seems to think you'll go along with whatever she has planned."

"Where is Kevin?" Andre interrupted, reaching toward where Kevin was standing.

Kevin gave Amber to Brenda, who slid out of the breakfast nook. Kevin stuffed himself into the bench seat and engulfed Andre's hand with his own. "I'm here."

Andre opened his eyes. Though he had neither pupils nor irises, Kevin felt Andre look into his eyes.

Andre whistled and said, "Man, you really are a monster, aren't you?"

Kevin knew what he meant and it had nothing to do with his teeth, claws and fur. He released Andre's hand. "Yes, Andre. I am. I assume you saw what happened in my... bubble."

Andre nodded. "And I can see it inside you. You'd do it again. You wouldn't even hesitate."

"No," Kevin said. "I wouldn't."

Andre closed his eyes. "Well, shit, and I was all worried about how you were handling it." He laughed. "I don't know what's right or wrong anymore."

"It's never been about that for me."

"Oh, I know that now. You've got tunnel vision. You've never been human at all. It's just a skin…"

Andre opened his empty eyes again and picked up the sword.

"The Swan Hilted Sword," he breathed. "It's amazing. Heavier than I thought it would be." He stood up and hefted the blade. "Brenda, you know how this thing works, right?"

"Not really," she said, backing away from him and shielding Amber with her arms.

Andre could obviously see the sword but nothing else. Kevin pushed himself to the back of the nook as the tip of the sword whipped inches from his face.

Victoria said, "Andre, please be careful with that thing."

Andre smiled. "Yeah. Blind guy with a sword. Probably scarier for you than me. Watch this, though. It's important."

He moved the sword in an arc. The air around the tip of the blade shimmered and split open, revealing a stone walled room hung with tapestries. He turned the sword at the end of the arc and the split closed.

"It's like a key," he explained. "It can open a path into Tir Naomh. It cannot, however, open a path back. Can you see what I did, Brenda?"

Brenda said, "Yes. But I don't think anyone else but you or me could do it."

Andre nodded toward the sound of her voice. "That's right. It's your special toy, for the most part. I can use it because I helped bring it here. It likes me. It likes you more."

He closed his eyes and fumbled the sword back onto the

table. Victoria winced as the blade gouged the wooden tabletop.

"You guys will have to leave before the sword decides to stay," Andre warned. "I don't really know what that means, any more than I know what the Hearth of Souls is. The spirit world works like puzzles. I suspect most of it is just smoke and mirrors. As always, free will reigns and you can choose to go or not to go. If you don't, Kevin's a dog forever. Now, I'm going back to bed."

He put his hand out and took a step toward the kitchen. Victoria took his hand and guided him in the correct direction. "I don't know if I'm ever going to get over the disorientation," he grumbled.

Brenda sat down across from Kevin. Amber climbed over the table and threw herself onto him. He let her crawl onto his shoulders and grab both of his ears.

"This is ridiculous," he said.

"'idiclus!" Amber mimicked. "Daddy dog mask. Anday has swo'd." She tugged his ears as if they would pull off. She was annoyed when they didn't.

"Please stop that," he said. She stopped pulling but still clenched his ears in her tiny hands.

Brenda laughed. "Yeah. Yeah, it is. So do we go to Tir Naomh or do you stay a Doggy Daddy for the rest of your life?" She pointed to the sword on the table.

Kevin smiled, which revealed all his teeth. Brenda stared at his mouth. She wasn't frightened of him at all, but her fascination was almost disturbing.

"Always to the point," he said. "What about the boys?"

Brenda shook her head. "I don't know, Kevin. Craig seemed so sure of himself when he left this morning. And Victoria does plan to go after him. She has to go to Tennessee first for some reason, but she said that the

Confluence was strong enough to protect him for now. Something about the number eight. I didn't really understand what she was talking about. Andre worries me more, though. He's been up and back to bed several times. I tried to talk to him. He's... I don't know. Changed. More than any of the rest of us, I think. It's like he's aged. But, Kevin, what are we supposed to do?"

Kevin didn't have an answer for that question, so he remained silent. Amber leaned forward and put her chin on the top of his head. "I a hat," she said.

Brenda smiled and said, "That's a hell of a picture. Let me get my phone."

Kevin barked, "No!"

Startled, Amber squeezed his ears, digging her fingernails into the soft flesh of their interior. Brenda froze.

Kevin removed Amber from his head.

"The rules are very clear about this sort of thing," he said. "Creatures like us have to operate in the shadows. Pictures and recording devices create pressure on us. When we get recorded in our true forms or doing something that can't be easily explained, events start to bend around us. If we become too exposed, we end up getting killed in some random way."

Brenda said, "Well, then, we don't have any choice at all, do we? You can't stay here if you can't change back into a person."

Kevin sighed. "That's probably true. Unless you want to live somewhere no one ever goes. My cabin is remote enough to hide out in forever."

Brenda snorted. "No. I don't. Also, I don't think the rules are the same in Tir Naomh. A Dog King isn't the strangest thing in that world by a long shot."

Kevin clicked his teeth together several times and said, "I

think, though, a dragon is still pretty far out."

"A d'agon?" Amber asked. "Daddy a doggy d'agon!"

Kevin smiled at his daughter. The features of his face contorted and the muscles protested the movement. He realized he'd never tried smiling in his true form before today. He would probably discover all sorts of social disadvantages to being himself. He sighed and said, "I better call my sister."

"There were once so many monsters in the world that humans were but another kind of monster," Clarence said to Craig as they walked among row after row of enormous incubation tubes. Craig kept his incredulity to himself, but internally his mouth was agape. This facility was several levels below ground yet occupied thousands of square meters. Robotic arms were mounted on a track system that covered the ceiling, three or four meters up. The amount of power necessary to run this facility would serve a quarter of Des Moines. Craig wondered how any of this was possible, but did his best to act unimpressed.

Clarence continued, "As humanity, like a disease, spread out over the planet and began to unlock its secrets, they wrote the other monsters out of their world. The human imagination, and its lack thereof, may be the most potent magic on the planet. al-Khwārizmī's systematic approach to mathematics was devastating. Paracelsus destroyed entire swaths of supernatural beings simply by proving that the human digestive system caused several illnesses. Humanity's tolerance for the supernatural declined as observation replaced superstition. Alchemy replaced magic and chemistry replaced alchemy. By the twentieth century, most magic had been destroyed. Some small pockets still remain. My life's work has been to bring magic back, Craig. You're one of us now. You're something different. Can you feel the tug? Can you feel the world rejecting you? Can you feel it trying to destroy you?"

"Maybe," Craig said, though he knew what Clarence was talking about. A teenage girl had caught him blipping at a truck stop in southern Minnesota. She stared at him as he seemingly materialized in the parking lot. He spent a half hour in the stall of the bathroom blipping backward as a result. Loretta had slept on the stall's convenient diaper changing station. As his atomic structure dismantled and reassembled itself over and over, he understood that if too many people saw him blipping, he'd tear himself right out of existence. Still, that entire speech seemed like bullshit. Something else was going on.

They stopped in front of a tube labeled PKΔ. The cylindrical glass rose from a stainless steel base. Clarence pushed a recessed button and a touch screen tablet slid out.

"This is a blank canvas," he said, typing into the tablet with a shaking hand. A green light illuminated the amniotic fluid and a small charge of electricity danced across the skin of the body inside. Its eyes opened and it lifted its right hand. "Once I take the genetic material from Amber and fuse it to the purine and pyrimidine bases in these organisms, they will be complete. They can then, like your bdelloid rotifers, absorb the DNA from any human they consume. They can even take the majority of their memories, providing the brain is eaten before it dies. There will be one difference, though, Craig, and an important one. They will be Awake. All of them."

Craig took the touch screen from Clarence and studied it. Biorhythms, vital signs, and mental activity all registered on active charts and infographics. A series of clickable tiles along the right side displayed various Coptic symbols.

"What are these symbols for?" Craig asked.

"Alchemy, boy," Clarence said. "We're going backwards in time. Once we release these creatures into the world, they'll consume their targets, become them, and begin the process of changing human destiny."

"I don't understand that," Craig said, handing the touch screen back to Clarence. "Why not just wake everyone up? Seems a lot less… cannibalistic."

Clarence motioned to a nearby desk. He walked to the chair, sat down, and pointed at the computer.

"These," he said, "have changed everything too quickly. I had amassed a small army of Awakened humans in 1990. By the year 2000, I had lost a quarter of them. At this point, I'm down to a fraction of what I once had. There are fewer and fewer to be found every year. The internet kills them. As humans take their Enlightenment farther and recording technology becomes more pervasive, we are running out of shadows to hide in. I didn't believe Moore's Law could be accurate. I was wrong. There is not time to try to wake up the collective of humanity."

Craig shook his head. "I dunno, Clarence. My newsfeeds read like the World Weekly News. Most of the information on the internet is either false or skewed. There should be plenty of shadows to hide in there."

Elpis sighed. "Not for us, Craig. We're too real. If we make it into your newsfeed, it's an obituary."

Craig thought about Victoria's radio and TV. Clarence's arguments still rang hollow.

A tall, gangly man joined them. His features were sharp and his eyes deeply set in his skull. A short goatee pointed down to a massive chest. He was wearing a white lab coat.

Clarence said, "Craig this is Number 8."

Alarm bells sounded in Craig's head, but he remained calm and extended his hand in greeting. In retrospect, he regretted this decision. Andre's warning had been for nothing.

Number 8 took his hand and twisted his arm, locking his elbow and shoulder. Craig maneuvered out of his grip, but Number 8 caught his other wrist.

Craig said, "Fuck this," and blipped, intending to cross the room, flip Elpis off, and leave.

But Number 8 moved almost as fast as Craig. The pair began a fighting dance similar to what had happened in the Small Comforts motel room. Craig knew that he was going to lose seconds into the battle, but he fought anyway.

As Craig blurred around the room with Number 8, Clarence said tiredly, "Amber was drugged with a very specific opium flower, Craig, which means that Victoria helped you bring her to me. I do not know why that *woman* would help you, but I suspect you haven't been forthcoming with me. I can also smell her stench all over you. She's helped you block me out. Craig, I'm not going to kill you, but I have ways of making you do what I want. One way or another, I'll get the information I need from you. Until then, you can remain as a guest of The Elpis Foundation. Perhaps you'll even lure that witch here, so I can deal with her as I've intended to for decades."

Craig was sweating and bleeding. Number 8 transformed as he applied various submission moves. The goatee on his face split and enlarged into fangs. His eyes separated into eight shiny, black orbs. His limbs elongated. Thousands of spiny hairs punctured his skin, which made it difficult to escape his grip. Each time Number 8 got ahold of him, Craig's skin lacerated as he twisted free. Craig realized that if Number 8 wanted him dead or broken he'd be both.

Finally, Number 8 spun in what appeared to be unexpected retreat. Craig blipped toward the door. He made it two steps before a gooey web encased him from his shoulders to his feet.

Craig's breath fled his lungs as he hit the ground. Clarence crouched above him and gripped his face with bony, thin-skinned fingers.

"I'm going to tear your mind apart, boy," Clarence growled. "Then I'm going to put it back together the way I want."

Clarence released Craig's face and stood, relying on his cane.

Craig sputtered, "Spider Man beat the Flash this time, but there will be a rematch."

Clarence ignored him and limped from the lab.

Octavio sat in a small examination room in the Medical Research Wing of Elpis Enterprises pretending to read the latest issue of *National Geographic*. The anesthesiologist was finishing with Clarence, who lay sleeping on a fancy gurney with a variety of electronic controls. As she injected syringes into Clarence's IV, she shot glances at Octavio. When she'd seen him last week, his right arm wasn't missing. She didn't ask about it and he wasn't in the mood to make up a story.

As his eyes slid across pictures of mountains and brightly feathered birds, he tried to figure out how Sheila's mad plan would play out. Neither Sheila nor Kimm were mentally stable. Sheila's transition from emotionless killer to... he had no idea what, really... was still hiccupping. At times, she seemed to be in complete control of herself. At others, she seemed on the verge of a freak out. She'd made him pull over twice on the trip from Minnesota this morning so that she could vomit. Her eyes flashed green each time, so he at least had some warning. She insisted that she would be fine, that she was just working through the change that Brenda forced upon her. Octavio was not convinced, considering she'd eaten his arm.

Kimm was faring much better. However, his antics at the car dealership raised questions. If Sheila could waffle between stable and unstable, so could Kimm. Oren had no such anxiety. He and Kimm had chatted in the back seat for the entire drive. Kimm drilled Oren for information about their family, which Oren gave in elaborate detail. Octavio suspected that Kimm was using pheromones to manipulate Oren. The entire situation was just too weird, otherwise.

Had Sheila not insisted that the Confluence be followed as she'd mapped it, Octavio would not be anywhere near the twin powder kegs of Elpis Enterprises and The Elpis Foundation. He knew he could keep his cool with Clarence. But how would the Térata react to coming home? His fate was in the hands of two emotionally unstable killing machines.

When the anesthesiologist finished and left, Octavio locked the door and took off his shirt and pants.

Clarence's jaw hung open and his breathing was rough but even. The first time Octavio had done this, two years ago, Clarence had still been full of life. His albinism made his skin papery as it aged, but his body was fitter than one decades younger. Now his skin sagged, looking as though it might fall off the bones it was pinned to. As Octavio removed Clarence's hospital gown, he grunted. Even in the two days he had been gone, the muscles and skin had suffered notable deterioration. Clarence would not live much longer.

"This will probably be the last time we do this," Octavio

said.

Thousands of thread sized tentacles twisted out of the skin all over Octavio's body. They danced together as if flowing with unseen currents. One at a time, the tentacles dipped and drove into all areas of Clarence's body. They found and devoured cancer cells. Instead of pumping the cancer back to Octavio, they digested it and regurgitated healthy cells. This process had worked well in the first year of Clarence's battle with leukemia. For reasons he did not understand, it had become less effective as time went on. In the last few months, it barely worked at all.

As Octavio guided the tentacles through Clarence's body, he brushed them against bones, which housed the source of the problem. Clarence was adamant that Octavio not disturb the marrow. That admonishment frustrated Octavio, since he thought he could cure the cancer outright by destroying and rebuilding the marrow. Clarence had reasons for his idiosyncrasies, so Octavio had always obeyed. This time, though, Octavio allowed a single tentacle to bore into the bone in its search of cancer cells. A pulsing blackness shot through the tentacle, killing it. Pain blasted into him, but he remained stationary. If he pulled away from Clarence now, Clarence would be torn to shreds. Octavio gritted his teeth and disconnected the tentacle from his core before the blackness could travel its entire length. Heaving breaths, he twisted the tentacle around his index finger and ripped it out of himself. It dropped to the floor, thrashing and blackened. He rebuilt the area where the tentacle had disturbed the bone in Clarence.

Well, he thought, *that was stupid.*

Had he not cut that tentacle the instant he did, he suspected that whatever was killing Clarence would now be killing him. *Isn't that what you want, anyway?* a little voice in his head taunted. Octavio shook his head. He did not want to die. His death wish was a fantasy, an illusion of depression.

Another hour passed before Octavio cleared out all the cancerous cells. Clarence looked better, but imminent death still clung to his features. Octavio draped the hospital gown back over him and put his own clothing back on. He pushed the call button for the nurse and left. Usually, he would remain until the anesthesiologist returned and woke Clarence back up. Today he could not afford the time.

A piercing hunger rippled across his muscles. He hadn't eaten since leaving for the Twin Cities. The energy he expended treating Clarence's leukemia coupled with the damage Sheila had done left him famished. He needed raw meat. The more alive that meat, the better. The Foundation made provisions for him.

Octavio crossed the hallways of Elpis Enterprises, nodding to a few people he knew. Most of them were startled by his missing arm, though he waved away any conversation. He should have put on a prosthetic. Sometimes bullshit explanations worked. They usually didn't. At least Halloween was coming up. He could claim it was a joke costume.

By the time he reached the agricultural facilities, he was grumpy with hunger. He swiped his ID badge through the security check point leading to an exterior compound. The security guard didn't look up as he entered.

The Elpis Foundation's livestock breeding programs were world class. They occupied twenty acres, housing all sorts of animals. To the public, the accessible areas contained run of the mill agricultural animals. In restricted areas, there was a zoo. Octavio had never visited it. He stalked across a grassy courtyard and into a curtain barn. None of the employees were close enough to notice his missing arm. They just waived and went about their various tasks.

Octavio locked the barn door and marched by the tack closet, feed room, and rows of farrowing stalls containing hogs of various sizes and colors. The pork production arm of The Elpis Foundation was a popular charity that supported 4-H groups across Iowa and other areas of the Midwest. It was usually a busy place, but he had called ahead, ensuring the barn was empty. Octavio stopped before the final stall. Inside, four females whose weight gain had not matched target lounged on a bed of woodchips. Octavio opened the gate and walked inside. The sows grunted and stood up.

"Hello, ladies," he said in a comforting voice as the hogs sniffed his shoes and pants. "How are we doing today? It's getting chilly outside, isn't it? Let's just cut down the draft a bit, shall we?"

Octavio flipped open a box lid on the wall and punched a code into the numerical pad beneath it. Steel roll ups descended from the ceiling on all sides of the sty. An overhead fluorescent flickered to life. The hogs grunted and kicked at the woodchips on the floor. Octavio kept up a litany of reassurances until the outside world was blocked out.

He removed his shirt and allowed four tentacles to slither from beneath his armpits, as he had done when he devoured Tim. The tentacles approached each of the pigs, careful not to cause the animals any additional stress. Hogs were loud when they were afraid. Octavio had learned to make this process as quiet as possible.

The tentacles sprung into the pigs' throats, tearing out vocal cords on their way to carotid arties. The animals stiffened and trembled as the tentacles sucked in their blood until their hearts stopped beating. One by one, they fell over.

The tentacles thrust into the flesh, grinding it up and pumping it back into Octavio's body.

A euphoric sensation enveloped him as the meat slithered into him. He slumped to the floor. The tentacles chewed through bone, skin, muscle, and bowels. As they consumed the last fragments of the hogs, a pleasant coolness settled over Octavio's skin. The euphoria faded as the tentacles retracted. Smaller tentacles burst from his right shoulder and knit his arm back together. With so much meat available, they worked quickly. In a matter of minutes, his arm was restored. He flexed new muscles and wiggled his fingers to ensure full connection to the rest of his nervous system.

Octavio put his shirt back on, stretching it over the new, massive bulge in his midsection. He tapped the code into the keypad to lift the roll ups. As they slid up, he was surprised to find Number 8 standing outside the stall waiting for him. He was in human form, thankfully.

"What's up?" Octavio asked as he opened the gate and wobbled out.

Number 8 said, "We have a boy you are supposed to take a look at. You'll need to talk to Clarence about him. Please come with me."

Octavio nodded. "OK. Where are we headed? I'm going to need to use the bathroom in about twenty minutes, and I think you know that isn't optional."

Number 8 inclined his head and looked down his nose. "We'll be in the sub-level labs," he said. "There are facilities there that will meet your needs."

"Oh, great," Octavio said. He disliked the labyrinth of mad scientist laboratories beneath The Foundation. As grotesque and demonic as he found his own condition, the stuff going on down there was worse. The science that created Clarence's numbered pets and the procedures he used to Wake Up humans were messy at best. Octavio had once seen Number 4 chase a small child covered with lizard scales through the halls. The child hadn't survived what Number 4 did to capture him. Octavio avoided the area whenever possible.

"I'm not going to be able to move very fast," Octavio said. "I currently weigh around four hundred pounds."

Number 8 smiled. "The way you eat is fascinating," he said. "May I watch sometime?"

Octavio shook his head. He'd had nightmares about the way Number 8 ate. "Nope. That's private. I'll follow you, but go slowly."

Number 8 shrugged and said, "We've got more in common than you think, Octavio."

Dios no lo quiera, Octavio thought.

An electric golf cart was parked outside the barn. It lurched to the right as he sat down and the motor bogged as it accelerated. Octavio's midsection grumbled. Moving was always uncomfortable after he'd gorged. The spare tire around his waist didn't make things any easier.

His new arm was not noticed. If anyone mentioned its absence before, he'd claim he had been playing a joke on Clarence. Even in Clarence's seat of power the rules held. Exposure was a problem.

Number 8 drove to the service elevators of The Foundation. He swiped his ID card on the panel to access the lower levels. The descent sent a wave of nausea through Octavio, but he could not throw up. His digestive system didn't work that way anymore. He inhaled deeply and closed his eyes. The doors of the elevator slid open and Number 8 drove through the forest of tubes that was Clarence's latest project. Octavio knew little about it and wanted to know less. They came to a work station where

Clarence was hunched over a microscope, muttering to himself.

Number 8 said, "Octavio is here."

"Good, good," Clarence said, not looking up from the microscope.

Number 8 tilted his head, indicating that Octavio should get out of the cart.

Octavio shook his head. "You're going to have to drive me to a wash station in about five minutes," he said. "I won't make it on foot. I usually use the one in the barn."

Number 8 grinned and sat back in his seat.

Clarence turned around and said, "I'm sorry to have disturbed your eating cycle, Octavio, but I need to clear some things up."

Octavia waved his hand and said, "No problem." A noisy rumble from his stomach belied him.

"There is a boy being held in one of the examination rooms," Clarence said. "He's managed to block me out of his mind and there is information I need from him. He brought a child to me this morning. I need to know every detail about how he came into possession of the child. Number 1 is involved."

"My report—" Octavio began.

"I read it," Clarence interrupted. "There's much more going on than you are aware of. I believe this boy, Craig, has information I need. Get it out of his head."

Octavio frowned. "You know what I'll have to do to get that information. He'll suffer severe brain damage."

"I don't care," Clarence said. "I need to know exactly what is happening before I enter the final phase of this project. I would torture him, but that always distorts the truth. Clean his mind of the last forty-eight hours and bring it to me. Be detailed. Put him back together as best you can when you're finished, but get the information."

"OK. I have to take care of this first," Octavio said, pointing at the bulge in his abdomen.

"He's in A-389," Clarence said, turning back to the microscope.

Octavio looked at Number 8 and said, "Unless you want a mess all over your nice golf cart, we need to get moving."

Number 8 nodded and drove to a room labeled Chemical and Eye Wash Stations. Octavio stumbled to one of four stainless steel doors. He flipped the door open and slid inside a cramped space containing a floor drain, shower head, and a pull chain hanging from the ceiling. Octavio stripped and hung his clothing on a peg on the back of the door. His abdomen contorted. He began panting.

"OK, OK," he said to his belly. "*Jesús Cristo.*"

Carefully, Octavio positioned himself above the floor drain. He propped one hand against the wall and grabbed the brass ring of the pull chain with the other. A large tentacle wriggled from his rectum. He guided it down to the floor drain and yanked the chain. Cold water hit him and he yelped. The tentacle disgorged a rust colored, pasty ball. Octavio smashed it with his foot, which allowed the water to dissolve it and wash it down the drain. Another ball followed, then another and another. Octavio stayed under the water until all traces of the paste balls were gone. The tentacle retracted. Pork was, besides human flesh, the most satisfying of meals. But it made a mess on the way out.

He released the pull chain, dried off with paper towels, and dressed. Now he had to deal with Craig. This was going to be tricky. Clarence would know if he held back anything.

Number 8 waited in the golf cart when Octavio came out.

"I was under the impression that you had somewhere else to be," Octavio said.

Number 8 shrugged. "I did. But Clarence wants me to help you with the kid. He's fast. Too fast for you to handle alone."

Oh, wonderful, Octavio thought as he slid into the golf cart, *because I needed this to be more complicated.* He considered his options as they drove to exam room A-389.

Sheila stood in the doorway of her apartment at the Elpis Foundation staring at the bed inside. "Apartment" was a generous term. This was a dormitory. A dormitory for Térata. "Bed" was also a generous term. It was a twin without its other, white sheets stretched harshly across a hard mattress. A grey blanket sat folded beside a flat pillow.

She was in her true form. Being otherwise would elicit questions from anyone who saw her. The tension of holding Sheila's form had vanished, but that wasn't something she could explain if she planned to survive here for long. She stepped into the room and closed the door.

A squat dresser and simple desk stood against the wall across from the bed. The room had a tiny closet as well as a small bathroom with a sink, shower, and toilet. The cinderblock walls had neither decorations nor windows. Sheila opened the drawers of the dresser and flipped through their contents. Underwear. Socks. Gym clothes. She rifled through the closet, finding generic outfits.

My life was barren, she thought.

Accruements of her identities were either bought and discarded or checked out and returned to The Foundation. Everything in this room was practical necessity.

The exception was the makeup case in the bathroom. It was a beige box edged with gilt, containing eye shadow, lipstick, rouge, and nail polish. Brushes, application pads, and other tools were tucked amid the cluster of sizzling colors. She took the box to her bed and spread out its contents. The sheet became a stark pallet splashed with almost every color, shade, and hue in the spectrum of visible light. At the bottom of the box she found what she was looking for: a snail shell brooch inlaid with mother of pearl and gold. The spiral of the shell was a lyrical golden line.

Sheila smiled as she turned the brooch over in her clawed hand. Memories cascaded through her mind. Since Brenda had spoken the words 'you're free,' Sheila's past was twisting and redefining itself. All the emotions she'd once faked were becoming real. The process was disjointed, paradoxical, and painful. She needed a strong memory to contextualize the emotional shit storm. This broach brought back the most powerful memory of Sheila's life. A woman named Hellena Stevens had given this broach to Sheila five years ago. A gallery owner in the Meatpacking District of New York City, Hellena had fallen madly in love with Sheila during an opening reception at her gallery. Sheila had hit her with pheromones to illicit the response, but in retrospect that had probably been unnecessary.

Hellena's brother had been a person of interest to Elpis Enterprises. Sheila only used Hellena to get close to him. But their affair was a blistering week of sexual intensity. During that period, Hellena managed to chip the emotional barrier that blocked Sheila's notions of sentimental attachment. Sheila remembered the woman's body, her too-white skin, her fading red hair, her expensive perfume, her supple lips… the taste of red wine, the smell of orchids always in bloom in her bedroom, the warm oils and soft bath soaps they shared.

A warmth flowed into Sheila's chest as she unlocked these precious memories. All the emotional sentiments she had feigned at the time became sincere. Giggles between the sheets. The innocent chatter of lovers with no thought beyond each other. The exploration of Hellena's body and the unbridled discovery of hidden joys. Green tears leaked from Sheila's eyes, trailing through the fur of her snout before dropping to the sheet. Stains spread where they fell. She'd never cried before, especially not in her true form. The green splatters were beautiful.

Hellena had given her the broach the night before Sheila broke her heart and killed her brother. Sheila imagined Hellena's pain as she read the brief note left on her pillow while she slept. That note and her retention of the broach were ample evidence of how deeply Hellena had penetrated Sheila's emotionless exterior. Sheila hadn't gone back to New York for a year after the affair, always finding reasons to be elsewhere. By then, Hellena had closed her gallery and moved to Italy. Sheila's obsession with Number 1's escape was driven by this episode of her life. The crack that Hellena hammered into her would not seal and her longing for freedom took on more distinction as she realized it might be possible.

Sheila sobbed, clutching the broach to her heart. She felt the stabbing wounds she'd inflicted on a woman who wanted nothing more than to hold and cherish her. The shattered illusions that she constructed to seduce Hellena were glass shards beneath her emotional feet. Her tears were the blood of those feet as she dragged them through her memories.

As she hoped, Sheila felt herself solidifying around the memory. Hellena became a focal point from which she could judge right and wrong. The week she'd spent in Hellena's arms had been right. Leaving her had been wrong. Such a thin distinction without emotion, but a sea of difference through the lens of love. Sheila's mind ordered itself around the affair. To her dismay, her entire life up this point was an unforgivable series of manipulations. Emotions were a curse to a creature such as herself. No wonder Clarence had blocked them.

Sheila stared at the explosion of colors on her bed. Tears streamed steadily from her eyes to the sheet, reminding her of the stained canvases of Sam Gilliam. She pulled the broach away from her heart and opened her hand. It rested against the blackness of her palm, shining dully in the fluorescent light of the room. The gold spiral mirrored the Confluence swirling around her.

Beauty, she thought. *I must live a life of beauty.*

As the thought trailed away, she felt something snap in her chest. The tears stopped flowing. Her guilt and self-loathing faded. If she reached for beauty, she could move forward. She couldn't undo her past. But she could live with it.

Sheila put the broach and her makeup back into the case. She put the case back in the bathroom and returned to the bed, where she lay down and stretched herself out. Her legs hung off from the calves down. In the past, she hadn't noticed such discomforts. Now, she couldn't believe she'd slept here night after night, just fulfilling her need to rest and rejuvenate.

Her hand slid between her thighs and she thought of Hellena. She masturbated, panting hard as she remembered the woman's smell, taste, and the feeling of her skin pressed against her own. When she climaxed, she thrust her finger deep inside and imagined Hellena smiling, assuring her that she would be OK. That, honestly, a broken heart and a murdered brother weren't the worst things that could happen to a person on the same day.

Kimm growled in frustration as he manipulated the interface of a computer in the common area of the dormitories that he used to think of as home. The I-Station, as it was known inside The Foundation, was a row of six booths divided much like stalls in a bathroom. Each stall provided some, but not absolute, privacy. A 32" touch screen, ergonomic keyboard, speakers, headsets, mouse, and other computer accessories were spread before him. Everything was oversized to accommodate the hands and bodies of the Térata.

Kimm's access to most of the Elipsis Network had been suspended. He could access his e-mail, which was obviously being monitored, and nothing else. He ticked his clawed fingers against the keyboard, using just the nails to type.

As he tried and failed to login to the Tracking Network for the fifth time, the door of the I-Station opened. He growled and turned to find Number 4 staring at him with unblinking red eyes.

"You are smaller," she observed.

"You aren't any smarter," he replied. A large portion of his memories had resurfaced when he walked into The Foundation, for which he was very grateful. Octavio's fabrication that Number 1 had drugged them was a solid cover, but it would only explain so much.

Number 4 gave no hint of annoyance. "Clarence wants you to brief me on everything that happened in the Twin Cities. He suspects that Number 1 may follow you here. He wants to be sure we're ready for him."

Kimm became distracted by the glistening red to orange transitions of her scales. Coupled with the yellow down of her eyebrows and hair, she was a stunning creature. Funny how he'd never been able to appreciate that before.

"Well?" she prompted, lifting a finger with a hooked claw. Her tongue flicked out of her mouth to lick the transparent membrane over her eye.

"I was drugged," Kimm spat. "The effects have not completely worn off." He returned his attention to the screen, where he posted a coded message on a dating website that said, "Can't do Friday night, but maybe Monday." Victoria and Kevin would see it and know he'd failed to access Elipsis. Number 4 watched the screen with interest. He clenched his teeth.

"I see," Number 4 replied. "We can discuss this in the conference room if you would find that more comfortable."

Kimm stood and gestured for her to lead the way. He lumbered behind her like a gorilla, unable to walk upright in true form. Number 4 walked like a human, but he'd seen her slither across walls and ceilings as if gravity didn't apply. The pads of her oversized fingers and feet were bristled like the feet of geckos. He tried to remember more details about her, but most of them were gone. He had a notion that he and she had been at odds on many occasions. He hoped whatever politics existed between them would take a back seat, since he couldn't remember any of them.

"I read that you were unable to transform," Number 4 said as she closed the door to the conference room and locked it.

Kimm spent a moment negotiating himself into one of the chairs, which were sized appropriately for the Térata but still didn't quite fit his body type. Number 4 had no such problems and sat down. She stared at him through red eyes with slit pupils.

"That was true," he said. "I am recovering slowly. I have limited shifting abilities now."

"Show me," she said.

Kimm kept his exterior calm, which wasn't difficult since his face looked like a cross between a bat and a wolf, but he felt a stab of resentment mingled with panic. He released a pheromone to mask his scent, thankful that he could manage it. He hadn't been sure he'd be able to. If Number 4 started smelling emotions come out of him, his game would be up way too soon.

"I cannot," he lied. The only other form available to him was Kimm and he'd already compromised that identity too much by walking into The Foundation in it. He didn't want any further exposure. "I barely managed to take on my true form when I arrived. I can't shift right now."

"And yet you can control how you are perceived," Number 4 said.

He nodded. "That happened when I tried to change," he said.

"Interesting," Number 4 said. "I wonder what drug Number 1 used on you."

"No idea," he said. "As Octavio put in his report, I am experiencing synesthesia, disorientation, and occasional physical paralysis. The effects lessen with time. I thought I'd have already been blood tested."

Number 4's unblinking red eyes regarded him for several moments. Her tongue slid out to lick them. She said, "You will be tested, but Clarence has other priorities right now. Did you have any direct interaction with Number 1?"

"No," he said truthfully.

"Did Number 7 have any direct interaction with Number 1?"

"Yes," he said. "That's how we know we were drugged. Octavio located both of us together in the hotel room at Le Méridien Chambers. I have no memories of how I got there.

You should be interrogating Sheila. She can tell you much more about Number 1."

Number 4 made a slight nod as he finished, as if confirming a suspicion. He wondered what she was up to.

"What do you know about Victoria Starks?" she asked.

Kimm was surprised by the question. Victoria had not been any part of Octavio's report. "Nothing," he said. "Is she involved?"

"Clarence thinks so," Number 4 said. She stood up and leaned forward. "You are lying to me, Number 7. Why are you lying to me?"

Her flat tone of voice and aggressive stance flared Kimm's anger. He snarled and his quills stood out straight.

"Lying?" he growled. "What do you know about lying, Number 4?"

Number 4's tongue flickered to her eye and she said, "You are having an emotional outburst. You referred to Number 7 as one of her identities. These are indications of a severely compromised nervous system. Coupled with your obvious physical lessening, I believe you are no longer a reliable source of information concerning Number 1."

She pushed a button on the desk. A speaker squawked, followed by a smooth voice that said, "Copy. This is Number 8."

"Number 9 is compromised and considered hostile," Number 4 said. "I am implementing plan CC802. Assume Number 7 is equally compromised and proceed as planned. Inform Clarence. I will bring in Number 9. Please bring in 7."

"Ten four," replied the voice in the speakers.

"If you think you can just package me up and take me somewhere, you've got another thing coming," Kimm said, allowing a nasty grin to spread across his face. "You didn't fare so well the last time we got into it." He had no idea if that was the case, but it seemed like a good way to throw her off.

Number 4 said, "That is true. So I learned. I had hoped you would become violent. I can now even the score."

She reached beneath the table and pulled out a pistol. Kimm laughed. "A gun?" he asked. "You know bullets won't stop me."

Number 4 squeezed the trigger. Kimm heard the decompression of a CO_2 cartridge. He honed his vision onto the tip of the pistol and watched a dart emerge. Spinning, he plucked it from the air. Before she could pull the trigger a second time, he threw the dart back at her.

Surprise registered on her face as the dart penetrated the scales on her neck. She hadn't learned enough. She fired the gun two more times, but the darts struck the wall and table top. Her knees buckled as she dropped the gun. Kimm pushed her into a chair and pulled the dart out of the table. Whatever was in it was powerful stuff. Were it etorphine, the dart would need to be large enough to contain a plunger system. This one could not have delivered a dose high enough to achieve the effects that Number 4 was experiencing.

"Can you talk?" Kimm asked, sending a wave of pheromones at her that should loosen her tongue and make her more pliable. She didn't even put up resistance. That drug was something else.

"Yes," she said. "But I am dying, so you don't have long to ask questions."

"Really?" he asked. "What the fuck was in that dart?"

"I don't know. Clarence said it would kill you without causing the explosion we usually experience at terminus. He wanted your body intact for study."

"That motherfucker," Kimm breathed. "Why did he want to kill me?"

"It was my decision," she replied, her voice weakening as she spoke. "If you were compromised to a point that we could no longer trust you... I was to kill you and bring you to the labs. I made the call when you blocked your pheromone signature. You were obviously... lying."

Her tongue flickered out, but didn't make it all the way to her eye before sliding back into her mouth. A gurgle bubbled from her throat and she coughed.

"Why are you telling me all this?" he asked. "For that matter, why didn't you kill me before you told Number 8 all that shit?"

"Because I wanted to be free like you," she said, managing a wry smile that for a moment made the features of her scaled face quite lovely. "I made errors, which is common when emotions are involved." She coughed again. "Number 7 is Sheila now," she mused. "Tell me... who are you?"

"Kimm," he said.

Her tongue flickered from her mouth, but fell limply across her chin. The red of her eyes faded to dull grey. The smile was still on her face.

Kimm frowned at her body and picked up the pistol. He could only fire it with the claw of his finger. Aiming would be impossible in this form. He released the clip. There were still 4 darts inside. He needed to get to Sheila before Number 8.

Craig lay on an exam room table staring at the tiles of the suspended ceiling. The brown vinyl pad stuck to his lower back where his shirt climbed up. The room had been stripped of everything but the exam table, including the sink. Craig entertained the notion of kicking the copper pipes sticking out of the wall to create a flood. He could possibly escape in the ensuing chaos. Except there wouldn't be any chaos. Even if there was, he was unlikely to achieve anything more than making a wet inconvenience for Clarence's ass-hat minions. He didn't shelve the idea.

Despite having what amounted to an awe-inspiring super power, he had been soundly routed every time he'd been put to the test. First, in the Small Comforts and then again by that spider monster.

Fuck that fucking fuck, he thought.

Number 8 had stripped Craig of everything but his jeans and t-shirt. The monster had even taken his shoes. The concrete floors were cold. More annoyingly, Number 8 had taken his cigarettes. Craig now understood why cigarettes had such a high value in prison.

Craig checked the door to ensure it was indeed locked. He knocked down two of the ceiling's drop tiles, hoping that a vent would facilitate his escape as if he were the hero in an action movie. He paced. And he sweat.

His mind turned to Elpis's mad scheme. He should have been more enthusiastic about asking questions. Who would those blank humanoids replace? Politicians? People of power? What happened if they were caught in the act of eating their intended victims? Would Clarence be able to control them? And, most importantly, why did Clarence want to bring back magic in the first place? That was the catch for Craig. Technology was expanding at a rate that made magic pale in comparison, and it relied on much better structures. Clarence was a master of both, so why would he want to change the paradigm? And considering how much control he already had over magic and technology, why in the world was he still sick?

He's probably just fucking crazy, Craig thought.

Clarence's explanation for the decline of magic and monsters was certainly crazy. It didn't hold water. The ancient Greeks and Persians had advanced mathematics at their disposal. Democritus had postulated the existence of atoms in the 5th century BC. For Clarence's explanation to be valid, history itself had to have been rewritten thousands of times over 40,000 years. Craig's mind didn't allow for such unattached, theological nonsense. Clarence's argument reminded Craig of the preacher at his father's church, who claimed God had left dinosaur fossils for humanity to find when he created the earth 6,000 years ago. There was something deeper, truer, and more logical beneath Clarence's bullshit.

In boredom, Craig blipped around the room. Time slowed down for him when he blipped, but not evenly. There was a wobble to the world as he moved. He couldn't control his speed with precision. This was why he he'd been losing fights. He took his shirt off and threw it into the air. As he turned on the blip, the shirt moved in slow motion toward the floor. Craig slid into it as it fell. The fabric resisted him with more force than its weight would imply. He had to be careful, or he'd tear it to pieces. So blipping pushed energy from his body into the environment. Though an object looked stable, it often disintegrated when he touched it. On his run to Des Moines earlier today, he'd hit a patch of loose gravel just south of the Twin Cities. He dug a hole in the ground before realizing that the gravel couldn't withstand the force of his footsteps. He wondered where such energy came from. A human body could not generate that much energy without burning up. And why didn't he create wind in the air when he moved?

He turned off the blip and sat back down on the bed.

It was stupid to get caught, he thought. *Given enough time, I could figure all this out and really understand it.*

He wouldn't have that chance. Clarence's threat scared the shit out of him. Craig had ignored Victoria's warning about "forfeiting his mind" when he drank the contents of the petri dish to seal his deal with Clarence. But his mind and its native intelligence were his refuge. He'd hidden in them throughout his childhood with his mother. He'd exploited them in college as the brick and mortar foundations of his identity. The idea that they would be taken away from him was terrifying.

A knock issued from the door.

How considerate, he thought in a panic. He hadn't known how long it would take for Clarence to address him, but he hadn't thought it would be today.

The door cracked and Number 8's silky voice said, "We're coming in Craig. If you do anything stupid, I will eat your testicles. They aren't necessary to us."

A chill spread out through Craig's skin. Number 8's voice made it clear that he was not bluffing. Craig considered blipping, but the arrogant smile on Number 8's face as he walked in erased the thought. That fucker *wanted* to eat his testicles.

Following Number 8 was a Hispanic man with a crew cut and a deep frown. The juxtaposition between him and Number 8 was striking. His skin, except his right arm, was dark while Number 8's was pasty white. He was muscular and short. Number 8 was tall and thin. His brow was furrowed with thought. Number 8's expression was cruel and lackadaisical.

"Jay and Mexican Silent Bob!" Craig said, spreading his arms and smiling.

The joke was lost on the pair, who came into the room

with businesslike indifference. Craig grimaced and backed into a corner. This was actually happening and his brain was about to get "forfeited". Sweat leaked from his armpits.

Number 8 curled his nose and said, "Your fear smells like shit."

Craig swallowed and stared at him.

Number 8 motioned to the exam table. "Sit here," he said. "Octavio needs to have a look at you."

Craig looked at the exam table and shook his head. Number 8 growled, his jaw splitting in two as his goatee grew into fangs.

Craig put his hands up and managed to sputter, "Fine! Fine! Jesus Christ!"

Number 8's face returned to normal.

The five steps he took to the exam table made Craig think of every man who'd ever walked to his death at the guillotine, electric chair, or firing squad. He'd never agreed with capital punishment anyway. He climbed onto the vinyl slowly, feeling it expel air as he sat down.

The Hispanic man, Octavio apparently, walked to the table and fiddled with the electronic controls until he figured out how to make the table descend. He said, "I'm going to need you to relax. The less you fight me, the less damage I'll do to you."

Craig squeaked, which caused his face to redden. Embarrassment in the face of getting his brain scrambled.

How funny, he thought, *I'm a big pussy and that's the bigger problem here...*

Octavio pushed Craig's knees apart so that he could bring his face within inches of Craig's own. He grabbed Craig's biceps in an iron grip. Craig became aware of Octavio's damp smell, as well as the details of his black hair and eyebrows. The entire experience was strangely intimate.

Craig found absurdity in the fact that he was having a homophobic reaction. He wondered if everyone felt so self-consciously idiotic directly before dying.

At least he's good looking, Craig thought in a desperate attempt to make himself laugh. The attempt failed.

Octavio's pupils expanded until his eyes were black. Out of the blackness, small tentacles slithered forward. Craig flinched and clamped his eyes shut. The tentacles tickled against his eyelids. Craig screamed. He'd have launched himself off the table if Octavio didn't have such a firm grip on his arms.

Octavio said, "Stay very still, Craig. Let me do what I have to do."

Something about Octavio's voice calmed Craig's nerves. He gritted his teeth and opened his eyes. The tentacles slid over the globes of his eyeballs. He felt them work into the back of his optic foramen and slither into the frontal lobe of his brain. He found it surprising that he had nerves to let him feel it.

Craig's brain exploded in light and pain. He screamed and flailed his hands until he caught hold of Octavio's elbows. His fingernails dug in. Blood ran into his palms. His legs kicked out and snapped back, slamming into Octavio's hamstrings. There was no context for the pain he was experiencing. It enveloped his head and ripped through the rest of his body. His voice gave out after the second scream, his vocal chords constricting with his throat. He couldn't breathe.

Trust me, Octavio's voice said in his mind. *I'm going to take the pain away a little bit at a time. You need to relax and go limp as I do this. We have to convince Number 8 that I'm fucking you up pretty bad.*

You are *fucking me up pretty bad!* Craig thought back. He was glad that his jaw was clenched shut or he'd have screamed that out loud.

The pain ebbed. Craig had once been beaten with a belt by one of his mother's boyfriends. That man had counted to fifty before he stopped. What Octavio had done was worse, but as the pain stimulation receded, a similar endorphic euphoria spread through Craig's body. He released Octavio's elbows and his hands fell into his lap. Blood dripped from his fingertips. His feet slid down Octavio's hamstrings, but the muscles had cramped so that they caught at the back of his knees and stayed there.

Nothing to do about that, Craig thought.

No, Octavio replied, *there isn't. Now, what I need you to do is recall everything that happened to you in the last 48 hours. Over and over again. I'm going to try to capture it without taking it away from you. I've never done this before, so things may go badly. You're just going to have to trust me.*

Craig began to panic again as the last of the pain vanished. Then he remembered what Andre said. "Trust the Number 8, but seek not the first." Octavio. Eight. Craig had already fucked up the second half of that admonition. Perhaps he could salvage things if he managed the first. He relaxed and thought, *OK. Here goes. I'll do my best to give you what you want.*

Octavio replied, *Bueno.*

Chapter 11
Térata

Elpis Enterprises, Oren found, was a complicated beast. He sat in an uncomfortable chair in a cheap hotel room in Ames with his laptop, searching the internet to better understand the company his dad worked for. Hours of research had yielded very little.

Elpis Enterprises existed as a publicly traded company on the NYSE with a board of directors who were related to GE, Monsanto, Pfizer, and other research firms. It held several patents used by other companies in contractual capacities. The exact nature of those patents was proving difficult to uncover. They seemed to be components of GMO and biotech research. The company was headquartered on a sprawling campus in the northern reaches of Des Moines. It conducted research, employed 7,000 people in six locations across the Midwest and South, and managed to elude media coverage whenever possible. *The Economist* mentioned Elpis Enterprises as an example of a "patent trove" in an article pertaining to intellectual property rights. The company regularly won industry awards for innovation, though it made no mention of them on its official website, which was vague and difficult to navigate. Its corporate slogan, "Hope For the Future", was generic.

Oren set the laptop down on the rickety desk. Hunger finally drove him away from the screen. He flipped through the local directory book in search of a delivery service. As he lifted his phone to call "Paisano's Pizza" it rang in his hand. The screen showed a St Paul number that wasn't in his contact list. He answered, "Hullo."

"Hi, is this Oren?" a male voice asked cheerfully.

"Yeah, who's this?" Oren replied.

"My name is Winton," the voice answered, "and I've been sucked down the same rabbit hole as you and a couple of my other friends."

"Rabbit hole?" Oren said. His dad had mentioned a woman named Victoria and several other people, but no one named Winton.

"Yeah, yeah," Winton said. "Monsters. Robots. All that stuff you knew was being done somewhere, by someone, but never knew who. Well, *we* know, don't we?"

Oren had not known any of this "stuff" was going on anywhere except movies. "So," he said, "What can I do for you?"

"Well, your dad was supposed to get some information from some company named Elpis Enterprises and send it to some friends of mine. Unfortunately for him, things didn't go as planned."

"They didn't?" Oren said. He stood up.

"Apparently not," Winton replied. "They needed passcodes to some proprietary intranet called Elipsis. I hate when companies give their software clever names like that. Anyway, that bombed so they brought me a laptop and asked me to crack it. I did, of course, but without being directly hooked into their system, I'm still blocked out of a bunch of shit. And, from what I've read so far, this is some deep shit. Does that make sense?"

"Yeah," Oren said. "It does. I mean, as much sense as it can."

Winton said, "What's it like to have a monster for a dad, huh? That's gotta be awesome."

Oren stared at the paisley wallpaper. "Yeah," he said. "Yeah, it is. What happened to my dad? Why didn't he get the info?"

"No idea," Winton said. "My buddy Andre dropped by with the laptop several hours ago. He left before I got it cracked. I called him once I got into it. I don't think he expected me to learn as much as I did. He told me that things weren't going well in Des Moines and somebody named Kimm—your dad, right?—couldn't get into this Elipsis System, and that's pretty important. You've got a laptop, right?"

"Yeah," Oren said.

"Well, first I need you to let me take it over. Don't worry. It's not hard. Just gotta install a couple programs you can download. I'll walk you through it. Then, I need you to go to this Elpis Enterprises place and figure out a way to get onto their Wi-Fi. As long as their Wi-Fi runs on the same connections as this Elipsis program, a script kiddie could crack it with the info on this laptop. It's loaded."

"I'm gonna have to call you back, man," Oren said.

"Wait—" Winton began, but Oren hung up.

Oren's dad had instructed him not to call or text him while he was at the Elpis compound. His phone wouldn't be on. There was no way for Oren to confirm anything that Winton just said. Andre was one of the people that Sheila mentioned being a part of the Confluence thing. He was supposed to show up in Des Moines after some people named Kevin and Brenda dropped their daughter off with Oren. Was the connection with Andre enough evidence to prove that Winton was telling the truth? Oren felt foolish for not getting Kevin or Brenda's number before his dad and Sheila left.

He paced the room, muttering through an argument with himself about whether or not to believe this Winton person. His hunger was forgotten. Ten minutes later, he called Winton back.

"It's totally rude to hang up on people," Winton said.

"Sorry," Oren said. "It's hard to know who to trust when everybody turns out to be someone else."

"That's so awesome," Winton said. "Anyway, I found you on Skype. I'm calling you now."

Liquid tones issued from Oren's laptop. He answered the call and Winton's plump, Asian face popped onto his screen.

Funny, Oren thought, *I pictured him as skinny and white.*

"OK," Winton said. "I'm going to show you a bunch of screen shots of what I need you to do. What kind of computer do you have?"

"MacBook," Oren said.

"Hippie," Winton said. "At least the battery will last. Is it fully charged?"

"Uh huh," Oren said.

"Good, good, good," Winton said. "Now, what I need you to do is..."

Oren followed Winton's instructions. An hour later he found himself in the lobby of Elpis Enterprises' medical facility, sitting in a chair by a plastic plant trying to look inconspicuous. Luckily, it was a large waiting room with heavy foot traffic. The receptionist handed him a card with the Wi-Fi information when he'd inquired about using it. She didn't even ask him who he was there to see. That was disappointing, since Oren had invented an elaborate, plausible reason to be there.

After he logged on, Winton yipped into Oren's earbuds, "Now we're cookin'. Keep your eyes open. Sooner or later, someone is gonna notice what I'm doing. By then, I should be able to get the access your dad needs and you can blow out. Until I do that, stay put."

"What are you going to do?" Oren murmured.

"I don't explain what I'm doing for people," Winton said. "It confuses them and annoys me. Just do what I say."

Oren grimaced at the computer screen. "Fine."

Kimm slammed open Sheila's door, shouting, "They—"

Inside, Number 8 sat in a desk chair. He was in human form. Sheila lounged on her bed, one knee tucked up, her arms resting on top.

"They what?" she asked, raising a furry eyebrow. Kimm found the expression absurd on her snouted face.

"Uh," Kimm said.

"He appears to be having an emotional response," Number 8 said. "How interesting. Where is Number 4, Number 9? She should be accompanying you in such a state."

"She didn't make it," Kimm said. "Do you plan on killing me, too, 8?"

Number 8 waved his hand dismissively. "Perhaps, but I'd like Number 7, or, I suppose, Sheila, to finish what she was saying before you interrupted us. Please close the door."

Sheila nodded to Kimm, so he shut the door and locked it. He skulked to the bed and curled up next to her.

"As I was saying," she said to Number 8, "we are tied to Clarence by heavy psychological lines, but each of us longs to be free of them. Number 1 found someone who can break Clarence's hold over us, but in the process, we begin to develop emotional responses to our environment. We always had emotions, they were just buried beneath Clarence's will. When we take control of them, it's like a child trying to aim a firehose. We aren't really built for it. It takes time for us to develop and we have to make very hard decisions throughout the process. If you want, Number 8, I can arrange for you to be free of Clarence as well. I know you want to be. I can smell it on you. I can see it in your eyes."

"Even in these eyes?" Number 8 asked, allowing his head to take its true form. His eyes split into eight black orbs arching up the sides of his forehead. He stood, unbuttoned his white lab coat, and kicked off his blue slip on boots. His body elongated and browned. Short, golden hairs sprouted all over it. His fingers and toes grew so that each resembled the leg of a tarantula. The lab coat fell to the floor. He spread his arms expectantly.

"What kind of emotions do you think creatures like us can really have?" he asked through two fangs.

Sheila stood. Number 8 towered over her by more than a foot. She reached up with her clawed hand and caressed the side of his face.

"We feel like this," she said. A blast of pheromones hit Number 8 so hard he fell back into his chair. Kimm was impressed with Sheila's ability to control so many various chemicals at once. Joy, sadness, lust, love, loneliness, loss… the entire spectrum of human emotion poured out of her. Kimm could almost feel Number 8's sanity begin to crack when Sheila cut them off.

Number 8's eyes, which could not convey emotions whether he felt them or not, stared into Sheila's.

"That was…" he said. "That was very interesting. I had always wondered what sex would be like if I actually felt it the way humans do… Very interesting. However, if I don't bring you both back to Clarence, he'll kill me, you, and probably Octavio for bringing you back and not reporting your true conditions. I have a… fondness… I suppose might best describe it… for Octavio. So unless you can give me a great reason not to kill you both now, I will do so."

Kimm growled and compressed his body onto the bed like a spring. Number 8 was powerful, but Kimm was confident he could be defeated. Especially with Number 7's help. The fight wouldn't last very long.

"You don't have to kill us," Sheila said, laying her hand on Kimm's head and stroking his fur. A shock of pleasure spread through him and he leaned into her hand. Thoughts of dismembering Number 8 vanished. She continued to stroke him as she spoke. "We will come with you. We just need a small piece of help from you in return."

"This seems illogical," Number 8 said, jerking back into human form and reaching for his lab coat.

"Don't touch that fucking thing," Kimm purred. "Or, I'll tear you to shreds. The darts in the gun he has will kill us without causing us to explode."

Number 8 slid back to his true form and hissed at Kimm, "How can you know I won't betray you?"

"We don't," Sheila said. "But when Brenda gets here, you will have a choice. If you kill or betray us, you'll never get that choice. She will come regardless. She can either free you or kill you. The choice will be yours. If you kill us, she will kill you. She is the end of the Térata, Number 8. Listen to my voice. You know this is the truth."

"I know you believe it is," Number 8 said. "Tell me more."

Andre hung up the phone with Winton and said to Victoria, "Winton has hacked into the Elipsis Network. That's what Sheila said we needed, right?"

"Yes," Victoria said.

Andre felt the truck decelerate as she pulled to the side of I-65.

"What are you doing?" Andre asked.

"Sending Brenda a text message with Winton's number. Kevin will need this information from him."

"You can't text and drive at the same time?" Andre teased.

"I prefer not to," she said. "I'm driving at ninety five miles an hour."

"Well, I can't text at all anymore, so I suppose I shouldn't give you shit," he said. "Wait a minute. We're doing ninety five? It must be nice to have an invisible truck. Beats the shit out of a radar detector."

Victoria ignored him, finished whatever she was doing, and pulled back onto the interstate. The sound of the engine accelerating seemed so much louder now that he couldn't see. Victoria's driving was manic, even when she wasn't in a hurry. She swerved through what he assumed was traffic, giving him no warning before the vehicle lurched right or left. The seatbelt carved an annoying burn into his neck. He kept his hand on the door grip to keep from bouncing around the cab.

Andre cracked his eyes and watched the spirit world fly by through the windows of the truck. Most of his surroundings were black void, but the sun overhead flipped between identities, sometimes appearing as Apollo and his chariot, sometimes as the Eye of Horus, and sometimes as the cutout of a childhood drawing on yellow construction paper. The road itself vanished and reappeared, changing from asphalt to bricks to the packed dirt of a cattle trail. Objects in the landscape ballooned into existence, or appeared in disjointed perspective. He'd been watching the approach of what looked like the St Louis Arch for the last hour. It hadn't gotten any bigger or closer as they moved toward it. Nothing was stable.

At least he could see the truck around him. When riding in Kevin's SUV that morning, he seemed to be floating any time he opened his eyes. Victoria explained that since she'd charmed so much of the vehicle, it probably showed up residually in the spirit world. She seemed out of her depth and reaching for an explanation, which put him a hundred leagues under the sea without a diving bell.

Where had that metaphor come from? He wondered. He'd never read Jules Verne and had no idea what a diving bell was. His brain got a jolt of symbolic imagery every time he opened his eyes. Sometimes that imagery came with all sorts of backstory, but it was unattached fragments of explanations that he could understand only if he knew every reference. He was well read for a college dropout, but the inundation of information far outstripped his knowledge base. Sometimes there were living spirits which tried to explain things to him. If he closed his eyes, he couldn't see or hear them. With his eyes closed, he existed solely, and blindly, in the really real world. That was a huge relief. Sometimes the spirits whispered some pretty scary shit. A gas pump told him he'd be dead by the end of the day.

"If Sheila and Kimm can't get us into Elpis Enterprises with the box, we're going to be in a pretty tough spot," he said. He'd made variations of this statement several times since Victoria's phone conversation with Sheila this morning.

"Yes," she said. "That is true."

"I'm going to be pretty worthless, anyway," he continued. "Do you think that Kevin can get the box inside, if we can't?"

"Kevin and Brenda have their own part to play," Victoria said. "And you are hardly worthless. Stop wallowing in self-pity."

Andre grimaced. Easy for her to say. She wasn't staring at the back of her eyelids in lieu of someplace that shouldn't exist.

"Andre," she continued, "your life is going to be something of a mess for the next few months, or even years. The possibilities of the world may seem closed to you now, but they will open up again."

"You know, I hate that shit," Andre said. "It's like..." His voice snapped, becoming chipper and upbeat. His hands danced, palms forward, in the space around him. "You've got to keep a positive attitude! Just work hard and you'll get your reward! Everything happens for a reason! It'll be OK in the end!" His voice collapsed, tinged with bitterness. "That's great, I guess, but I'm fucking blind, Victoria. I'm not brokenhearted 'cuz my prom date ditched me for the football star. I'm not bummed 'cuz I didn't get my dream job right outta college. I'm not angry about global warming. I'm fucking blind, OK? I didn't ever want to be Stevie *fucking* Wonder! I hated piano lessons. Give me a few days to just be pissed about it."

A thick silence followed his rant.

"You're laughing at me, aren't you?" he accused.

"Yes," she admitted, a pent up giggle escaping as she spoke. "I am. You are quite entertaining."

He laughed. None of the bitterness he felt tainted that laughter. "Yeah. I know. The angrier I get, the funnier I get.

It's like a defense mechanism or something. My best nights at the comedy club were after terrible days. Craig used to do shit to piss me off on purpose, just to get me going at parties."

He was saddened by the past tense of his last statement. Those times had been as recent as last week, but in this context they seemed like ancient history.

They sat in silence for a while. Andre imagined the real road flying by. Cars in all shapes and colors. The shadows of telephone poles and their lines dancing in the ditches. Sunlight on everything. He missed sunlight more than anything else. The sun in the spirit world didn't brighten it. It was just a thing suspended in void.

"I haven't told anyone this," Victoria said, breaking the silence. "But I did kill Billy Dillon and Nellie Brown."

"Really?" Andre said. He supposed that wasn't surprising, except for that vow she'd talked about when she tried to kill Craig. If someone stabbed his dad with a kitchen knife, he'd kill them given the chance. He might feel bad about it later, but knowing that probably wouldn't stop him. He loved his dad. He really wished he could call him and talk to him about all this shit.

"Really," she said.

"Well, what did you do to them?" he asked.

"Things I shouldn't have," she said, and told him the story.

Mam-maw had not believed a word Victoria said about the jade box in the second subterranean room. The spiral headed key no longer opened the lock to the door. When Victoria showed her the tarot cards, Mam-maw dismissed them as something Victoria had ordered from one of those vapid women's magazines she liked to read. Her tattered clothing and the lack of a fetus also didn't impress the older woman. She assumed that Victoria had created the entire scenario as an elaborate fabrication.

The thing in the box must have lied about making any deals with Mam-maw concerning the sheriff. The woman had never set foot in the room with the box, nor did she have any knowledge of the occult or supernatural. More than having no knowledge of such things, she disavowed their existence. She was nothing more than an herbalist and wise woman. Any hoodoo she performed was a pure affectation for the benefit of her patients.

Victoria could have demonstrated her new strength and durability in a further effort to convince her grandmother that she had encountered a demon. But her heart had broken when Mam-maw refused to believe her. Victoria packed her things and left Pikeville. Mam-maw sat on the porch in her rocking chair and coldly watched Victoria drive her father's truck away. Abortion was a betrayal for which Mam-maw would never forgive her. Victoria felt a press of guilt as she bounced along the dirt roads toward Knoxville. Though she hadn't aborted the child herself, she had chosen the path that led its premature removal. What was the difference? Wasn't an abortion justified, anyway, since she'd been raped? Not by Mam-maw's standards. She cried the entire drive to Knoxville.

The house she had shared with her father in the Mechanicsville neighborhood was a camelback shotgun. The upper floor had been her bedroom. She sat on her bed, staring at the accruements of her childhood. Compared to others in her neighborhood and school, she'd been "spoilt rotten" as they loved to point out. With no siblings and a well-to-do father, she'd enjoyed more space, more clothing, and more of everything than most of her classmates. Sitting on the bed, tears welling in her eyes, she marveled at the girl she had been. Distant from those around her. Unabashedly intelligent and condescending. Popular but cold and, at times, cruel to those with so much less than her. They had been equally cruel to her, but in retrospect their angst seemed more justifiable than her cool disdain. Many of her peers lived in shacks without running water or electricity, packed into bedrooms with all their siblings and sometimes aunts and uncles. They wore the same clothes daily, often washed without soap. Still, she'd carved a successful path through the social turmoil and class stratification of her high school years. She'd been a bright star among her peers. Until Billy Dillon and Nellie Brown crashed into her world.

She opened the drawer of her dresser and pulled out her diary. In neat cursive script, she read her last entry:

"Tomfoolery. That's just what it is. Logan Braxton wants me to go the senior dance with him, but I'm not obliged to take him up. He has been seen with Abigail Dupree, a girl of no virtue. I am certain he means only to impinge upon..."

She closed the book. The words had been written by someone else. A bright, young, stupid girl with no notion of the darkness swirling all around her. Victoria pulled a milk crate from her closet. She dumped its contents, shoes mostly, onto the floor. She gathered several items from her bedroom and placed them in the crate. Her diary. A scarf. A necklace with a seashell pendant. She went to her father's bedroom and sorted through his belongings. He'd been a simple, direct man. She left all his clothing hanging in the closet. In his dresser, she found sentimental letters he'd received from Tabby during their good years. She also found letters from Nellie Brown. She didn't read these, but tossed them into the crate. He had no jewelry. His shaving kit was very nice, so she put it into the crate. She stood in the middle of his room in splendid disappointment. Her father was reduced to a few letters and a straight razor. No wonder they never lacked for money.

In the living room she collected the photo album from its stand, along with the cuckoo clock. She left the Monopoly game. Neighbor's faces appeared in windows as she locked the front door of the house. She didn't acknowledge them and no one approached her. She put the crate into her truck and drove to the solicitor's office. There she made arrangements to sell the house and all of its contents. This was the last anyone in Knoxville ever saw of Victoria Starks.

Wrapping her head in a scarf that covered half her face, Victoria rented a room at a hotel in the Bowery district. She was admonished by the proprietor that he usually didn't take stray young ladies, especially black ones. She assured him that she was not a prostitute and greased his palm with a twenty dollar bill. The gold in his teeth sparkled with the smile her money produced.

For the next few days, Victoria sat in the hotel room playing with the tarot cards she'd taken from the jade box. She found that if she focused as she shuffled the cards, she could glimpse hidden truths through them. The proprietor's wife was carrying on a secret affair with the cleaning woman. The proprietor himself was impotent. The maintenance man who came to repair the continually leaky roof was the inbred result of his mother's father's unwanted sexual attention, making his father and grandfather the same person. The subjects of her inquiries needed to be nearby when she turned the cards. If they were in the room with her the readings revealed even more. She invited the proprietor's wife for a private reading. She found that when a person was actively involved in the reading, the amount of information the cards revealed was staggering. The proprietor's wife was so taken with the experience that she brought her friend the next day. By the next week, an onslaught of locals arrived daily, demanding readings. Victoria never divulged her identity to anyone in the Bowery, insisting that everyone call her Madam Ankaboot.

The story of her father's murder was still a topic of discussion in Knoxville and her reappearance at the Mechanicsville house had stirred rumors that made their way back to her. She had taken to affecting a Persian style, with heavy make-up on her eyes and a veil over her mouth and nose. She rarely left her room. No one connected her with the "poor wretched girl" whose father had been stabbed to death. Or, in one variation of the story, the "evil bitch" who'd murdered her father to claim his estate before he could remarry.

Victoria spun her own rumors through the Bowery, creating a mystique around Madam Ankaboot. As her reputation grew, the hotel afforded her its nicest room, with its own bathroom and electricity. The proprietor charged her visitors his own fee, in addition to what Victoria charged for her readings.

Victoria hired a local girl to clean, serve her meals, and draw her baths. She installed oriental screens and burned incense. She bought pillows and arranged the furniture in the room so that she and her clients could sit on the floor for the readings. Candles set into skulls sat to her right and left. Her face, thick with make-up, remained half-hidden by the silk veil at all times. Two weeks after she began her profession as a fortune teller, Nellie Brown walked into the room.

"Good afternoon, Nellie Brown," Victoria breathed from behind her veil.

"You's the witch who kin tell mah fate?" Nellie asked, closing the door. She drove into the room and squatted on the pillows across from Victoria. Her face was bent in a suspicious frown. Like most of Victoria's clients, Nellie wanted to believe Victoria could tell the future, but she didn't want to look like a fool.

Victoria said, "I'm Madam Ankaboot. I can tell your fate." She shuffled the cards. Nellie, like all those before her, was stunned by the grace of her hands. This was the moment her clients dropped pretense and believed in earnest.

"You must think on the matters that concern you most," Victoria purred. "Clear your mind." She fanned the deck on the blanket between them. "Pick a card. Any card."

Nellie scrunched her nose up and drew a card. The Raven.

Victoria said, "Death haunts you, Nellie Brown. A grave injustice hangs over your head. Pick again."

Nellie's hand shook as she drew another card. The Tower.

"You are very worried that your soul may be lost," Victoria intoned. She kept her voice even, but she was becoming agitated. The cards said much more than she was revealing. Nellie Brown was thrashing with guilt over the murder of Basil Starks. She had not known how far Billy would go that night. Her feelings for Basil had not been as feigned as she imagined them to be. His dead eyes stared at her in dreams. She suffered night terrors and lost the taste for food. In a year, she would be dead unless she could cleanse the blood from her conscience. Victoria saw a fork open in the reading. If she wanted, Victoria could draw out a path that would lead Nellie Brown to redemption. She could also obfuscate that path to such a degree that Nellie would never find it.

"Draw another card," Victoria said.

Nellie pulled a third card, her hand quaking even more.

The Fool.

Victoria gasped, but quickly recovered. "You must send the man responsible to me, Nellie Brown. The cards have nothing more for you. I will not charge you for this reading, since it is so spare. Bring me the man, Nellie Brown."

Nellie's head bobbed and she scurried from the room. Victoria reclined on her cushions and tapped her lips with her index finger. Nellie Brown would die from guilt. There was no turning back from the fork Victoria had chosen for that woman. What fate, she wondered, could she coerce from the cards for Billy Dillon?

She didn't have to consider the matter long. Billy arrived an hour later and interrupted a reading with a prominent white politician. Even in the Bowery, Billy knew better than to push his luck too far. He excused himself and closed the door. Victoria made him wait, dallying with the politician for another hour. That man left happy. He would win his next election if he followed her advice, which she knew he would.

Billy barged into the room after the white man was safely out of the hallway and spat, "I hear you been messin' wit' my girls."

"Please have a seat, Mr. Dillon," Victoria said, her voice smoky. "I have a reading for you."

"I ain't studyin' no witch," he replied. "I jes came over here ta tell ya off my girls, lest I black ya eyes out."

Victoria picked up the deck and began to shuffle. "Shame," she said. "I see big things in your future, Mr. Dillon."

He watched as she separated the deck and twisted it so that it collapsed back into itself with one card sticking halfway out. She held the deck up and said, "Pick a card, Mr. Dillon. The future is a mystery everyone wants to solve."

Billy reached down and drew the protruding card. The Carnival King.

As the card turned, Victoria felt the world around her lurch sideways. Pathways exploded in her mind. Billy Dillon was more complex than she could have imagined. His future was a series of prisms, each possibility turning in time with other possibilities. She saw that he could change, that underneath layers of hate and rage lurked a bruised boy who really wanted to do good in this world. In one angle of the prism, he sat in church with a family, his son staring up at him in adoration as they sang a hymn together. He died surrounded by great grandchildren in that vision. Conversely, she saw him beating women and killing men in hundreds of ways. He died violently in all those possibilities. Victoria realized that Billy Dillon was much more than just the man himself. He was the sum of everyone whose life he would touch going forward. Doubt crept into Victoria's mind but she hardened her heart.

"You will be rich," she lied. "You are being taken advantage of. Fight back. Take what is yours."

Billy smiled a lean smile and dropped the card onto the floor. "Well, ya know yer ways, then. But step back offa my girls."

He swaggered from the room. Victoria picked the card up and considered it. She had condemned him. Tonight, he would confront the head of the prostitution ring in the Bowery and be gunned down. His body would be tossed into the Tennessee River and never recovered. Nellie Brown would starve herself to death and be buried in a pauper's lot with a white transient from Indiana.

Victoria put the deck back together. As she returned it to the box, the Fool card slipped free and fell to the floor. When she picked it up, her own future spun out like a tangled cable. Possibilities within possibilities flashed before her. She realized that she had chosen paths not only for Nellie Brown and Billy Dillon that day, but also for herself. Her father's disappointed eyes bore into her mind. An immense pressure built up in her skull, which felt as if it might crack from crown to forehead. Tears streamed down her face as she tried to imagine a way out of the warping possibilities that danced across the inside of her eyes. Each became worse than the last and she could not stop the torrent of images and emotions. Death would surround her, cursing her to walk the earth forever in complete isolation. Her body would become riddled with scars and warts, making her look like the witch that Billy had called her.

"I will never lie in a reading again," she grunted. The pressure in her head receded. That wasn't enough.

"I will never willfully take a life," she promised. Her father's eyes vanished. The pressure faded and she collapsed onto her pillows, clutching the Fool card to her chest.

She had reset her future with those vows, but she knew she could never betray them. Even if she wanted to. They were now woven into the fabric of her destiny by bonds she had no power to break. That was fine. Two rules gave her the freedom of her life back. It was a good bargain.

The next day, Victoria gathered her milk crate of possessions and rang for a car to take her to the train station. She broke the hotel proprietor's arm in two places when he tried to stop her from leaving. She shed the identity of Madam Ankaboot. Chicago was calling to her. She wouldn't have many chances to see her mother again, so she decided that now was as good a time as any to track her down.

When Victoria finished talking, they drove in silence for a while. Andre wasn't sure how to respond to the story.

"So how did it go in Chicago?" he asked.

"Not well at first," Victoria replied. "I found my mother, who was overjoyed to see me. That's a story for a different time, though. I just want you to understand that you are not alone. I remember feeling very alone in the beginning."

"Am I going to live as long as you?" Andre asked.

"I don't know," she said. "I doubt it. I was Awakened when I drank that potion, but something was also added by the demon in the box. Most people who Wake Up aren't like me. They will have one primary ability, like Craig's speed or your visions. These days, there are hardly any people who Wake Up. I don't keep in touch with any of them."

"So we don't have a support group or anything?" Andre asked.

"I suspect there are places people like us gather, but I have never felt a need to find them."

"You've spent your entire life alone, huh?"

Victoria was quiet for a long time. Andre was annoyed with his inability to see facial expressions. Every silence in a conversation felt like the person was judging him. He knew the sensation was inaccurate, but knowing that didn't help much.

"No," she said. "I have been alive a long time, Andre. I have spent long periods alone. I have spent long periods near people. I had a lover for almost twenty years in Washington, DC. He was an artist. An amazing person. I stopped telling fortunes until he died so that I could work in a gallery. That was the happiest time of my life." She paused again. He imaged she was collecting her thoughts, but he couldn't know for sure. "I have avoided the Awakened and most supernatural creatures for the majority of my life. As you can see, when we are close together, events tend to be unstable. I do not like unstable. So I live in isolation or in the company of normal human beings. I do not feel alone."

Andre turned her words over in his mind. He said, "You may not be able to tell lies in your readings, but you certainly can outside of them."

"That is a cold accusation," Victoria said.

"But it's true. You're lonely. You're empty. You've been hiding for a long time, and you're tired of hiding. Otherwise, you would have left Minneapolis when that monster raped you. You don't need to be here to figure out what's going on with your pregnancy. You could figure that out from Alaska if you wanted. You came back because you knew it would lead you to us. You're lonely, Victoria. Admit it."

She was silent again.

"You know," he said, "I can't see you, so I actually have no idea how what I say effects you."

"I'm crying," she said. Her voice quivered, but he had trouble imagining more than one or two tears sliding down her face.

"Oh," he said. "Sorry. I wasn't trying to make you cry."

"Now who is lying?" she asked, sniffing. "You are in pain. You are lashing out. You had every intention of hurting me, and you did it. But you are correct. I need you, Andre, and I need many of the others. Even the monster who raped me, as horrific as that seems. A circle has completed and I want to start over differently than I have in the past."

Andre squirmed in his seat as she spoke. He knew he could be cutting and brutal when he let his tongue loose, so he often kept his actual thoughts to himself. Nobody liked an asshole. Jokes allowed him to flitter through conversations without upsetting anyone. Now that he was blind and surrounded by supernatural nonsense, keeping things light wasn't easy.

"I really am sorry," he said. "I'm tired. I'm going to try to sleep now. Thank you for telling me your story. It does help to know I'm not alone."

She said, "That's a good idea. We've still got another seven hours until we get to Pikeville."

Halfway to Des Moines, Amber began the kind of wailing that was a precursor to a full scale melt down. She had been fussing for the last hour.

"Please, honey," Brenda said, "We'll get to Ames in another hour. Try to take a nap, huh?"

Amber screamed, "No nap! No nap!"

Brenda said to Kevin, "Can't you do something about this?"

Kevin was too big to ride in the front seat, so he was stretched out in the third row. He poked his head over the back of Amber's seat and licked her face. She stopped screaming and stared at him. He licker her again and she smiled.

"Do you want some milk?" Kevin asked.

"Milk!" she said. Kevin handed her the sippy cup that she'd thrown on the floor minutes ago. She stuck it in her mouth and smiled at him. "Doggy daddy," she said around the nozzle. He licked her face again and she burst into giggles.

"I meant could you do something like you did when you put her to sleep," Brenda. "That works, though."

"I don't like doing that," he said. "I never worried about what side effects using pheromones had before, but like any kind of mind altering substance, there have to be problems. I'd rather not risk it with our daughter."

"Ah," Brenda said. "I hadn't thought of that."

Amber chewed on the sippy cup, her eyes glued to her father.

Brenda's phone beeped.

"Here," she said, handing her phone to Kevin. "Call someone named Winton. Victoria said he got the information we need. It's in my text messages."

"Good!" Kevin exclaimed, taking the phone. He fiddled with it for a few minutes before grunting in frustration. "Stupid touch screen phone. It doesn't recognize my claw and my fingers are too big to select anything." He handed the phone to her. "Can you dial him?"

She did and handed it back. He put the phone to his ear. She nearly drove into the ditch staring at him. It was like a cartoon. *Werewolves on cell phones*, she thought and laughed out loud.

"Watch where you're going, dammit!" he snarled.

"Wee!" Amber squealed as Brenda jerked the wheel, bringing the vehicle back into the lane.

"Hello?" he said into the phone. "Yeah, Winton?...I remember. At that barbeque at Andre's parent's cabin last summer...Uh, huh...No...Fine, thanks...Number 1, yeah. Look, I know it's a lot to take in, but I just need a universal pass code for the doors at The Foundation...Wow. Really? Perfect...Good job...Text it to me. I can't write things down right now...Yeah...Yeah, OK. Well, Craig can probably fill in the details once we get this straightened out...Well, I don't really know. Thanks for your help."

He pulled the phone away from his ear. Brenda could hear a voice continue speaking. Kevin mashed his finger on the screen until the voice cut off.

"Jeezus!" he said. "That kid is excited. He did exactly what I wanted, though. We've got a pass key. Once we drop

Amber off with Oren, we can go in through the loading docks at The Foundation. Sheila said the dedicated entrance for the Térata is still in service, so we should be able to get in there."

"Can you tell me exactly why we're driving to Des Moines, now?" Brenda asked, peering at him in the rearview mirror.

Kevin rested his elbows on the second row of seats, his clawed hands dangling. He caught her eye in the mirror and pointed at the road.

"Sheila believes that if you don't 'save' the Térata, they'll all go feral when Clarence dies," he said. "She is assuming that Victoria and Andre can stop him and get whatever is in him back into the box. And she's assuming he'll die when that happens." He took a deep breath and leaned forward until his head was beside hers. "This is the part where you have to make a decision. I can't let Sheila do this on her own, so I plan to get into The Foundation and... I don't know... do whatever I can to help her out. But you don't have to do this. You and Amber can wait at the hotel with Oren until I get back."

"*If* you get back," Brenda said. She stared straight ahead, her hands at ten and two on the steering wheel. "What am I supposed to do at The Elpis Foundation?"

"The same thing you did to Sheila," he replied. "Tell the Térata they are free. That way, when Elpis dies, they can start their lives over. I have no idea why Sheila thinks this is so important, to be honest with you. I didn't care about them at all when I left. Of course, when I left, I had you to focus on. I don't know what it's like for her. She's certainly become a lot more sentimental."

"So we just show up and start telling monsters they're free?" Brenda asked. "Sounds like a dodgy plan. Don't they have video cameras and things?"

"Not in that area of The Foundation," Kevin said. "It's too risky to video anything, even if it's not being recorded. Video is bad for creatures like us. We all have tracking chips, but I tore mine out years ago. If we can get to the dormitories, we should be able to find most of the remaining Térata. Sheila said she'd send them to us once we set up shop inside."

"That sound optimistic," Brenda said.

"Well, there aren't many people in those areas of The Foundation. Normal people freak out when they see the Térata in true form, and it's usually uncomfortable for us to maintain other forms. From what Sheila says, there are fewer Awakened now than there used to be, so we should be able to get inside without too much fuss."

"What happens if we both die, Kevin?" she asked.

"Yeah. That's why you have to decide," he said. "Amber has no one."

Brenda drove, staring hard at the road. Amber drifted off to sleep. Kevin caught the sippy cup as it slid from her fingers.

"What do you think happens if Clarence dies and I don't do what Sheila wants?" she asked.

"I think they'll go mad," Kevin said. "Without a focus, they don't really have their own will. Clarence is their focus. If he dies, I suspect they'll end up getting exposed and killed very quickly."

"Is that such a bad thing?" Brenda asked.

"No," he admitted. "But it's slightly deeper than all that. Sheila doesn't think that she or Kimm can survive if you don't free the Térata. She's probably right. The Confluence has us bound up in ways I don't understand, but Sheila seems to think she knows how it has to go. If you don't free the Térata, the Confluence will be interrupted."

Brenda said, "Is this like fate or something? This Confluence?"

"Not really," he said. "It's just a way to describe powerful relationships. Confluences affect fate. They are powerful pathways between people that make events more or less likely to happen. But at the end of the day, they're just relationships. Fate is always in our own hands."

"Well, fuck," she said. "I don't know what to do."

"I have to go in," Kevin said. "I can feel it. I owe Sheila this. In a way, I owe all my brothers and sisters this. If I don't go, I will spend the rest of my life regretting it. I'm sorry it has to be this way."

"Me, too," she said, though her voice was gentle. "I just hope, for Amber's sake, we can get back out of this mess. My will leaves Amber as a ward of the state with a trust fund. The thought of her ending up in the foster care system makes me kind of sick."

Clarence reached into his desk and pulled out a pistol. A low growl rumbled deep within Kimm's throat, but Sheila hissed at him, so he relaxed. His arms were tied behind his back with cords he could break, but it would be a challenge to dodge the darts if Clarence started shooting. Sheila was so relaxed that Kimm suspected her of mental instability.

"That won't be necessary," Number 8, who was also in his true form, said. "They are cooperative. Whatever was done to them is wearing off. I recommend putting them into holding cells until we can run a full battery of tests. Octavio's report is accurate."

Clarence asked, "Where is Number 4?"

"I found both of them in Sheila's room," Number 8 said.

"I'll inform Number 4 that she can stop searching."

Clarence said, "She's been in the conference room for the last fifteen minutes, but she isn't answering when I call the room."

"Odd," Number 8 said. "I'll investigate as soon as I get these two into the cells."

Clarence stared at them with a stony expression. Kimm felt like a child trying to lie his way out of trouble. In the past it would have never occurred to him to deceive Clarence. Clarence was the only person Number 9 ever wanted to please, according to his fractured memories. He couldn't remember Number 8 very well, but his esteem for his brother was growing. Number 8 didn't betray a hint of unease.

Clarence put the gun back in his drawer, but stared into Kimm's eyes.

"Tell me, Number 9, how do you feel right now?" he asked.

Kimm almost answered, but stopped short. That was a barbed question. He needed to think about it for a moment. For the Térata, there would only be one way to answer that question.

"I am physically fit, but mentally compromised," he reported as a matter of fact.

Clarence pulled the gun back out of the drawer and pointed it at Sheila. Kimm tensed. This was another test. He could not fail. With an immense effort of will he remained calm. His senses were sharp and Clarence knew that. Clarence began to squeeze the trigger of the gun. Kimm's mind exploded with the need to act, but he stifled it. Having emotions was a severe pain in the ass. Clarence's finger relaxed.

"Do you think I should have shot Number 7?" Clarence

asked.

"No," Kimm replied.

"Why not?" Clarence asked.

"It would be wasteful," he said. "Number 7 is useful and will make a full recovery."

Clarence pointed the gun at Kimm and pulled the trigger.

Kimm suspected that would happen, or he would have died right there. His eyes followed the dart as it left the tip of the gun. He dipped his head and snapped his jaw, catching the dart in his teeth. Its needle tip was millimeters from his tongue. His balance was precarious, but he managed not to fall over as he spat it onto the floor.

"I also think it would be wasteful to dispose of me," Kimm said.

Clarence smiled.

"You are my favorite, Number 9," he said with genuine fondness. "I broke the mold with you." He turned to Number 8. "Take them to the holding cells. Make sure they are fed and cared for. And find out why Number 4 isn't responding." He turned back to his desk and the computer screens arrayed around it.

Number 8 put them in one of the reinforced holding rooms used for rogue Awakened. A toilet and sink occupied the corner. A double bed was tucked into a niche in the stainless steel wall. They had agreed earlier that Number 8 should put them in the same room rather than separating them as would be normal protocol in this situation.

"I thought that you would be weak since you are so physically diminished," Number 8 said to Kimm has he ushered them into the room. "I was wrong. I'm glad I did not decide to attack you earlier."

Kimm nodded and said, "Please remember that. I don't want to have to prove it to you again."

Sheila said, "When the blonde woman, Brenda, arrives, find her quickly. Tell her exactly what I told you. Our fate hangs on you now, Number 8. Do not fail."

"I will not," he said. He closed the door and locked it.

Sheila sat on the bed and put her elbows on her knees with her claws hanging between them.

"Now we wait," she said.

Kimm asked, "How can you be so certain we're doing what is right?"

She sighed. "I'm not, really. But I know that we aren't necessary right now. Oren and Craig are important. Some other kid I don't know is important. Brenda is important. Andre and Victoria are important. The other Térata are important. We're not. I figured it was safest for us to be out of the way so we couldn't throw anything off. We've done what we were supposed to do."

"What was that?" he asked.

"We planted a seed," she said.

He curled up on the bed next to her and put his head in her lap. "A seed?" he said.

"That's what the vision I had when I saw the Confluence said I had to do," she said, absently running her claws through the fur between his ears. Before she'd rubbed his head earlier today, Kimm had never even imagined the pleasure that being petted could bring. A tingle started under her fingers and traveled down his spine. Something in his chest began to loosen. She continued, "I had to plant a seed for Brenda to water so that the Térata could grow. I hope I chose well in Number 8."

"I think so," Kimm said. "He's in love with Octavio. He doesn't know that. But he is."

Sheila laughed. "Octavio is easy to fall in love with."

Kimm turned over and exposed his throat. Sheila ran her

fingers from his chin to his collar bone. A heavy purr issued from his chest. That was new. As air traveled down his throat a small portion of it diverted, causing a deep rumble. The rumble itself vibrated through his muscles, relaxing them. He felt an almost ecstatic contentment.

"You're purring," Sheila said. "I didn't know you could purr."

"I didn't either," he said. "Clarence must have used some cat DNA when he put me together."

"How odd we are now," Sheila said. "All these new feelings. Our bodies are changing. But I can't help thinking that we can't really know what love is, yet. It's too soon. We're just confused."

Kimm said, "I love Oren. I know that."

Sheila stared into space for a few minutes. "Yes, I suppose you do. But your DNA is consuming Kimm's. He really is your son. That's biological impetus. It's not like romantic love."

Kimm pushed himself across her legs until her hands were on his belly. His purring intensified as her claws worked over his abdomen. His penis, already erect through the tuft of hair that usually covered and protected it, began to ache.

"I don't really know about that kind of love," he said. "But I know about lust. It's like being hurt and tasting sugar at the same time. I felt it the first time in the Twin Cities after I'd been watching Brenda for a while." He began rubbing his crotch like he had while waiting for the kids to exit the van in Minnehaha Park. His breathing became pants as pleasure spread from his groin to the rest of his body. Sheila kept rubbing his stomach. He leaned up and licked the green discs on her chest. She gasped.

"Oh," she said. "I didn't know..." He began licking all the discs plating her chest and stomach. She dug her claws into the fur of his belly and pulled. He grabbed his penis and squeezed. Semen shot out, covering her arm and his chest. His purring became a roar.

Sheila slid her free hand underneath of him and into her crotch. She groaned as he lapped at her plates, finding sensitive areas where they met the flesh. Green drool dropped from her mouth onto his snout. He turned his face upward and licked her chin, sliding his tongue along her bottom lip. She let out a low moan and thrust her hips into his back, digging her claws into the skin of his belly as she climaxed. Blood flowed beneath her claws, mingling with the semen on his chest. When her orgasm finished, she sucked the blood from her fingers and the licked the semen from her forearm. She bent down and licked his wounded belly, her rough tongue pulling blood and semen out of his fur. The punctures closed, leaving small, puckered marks on his jet black skin.

They lay together stroking each other.

"This isn't love," she said with some disappointment.

"No," he replied. "But it is nice. What are you worried about?"

"Octavio," she said.

"What about him?"

"I don't love him, either." She sighed.

"So?"

"Well, I tangled him into all this and I think he might have expectations…"

"Maybe he'll be interested in Number 8."

"No," she said. "He isn't like that."

"Too bad," he said. "That would be an easy way out."

"Listen to us, Kimm Peters," she said. "Can you imagine this conversation before we ran into Brenda?"

"I can't remember most of what happened before I ran

into her," he confessed. "I don't really like remembering what I can."

"I can remember it all," she said. "And we were nothing like this. I'm *worrying* about how Octavio *feels*. I am an entirely different creature than I was two days ago."

"Octavio is a good man," Kimm said. "You sense that and you care about him. But that's not just you. What's funny is that Kimm Peters wasn't as good as I am. Actually, he was a self-centered prick. You simplified what Brenda does to us when you described it to Number 8. We don't just become free, or who we decide to be, when we encounter Brenda. In a way, we also become what she wants. She's a powerful woman, Sheila Barnstock, with a very strong sense of right and wrong. You and I aren't feeling what we would have felt without Clarence. We're feeling what Brenda thinks we should feel. It's like she wrote our emotional code. Programmed us. We're just sorting through the code trying to make sense of it."

Sheila was using her claws like a comb to straighten the thin, damp fur on his chest. He was still purring. "And now," she said quietly, "I've unleashed her on our brothers and sisters."

"It's not so bad," Kimm said. "Having emotions is dangerous business. But we wouldn't be able to enjoy things like this without them."

He began licking at her discs again. She groaned with pleasure.

Oren watched Brenda explain to Amber for the fifth time that she would be back in just a few hours. The toddler was handling this entire situation much better than her mother. Kevin remained in the Suburban. He'd demanded that Oren come down to talk to him before Brenda brought Amber up. The shock of seeing such a large, hairy beast in the back of a black SUV was disorienting, but Kevin's interview process had been even more bizarre. He had sniffed every crevice of Oren's body, spending an uncomfortable amount of time in his armpits and crotch. The world of monsters and robots, as Winton put it, had lax rules concerning personal space. Apparently Oren passed the smell test, so Kevin agreed he could baby sit Amber while they did whatever they were going to do at The Elpis Foundation.

Brenda was another matter. She pulled Oren aside as Amber became engrossed with a cartoon on the TV.

"How old are you?" she asked.

"Twenty one," he said.

"Do you have any experience with kids?" she asked.

"I've got two little sisters and I used to volunteer in the church nursery at Sunday school when I was a teenager," he replied.

"Where do you work?" she asked.

He didn't respond for a moment. It was a tough question. He hadn't had a job until yesterday and that had been sidelined. "Kimm's Auto World," he said. "I help my dad with the books."

"Are you in college?" she asked.

"Yeah," he said. "I'm majoring in Finance at Hamline."

She relaxed and almost smiled. "Nice. I graduated from Carlson with a degree in Finance."

He nodded. "That's a great school."

She said, "It is. Anyway, Amber won't nap for another couple of hours, but she should go down pretty easy. I don't usually let her watch TV with commercials, but in this case do whatever you need to do to keep her happy. She seems fine now, but two year olds can be really moody..." She continued a litany of childcare advice that he didn't pay much attention to. He'd changed plenty of diapers.

"...and I want to be clear about one thing," she continued, jerking her thumb toward the window overlooking the parking lot. "My husband out there? He isn't just a big, fury pet. He's a full scale monster. Teeth. Claws. The works. Like one of those werewolves in the movies, only I think a lot more dangerous. So don't let anything happen to our daughter, OK?"

Oren nodded and said, "Yeah, I have, uh, experience with monsters. Dad is one."

Brenda's eyes flicked back and forth as she looked from one of his to the other. He felt like she could see all his insecurities when she did that.

"You seem like a good kid," she said. "I'm sorry you're involved in all this."

"I'm not," he said. "Two days ago I thought life was just a series of small disappointments. Now it's something terrible and beautiful and strange. I have a feeling I might get killed before all this is over. But, you know, now it will be worth it."

"You're pretty mature for your age," she said.

He shrugged. "I get that a lot. Mom says I compensate for a having a man-child father."

He immediately regretted saying that, but something about Brenda made him want to expose himself. Her tone of voice dug into his self-confidence. She nodded at the extraneous information as if it was what she wanted to hear, though, so he felt better about it.

"I don't pretend to understand what's happening with your Dad," she said, "but I doubt he'll be a 'man-child' going forward."

"Let's hope not," he said. "The way he was before was monstrous enough…"

She smiled. "We didn't choose this, did we?"

"Actually," he replied, "I did."

She stared at him for a few moments, causing his unease to return. "Well, Oren, I hope you chose wisely. There is no going back."

He shrugged again. "That's fine with me."

Amber stood up and began jumping on the bed. "O'en, watch me bounce!" she shouted.

He smiled. She put her arms out and he picked her up.

"Are we going to have fun today?" he asked, tapping her nose with his finger.

"Yes!" she answered, grabbing his finger.

"What are we going to do?" he said.

"Tell sto'ies!" she exclaimed.

"OK," he said. "We'll tell stories."

"There is one more thing," Brenda said. She pulled something wrapped in a blanket from Amber's pile of necessities. "This is very, very important to me. I do not want to take it with me to The Elpis Foundation. Don't let anything happen to it."

"What is it?" he asked.

"A sword," Brenda said. "Don't mess with it. Just make sure it stays safe. Make sure my daughter stays safe."

Brenda almost needed to be pushed from the room to leave. She said, "I love you," to Amber three more times before Oren closed the door on her.

The next couple of hours were more laid back than he expected. Amber was a very well behaved two-year-old. Brenda left food, diapers, and a smattering of toys in a large bag. They played with matchbox cars and baby dolls. Oren was surprised at Amber's developed sense of storytelling.

Every game with the toys was a story. The cars married the baby dolls who lived in castles in fairy lands. Though her vocabulary was limited, she always knew what was going to happen next. True to Brenda's word, Amber crashed out on the love seat two hours later at 5:00 p.m.

Oren ate most of the bag of Cheerio's Brenda left as he surfed the internet, looking for more clues about Elpis Enterprises. As he was reading an article about viral DNA replication, his Skype window flashed. Winton was calling.

Oren clicked his mouse to answer. "Hey, Winton, what's up?"

Winton's panicked face popped up on his screen. "You've got to get the fuck outta that hotel! They figured me out. It'll be a matter of time before they trace the IP address of your computer and figure out where you are. I'm blowing out, too. You've got my number. Call me in an hour when you're somewhere else. Turn your computer off and don't turn it back on again!"

Oren coughed Cheerio's into his lap. "Who found us?" he sputtered.

"Someone in the Elipsis Network," Winton said. "I don't really understand how. I can't back trace the account that pinged my computer, but they definitely know I've been poking around. I covered my tracks, so they don't know what I changed, but they can find both of us now. Get out now. Don't use your credit card. Find somewhere safe and call me."

Oren's heart pounded and he looked out the hotel room window at the parking lot. It was empty. The possibility that anyone could track him to this hotel hadn't occurred to him. When he left Elpis Enterprises four hours earlier, he felt a complete sense of relief. That seemed silly in retrospect. Being a spy was obviously something he wasn't cut out for.

He turned his attention back to the computer screen.

"Jesus Christ, Winton, look out!" he shouted. Just over Winton's left shoulder hovered an insectoid face.

Winton turned his head and screamed. The computer tipped sideways, landing so that the camera faced the ceiling. Crashes and more screaming came through the speakers. A few seconds later, the insect face appeared in the Skype window. The screen went black.

"Oh, shit, oh, shit, oh, shit," Oren said, slamming the screen down. He phoned a cab and piled everything, including the sword, into Amber's car seat. It was goddamn lucky Brenda had thought to leave that thing.

He woke Amber who wanted to know if it would be OK to sleep in the car. He assured her that would be fine as he repeatedly mashed the "down" button to call the elevator. When he reached the lobby, he threw his keycard on the front desk and said, "Checking out early. Thanks."

The clerk raised his hand, but Oren ignored him and stared out the plate glass doors of the lobby.

Amber waved at the clerk and said, "Bye, bye."

Five agonizing minutes later, a cab pulled into the circle driveway. Oren stuffed Amber and her car seat into the cab's back seat and jumped in.

"Get us out of here," he commanded as he closed the door.

The radio was playing jazz music so loud that Oren wondered if the driver heard him.

"Sure thing, man," the cabby said.

As they pulled out of the hotel's roundabout, Oren felt like he'd just dodged a huge bullet. His fingers felt weak and his throat was tight.

What in the hell do I do now? he wondered.

Chapter 12
The Swan Hilted Sword

Victoria held Andre's hand and surveyed the collapsed shack she and Mam-maw had called home. Upon Mam-maw's death in 1950, she bought the property as well as the adjoining land her father had farmed. However, she had not returned since driving away from Mam-maw's cold disapproval in 1938. The acreage had returned to its natural state. There was no sign of the vast vegetable garden where she'd spent so much of her childhood weeding and cultivating. The hunting lodge was gone. The shack itself was reduced to an overgrown lump of collapsed timber. Close inspection was required to see that it had ever been a building.

The air was warm and heavy beneath a blazing late afternoon sun. She'd been away from the South a long time. October in Tennessee was like June in Minnesota.

Andre stabbed at the ground with a hiking pole. "I can see how the shack used to look, sometimes," he said. "It flashes in and out of existence in the spirit world."

Victoria nodded, despite the fact that he couldn't see her. Over the last ten hours, she'd been forced to realize how much of her communication was nonverbal.

She said, "Let's hope that the entrance to the root cellar hasn't been filled in."

"It's right there," Andre said, pointing with the pole.

Victoria led him to the far side of the mound. The cellar door was tucked amid a tangle of vines and weeds. Unlike the rest of the building, it appeared as it had seventy years ago.

"You can see this door in the ground?" Victoria asked.

"Yeah," he said, "I can. Most people wouldn't notice it. It exists in both worlds, somehow, but sort of switches between the two sometimes. For me, it's floating in black space. You have no idea how disorienting it is to feel ground but see nothing but emptiness beneath you."

"No," she said. "I have no idea."

She reached down and pulled the cellar door open. The hinges screeched as it opened. Spider webs pulled apart and insects scurried away from the light.

"Do you see the stairs?" she asked.

"Yes," he answered. "They are frozen in time and will never rot. I wonder if I could get something like that for my parents' deck. They've replaced it twice. Although I think my dad just likes building decks."

Victoria laughed. "Do you see anything about the cellar that we should be aware of?"

"The box is here. It wants you to find it. It's missing something and it wants that something back."

"It's missing its prisoner," Victoria said.

Victoria clicked on the headlamp she'd bought at the same place they'd picked up Andre's pole. She strapped it over her cotton do rag. The LED light flooded the cellar as they descended.

"I can see everything down here!" Andre exclaimed,

letting go of her hand. His irises and pupils returned to his eyes. "I can even see *you!*"

"That must be nice," she said.

"It's fucking great!" he said.

"I don't think your sight has returned permanently," she cautioned.

"I know," he said, but his grin stayed wide. "It's just really great to see again!"

Bail lid jars full of preserved fruits and vegetables still lined the walls of the shelves, just as they had so long ago. Andre pulled down a jar of red peppers and said, "According to the lid, this is over sixty years old. I wonder if we could eat it."

"Probably not," Victoria said. "My Mam-maw canned it. I bought the property following her death, so no one else has been here. She was gifted in the art of pickling."

"My mom does that, too," Andre said. "Every summer she spends a week jarring everything she can get her hands on. I used to tell her that she should jar my older brother."

Victoria smiled. She released the hidden latch and the shelf swung in.

"Oh, God!" Andre exclaimed, taking a step back.

"What is it?" she asked.

"It's a mouth!" he said. "We have to go into a human mouth. It has big, stained teeth and the floor is a tongue... and the lips are chapped and bleeding."

Victoria saw only the tunnel leading to the two subterranean rooms. "I don't see that," she said.

"It bends space," Andre continued. "You walk into the mouth and space just stops mattering. But if the mouth ever decides to close I don't know how you get out."

"To my knowledge," Victoria said, "the mouth has never closed."

"No… No. It wouldn't," Andre said. "At least I don't think it would. It's waiting. But it isn't waiting for us. We should be fine." He grimaced at the opening.

Victoria marched forward. Andre followed, cringing away from the walls.

"This is so gross," he said.

They came to the fork and turned left. Andre muttered under his breath as the tunnel shrank. By the time they reached the small, oak door, he was hugging himself and cursing. Victoria reached into her pocket and pulled out the spiral key.

"I don't know if this will work," she said. "It didn't last time."

"It should," Andre said. "It looks… ready." He reached toward the lock but jerked his hand back. A glimmer of blue light sparked in the air before the door.

"What's that?" he asked.

With a flash, Mam-maw's frowning face resolved in the air. Her wrinkles were like canyons and her hair whipped wildly in a wind Victoria could not feel. The veins beneath her skin throbbed with a blue pulse.

"Stop!" Mam-maw commanded.

"What the fuck!" Andre sputtered.

A lump rose in Victoria's throat, but she said, "Spirit, leave us in peace."

"I'll do no such thing, chile," Mam-maw said. "You've come again ta make deals wit' the devil! I'll not stand by an' let ya do such. Not as I have the power."

Victoria said, "Why didn't you believe me before?"

"I did," Mam-maw said. "But you knew what ya'd done were wrong. Sellin' a chile into slavery jus' ta be rid of it? Just for petty revenge? Don' tell me ya' don't feel the guilt, chile. You was raised better'n that."

A tear slid down Victoria's cheek. The lump in her throat threatened to become a sob, so she swallowed hard. "I love you Mam-maw," she said.

"I love you, too, chile, so I'll not let ya take the second path twice."

Victoria raised her hand. She felt more tears slide down her cheeks. "I'm sorry, Mam-maw," she said, "but I have to do this." She waved her hand in an intricate pattern and said, "Begone!" Her voice boomed and Mam-maw's specter collapsed into a thin cloud of light that faded away.

Andre said, "Well, that was unpleasant."

"Yes," Victoria said after clearing her throat. "Yes, it was."

"The door will open now," he said.

Victoria put the key into the lock and it popped apart. Crouching, she opened the door. For a moment, time fell away and she was transported back through the decades to the first time she'd been here. She shone the light around the room before aiming it at the bottom shelf under the bones. Everything was the same. The jade box glowed dully once more.

"There it is," she said.

Andre came in behind her. "Yeah, yeah," he said. "Right where I saw it in that vision thing back home." He crossed the room and rummaged through a drawer in a curio cabinet. "Can you bring that light over here, please?"

His voice was a pitch higher than usual. Almost giddy.

She retrieved the jade box and opened it. Bottomless void greeted her. The light from her headlamp did not penetrate the bottom of the box. She dipped her finger inside. It vanished up to the knuckle.

"C'mon," Andre insisted, waving his hand at her. "I need to see to find it."

She aimed the light at the drawer he was searching and

walked over to him.

"Point the light inside," he said. His face was intense. Inside the drawer was a collection of oval clamshell boxes. Andre plunged his hands into the drawer and turned its contents over.

"Aha!" he exclaimed, pulling out a brown leather box with guilt edges. He flipped it open. Inside was a pair of nineteenth century spectacles. The rims were perfect circles with what appeared to be tiny gear teeth around their edges. "Something is missing..." he muttered, closing the box and thrusting his hand back into the drawer. After a few seconds he pulled a second, matching box from the drawer. Inside were various lenses that fit against the rims of the glasses in the previous case, clicking into the gears.

"Yes!" Andre exclaimed. "This might work!"

"What is it?" Victoria asked.

"I'm not sure," he said, "but it might be a way for me to see again."

"That would be wonderful," Victoria said.

"Yeah, it would," Andre said. "Let's get the fuck out of here and try it!"

"Language, Andre," she said.

Clarence sat at the control terminal in his lab and tapped the enter button on his keyboard without fully depressing it. Everything was ready. The final tests showed all systems were functional and primed. Amber was strapped into a stainless steel gurney with an IV in her arm. Electrical diodes ran from her temples into a series of Tesla coils and computers. From those terminals, every blank canvas would receive the charge of information necessary to complete their formation and Wake Up.

She looks like the Child of Frankenstein, Clarence thought with uncharacteristic humor. He was nearly jubilant, which was the reason he hesitated to press the button and begin the genetic transition that would finalize years of work. He tried to never act when in the throes of an emotional surge.

Craig sat in a wheelchair beside the terminals, staring into space. His head was propped up by a pillow. Drool soaked this t-shirt and tears leaked from his unblinking eyes. Clarence's humor faded as he glanced at Craig. When he told Octavio to get the information at any cost, he had been too hasty. Octavio had lobotomized Craig. Impatience and urgency led to mistakes. Craig could have been one of the most valuable Awakened that Clarence had ever found. It hurt Clarence to delve into Criag's mind and see the devastation that Octavio had caused.

On the bright side, Octavio regurgitated everything he'd taken from Craig directly into Clarence's brain. What Octavio revealed was sufficient to still most of Clarence's concerns. Following Clarence's expulsion from his mind at Phalen Park, Craig had retreated to Victoria's cabin with everyone involved. Nothing of great interest had happened there, but he had managed to grab the child this morning unbeknownst to anyone in the house besides Victoria. In his memories, Brenda and Number 1 were sleeping. Victoria had helped him for reasons even Craig didn't understand. They must have made an arrangement that she caused him to forget. She was a tricky woman who had her own agendas now. Her pregnancy was a juicy bit of information. For the first time in four years, Clarence began to plan for a future beyond the immediate. Children of the Térata. What an interesting development. Whatever Victoria was up to could wait. Clarence had what he wanted.

Tests on Amber revealed a high opium content in her

blood, but no other abnormalities. Her genetic profile contained the exact traits Clarence suspected would be necessary for her to exist. Gaps in her DNA strands were held together and methylated by magic. The sequencing of that magic allowed her to form proteins and prions that nothing else on earth was capable of producing. Those proteins were what he needed to make it possible for his blank canvases to sustain a full memory transfer of their victims. Without that transfer, they would be useless. With the push of one button, he could start this process. Seven hundred vehicles waited in the parking garage, ready to transport his new children all over the country. This was only the first wave. He could grow batches of these creatures in less than two weeks, continually replacing humans across the globe with Awakened homunculus. Scientists, politicians, religious leaders. The first generation would infiltrate the lower echelons of governments, corporations, and religious institutions. Subsequent generations would fill in higher positions until every political structure on earth was under Clarence's control. At that point, he could release the god in his bones, having fulfilled the purpose of his life. The god could fulfill the Rattlesnake Prophecy and control the most powerful Confluence in two millennia. Clarence could then repair the damage done by the leukemia and continue his life. He hoped.

"I'm sorry, Craig," Clarence said to the boy. "I may be able to repair your brain, given time, but I'm afraid you'll never be what we both knew you could be."

Craig didn't respond. He never would, unless Clarence could find a way to reconstruct his entire frontal lobe and a significant portion of his hippocampus. That was a challenge for later. In the meantime, Clarence kept Craig nearby as a reminder of the consequences of hasty decisions. His finger hovered over the enter button, but he continued to turn the matter over in his mind.

Up to the moment she pulled the Suburban into the parking garage beneath The Elpis Foundation, Brenda felt clear and calm. As the shadow of the building covered the hood and windshield of the vehicle, her throat constricted. Her hand shook as she entered the code that Winton had provided into the keypad leading to the parking ramps.

"Shit!" she said after entering a 2 instead of a 3. The touchscreen blinked red three times and prompted her to enter the number again.

Why does it have to be nine *characters?* she thought.

The screen turned green and the traffic bar flipped up.

"Which ramp do I take?" she demanded. "A? C? What?"

From the back seat Kevin said, "Just follow the yellow arrows to the sublevels. Relax. You're doing fine."

"I don't see security guards anywhere," she said, driving down the ramp.

"Do you really think a place like this needs security guards?" he asked.

"I suppose not. And no video cameras, right?"

"No. Like I said, creatures like us don't like to be recorded. Ever."

"Yeah," Brenda said. "The rules. God, this is a lot to remember."

Kevin nodded. "We should be able to move around without being tracked."

Brenda wished such repeated assurances made her feel better. She flipped the sun visor up and said, "OK. Does anyone know we're here?"

"Yeah," he said. "That code you entered will be logged on

a security account. If Winton did his job right, it won't flag anything and no one will worry about us. We have to hope he knew what he was doing. I also released a pheromone making us smell like a food delivery truck to anyone who's paying attention. We are safe. For the moment."

Brenda continued driving. "Jesus," she said. "How far down does this go?"

"You don't really want to know," Kevin said. "When you get to sub-level F, park somewhere near an entrance. If anyone sees us, just sit tight until they go away. Unless they're Térata. Then hit them. Hard."

"How will I know if they're a Tér-whatever?" she asked.

"I'll tell you," he said.

She took a deep breath and said, "Ok. I can do this. Then we can get out, get our daughter, and get on with making you human again."

She had no anxiety whatsoever about returning to Tir Naomh. She suspected that was because she didn't have a job in this world anymore. In that world, she had a country to run. The idea of being unemployed upset her more than the idea of living in an imaginary fairy tale land that could cease to exist at any moment.

"Here it is," Kevin said.

She pulled the SUV into a parking spot near the entrance.

"What now?" she asked.

"We get out and head inside," he replied. There was a wobble to his voice.

She turned around and squinted at him. His mouth was open but his eyes were slits. "What's wrong?" she demanded.

"This was my home for decades. I haven't seen it in four years. The doors have been painted blue. They used to be green. It's just odd to see it is all."

Brenda said, "Oh. Sorry."

He waved his clawed hand. "Not a big deal. Let's go."

Brenda glued herself to Kevin's side as they walked toward the door. This whole idea seemed more reasonable before she found herself hundreds of feet under a shimmering glass building.

Kevin opened the door into an empty cinderblock hallway.

"This hall leads to the dormitories I grew up in," Kevin said. "We will find several of my brothers and sisters here. We're prone to inactivity when we're not in the field, so some of them will be napping in their rooms. Beyond the dorms, there is a sprawling complex of laboratories and other... rooms. I'm not sure how many of my siblings we need to set free, but I have a feeling we'll end up in some pretty strange places. You are going to see things that you probably haven't ever imagined. Are you ready for this?"

"No," she said. "I'm not ready at all. But I'm here, so let's get it done."

His lips pulled away from his teeth in a way that made him look like he was going to bite her head clean off her shoulders. She had trained her mind to understand that as a smile.

They walked down the hallway until they came to another steel door. Kevin opened the door into a man-sized spider. Brenda screamed, threw her hands up in front of her face, and squeezed her eyes shut. She hated spiders. Truly, utterly hated them.

"Brenda!" Kevin yelled. "You're killing him! Brenda! Stop it!"

Brenda cracked her eyes, peeking through her fingers. The spider thrashed on the floor. Actually, it wasn't really a spider. It had a human's arms, legs and torso. It was, in fact, a he. His face wasn't human at all. Eight eyes. Fangs. Hairy skin like a tarantula. His fingers and toes were elongated.

"I'm sorry," she said. The monster stopped thrashing. For the first time, she felt a solid wall of something move out of her and into the monster on the floor. She watched as it entered his body and began to alter him. She didn't even need to speak to do this.

Wow, she thought. *It's like I'm rewriting his entire existence. This is...* She didn't know what it was, but it was very powerful. He was under her complete control.

The giant-spider-man-thing sat up.

"Hello, Number 8," Kevin said. "Sorry about that."

"It's fine," Number 8 said.

Brenda squeaked when he talked. His voice was smooth like a DJ. Coming from the mandibles and fangs on his chin, that voice was upsetting.

"I expected something like that," Number 8 continued. "But it isn't over yet, is it?"

"No," Kevin said. "It's far from over. You expected it?"

"Sheila told me you would be coming. I've been watching the security logs. The code you used to get in wasn't familiar, so I thought it might be you. I came to meet you. I want to be free like Kimm and Sheila. And you."

Brenda said to Number 8, "Why didn't Kimm just get your security codes?"

He said, "Because I'm already here. If my tracking chip shows I'm in The Foundation and someone uses my codes at the docks, it will trigger a flag for investigation."

She nodded and asked, "Can you, you know, change into a normal person, please?"

"Sure," he said. "At this point I don't really have a choice if you tell me to do something. You really pack a whallup."

A spider just said "whallup" in a voice like Casey Kasem,

Brenda thought. Of all the strange and terrifying things that had happened in the last two days, that was the one that disturbed her most. How she hated spiders.

His body convulsed and his fangs spread wide in what appeared to be extreme pain. He took deep breaths, she supposed in an effort to manage the change. His eyes congealed together into normal sockets. His skin paled to a glassy white and the hairs slid beneath it. His mandibles and fangs melted into a sharp goatee. He was tall and thin with ropey muscles and jet black hair.

"Oh," he said, shakily. "This wasn't the identity I was going for."

"Get used to it," Kevin said. "You may not be able to change into anyone else."

"That would be unfortunate," Number 8 said. "I have more attractive forms."

Brenda stared at him. He was worried about how good looking he was? He was a hell of a lot more attractive than he had been seconds ago.

"I thought," she said to Kevin, "that they would all be like you and the other two. You know, kind of canine. Like werewolves."

He shook his head. "Nope."

Number 8, whose nudity did not seem to occur to him at all, said, "Please come with me. I want you to look at Number 4. I think she's dead, but—Brenda, is it?—maybe you can do something."

He stuck out his hand and smiled. After glancing at Kevin for approval, she took it. Number 8's grip was tender.

"What do you mean dead?" Kevin asked. "If so she should be cinders."

Number 8 shrugged. "Clarence created a chemical that kills us without making us explode. He wanted to dissect

Number 7 and Number 9."

"And he didn't?" Kevin asked.

"No," said Number 8. "They're in holding cell A802."

"Together?" Kevin asked.

"Yes," Number 8 said. "Apparently, once we get access to emotions, we get lonely." He began to smile, but burst into tears.

"Oh, oh, oh," he said. "It hurts." He clutched at his chest, digging his fingers into the flesh as if he could tear something out. "Why does it hurt? I don't understand. What am I doing?"

"Crying," Kevin said. "It will take time for you to figure out why. Probably because of all the horrible things you've done."

Number 8's eyes widened. "Oh, oh, oh," he said again. "I'm a monster. I'm a terrible thing. I can't live like this! I've done… *things!*"

Brenda frowned and sent a wave of energy to calm him. Number 8 shook as it hit him.

He yelled, "No! No! Don't make it go away!"

She stopped.

He buried his face in his hands and sniffled. After several deep breaths, he collected himself.

"I'm going to have to deal with that sooner or later," he said to her. "If you stop my transformation now, I may not ever connect the dots. It hurts. I don't understand it. But I'll figure it out."

She felt a pang of respect for Number 8. Watching him suffer was hard. The suffering itself must have been immense.

"Take me to Number 4," she said. "And do you have a name?"

"Connor," he said. "In this identity, anyway."

"It's a good name," she said.

"Why do you remain in your true form?" Connor asked Kevin. "I don't feel any tension outside my true form, anymore. It must be the same for you."

"Long story," Kevin said. "Don't worry about it now."

Connor led them down a series of cinderblock hallways under fluorescent lights. Steel doors lined each hall. He stopped several times to cry or take deep breaths.

What a bleak place, Brenda thought.

As if reading her thoughts, Connor said, "This is a sterile place, isn't it?"

"Yeah," she replied. "How do you live here?"

"We don't see it," he said. "I am noticing cracks in the concrete for the first time in twenty years. It's overwhelming." He coughed and spat up a wad of blood. It splattered on the gray floor. He stared at it with fascination.

She realized that she had physically injured him when he'd surprised her at the door. Intuitively, she reached out and touched his shoulder. Instead of sending a wave of something at him, she sent a series of small vibrations into him.

"Does that feel better?" she asked.

He said, "Yes. Much. Thank you."

They exited the hallway into a room containing what looked to Brenda like six large photo booths. They were packed with oversized computer equipment.

"I-Stations," Kevin muttered. "I forgot about them."

"Number 4 is here," Connor said, leading them into a conference room.

A large round table stood in the middle of the room, surrounded by rolling chairs that looked like they were designed for giants. In one of the chairs, a lizard-like female lay staring at the ceiling. Brenda gasped. She was beautiful.

Her scales glistened from red to yellow. Patches of yellow feathers covered her head and sprouted from her armpits and crotch. Brenda approached her slowly.

"Be careful, Brenda," Kevin warned, shadowing her. "She is deadly."

"She is dead," Brenda said, running her fingers along the feathers of the creature's eyebrows.

Connor said, "I had hoped not."

Brenda pursed her lips and ran her fingers along the scales of the creature's face. They felt like plastic. Not exactly sure what she was doing, Brenda sent the same vibrations she'd used on Connor. The only warning she had was the spark of red that lit the depths of the creature's grey eyes. Luckily for her, that was enough for Kevin.

Number 4 sprung from the chair, her tongue thrashing. Her clawed fingers grabbed at Brenda, but Kevin had already moved her out of reach. The claws raked Kevin's side. Blood splashed onto the conference table. He snarled and kicked her back into the chair, which flipped over. As if levitating, she flew from the chair and scampered up the wall. She hissed through small, pointed teeth. Faster than Brenda could follow, she slithered across the ceiling, almost making it out the door before a wad of silver webbing splattered all over her, tacking her to the doorway. Connor, back in his spidery form, squatted on the tabletop with his rear in the air. A set of spinnerets whirled directly above his anus.

"That won't hold her long!" Connor yelled.

"Brenda, you've got to hit her," Kevin said, clutching his side.

Blinking, Brenda turned her attention back to Number 4, who was indeed tearing her way out of the webbing with alarming speed.

"Stop!" she commanded.

The creature went limp. Her calm, red eyes regarded Brenda with blank disinterest. But just beneath the surface Brenda could feel emotions roiling through Number 4's mind. She sent a series of waves meant to weaken, rather than shatter, the barriers that kept those emotions distant. Number 4 choked and began struggling again.

Well, so much for the nice way, Brenda thought. She sent the same wave of instructions she'd hurled at number 8. Number 4 cried out and grabbed her head.

"What are you doing to me?" she screamed. "Is this what freedom is?" She dug her fingers into the feathers of her hair. "Make it stop! Make it stop!" Blood trickled down her fingers and dropped onto the floor.

Kevin looked at Brenda and shook his head.

Connor said, "No, Number 4. You cannot stop it."

"I'm sorry," Brenda said, "but there is not a nice way for me to do this. Stop hurting yourself."

"You!" Number 4 exclaimed, pulling her claws out of her scalp.

Kevin turned to Connor. "Let her down."

Connor teased his large fingers along the webbing that kept Number 4 suspended in the doorway, unraveling it. He caught her as she fell and deposited her in one of the chairs. She curled into a ball and began rocking.

Connor scuttled away from her. "Arrgghh," he said. "Why does doing anything hurt so much? I'm upset because I like the color of her skin, but I might have to kill her if she doesn't calm down! This is ridiculous!"

Silently, Brenda agreed. She had imagined walking into The Elpis Foundation, yelling at a few wolf-people, and walking out. What was happening was a big mess. A stinging weariness set in behind her eyes. This was exhausting work. How many more of these creatures were there?

Kevin grunted and sat down next to Number 4, keeping his eyes glued to her.

"Oh my God!" Brenda cried.

Kevin's flank looked like hamburger. How much damage could Number 4 have done with only one swipe? The wound had a sobering effect on Brenda. These were monsters. No matter how much empathy she felt for them as they changed, they were terrible, powerful creatures designed to kill.

"Don't," Kevin said as she reached for him.

She pulled away. "Why not?" she demanded.

"I don't know what will happen," he said. "I'm in no danger of dying and Number 4 is still very dangerous. We all respond differently to what you do, Brenda. And the process is unpredictable no matter what."

"That would have been nice to know before we got here," she said.

"Yes," he agreed. "It would have. But everything was just speculation. I didn't want you to make any assumptions. Your physical presence does seem to help the transition. There is that."

Brenda snorted in frustration.

Number 4 looked up at Brenda, the red orbs of her eyes pulsing. "I don't know who I am. Help me," she pleaded.

Brenda frowned at her and said, "Take a human form."

Number 4's limbs splayed out and she gulped at the air like a fish. Her scales smoothed over and her feathers split into bright yellow hairs. Her face resolved into Asian features. Her eyes, though, remained red.

"What's your name?" Brenda asked.

Number 4 shuttered and said, "Michiko."

"You are free, Michiko," Brenda said. "Please behave yourself."

Michiko curled back into a ball.

Brenda considered Kevin for a moment. Despite his protests, she touched his shoulder and sent vibrations into him. Surprisingly, information came back to her. The wound on his side was much, much worse than he'd let on. There was poison in it. She scowled at him. That poison very well could have killed him. He grunted as she continued pushing vibrations into him, cleaning and repairing the damaged tissues.

I'm starting to understand how this works, she thought. *I'm also reaching some kind of limit, too.* The exhaustion she felt earlier was now an acute throbbing that had signs of becoming a migraine. When she finished fixing Kevin, she crawled into his lap and rested her head against his chest.

"I can't keep doing this," she said, picking at the blood matted fur on his side. "It's starting to hurt."

Kevin covered her shoulders with one of his clawed hands. "Then you're done."

Connor crawled over to Michiko and brushed his spider-leg fingers over her skin. She leaned into his caress.

"It feels good," she said. "I never thought about anything feeling good like that."

Brenda found the scene unsettling. She had quickly begun to like Connor, but she would never like looking at him in this form.

Connor said, "We need to find Octavio. He has access to the location of all the Térata on Elipsis."

"It doesn't matter now," Kevin said. "Brenda is finished."

"No, no," Connor said. "That's not what I meant. Not now. But we need to be able to find them. For when Brenda has recovered."

"There isn't time for that," Kevin said, putting his other hand around Brenda. "I won't risk it."

"But what will become of them?" Connor asked.

"I don't know," Kevin said. "I don't really care."

"That's easy for you," Connor said. "You have a family. We have nothing but each other. Brenda gave us the ability to care. We can't just stop. You know how this *feels*."

Brenda said, "I don't know how much more I can do."

Michiko said, "You're everything to us now, you know."

"No," Brenda said. "I don't know."

Michiko straitened herself in the chair and ran her fingers through her short, yellow hair. She pulled her hand away and stared at it. When she looked at Brenda, a series of emotions trembled through her eyes. Anger first, followed by what could only be described as desperation.

"Clarence made us with science, but he started with magic," she said. "Human-animal chimeras were real long ago. He found the remains of one. Our DNA is based on the fragments that remained. Back when chimeras were common, some humans could control them. It was humans like you, Brenda, who had dominion over them. Those humans were charged with protecting chimeras, and in return they lent their powers to your causes. Wars were won and lost with the help of such creatures."

Kevin asked, "Where did you get all that?"

"Clarence suspected something like this had happened to you," she said. "I was sent to find you on several occasions. He told me the story so I wouldn't get too close if I located you. When I finally found you, I tasted just a sip of what Brenda can do. Emotions are like fire, aren't they? Like fire you can't resist touching. I barely made it out of the Twin Cities psychologically intact. Clarence thought Number 9's DNA was far enough removed from the original chimera to avoid Brenda's powers. He was quite wrong."

Brenda buried her face in Kevin's chest. His fur smelled rich and musky. She didn't want to hear any more.

"But we aren't chimeras," Kevin said. "Those are legends. Like the Minotaur. Or the Sphinx. We're something else entirely. Those creatures couldn't change forms. They didn't have metal hearts."

Michiko shrugged. "A big enough part of us is still like those creatures. Brenda is like those humans who used us in ages past. You've taken her as yours, but she belongs to all of us. And we to her."

Brenda looked up.

Connor nodded in agreement. She found his bobbing, eight-eyed head irritating.

"You are not children," Kevin said. "Do not act like it. Trading Clarence for Brenda is not an option."

Michiko began to cry. Connor put his arms around her.

"Oh, for Pete's sake," Brenda said. "I'm not going to lead you all around like a bunch of dangerous pets. That's absurd. In fact, I'm leaving the whole fucking planet shortly."

Michiko looked as though she'd been struck, and even with the emotionless face of a spider, Connor managed to appear wounded.

"But," Brenda continued, "I can put my big girl pants on and free the rest of you. It'll be like that time I worked seven doubles in seven days at the Pit Stop."

Kevin said, "That is not a good idea. This isn't physical exhaustion. You could damage yourself."

"If you think working seven doubles in a row is just physical exhaustion, you've never worked in the food service industry," she replied.

Kevin laughed. She felt the deep rumble roll up from his

chest.

"Just, would somebody get me some water?" she asked. "And maybe an aspirin. I'll be fine."

Connor jumped up and said, "I'll get water. I don't think we have aspirin, though."

She waved her hand and laid her head back on her husband's chest. "Fine. And turn back into a human. Looking at you gives me the chills. And, both you, find clothes."

Though she would never tell him, it was Kevin's words that galvanized her decision to continue. He was wrong. The Térata *were* children. Deadly, deadly children. But children all the same. She couldn't leave them.

"*¿Que...?*" Octavio said as he stared at his ringing mobile phone. The name on its screen read, "Timothy Shelton."

"Hello," he answered.

"Hello, Octavio," Tim replied. "I think you and I have some things to talk about."

"What the fuck?" Octavio said.

"Why don't you come down to my office for a quick chat, huh?" Tim said.

"Why in the name of God would I do that?" Octavio spat back.

"Because you're Clarence's last man," Tim said. "And if you don't come here right now to negotiate on his behalf, I'm afraid a lot of decisions are going to get made that will put you in a, shall we say, untenable position."

"Fuck you, Tim," Octavio said. "I ate you."

"Well, and I'm trying to be nice about that, aren't I?"

"I assume you'll just try to kill me again, Tim."

"If I wanted to kill you again, I would have done it the

minute you got back from the Twin Cities with Clarence's numbered pets."

Octavio cringed as Tim used the same words he did to describe the Térata.

Tim continued, "We both know the old man is at the end. He's got that mad scheme going on down in the sublevels, and I need information about that before his inevitable demise. I'm offering you a chance, Octavio. Help me. Oh, and I'm not sure what you've got going on in the Twin Cities, but it may interest you to know that we've got a couple of kids in custody. Winton and Oren, I think? Something tells me you'll be a bit more pliable knowing that, eh?"

Octavio's stomach lurched, but he kept his voice smooth. "Fine, I'll come down there, Tim. But don't forget how it went for you—or whoever that was—last time you tried to pull shit on me."

"I wouldn't dare," Tim said.

Octavio hung up the phone and tossed it onto his desk. It knocked over the Quetzalcoatl figurine. He picked up the carving and rubbed his thumb across its surface.

"What the fuck?" he said.

Octavio had no idea who Winton was, but if Tim had Oren, things were going sideways. How in the world had Tim figured out that Oren was here? Why would he want him? Kimm and Sheila were in a holding cell in the sublevels of The Foundation. Tim didn't even have access to that area. Octavio regretted avoiding the politics that were rumbling through Elpis Enterprises. It would have been nice to know a bit more about what was going on. Mostly he blamed his depression for this. He had plenty of opportunities to at least pay attention to the fact that his place of employment was cracking to pieces, but he'd spent most of his free time moping in the gym.

His phone beeped. A text message scrolled across the top of the screen. "When i said now i meant in less than 5 mins," it read. Octavio grit his teeth to keep from punching the screen of the phone. He left his office and stalked down the hallway. He'd had a very, very trying day already. In the normal world outside the Elpis mess, he would have clocked out an hour ago and gone to a bar with friends. He'd done stuff like that in the Marines. Even in combat zones, there was an end to a bad day if he survived. This day was wearing him thinner by the minute. He wanted to sleep. He wanted to drink beer and get into an honest fight in a shitty bar near a military base because some gringo called him a wetback. He wanted to see his mother and sister and his nieces and nephews. He wanted his life back. Or he wanted to die. The middle ground was no good.

He swung Tim's office door open without knocking. Tim sat behind a polished, oak desk with a glass surface. Non-objective canvases adorned the walls. The carpet was slate grey. Behind the desk, a large window overlooked a courtyard, green fields, and the Enterprises Building. The only evidence of a computer was a large LED screen sitting on the desk next to a wire sculpture of a horse. Tim pushed his glasses up his nose as Octavio entered and motioned to one of the sleek, postmodern chairs in front of the desk. Octavio kicked the chair at a painting, which fell off the wall.

"What do you want to talk about?" Octavio asked, folding his arms across his chest.

Tim sighed. "A lot, really. I do wish you'd sit down."

Octavio didn't move.

"Well, to start, we both know Clarence is at the end of his battle with leukemia. We both know he is obsessed with some apocalyptic plan to undo the rules that govern our kind."

"*Our* kind," Octavio interrupted.

"Of course," Tim said. "You don't generally meet people you've eaten again, do you?"

He had a point. Octavio had always thought of Tim as a very competent, very annoying pencil pusher. He would have to reevaluate.

Tim took off his glasses and motioned to the remaining chair. "Please, have a seat. I'll get a crick in my neck looking at you. There is a lot more going on than you're aware of."

Octavio pulled the chair away from the desk and sat down. His arms remained crossed.

"Thank you," Tim said. "Now, I assume you know something about what's going on in the sublevels where the Térata generally lurk. Despite my best efforts, I remain yet in the dark about what is going on down there. What I propose to you is something of a hostage negotiation. You tell me what's going on and I'll free the pair of hackers who somehow managed to get into Elipsis. I'm not actually all that interested in what they were doing. Nothing was damaged and no sensitive files were leaked. I *would* like to know why you're involved with them, but that's secondary."

Octavio frowned. "So you want me to tell you about Clarence's latest project? In exchange for Oren and the other guy?"

"Yes. And there is a small child, too. Clarence has been so very secretive about what he's been up to in the Twin Cities these days."

"What, exactly, do you want to know?" Octavio asked.

"To start, just give me a broad picture of what's going on."

Octavio shrugged. "Basically, he's got seven hundred genetically engineered humanoid figures in a bunch of very big test tubes. He calls them 'blank canvases'. I think he means for them to take the place of specific human beings. I have no idea why."

Tim smiled and nodded. "When does he plan to do this?"

Octavio shook his head. "I'd actually like some information first, if you don't mind."

Tim put his glasses back on and spread his hands, "Sure. What would you like to know?"

"How are you alive?"

Tim smiled. "Like you, Clarence found me when my life had taken something of a downturn. There was an auto accident. I was sixteen and my parents were killed. I should have been dead, too, but instead of dying, I grew a second me and repaired myself. The cops thought we were twins when they arrived. I'm a replicator. I can grow clones of myself by removing a body part. Those clones are not me and they have only the functionality I give them. I use them for all sorts of purposes that might otherwise expose me to danger or boredom."

"Like assassination?"

"Oh, yes," Tim said. "Among other things. How do you think I have managed so much over the years? When people wish they had two of themselves, they wish they were me."

"Must be nice," Octavio said.

"I've found it to be," Tim said. "Now, when does Clarence plan to unleash these things?"

"Probably today," Octavio said.

Tim frowned. "Today?"

"Yup," Octavio said.

"Do you know how the process works?"

"I'm a camp counselor," Octavio said. "Isn't that what you always call me in your e-mails? How on earth would I understand any of that stuff?"

"True," Tim said. "But I believe you're more than you appear to be, Octavio. You're quite remarkable, actually. I'd like you to take me to the sublevels. You've got the clearance. I'd like to see for myself what Clarence has spent billions of dollars developing."

"Bad timing on that," Octavio said. "You should have asked me last week, instead of trying to kill me."

"In my defense," Tim said, "I had planned to kill you for your clearance badge and fingerprints to get down there. It was nothing personal."

"Why should I betray Clarence for you, Tim? The hostages? Do you really think that's enough to get me to cave? You obviously don't know me. Tell me why I should take you down there."

Tim stood up and leaned forward with his hands on his desk. "Octavio, this company is about to fail. Our balance sheets are bleeding red. Everyone employed here is going to lose their jobs. The entire campus will be shuttered and abandoned to some God forsaken banks. At Clarence's request, I've kept the board of directors in the dark, but at the end of fourth quarter reporting, I'm not going to be able to hide the damage any more. Despite all I can do, despite everything *all* of the Awakened can do, we can't save this company. Clarence has destroyed it. He is going to die anyway. I've got just over two months to patch this back together. I'm desperate, Octavio. Elpis Enterprises is our life. If it goes under, none of us will have a place. Clarence couldn't save us with the Térata. He won't save us with this fool notion he has of making it safe for us to expose ourselves to the world. Everything good will be lost. I'm no villain, Octavio. I'm a pragmatist trying to save the only place of safety I know in this world!"

Tim's face was red and veins stood out on his neck.

Nice speech, Octavio thought.

"No," Octavio said. "I won't take you down there. Ever. It's off the table."

"What about the kids?" Tim asked.

"What about them?" Octavio countered.

Tim looked down at his desk and blew out a breath. He looked back up and said, "Fine. We'll do it the hard way."

Octavio heard the tinkling sound of glass breaking. A small hole appeared in the window behind Tim. A wet sensation dribbled from his forehead to his nose. He slumped forward in his chair and tumbled face first to the floor. Blood stained the grey carpet in a widening pool.

Tim picked up the phone and dialed. "Hi, Aaron... Yeah. He's dead... Theodore. Shot him from all the way across the courtyard... Yeah. Call Number 6 and tell her she can do whatever she wants with that kid. Kill the other kid at the warehouse. Bring the child to me... Yeah. Fine."

Tim turned Octavio over with his foot. "You know, you stupid wetback, I was going to kill you, anyway. You're an idiot." He pulled Octavio's security badge off his shirt. Using a surgical saw he pulled from his desk, he chopped off Octavio's right hand. He put the hand into a black plastic bag and left the office, locking the door on his way out.

Octavio lay on the floor, eyes wide and blank. His phone rang. After ten minutes, a tentacle squirmed out of the hole in his forehead. It spit a smashed rifle slug onto the floor and retreated back into the hole. Small tentacles emerged and began rebuilding his skull and hand. Octavio pulled in a huge breath and sat up.

"*¡Ay!*" he yelled, rubbing his forehead with the palm of his left hand. His right hand would have to wait to be reformed. He didn't have time to do it correctly.

Octavio scrambled behind Tim's desk and slid the

keyboard out. He logged himself into Tim's terminal. Once in, he activated Elipsis' tracking network and typed in Aaron Black's name with his good hand. A map rotated onto the screen. A blinking green dot showed Aaron on I-35 southbound. *He's going to the warehouses in Ankeny*, Octavio thought. He sent the tracking beacon to his phone. If Octavio hurried, he might be able to save Oren. Either way, he could get Amber before Aaron got back with her.

He dialed Number 8 on the computer. No answer. *What the fuck?* Octavio thought. Number 8's beacon showed him moving in the Térata dormitories with Number 4. Octavio dialed the phone in an I-Station near him.

Number 8's smooth voice answered, "Hello?"

The voice was right, but Number 8 had never answered with that word before.

"Number 6 is compromised," Octavio said. "I'm revoking all her accesses. She's to be considered hostile. Timothy Shelton and Theodore Hodges and any other Awakened human are also to be considered hostile. They have my security badge and my hand, so they may try to access the sublevels. Be aware. Protect Clarence."

"Understood," Number 8 said, sounding more like himself. But then he said, "So are you coming down here now?"

"No. I have to go to Ankeny."

"Well, it would be nice to see you."

"What?"

"Oh, never mind. Can't you revoke your own access to the sublevels?"

"Yes, but if I do that I can't reinstate it. I'm going to need to be down there. Soon."

"Does this have anything to do with Kevin? He wants to know."

"What? What in the world is going on down there?"

"The end of the Térata, I think," Number 8 said. "Or something like that. Anyway, Kevin wants to know if this has anything to do with him being here."

"Put him on," Octavio said. If Number 8 was with Kevin, that meant Brenda was probably there, too. That meant things were about to get very messy in the sublevels. Sheila had been very insistent that this happen. He couldn't tell them Amber was in danger. It would interrupt everything.

"Octavio?" Kevin said. "Sorry, I haven't met you, but Sheila explained quite a lot to me this morning. What happened with Timothy?"

"He's coming to the sublevels to see for himself what Clarence is up to. I doubt that's going to sit well with the Confluence that Sheila was talking about. She never mentioned him or any of the other Awakened to me."

"Me neither," Kevin said. "Why aren't you coming down here? Connor seems disappointed."

"Disappointed? Who is Connor?" Octavio asked. Wait a minute. Connor was one of Number 8's identities. "Forget it. I have to go to Ankeny. They've got… some things in a warehouse there that I need to get." He wanted to kick himself for pausing.

"Things?" Kevin asked.

"Yeah, but I don't have time to get into it. Just be aware that you're about to get some heat down there. These guys aren't going to be fucking around. I think you know Theodore, right?"

"Oh," Kevin said. "Yeah. That's heat. OK."

"And get Number 8, or Connor, or whatever he's calling himself, to find his fucking phone so I can get ahold of you when I get back."

"Will do," Kevin said. "Can you give Number 8 access to

the tracking system, please? It would make our jobs down here a lot easier."

"Sure," Octavio said and disconnected the call. Time was not on his side. Cursing his lack of a right hand, he upgraded Number 8's security clearance. When he was finished, he punched the computer screen, sending it to the other side of the room. It knocked another painting off the wall.

The door was locked, requiring him to kick it off the hinges to escape the office. Luckily, no one was in the hallway outside. He ran from the office and down the stairs. Once outside, he sprinted to his car. If he didn't get Amber back before something happened to her, Kevin would likely kill him. If he didn't save Oren, Kimm would likely kill him. Octavio laughed as he peeled out of the parking lot. Monsters were troublesome friends.

Oren managed to get Amber's car seat situated and buckled into the cab before it left the parking lot. The cabby, a muscular man with black hair and a well groomed mustache, asked, "Where to, pal?"

"I need another hotel," Oren said, smiling at Amber, who was fiddling with her toy pig.

"In Ames?" the cabby asked.

"Yeah," Oren said. "That's fine."

"This one didn't work out, huh?"

"No," Oren said. "Not at all."

"You want something nice or cheap?"

"A Super 8 or whatever is fine," Oren replied.

He pulled out his mobile phone and scrolled through his contacts. Every relevant number he had was for someone who was currently at The Foundation. And Winton, but he was probably dead. Oren would need a credit card to check into the hotel room. Winton had advised him against using his own. He stopped under the entry for "Mom", but hesitated calling her. It would be easy to get her to pay for the hotel, but she'd be angry about the whole affair. It wouldn't be the first time she had to float a bill for his Dad. He sighed. He'd call her as a last resort if he couldn't talk the front desk person into taking cash for a room.

The cabby pulled onto the interstate and headed south. That was odd. They were already on the south end of Ames. There must be another cluster of hotels in the next couple of exits. Amber faded back to sleep as the car sped down the highway.

The cabby answered his phone, something that had always annoyed Oren about cab rides. "Hi, Tim, did you take care of our friend? ...Wow, nice shot! ...Will do... Should I leave him there? ... Later."

He hung up the phone and dialed another number. "He's all yours, honey," he said. "See you back here in a few hours. We're in." He hung up the phone and slid it into his sport coat. Oren had never seen a cabby wear a sport coat before.

"Is there a hotel this far south in Ames?" Oren asked.

"Actually, I just thought of a great place in Ankeny," the cabby said. "It's got hot tubs in the rooms for the standard price."

Oren frowned and nodded. He had been to Ames to party with some of his buddies who'd come to Iowa State, but he didn't really know the area well enough to argue with the cab driver. He kept his eyes on the meter.

They exited the interstate to an industrial area. A large sign read, "Tax Free Economic Development Zone". There were no signs for hotels anywhere. Oren's stomach began tying itself into knots.

"Um," he said, "is there a hotel in here somewhere?"

"No," said the cabby, or whoever he was, as he pulled into an industrial complex. "We're going to a storage warehouse, where I'm going to ask you some questions. If you answer them, I'll drop you off at the hotel later."

The cabby pulled the car into an open overhead door and used his phone to close it. He stopped the car and turned around. In his right hand, he held a gun.

"Before we get started, I need you to answer one question. If you lie to me, I'll know, and I'll shoot this little girl. Are you Awake?"

At first Oren had no idea what the man was talking about. His heart was pounding in his ears. The man pulled the hammer back on the gun.

"No!" Oren said, louder than he'd intended. Amber woke up with a start. She stared at the gun but didn't say anything.

"Figures," the man said. "Well, get out of the car. Leave the kid. And your phone."

Oren unbuckled his seatbelt, dropped his phone onto the seat, and stepped out of the car. He left the door open. The guy grabbed the collar of his shirt and threw him more than ten feet forward. Oren stumbled to the concrete floor.

"Stay down," the man commanded.

Oren complied.

The warehouse was filled with shipping containers for trains and barges. The cab was parked in the middle of what appeared to be a loading area. Oren cast about for something, anything, that might be useful in this situation. There was nothing.

"Why did you hack into our system, kid?" the guy asked. He pointed the gun at Oren's chest.

"If I tell you, you'll let me and Amber go?" Oren said. He

was happy to find that his voice was firm. He settled himself on his heels and faced the man with his shoulders straight.

"Yup, sure," the guy said.

"What's your name?" Oren asked.

"Aaron Black," the man replied. He twirled the gun. "No more questions. Just answer me if you want to live through this."

There was no way Oren was living through this and he knew it. In a way, he'd known it the moment he saw his short line in the Confluence that Sheila had drawn.

"My friend and I do this kind of stuff," he lied. "We're eco-terrorists. Your company is seriously fucking up Mother Nature. We were hoping to crash your servers."

Aaron Black smiled. "I'm going to give you that one," he said, "because I respect your gall and creativity under pressure. Now answer me, or I'm going to shoot your dick off."

He pointed the gun at Oren's crotch.

Oren's mind spun. He tried to think of something to say, but it was obvious that Aaron wasn't going to buy anything but the truth. He froze, unable to think forward. Telling the truth was out of the question. Aaron lost his patience and fired the gun. A chunk of concrete exploded beside Oren's leg. He yelped and shielded his face with his arms.

"Talk. Now."

"Kill me," Oren said, dropping his arms to his side. "It's really the only reason I'm here, anyway."

Aaron frowned at him. "It's not that easy, kid."

He pointed the gun at Oren's leg and pulled the trigger. Oren's right quadriceps exploded in blood. He screamed and fell over. The concrete felt cool against his face. He focused on that in an effort to block out the searing pain that stabbed up from his leg, reached into his chest and spread to his arms. How could so much pain be so many places when he'd only been shot in the leg? How could so much blood be coming out of him?

"I'm going to give you a moment to collect yourself," Aaron said, "then you're going to answer my questions or I'll shoot your other leg. Then your feet. Then your hands. If you want to die, the fastest way to do that is—"

A small, grey blur shot from the open door of the cab and hit Aaron in the back of the head. Its momentum did not slow with the collision, so Aaron's head ripped off his neck. Blood fountained upward as his body fell forward. Groaning, Oren rolled to avoid being soaked. He twisted his head. A small, grey monster was holding Aaron's head thirty feet way. In Amber's voice, the monster said, "Bad! Bad! Hu't O'en! Bad! Bad!"

"Amber," Oren sputtered.

Amber dropped the head and bounded to Oren on all fours.

"Amber," Oren said, panting. "Listen to me. I think I'm going to bleed to death." Oren was pretty sure that one of his femoral arteries had been damaged, judging by the amount of blood that was pouring from the bottom of his jeans. His hand was pressed firmly against the entry wound, but that didn't seem to be helping. His head felt light. "Honey, can you bring me my phone?"

The monster, which looked like her father without a snout, smiled. "Phone!" she said, and bounded back to the cab. A moment later she emerged with the blanket wrapped sword. She propped it on Oren's side.

"No," Oren said, gritting his teeth. "No, honey, I need the phone. The *phone*."

Amber shook her head. "No phone. Swo'd."

Oren let his head fall back against the concrete. He was

going to die because a child wanted to play. Well, and because someone had shot him in the leg. Dodged bullets, huh? This was silly.

Unwrap me, a distant female voice commanded.

Oren's head snapped up from the floor. "What?" he asked.

Unwrap me, the voice repeated.

Amber nodded at him.

With the hand that wasn't pressing his wound, he pulled the blankets off of the sword. It was a beautiful thing. Two swans climbed the golden hilt, their wings meeting at the top. He sat up, wheezing with pain.

You know what to do, the voice said. It carried a gentle, maternal note.

Amber nodded again.

Oren turned the sword so that the hilt rested against the floor. He positioned the point of the blade on the left side of his chest and fell forward. The pain in his leg receded. As the world spun away, he saw Amber, a two year old girl once again, clapping her hands and smiling. She was covered head to foot in blood.

Chapter 13
Hope for the Future

Clarence cradled his face in his hands as he listened to Octavio's voicemail greeting for the third time. On the computer screen in front of him, Octavio's beacon was flashing red. The location tab indicated he was in Timothy Shelton's office. Clarence's top executive assistant had finally made a hard move. Clarence had not expected him to do so until next year, when the financials of the company would be threatened. By then, Clarence had planned to license a new string of patents on bioelectrical information transfer that would stabilize the balance sheets, thus calming Timothy and the other Awakened. They had legitimate concerns about their futures without Elpis Enterprises.

Since Clarence still trusted him, Octavio was an obvious target in a coup attempt. The boldness of Tim's move was still startling. The man was as ambitious as he was afraid of losing Elpis Enterprises to financial ruin. He and the rest of the Awakened would have to be dealt with harshly. The situation saddened Clarence.

More problematically, Clarence's ability to stave off the carcinogenic poison oozing from his bones died with

Octavio. Coupled with Timothy's sudden movements, Clarence had no more options. He depressed the enter key on his keyboard.

A high pitched whine issued from machinery throughout the vast laboratory housing his blank canvases. Pulsing waves of electricity traveled from the diodes on Amber's head to the Tesla coils behind her. The solution in the tubes began to glow, casting pulses of green light. The homunculus inside opened their eyes in unison.

Clarence turned to Craig and said, "It has begun. Let us hope, my boy, that when the god that is killing me tears his way out of my bones, he finds my work worthy of a continued life. Otherwise, we are both doomed."

A tear dribbled down Craig's slack face as the fluid in his lacrimal ducts began to drain.

In less than an hour, transmission of the information stored in Amber's genetic material would be fully infused into the forms in those tubes. They would all Wake Up. If they could find their targets before Clarence died of Leukemia, he might yet change the course of his fate.

Hope, Clarence thought ruefully, *is all that I am left with.*

Octavio pulled into the parking lot of the Elpis Enterprises staging warehouse where Aaron Black's flashing red beacon indicated he should be. Octavio could not imagine a scenario in which Oren killed Aaron Black. That man could move like lightning. He was one of the best soldiers Octavio had ever met. Something else had happened. It probably wasn't good.

The parking lot was well lit but deserted. Octavio parked in front of one of the overhead doors at the loading docks. He fiddled with the security code until the door lifted. His hand had grown back, but the nerve endings hadn't fused properly. He'd need to remove and regrow it, but he didn't have time for that now. Inside, a yellow taxi with open doors sat in the middle of the bay. Aaron Black's body lay next to the cab. His head was twenty feet away. A small, naked girl was driving a toy car over Aaron's legs, making "voom" sounds. The concrete floor around her was coated in blood, which also streaked her skin and hair. A gun lay next her, covered with small, bloody fingerprints. She looked up at Octavio.

"I Amba'," she said.

"I'm Octavio," he replied. "It's nice to meet you, Amber. Can you tell me where Oren is?"

"In swo'd," she said, pointing to the other side of Aaron's corpse.

Octavio approached the child slowly. He picked up the gun and slid it into the pocket of his jacket. On the other side of Aaron's body lay a broadsword like he'd seen in fantasy movies. The hilt was entwined with two golden swans. The blade was covered in blood for three quarters of its length. Octavio lifted the sword. Amber nodded as he did so.

What did Amber mean? Oren was *in* the sword? Octavio wiped the blade on Aaron's jacket and held it up in the fluorescent light. Oren's face flickered across the blade and vanished. He appeared to be sleeping.

Oh, great, Octavio thought. *He's actually inside the fucking sword. How did* that *happen?*

Octavio set the sword down and crouched in front of Amber. "Amber, I would like for you to come with me. Is that OK?"

Amber looked at him and crossed her arms. She leaned forward and sniffed his hands. Continuing to sniff, she pushed her face into his armpits. When she pulled her face away from his chest, she was smiling. "Octa OK!" she said.

"Go see Mommy and Daddy?"

"Let's get you cleaned up first, huh?" he said.

Octavio rummaged through the back seat of the cab until he found baby wipes, diapers, and a change of clothes. Thankfully, none of the blood he wiped away was hers.

"All clean!" she said as he tossed the last bloody wipe onto Aaron's body.

She insisted on putting her own dress on, which slowed the process down. A pang of nostalgia wormed through Octavio's chest as he slipped her socks and shoes on. His niece had been this age when he'd shipped off to Afghanistan.

The straps for Amber's car seat were torn out and pieces of fabric were scattered throughout the back seat. The rest of the car seat was intact. He moved it to his car and strapped the seat belt over it with Amber sitting inside. He knew what his sister would say about improper use of car seats, but he didn't have many options at the moment.

He returned to the cab to retrieve the sword and the rest of Amber's things from the back seat. On impulse, he opened the trunk. The body of a middle aged white man was crammed inside. Octavio had suspected the cabby would be there. Aaron wasn't subtle, but he had been a master of field improvisation. Octavio closed the trunk.

He knelt beside Aaron's body and inspected his neck wounds. At first, Octavio assumed that Aaron's head had been chopped off by the sword. But the jagged wound indicated tearing, not chopping. Considering who her father was, Octavio decided Amber had most likely killed Aaron. Disturbing.

Amber was dozing when he got back to the car.

"*Sueña con los angelitos,*" Octavio said, running his fingers through her thin black hair.

He pulled the car out of the parking lot and dialed Number 8 on his phone. That bastard better answer. This was getting weird.

Andre blinked his eyes. The Tennessee night was gorgeous. Shimmering white stars in the sky. Dark green foliage in the surrounding forest. Metallic red paint on Victoria's pick-up. These were the most wonderful things he'd ever seen. The spirit world was graphic and startling, but it lacked the substance of the real world. Details had never seemed so important. Through the lenses of his new glasses, Andre could pick out the individual pieces of gravel in the overgrown driveway, despite near darkness.

"This is really, really great," he said to Victoria.

"I am happy for you, Andre," she said. "I wonder, though, if there is a price for these glasses. Few things come for free."

Andre shrugged. "Maybe there is. I don't know. I don't really care. When I walked into that room full of stuff, I knew they were there. There wasn't a price tag."

"There is rarely something as obvious as a tag. Shall we head to Des Moines?"

"Wait," Andre said. He opened the case of lenses and selected a pair with a spiral etched into the glass. He took off his glasses and set them on the hood of the truck.

"Can you still feel the Confluence?" he asked.

"Yes," Victoria replied. "It's faded, but still very powerful. I can feel it demanding we go to Des Moines."

Andre screwed the new lenses onto the frames of his glasses and put them on.

"With these lenses, I can't see anything but the Confluence," he said. "It's like a swirling river of golden mist. I can touch it, too. Even in this world, I can touch the

Confluence."

"The last time you did that, the results were unexpected and unpleasant," Victoria said.

"The last time I did it, I didn't understand it at all," he said. He gathered the cases from the hood of the truck by touch. "Get your purse, Victoria. And bring the box."

Andre stared at the river of the Confluence stretching northwest toward Des Moines. It reminded him of the arm of a galaxy in one of those pictures sent back from the Hubble Telescope.

He felt Victoria take his hand. "I think I know what you intend to do," she said. "Be careful, Andre. If you are wrong, we will die and your friends along with us."

"If we try driving back, they will die, too," Andre said. "Something went wrong. The Confluence is bursting. If we aren't at its center when it goes, very bad things will happen."

"That may be," Victoria said, "but I've been caught up in Confluences before. I've never found one I couldn't just walk away from."

"Have you ever felt one like this?" he asked.

"No," she said. "No, I haven't. And even without the Confluence, I believe I would go back for your friends."

Andre smiled and squeezed her hand. "Then you can think of them as your friends, too."

"Perhaps," she said.

Andre reached forward and thrust his fingers into the flow of the Confluence. His digits disintegrated and joined the golden lights. He took a step and was jerked upward. Every atom in his body separated and spun into the swirling mass. Victoria was pulled along with him. They joined together as they flowed, moving into and out of one another's atomic structures. He could feel all of her in microscopic pieces. *Such comfortable intimacy*, Andre thought as they sped along the glittering path to Des Moines.

Kevin held Number 2 in an arm bar as he finished taking a human form. Kevin recognized the identity as Reginald Thurston, a heavily muscled black man with a flat nose and deep set eyes. Reginald ceased struggling, so Kevin let him slump to the floor. There he panted and hugged himself. Brenda was becoming surgical with her abilities, making the Térata's transitions to emotional awareness easier each time. Number 5 had gone much better than 8 and 4. Number 3 had been almost as clean as Number 2, who was now Reginald.

A small crowd was gathered in Reginald's dormitory.

It feels like an intervention, Kevin thought.

"That is the last one in the facility," Connor said, consulting his phone. "Number 6 is in the Twin Cities. Numbers 10, 11, and 12 are dead."

"Thank God," Brenda said, slumping onto Reginald's bed.

Kevin sat next to her and gathered her in his arms. Her breathing was ragged, as if she'd been running for hours. Her face was ashen. Chills shook her body.

"Where is Tim now?" Kevin asked.

Connor swiped his screen several times. "Still in a conference room at The Foundation. He's got twenty-three others with him. All of the military branch, unfortunately. I think he means to invade the sub-levels."

"We could just let him do it..." Kevin mused aloud.

"I think we should talk to Sheila, first," Connor said, slipping his phone into the front pocket of his shirt. "I can feel the Confluence she was talking about now. I know you can, too. It's very, very powerful."

Kevin sighed. Connor was right. But all he wanted to do was take his wife out of this nightmare, gather their daughter, and leave the entire world of The Elpis Foundation far behind.

"What do we owe Clarence, now?" Number 3, now Wendy Frisk, asked. She looked like a librarian, her brown hair tightly bunned and thick glasses resting on her thin nose. "We could just leave him. I can feel the Confluence, too, but I've never paid much attention to those before." She adjusted the belt on her slacks for the tenth time. Apparently getting dressed quickly wasn't something she was used to.

"We owe Clarence nothing," Connor said. "But we owe Brenda a great deal. If she wants us to resolve this Confluence, then we should."

"What is happening?" Reginald interrupted from the floor. "Why am I crying? Who are you people?"

Michiko took him by the hand and led him to the bathroom. "We're your brothers and sisters. It will help if you take a shower. You seem to have... soiled yourself. I'll get you some clothes."

Number 5, who had taken a human form named Sean Flynn, combed his fingers through his red beard. "So we're goin' to help Clarence? I can take five or six of the Awakened myself, but if Tim gets too many more, we're goin' to have problems. And I think I like some of those folks. I'm not sure. Is it OK to kill folks you like?"

Connor's phone rang. He pulled it out of his pocket and smiled. "Hello, Octavio," he said.

"I'm heading your way," Octavio said. "Tell Kevin I have Amber with me. She's fine. I need to meet you as soon as I get back. Has Tim moved yet? Is Clarence still alive?"

"Slow down a bit, Octavio," Connor said. "No, Tim hasn't made a move. He appears to be amassing an army—"

Kevin snatched the phone from Connor's ear and yelled, "Why do you have Amber? What happened?"

"Aaron Black got to her and Oren," Octavio said.

Kevin felt his stomach cramp. Brenda pulled on his chest hair in an attempt to right herself.

"She's fine," he whispered to her.

"I got to her before he did anything terrible," Octavio continued. "He's dead now."

"What about Oren? How did he get to them?"

"That's a bit more complicated," Octavio said. "What do you know about a sword with swans on its hilt?"

"What about the sword?"

"Oren's inside it," Octavio said, exhaling a breath. "I'm not sure how or why. But he's sure as hell in that sword."

Kevin looked down at Brenda. She was straining to hear the other side of the conversation, but had not heard that. "We'll deal with that later," Kevin said. Brenda did not need any further stress right now. "Bring the sword with you. We're going to get Sheila and Kimm. Meet us in the holding cell area. What's your ETA?"

"Twenty minutes to the sub-levels," Octavio said.

"See you then." Kevin hung up the phone and handed it back to Connor.

"What's happened with Amber?" Brenda asked. Her voice sounded like gravel grinding under a car tire.

"She's fine," Kevin said. "Octavio has her."

"And Oren?" she asked.

"Fine, too," he said. "We'll deal with him later. Octavio will be here in twenty. Let's go get Sheila and Kimm. If this gets too hot, we're going to need all the help we can get."

Reginald stepped out of the bathroom and said, "Does anyone know why this happens when I touch myself here?" He pointed at the erection standing up between his legs. "I used to be able to make it go up and down whenever I wanted."

The rest of the Térata looked from Reginald to Kevin with piqued interest.

"It's called a boner," Kevin said, picking Brenda up. "You're going to have to start dealing with things like that now. Inconvenience of emotional access. Get dressed. That'll help."

Michiko said, "It's much bigger than it was," as she handed him a pair of jeans and a t-shirt she'd found in his dresser. "I remember seeing human men do this in bed with me. It was a great way to get what I wanted from them. But now it seems... it *feels* funny to look at it."

"Yeah, it does," Connor said. "Kinda like a tingle."

"I don't feel anything," Flynn said. "And I think mine gets bigger than that. Does that really matter?"

"I would think so," Wendy said, peering over her glasses at Reginald as he put on his clothing.

Brenda began shaking in Kevin's arms. He looked down. Though her features were haggard, she was laughing.

"They *are* just like children," she muttered.

Sheila awoke with a start as the door to their cell opened. She and Kimm were curled together on the small bed. Kimm's head rested on her thigh. Hers had been on the small of his back. Kimm did not wake up, so Sheila poked him. He yelped and growled at the door.

"Relax," Kevin said as he walked into the cell. He had Brenda in his arms. She looked quite ill.

"What happened to her?" Sheila asked.

Kevin sniffed the air and scrunched his nose up. "She's been freeing the Térata," he replied. "It takes a toll on her.

What have you two been doing to kick up such a smell?"

"None of your business," Sheila said. He knew exactly what that smell was.

"You didn't soil the bed, did you?"

"No," she said. "We were tidy."

"Good," he said. "Hop up. I need it."

Kimm and Sheila crawled from the bed. Kimm stretched his body out, flexing his muscles and opening his mouth as wide as it could go. His knife-like teeth protruded as his lips curled above his gums.

Kevin wiped fur from the sheets, lay Brenda on the bed, and tucked her into the blankets. In low tones he explained to her that she should sleep here until he came back to get her. She protested, but he convinced her. Sheila felt a lump form in her throat, so she turned from their conversation to the open door.

An Asian woman came into the room carrying two changes of clothing. "Brenda prefers us to be in human form and wearing clothes," she said. She cocked her head to the side. Like Kevin, she would be able to smell the fornication in the air.

"Who are you?" Kimm asked.

"Michiko," the woman replied. "I used to be Number 4."

"Really?" he said. "I thought I killed you."

"Not quite," she said. "The drug slows our metabolism to the point of death. That's why we don't explode. It's as good as dead for all practical purposes. Brenda brought me back. She's the only one who could do such a thing."

"Fascinating," Kimm said. He shifted into his human form and took the clothes Michiko was offering. "I didn't really feel bad about killing you, but I am glad you're still alive."

"What were you doing in here to make that smell?" she asked.

"None of your business," Kimm said.

Sheila smiled and shifted forms. If the rest of the Térata were becoming aware of their emotions, a hormone jungle was growing in the hallway. After she dressed she stuck her head out of the door and took a sniff. Jungle was an understatement.

"Oh, Christ," Kimm said, joining her at the door. "What a mess."

The group in the hall included some identities Sheila knew. Number 8 was Connor. Number 5 was Sean. Number 3 was Wendy. By process of elimination, she assumed that the wide black man was Number 2. Number 6 was female and absent.

"Where's Number 6?" she asked.

"In Minneapolis," Number 8 answered. "She seems to have joined the Awakened in a coup attempt. I don't know how that's possible, but she's no longer one of us."

"And what's your name?" Sheila asked Number 2.

"Reginald Thurston," he said. "You can call me Reggie. Who are you?"

"I'm Sheila and this is Kimm," she answered. "You guys look like you're in pretty good shape, considering what Brenda does to us."

"Brenda is learning to make things go more smoothly," Kevin said from behind her. "As messy as it is may smell in the hallway, you both had it harder than they have."

Sheila said, "If you leave Brenda here, what will happen to them when she's not around to guide them."

"She already put a lot of work into them," Kevin said. "She's figured out what she was doing since she hit you two. I think they'll be fine. For now, anyway. Who knows in a week?"

Sheila asked, "Where is Octavio?"

"On his way," Kevin said.

Kimm said, "Hey, Number 8, let me use that phone in your pocket."

"My name is Connor, if you don't mind." He handed Kimm the phone.

Kimm dialed Oren's number. After ringing several times, the connection went to voicemail.

"Hey, Son, give me a call at this number when you get this. Love you." He handed the phone back to Connor with a frown.

"Clarence is probably wondering why so many of us are gathered here," Connor said. "He'll also not be happy to see the two of you leaving this cell." He turned the screen of his phone around. A cluster of green dots blinked on the screen.

Kevin said to Sheila, "You seem to have the best line on this Confluence. What are we supposed to do now?"

"I'm not certain," Sheila said. She closed her eyes and the image of the spiral formed in her mind. New lines interfered with the structure of the Confluence. She traced each path carefully for a few moments. "The paths all lead to Clarence. I think we should go to him now. The Confluence is becoming unstable. It will rupture soon."

"I thought Victoria was the center," Kevin said.

"You never were very good with this kind of thing," Sheila said.

He frowned at her, but nodded. "We need to wait for Octavio," he said.

"Yes, we do," she said. She eyed Kimm sideways. Connor had been visibly apprehensive about Kimm's phone call. "And others."

"Speaking of others," Connor said, "it appears that the Awakened will all be down here in a minute. They're moving from the conference room now."

Kevin said, "How many?"

"All of them," Connor said.

"All of them?" Kevin demanded.

"Well, except for Octavio, but he shows up as dead in Elipsis. That can't be accurate."

"How many is all of them?" Kevin said, waving his hand.

"Fifty-four."

Sean said, "That's too many. We can't beat them if it comes to fighting."

"What are they up to?" Sheila asked.

"Tim has decided it's time for a leadership change at Elpis Enterprises," Kevin said.

"Really? Now?" Sheila said with annoyance. "That guy is a douche bag. He could ruin everything. We have to go to the center of the Confluence. If we don't, bad things will follow."

"What kind of bad things?" Wendy said. "I'm just now discovering that I *can* care about things. One of the interesting points this illuminates is that I care about my own well-being. I'd rather not die in a wasteful attempt to defend a man I am no longer bound to."

Sheila had never liked Number 3. Apparently she never would.

"You all have free will now," Sheila said. "You can leave if you want."

"No, actually," came a quiet but strong voice from the door of the holding cell. Brenda leaned against the door frame. "You cannot leave if you want. Nothing is free, including your freedom. You will follow Kevin's lead in this matter. You will protect him. You will bring him safely back to me. Do you all understand?"

A wave of energy pulsed through the group of monsters. In unison, they all, including Kevin, nodded their heads.

Brenda faded from the doorway and went back to bed.

Well, Sheila thought, *that's an easy way to avoid an argument.*

"Octavio is coming," Connor said. "I can smell him."

Moments later, Octavio marched into the hallway, carrying Amber on his left hip and a large, ornate sword in his right hand. He didn't look at Sheila.

Amber squirmed out of his grip and ran to Kevin, who gathered her in a single, clawed hand so that she could hug his neck.

"That's adorable," Michiko said. "I never thought of children like that before." A tear ran down her cheek. Her tear wasn't the only one.

"Where is Oren?" Kimm demanded. "Wasn't the plan for him to watch Amber?" He strode to Octavio, who grimaced and looked down at the sword.

"He's in this sword," Octavio said.

Kimm roared into his true form and grabbed Octavio's shirt. His clothing fell away in pieces. Michiko tsked.

"What do you mean he's *in* the sword?" Kimm demanded.

Octavio slid the blade of the sword between their faces. "Look into the blade, Kimm. He's in there. I do not know how. He seems to be safe. Sleeping, I think."

Kimm grabbed the hilt of the sword and stared into the blade.

"My God," he breathed. "Oren, how did you get in there?"

Kevin put his hand on Kimm's shoulder. He held Amber in his other arm. She watched him with calm, childlike distance.

"This sword comes from the world of spirits," he said. "It can open pathways between worlds. I also think it might be alive in its own right. It's Brenda's. I think she might be able to explain it. But, Kimm, she's very sick and I don't want to wake her. We can figure it out after we sort out this business with Clarence."

Kimm searched his brother's eyes and looked back at the sword.

"I think he's hurt," Kimm mumbled. He stared at the blade for a few more moments. "OK," he said, handing the sword to Kevin. "Brenda better know how to get my son out of that sword."

Kevin nodded. He took the sword and his daughter into the cell and shut the door.

Kimm returned to his human form and picked up the pieces of his shredded clothing.

Sean laughed.

"What's so funny?" Kimm spat.

"I—I don't really know," Sean said through a grin. "I just saw you picking up your clothes and... it came out." He regained control of his facial expression. "I think that was funny. Was that funny?"

Sheila hid her own grin. It hadn't been so funny until Sean laughed. Now it was hilarious. The other Térata were all fidgeting. *They do have it a lot easier*, Sheila thought. *When I lost it, I tried to eat Octavio.*

"Here," Michiko said, handing Kimm a pair of sweat pants and t-shirt. "I brought extras just in case."

Kevin returned to the hallway. He shut the door to the cell and ensured it was locked.

Octavio addressed everyone, "Tim and his crew are coming down in the service elevators. I'm going to go to Clarence to warn him about what's going on. I can't let the Awakened kill him. I will call you when it is time to stop them. Hopefully we can use you as a bargaining chip to keep this from going completely Costa Rica."

Wendy snorted. "I'm not all that interested in being a

bargaining chip, but I guess I don't have a choice. Brenda's commands are stronger than Clarence's were."

Sheila thought, *No, honey, you don't have a choice. Even without Brenda's commands. We all die if separated. This is our only chance out of here.*

Sean said, "We will need a plan if they attack us."

Sheila said, "This is where we must defer to Kevin. He is in charge, after all."

She smiled as Kevin laid out a general plan to defend Clarence from the Awakened. He had Connor pull up a diagram of the laboratory on his phone. Using that layout, he set positions for everyone. Never before in their history had this many of the Térata worked together. Though they had always called each other brother and sister, it wasn't until this moment that they acted like a family. Sheila knew these new bonds were liable to be shredded in the next hour, so she savored the moment.

She noticed Octavio slip away as Kevin spoke. He winked and smiled at her as he left. Kimm was right. He was a good man. Too good of a man for her.

Octavio ran between the tubes of blank canvases. The liquid in the tanks was almost drained and the genderless beings inside were standing on their own. Their eyes followed Octavio as he ran. Whatever Clarence had planned was moving forward.

"Clarence!" Octavio yelled, seeing the old man slumped over his desk at the head of the room. The false Amber lay to his right in a gurney. Electrical pulses radiated from her head, encircling her body and launching back into a series of complicated metal coils behind her. Craig sat in a wheelchair to Clarence's left. An IV was hooked to his arm and a catheter ran from his pant leg. His eyes considered nothing.

Clarence lifted his head and turned. "Octavio!" he exclaimed. "Oh, my dear man. I thought you were dead!"

"I almost was," Octavio said, climbing a short staircase to the platform where Clarence sat. "Theodore shot me in the head. But most of my brain is no longer located only there. It took a few minutes to get past the shock, but I'm fine."

"It still says you're dead on Elipsis," Clarence said, wobbling to his feet.

"There's no protocol for that to switch back," Octavio said. "Usually death doesn't undo itself." That hadn't been very true recently. The system should be updated. "Anyway, the Awakened are moving, Clarence. They're coming down here. I've got the Térata assembled, but I don't know if we can stop them."

Clarence sat back down. "I'm afraid everything has changed, now, Octavio. I don't need the Awakened or the Térata anymore."

"What do you mean?" Octavio asked.

"I've been negotiating with the god inside of me," Clarence said. "I think he is pleased with the results of my new plan. I'm not quite ready to let him out, though, so it is wonderful that you've survived. The more time I have, the more leverage I have."

"God?" Octavio asked. He sat down on top of the desk, blocking Clarence's view of Craig. "In your bones?"

Clarence waved his hand. "Yes. That's what is killing me."

"That's why I couldn't get to the marrow to cure you, then?" Octavio said. A small tentacle slid out from the back of his shirt and snaked its way to Craig. It followed the line of the catheter up Craig's pant leg before drilling into his abdomen and slinking its way up to his brain. Octavio put the tentacle to work, hoping he could finish the job before

Clarence noticed.

"Yes," Clarence said. "But, hopefully, I'll be able to broker a new deal with this creature before I die. Having you by my side again gives me many more options."

But if you don't need the Térata or Awakened anymore, Octavio wondered, *what do you plan to do about the situation happening right now?*

"Number 1 is here," Octavio said. "He showed up looking for her." Octavio pointed at the false Amber. "I told him we would negotiate for her if he helped us deal with the Awakened. He agreed."

"You are the best of my people," Clarence said smiling. "Tim always underestimated you. Bring the Térata here, Octavio. We might as well get everyone together. The Awakened will be coming in from the freight elevators shortly."

Octavio pulled out his phone and dialed Number 8, or Connor, or whoever he decided he was.

"Hi, Octavio! Is it time for us?" Connor answered.

Octavio could not figure out why the monster was so excited every time he answered the phone today. "Go ahead and bring everyone in. Including Number 1. Be ready. The Awakened will be here in a few minutes."

"You got it," Connor said.

Octavio hung up.

"Number 8 seems excited," Clarence said.

"Yeah," Octavio said, shrugging. "He's been acting weird all day."

Clarence nodded. The Térata, in their true forms, began appearing among the tubes. They set up a defensive position between the elevated platform where Clarence and Octavio sat and the wide hallway leading to the freight elevators. The overhead door to that hallway was down. Octavio had barred it from the inside on his way to Clarence.

Kevin directed the Térata. He had a great eye for defensive strategy. For the Awakened to make it to Clarence after getting through that door, they'd fall into multiple traps. It would be a blood bath.

"Aren't they beautiful," Clarence said.

Octavio shrugged. They were impressive. Eight hulking creatures designed to hunt, kill, and destroy. Their movements were fluid and efficient, reflecting their intense physical intelligence. Each one could have laid waste to hundreds of humans, even if they were armed soldiers. But Number 4 was the only one Octavio thought had any beauty, and that was only because the color of her scales changed from yellow to red as she moved. It reminded him of the paint job of his cousin's '69 Camaro. The rest of the Térata were only monsters. Frightening. Not beautiful.

A resounding knock came from the overhead door. All eight of the Térata froze and focused on the door, which exploded. Flaming shrapnel flew through the rows of tubes. Apparently Clarence had used ballistic glass to construct them. The shrapnel bounced off the tubes like pinballs. The Térata moved almost lazily to avoid it. They slid back to their positions as the dust and rubble settled.

Tim Shelton marched out of the billowing smoke. Two more of him followed. His eyes scanned the room until he saw Octavio and Clarence on the far side.

"Wow, you are hard to kill!" he yelled to Octavio. All three of him waved. "Hello, Clarence! You've been ignoring my calls and e-mails, so I thought I'd pop down for a quick meeting. I hope I haven't interrupted anything."

More figures emerged from the smoke. Men and women wearing SWAT armor and carrying automatic AP4 Panther rifles fanned out behind Tim. Octavio counted fifty-six of them, including the three Tims. A tall man wearing a black beret barked orders, directing the Awakened into a quick but solid line designed for assault. Theodore. Octavio hoped that guy did not make it all the way through the Térata. Theodore was the only person in the organization that Octavio knew he couldn't beat in a fight. He was too fast, too strong, too well-trained, and he had all sorts of strange tricks up his sleeves. Octavio had lost every sparring match with him. Those matches hadn't even been close.

"Tell him that I'm not very happy to see him," Clarence said to Octavio.

"Your meeting request has been declined!" Octavio yelled.

Tim turned to Theodore and motioned forward. Theodore shouted to the Awakened, who broke into smaller groups and began zig-zagging between the tubes. *Smart*, Octavio thought. They knew an ambush waited for them. Their movements were designed to flush out the Térata one by one. He also appreciated their courage. Precious few of the Awakened could match a Térata in combat. Some of their abilities weren't even physical. But they willingly put themselves in a situation where they knew the enemy had an upper hand. They may have been misguided, but they were good soldiers. Most of them were about to die and they had to know that.

"Oh, let's not bother with all this," Clarence said. He stood up and spread his arms.

Two shock waves blasted forward from Clarence's body. The first wave felled every single one of the approaching Awakened. They hit the ground squirming. The second wave knocked over the Térata, who also thrashed on the floor.

"What are you doing?" Octavio asked, keeping his voice calm.

"Killing them," Clarence replied. "They all belong to me. I don't keep possessions that try to destroy me."

Clarence sent more waves into the thrashing bodies below. Screams filled the high ceiling of the laboratory. Some of the Térata roared in agony, causing the tubes to quake.

"But why the Térata?" Octavio shouted.

"Someone like me, someone who can control them, has altered them," Clarence replied. His voice floated above the cacophony raging through the room. "They are no longer just mine, and they are no longer useful."

Octavio surveyed the dying mass of bodies below. Blood ran from ears and mouths. Some of the Awakened lay still, eyes wide in agony. The screams abated as throats constricted with blood. Clarence sent wave after wave into the monsters and people below.

The stars in the sky above the Boundary Waters whirled into Octavio's mind's eye. He could almost feel the cool breeze and smell the forest around him. A decision formed around that image of the Milky Way. He couldn't let Clarence kill all those people. He dove into the lake beneath the stars. The water of Octavio's imagination brought him peace for the first time since he Woke Up.

Octavio withdrew his tentacle from Craig's body and leaned into Clarence's ear. "This will only hurt for a moment," he said.

Clarence glanced at him with a question on his lips. Octavio drove four tentacles into Clarence's chest. They chewed through his heart and lungs. Octavio pushed more tentacles into Clarence, sending them to chew everything they could reach. The bones of his body disintegrated. A vast blackness shot back through the tentacles. Octavio grit his teeth and plowed in more tentacles as others withered and died.

Clarence's hand fell on Octavio's shoulder. Octavio caught him in his arms. Clarence's eyes were wide open, shocked. Blood dribbled from his mouth. Octavio felt the blackness in Clarence's bones bore into his core, his center. The part of him that had not been blown apart by a roadside bomb. The blackness dismantled him, vaporizing everything it touched. Just as Octavio expected to lose consciousness, a serpentine voice said, *You have a choice, Octavio. Let me in. I will let you live.*

"*Vete a la chingada,*" Octavio spat.

The blackness surged and Octavio fell backward.

It's happening, Andre thought. A current of black slime bolted through the Confluence, scattering the golden dust. He and Victoria avoided it, but more came. As the blackness oozed and expanded, the Confluence began to unravel.

We're almost there! Andre thought desperately.

He felt Victoria's hand solidify under his. The calm peace of forward momentum evaporated. With a concentrated effort, Andre maneuvered through ever narrowing passages of golden light. Darkness tore apart the currents of the Confluence. When he didn't move fast enough, a sliver of the darkness burned a strip of his stomach away. Andre focused his mind on the patterns unraveling before him. Every turn became a hairpin. He drug Victoria through miniscule specs of the Confluence's dust to continue forward. At times he raced against ebbing flows, avoiding walls of blackness by fractions of seconds. His corporeal body, which had been but a memory, was now mapped out in dots and matrixes against a continual barrage of destruction. As he twisted and turned to continue forward, he felt Victoria behind him, safe as long as he avoided the contracting blackness.

After swirling sideways to avoid a black bubble that should have consumed him, Andre paused to plot his forward progress. His heart sank as he saw an unstoppable wall of darkness surging forward.

I'm sorry, he said to Victoria.

I am as well, she replied. He felt her squeeze his hand.

The moment before that wall hit them, it exploded into mist. The Confluence stabilized, showing a clear path to Des Moines.

His name was Octavio, Andre said, blurring forward. *His decision saved us.*

May it be written in the stars, Victoria said as they burst out of the Confluence.

Craig opened his eyes as Octavio's body hit the floor. He stood up and blipped. The IV tore from his arm, spraying spherical droplets of blood that splattered against him as he walked forward. The catheter ripped away, dragging urine and blood in its wake.

Before him, a shadow exploded from Clarence Elpis. It ballooned into the laboratory, darkening every element of the space. At first it felt like a sticky mist, but it quickly resolved into a gel. The darkness hissed into Craig's mind, *Let me in. I will save your friends. I will make you immortal.*

"Go fuck yourself," Craig said.

Seconds seemed to prolong into hours as Craig ran through the blackness, but he ignored time. He was moving faster than he ever had before. Faster than he thought possible. He had to move faster than the darkness. He grabbed Clarence's body and threw it into the Tesla coils.

The body atomized. For a precious moment, the shadow screamed and light flared in an electrical surge. Lightning forked from the point of Clarence's impact, dancing in purple bolts. A hole in space ripped open where Clarence struck the coils. Andre and Victoria materialized inside the hole and tumbled out, trailing golden dust in slow motion. The hole snapped shut.

Victoria stood up and pulled a translucent green box from her purse. She flipped it open.

"Return!" she commanded. Her voice reverberated as it did when she read tarot cards. Each syllable was elongated by the blip, the sonic waves stretching, peaking, and pounding.

The blackness howled and thrashed as it was dragged by unseen forces toward the open box. Tendrils of black smoke solidified and wound themselves around objects in the room. Wires tore loose, tubes capsized, and scaffolding collapsed as the darkness receded further and further into the box.

"Release this world," Victoria intoned, "and return!"

With a final, bitter howl, the blackness let go and dove into the box. Victoria snapped it shut.

Craig smiled and stopped the blip.

Kevin spat a wad of blood onto the floor and dug his claws into the metal base of one of the tubes housing Clarence's project. He tore the metal to shreds as he stood up. He looked up at the platform where Clarence had been standing. Craig, Andre, and Victoria were crouched around something. Clarence was gone. Kevin whipped his head around. The other Térata were pulling themselves from the floor. All of them had survived.

"Guard them," Kevin said, pointing to Victoria, Craig, and Andre.

The Awakened had not fared so well. Half of them were on hands and knees, coughing and sputtering. The other half lay unmoving on the floor. Only one, Theodore, was still standing. He leaned against a tube with his hand on the butt of his rifle, surveying the destruction.

Half of the tubes in the laboratory were shattered. Those that weren't tipped over were empty. Their previous inhabitants were nowhere to be seen. A trail of green ooze led to the destroyed overhead door. Clarence's plan had been executed. Kevin had no idea what to do about that. He decided it was not his problem.

Kevin limped to Theodore and said, "Are you finished here?"

Theodore dropped his gun and reached into a pocket on his flack vest. He pulled out a pack of cigarettes and lit two of them. He handed one to Kevin.

"Yeah, I reckon," he said. His stony face was white and tears of blood stained his leathery skin. His beret was askew.

Kevin looked at the cigarette pinched between his huge fingers. There was no way he could smoke it in his current form. He threw it into the wreckage of a nearby tube. It hissed as it hit the green liquid inside.

"We're leaving," Kevin said. "Elpis Enterprises is yours."

"That's right nice of you, Number 1," Theodore said. He blew out a large cloud of smoke. "For the record, I really didn't want to do any of this."

"For the record," Kevin said, "neither did I."

Theodore barked a short laugh, smoke billowing from his mouth.

"Get what's left of your people out of here," Kevin said. "We'll be gone in three hours. After that, the place is yours."

Theodore nodded and dropped his cigarette into a puddle of green slime. He turned and began checking bodies.

Kevin limped back to the platform. The Térata were gathered at its base. Connor was sobbing. Somehow, tears streamed from all eight of his eyes. Michiko tried to comfort him, patting his back with a clawed hand. Sheila stared at Kevin. The other Térata watched the Awakened with razor-like awareness.

"Octavio is dead," Sheila said.

Kevin nodded.

"Are they going to be a problem?" she asked, motioning to the Awakened.

"No," Kevin said.

"Good," Sheila said.

Kevin pushed through the Térata and climbed the steps to the platform. Craig held Octavio's head in his lap. The rest of his body was blackened with char, but his face was undamaged. Tentacles lay limply around him.

Kevin knelt and put his hand on Craig's back. "I saw what you did, Craig. You saved us all."

"Octavio saved us all," Craig said. "He took my mind out of my head and put it all back the way he found it, just in time for me to help. He was an incredible person."

"He saved Andre and me as well," Victoria said.

Kevin squeezed Craig's shoulder. "Connor, please collect Octavio. The rest of you, get your things together. We're leaving the Elpis Foundation. We won't be returning."

Connor climbed the stairs and knelt beside Octavio. He looked at Craig, who nodded. Gently, Connor gathered all of Octavio's tentacles and lifted him off the ground.

"You were a good man," Connor said. "I'm sorry I only knew you when I couldn't appreciate that."

Andre grabbed Kevin's arm. "What do we do now?" he

asked.

"I'm not sure," Kevin said. "Nice glasses."

Andre sighed. "Thanks. Are Brenda and Amber OK?"

"Yes," Kevin said, "They're—wait a minute." He pointed at the gurney. "Where did she go?"

Victoria asked, "Who?"

"Loretta, or whatever she was called. Amber's double."

"She was not here when Andre and I arrived," Victoria replied. "I would have sensed her. She's nowhere near now." Victoria tapped her lips with her fingers. "Perhaps she was disintegrated by Clarence's process."

That would be convenient, Kevin thought.

"Let's get out here," he said. "We can sort the rest of this out later."

Kimm didn't bother to turn on the Open sign in the window of Kimm's Auto World when he unlocked the door and walked in. In fact, he relocked the door. This wouldn't be the first time the dealership wasn't open during posted hours. Yesterday, he thought it fortuitous that car dealerships must be closed on Sundays in Minnesota. Now it didn't really matter. The only people likely to show up this Monday morning were bill collectors, anyway.

Kimm went to the office and began sending e-mails. To his lawyer. To the shady accountant in Apple Valley. To several of his creditors. He told them that he would be out of the country on business for a week and that, upon his return, he would settle all accounts. He sent a document to his attorney allowing him to act in stewardship of the business in the case of his demise. He sent an e-mail to his ex-wife explaining that he and Oren were heading to Mexico for a father/son vacation. That would irk her, but at least she wouldn't lose her mind with worry for a week or two.

Kimm had no idea how long he'd be gone or whether he'd ever be back. Brenda didn't understand why Oren was trapped in the sword. She had not wanted Kimm to accompany them to this mystical Tir Naomh place. Kevin had talked her into it, which dispelled a tense situation.

Kimm heard the click of the front door lock. He'd laid-off his only employee last Friday. No one but he and Oren should have keys now. He stood up.

Victoria's scent wafted into the office. Kimm exhaled and sat down.

"Hello," he said as she walked in. "How can I help you?"

"You and I have unfinished business, Kimm Peters," Victoria said.

"I suppose you aren't too happy with me," he said. "I can understand if you want to kill me, but I'd really appreciate the opportunity to get Oren back, first."

She waved her hand and sat across the desk from him. "No. Forget that. You were a different... *thing...* then. That circle has resolved. But we are still left bound together." She motioned to her belly. "And you have one more reading. I think it will help us both clarify how to move forward."

Kimm nodded slowly. She was more forgiving than he'd anticipated. Or perhaps more practical. He'd avoided her after the events at The Foundation yesterday. Now he felt foolish for doing so.

"Please clear your desk," she said, pulling her tarot cards from her purse.

Kimm slid paperwork and his computer monitor to the side. Victoria laid out the same cloth he'd seen on her floor in south Minneapolis and began to shuffle the cards.

"I am surprised to see that cloth," he said. "I thought it had been destroyed."

"It's very hard to destroy anything I love," Victoria replied.

"I see," he said.

Victoria's voice filled with power as she finished shuffling the cards. "I will ask the first question. You will ask the second. I, the third. You, the fourth. Prepare your mind, Kimm Peters."

Victoria said, "Will Kimm return from Tir Naomh?"

She turned the The Anchor. "Yes," she said.

Kimm grabbed the edge of his desk with both hands and studied the cards. "Will Oren return from Tir Naomh?" he asked.

She turned the next card. The Scales. "If he passes the tests."

Kimm frowned. That was an annoying answer.

"Will the child in my belly come to full term?" she asked.

The Raven. "Yes," she said.

"Who will determine if Oren passes the tests?" Kimm asked.

The Fool. "I will," Victoria said.

She gathered the cards and put them back into the box.

"You can see more than you say," Kimm said. "Tell me more."

"When your son completes his tests," Victoria replied, "call my name three times. I will pass judgment then. I can tell you no more without damaging your path."

Kimm sat back in his chair. "Why are you tangling yourself up in this?" he asked.

"Because it is time for me to change, too," she said, standing. "Longevity has given me many insights, but I have hidden for most of my life. I wish to emerge from the shadows, Kimm. And I cannot do that alone."

"Well, I appreciate your help," he said.

She nodded and said, "I assume you'll be at Octavio's funeral tomorrow?"

"Sheila thought I should go but I was uncertain until now. I will be there."

She looked at him for a few moments, tapping her lips with her index and middle finger. Without a word, she turned and left. The door locked behind her on the way out.

Kimm put his desk back together and finished his correspondences. He selected several suits from the closet. *What do you bring with you when you go to a fairy tale land?* he wondered. Several pairs of underwear were probably advisable. As he rummaged through the top shelf of the closet, an envelope full of photographs fell. Pictures of a Mexican vacation from years ago scattered to the floor. The first picture he picked up was of a rattlesnake, coiled on a hiking trail. The next picture was of Kimm holding the snake, now quite dead.

Craig smoked a cigarette with Andre on the porch of Victoria's cabin. The day was bright and clear with a stiff, cold breeze.

"You're going back to Des Moines today?" Andre asked.

"Yeah," Craig replied.

"What made you decide to do that?"

"Some guy named Tim Shelton called me," Craig said. "He offered me a job at The Foundation."

"What about school?" Andre asked.

Craig barked a laugh. "I don't know how I could go back, now. Classes would be difficult. I mean, it would be like, 'Excuse me, Professor; I know we're supposed to use the scientific method and all, but it turns out that half the universe is magic, which doesn't seem to have any set laws at all.' I'm not sure I can deal with it. Plus, I died and came back. And then I had my brain sucked out and put back. I don't think I can focus on school right now. I've got a lot of shit to sort out. I can probably do well with other people like me. Apparently Clarence had a file on me that impressed this Tim person. It's the best option I've got right now." He took a drag of his cigarette. "You should come with me, Andre. Somebody needs to do something about all those androids, or whatever they are, that escaped when Clarence went nuclear."

"I don't like science so much," Andre said, "and that place creeps me the fuck out. The androids are The Elpis Foundation's problem. I've got problems of my own." He tapped his glasses.

"You gonna hang out with Victoria, then?"

"Yeah. I didn't like her at first, but she's not so bad once you get to know her."

Craig grinned. "You gonna go for it?"

"Shut up, asshole," Andre said, laughing. "It's not like that. She's old enough to be my great, great grandma."

"GILF," Craig said.

"You're sick," Andre said. "And sexist."

"Says the beacon of contemporary feminism!"

A car drove up the dirt road toward the cabin, trailing brown dust in its wake.

"That'll be the priest," Andre murmured. He slid open the glass door and said, "The priest is here."

Craig watched the car approach and turned his eyes to the casket in the yard. Sheila had done an amazing job with Octavio. White roses lined the interior of the coffin, leaving only his chest and face exposed. He looked like he could wake up at any moment. Sheila had also built a trellis entwined with flowers which framed the lake. An American flag was draped across the coffin. She spent hours researching how to do that correctly. Octavio was a war hero of some sort. The final product was picturesque.

Andre walked over and met the priest, who his father had somehow managed to wrangle up for a non-traditional funeral. Octavio had been Catholic, so Andre was insistent that certain procedures be followed, despite the fact that they could not have a funeral mass. According to public records, Octavio was already dead. Having an official funeral was not possible. Sheila had checked into it. His family thought he'd died in Afghanistan two years ago. *So many shadows*, Craig thought.

Brenda, Kevin, Amber, Victoria, Sheila, Connor and Kimm filed out of the cabin wearing black suits and dresses. They had been discussing the ramifications of Tir Naomh all morning. Craig hoped to never leave the Earth again. Just knowing that entire worlds could exist within other worlds caused his scientific mind to seize up with the contradictions. He had a lot to learn, but his interest in magical geographic paradoxes was nil. The extent to which scientific processes could be applied to magic was of great interest to him, but he'd start in his native field of biology, roughly where Clarence left off. Tim Shelton seemed to think that was a good idea.

The funeral was shorter than Craig anticipated. The priest was not pleased that Octavio was not being given a full mass. Andre managed to placate the priest, who ended up saying a series of prayers over the body and giving a small sermon about the brevity of earthly life compared to its eternal, posthumous counterpart. Craig had little patience for religion, so his mind wandered as the priest made his way through a truncated version of Catholic funeral rites.

He couldn't remember anything from the point Octavio sucked out his frontal lobe and hippocampus until he put them back. But Octavio had left a trail of information that allowed Craig to react appropriately to the situation he awoke into. Craig hoped that the other Awakened at the Elpis Foundation were like Octavio. The man had been incredible. Seeing him dead in the casket was depressing, despite Sheila's impressive efforts.

Craig thought about his father for several minutes. He'd left a voicemail message for his dad about the minivan, but hadn't looked at his phone since. Eventually, he'd need to call and let him know that he planned to drop out of college and move to Des Moines. That would be a bombed moment. But, in the context of what he'd gone through in the last few days, his Dad wasn't the scariest part of what he'd be doing next.

The priest finished the ceremony and left, spending very little time with the bereaved. Connor cried and wailed. He must have known Octavio really well. Everyone else paid their respects with much more reserve. Sheila kissed his forehead before she closed the casket. All of them but Amber acted as pallbearers, carrying the casket into the woods where a grave had been dug. They lowered it into the ground and stood looking down.

"I have never known a finer man," Sheila said. "May we all strive to live up to his standard."

Sheila and Conner relaxed in a hotel room in downtown Minneapolis after the funeral. She lounged on the bed with her back against the headboard. Connor peered into the mirror on the lid of her make-up case, applying the last touches of lipstick from the tube that she'd recommended.

He stood and stared at himself in the body mirror on the back of the door.

"You look fabulous," she said.

He wore a sparkling gold dress that clung to his waist and fell in tassels just below his knees. The wig she'd bought framed his face with black curls and fell over his neck. His shoulders were too broad and his hips were too skinny. He was also a towering figure for a woman. But his makeup was perfect, erasing the masculine line of his jaw and shaved chin. He hadn't needed extensions for his eyelashes, which he batted at the mirror. Sheila had painstakingly shaved his entire body. The hair would regrow next time he changed forms, but for now he had the sleek look he'd wanted.

"I feel... I *feel* fabulous," he said. "But I'm scared. I've never been a woman before."

"You'll never be a woman, dear," Sheila said. "Even if you tried. Can you imagine what hormone therapy would do to things like us? But you can look like one."

"I don't know," he said. "It's like I'm a painting of a woman. I don't feel real. I feel good. But I don't feel real. Is this normal?"

"I don't think there is such a thing as normal," Sheila said. "There is ugliness. And there is beauty. And, honey, you are beautiful."

"All dressed up with nowhere to go," he sighed. "Tuesdays are probably not the best night to drag my way across downtown."

"Oh, I know a couple of places," Sheila said with a grin. "I'm known as something of a fag hag in this identity. You'll raise a few eyebrows, but I think I can keep you out of too much trouble."

"Really?" Connor said. He looked like a kid with a new toy and it was no fun to play with by himself.

"Yeah," Sheila said. "Let me get dressed, too. I can't have you outshining me."

When she was dressed, Sheila dug through her makeup case for the broach Hellena had given her. As she pulled it out, she noticed another one. This one had been given to her by a man in Taos, New Mexico. He had been a Pueblo metal smith. She had represented him before he hung himself in his barn studio. The broach was a golden rattlesnake inset with turquois. It was large and tacky, but the blue in the stones complimented her dress nicely. She dropped Hellena's broach back into the makeup case and pulled out the golden rattlesnake.

"That's gorgeous!" Connor exclaimed.

Sheila smiled. "It's appropriate," she said. "You've got a lot to learn, honey. The first thing being how to walk in those heels…"

Loretta peeked through a small hole in a box in the back of a UPS truck. She'd been tossed from truck to truck for the last two days. This box was supposed to contain a piece of "FRAGILE!" medical equipment. Loretta had removed its contents and replaced them with herself, four candy bars, and two bottles of water. She rigged the inside of the box to open and reseal from the inside, allowing her to sneak out to use the bathroom and scrounge for more food while remaining undetected. This seemed to be the final destination for the package, so she was going to need to figure something out quickly. By now she must be far, far away from that horrible woman, Victoria Starks.

Two men grabbed either side of her box and carried her into a large building. There, she was staged with several crates on a loading dock. After a few minutes, she pushed the top of the box open and crawled out.

"Oh my God!" a woman's voice shouted. "There's a kid in that box!"

Loretta froze. She crawled back into the box and sat down. There was nothing to do now but wait and see what was going to happen. Hopefully she was far enough away from Victoria.

Two hours later, Loretta sat at a table at the local police station. An officer was asking her questions, which she did not answer. Eventually, he gave up.

"Here's some paper and a pen," the cop said before he left. "Hopefully that'll keep you busy until we can get a case worker down here."

Loretta smiled at him. She took the pen in her hand and began to draw. Two year old fingers were not very coordinated, but she still managed to draw a pretty good picture of a rattlesnake in a field of stars.

Brenda stared at the Swan Hilted Sword. Oren's sleeping face flickered across the blade, as if reflected. She grimaced. Why was Oren in the sword? He was injured, though she didn't know how.

Everyone from Octavio's funeral except Sheila and Connor were gathered in the living room of Victoria's cabin. Their faces were expectant, except Kimm's. His was etched with anxiety. Backpacks were piled on the couch. A great deal of discussion and debate had gone into determining what to bring.

Andre removed his glasses and said, "The sun has set. Now is the time."

Brenda nodded and swung the sword. A gash opened in the air and expanded, creating a doorway floating in space.

On the other side was Kevin's tomb in Tir Naomh.

Kevin approached the doorway and said, "I'll go first, followed by Kimm. Once we determine everything is safe, Brenda can follow with Amber."

Kimm nodded, removed his clothing, and shifted into his true form.

Kevin took a step into the doorway and was blown backwards as if slapped by a giant hand. He collided with Kimm. Both hit the wall of the cabin so hard that the dishes in the cabinets rattled. The cat lamp fell from its table and shattered on the floor. Rubbing their heads, both crawled from the floor.

You knew that would happen, a disapproving woman's voice said from inside Brenda's head.

Brenda frowned and stepped through the doorway and back several times.

"What the fuck just happened?" Kevin coughed.

Brenda said, "I... I think..." She sighed. "It won't work that way."

Andre put his glasses back on and sat down. "Oh, God," he said. "Oh, God."

"What do you mean it doesn't work that way?" Kevin demanded.

"You... I... You can't come through unless you're in the sword," Brenda said.

Kimm's red eyes narrowed. "*In* the sword. Like Oren? But we don't know how Oren got in there!"

With his hand on his forehead, Andre said, "I do. You're not going to like this." His voice resonated unnaturally. "Only through the pure heart can the voyage be made."

"What does that nonsense mean?" Kimm asked.

Victoria was gathering the pieces of the cat lamp. "Tell them, Brenda," she said.

"I have to pierce your heart with the sword," Brenda said. "If your heart is pure, you'll enter the sword with Oren. Then I can take you to Tir Naomh. If your heart is not pure, you will die."

Kevin's eyes widened. "Even Amber?" he asked.

"Yes," Brenda said.

From Craig's lap, Amber clapped her hands and said, "Go in swo'd!"

"This may present a problem," Kimm said. "Our hearts are metal."

Andre waived his hand, "That doesn't matter. Unless your motivations are unpure. Then it will matter a lot. Don't you explode when you die?"

"Yes," Kimm said. "We do." He glanced around the living room for a few moments and turned to Brenda. "I'm reasonably confident that my heart is pure, but just in case, we better do this outside."

They filed out onto the patio. A chilly breeze swept off the lake, ruffling Kimm's fur. Brenda lifted the sword, but did not have the will to stab him.

Kimm smiled. Like Kevin's, his smile was all deadly teeth. He took the blade of the sword in his clawed, black hand and squared it against his chest. He said, "If I don't go into this sword, Kevin, throw my body in the lake. And take care of my son."

Kimm put his hand over Brenda's and pulled the sword into his chest. As the blade sunk in, his body folded like a piece of origami paper. The resulting shape matched the blade of the sword. A moment later, Kimm was gone. Brenda could see his reflection next to Oren's in the blade. She expelled her breath.

"Wow," she said.

Amber clapped her hands. "Kimm in swo'd!" she shouted.

Kevin took Brenda's hand and said, "We better do this at the bank of the lake."

"Why?" she asked, refusing to be pulled.

"My heart may be in the right place, Brenda, but I don't know if it's pure. The last time I left this world, I killed hundreds of innocent people to get back. I don't regret it. I'd kill them again. Does that sound very pure to you?"

Brenda looked at Andre. "Can't you see if this is going to work ahead of time?" she asked.

Andre took his glasses off, but shook his head. "No," he said. "I'm sorry."

Brenda turned to Victoria. "You?"

Victoria said, "The Dog King must be crowned if Oren is to return. That's all I know."

"That's good enough for me," Brenda said.

"Let's still do it by the lake," Kevin said.

They all walked to the water's edge. Victoria and Andre brought the backpacks. Craig carried Amber. An explosion of stars was visible in the sky. The water of the lake rippled in the wind and small waves lapped at the shore.

Brenda bit her bottom lip as she rested the blade against Kevin's chest. He took her hand the same way Kimm had done.

"I love you," he said and plunged the sword into his chest.

Like Kimm, he folded into the shape of the blade and vanished. Brenda looked into the sword. Kevin's reflection rested with Kimm and Oren's. She heaved a sigh of relief.

"Me next! Me next!" Amber said, bouncing around Craig's leg. He had a firm grip on her hand.

"This is seriously messed up," Craig said.

Brenda agreed.

Amber stopped bouncing and pointed at her chest. "Swo'd he'e!" she said.

Brenda swallowed. A two-year-old heart could surely be nothing but pure. The idea of stabbing her daughter sill rankled. What if there were more rules?

You know what must be done, the voice in her head said.

Taking a quick breath, Brenda stabbed her daughter in the chest. Like her father and uncle, Amber folded up and vanished. Her reflection joined theirs in the dull gleam of the blade.

Brenda turned to Craig, Victoria, and Andre.

"Good-bye," she said. Then she cut a hole in the air, threw the backpacks into it, and walked into Tir Naomh.

Next: The Rattlesnake Prophecy

ABOUT THE AUTHOR

Michael A. O'Leary Jr. was born in Norton, Kansas. He now lives in Minneapolis with his two kids, two scorpions, three frogs, and a snake. He graduated from Kansas State University with a BFA in Printmaking. An artist, musician, and writer, he has worked as an art handler, licensed general contractor, restaurant manager, deep-earth construction slurry plant operator, biology lab assistant, tire shop technician, and software development quality manager. He's sang and played bass in more rock bands than he can remember. In 2017, he released *Choices & Metamorphoses*, a short story collection. His next novel, *The Rattlesnake Prophecy*, will be released in 2018 or 2019.